Two Crowns, Three Blades

Robert A. Walker

For Suzanne,

My wife and queen

Contents

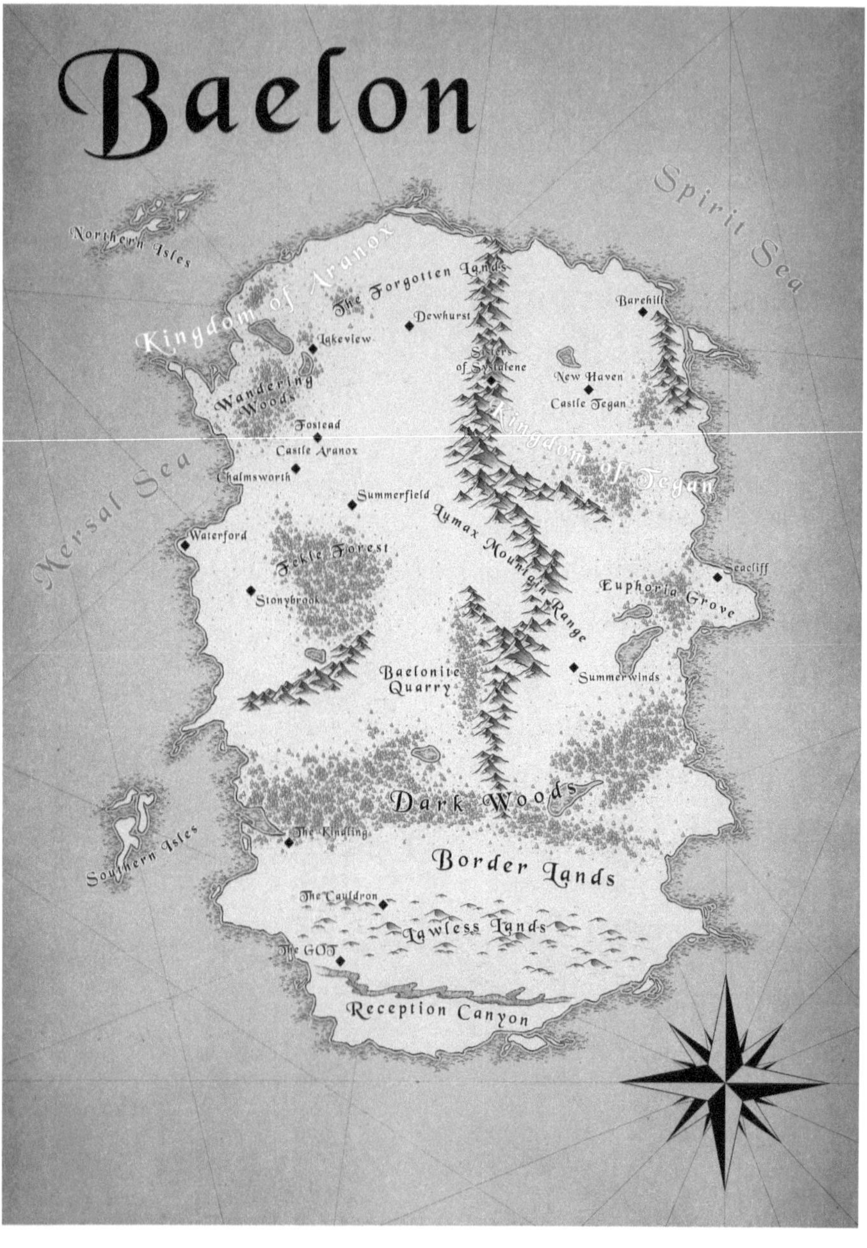

Baelon
Spirit Sea
Northern Isles
Kingdom of Aranox
The Forgotten Lands
Dewhurst
Barehills
Lakeview
Sisters
of Systalene
New Haven
Castle Tegan
Wandering Woods
Kingdom of Tegan
Fostead
Castle Aranox
Mersal Sea
Chalmsworth
Summerfield
Lymax Mountain Range
Waterford
Fickle Forest
Euphoria Grove
Seacliff
Stonybrook
Baelonite Quarry
Summerwinds
Dark Woods
Southern Isles
The Kindling
Border Lands
The Cauldron
Lawless Lands
The GOT
Reception Canyon

THE PROMISE OF A TEMPTRESS

"Some things are worth pursuing even though they don't exist."
Mari Dunn, to her daughter, Sibil, age nine.

Sibil Dunn

A long, low growl in the skies above Tegan carried across the Lumax mountain range, rumbling softly into Aranox. *One of the gods clearing his voice, no doubt, and surely what woke me.* Sibil wriggled her toes in a carpet of damp moss as forgiving as a sponge. Thick tree trunks with roughly fissured bark rose to a high ceiling made of heart-shaped leaves the size of her head.

Euphoria! She searched the distinctive foliage for signs of her mother while waiting for a cascade of purple flowers that never came.

Pit... pat... pit... pat. Small drops began to fall onto the waxy leaves above.

"Are you confused?" A dark, hooded cloak rendered a huddled figure nearly indistinguishable from the base of a knobbly tree trunk.

There's no mistaking that raspy voice! It belongs to the old woman who dressed the wounds of both my mother and Rolft Aerns—a Sister of the Systalene.

"I am." Sibil tightened her grip on a small blank card the woman had given her when they first met, its heart-shaped wax embossment pressed into her palm.

Pitta pat, pitta pat, pitta pat. The drizzle turned to light rain.

"About what?" the old woman asked.

"About a lot of things."

"Such as?" The crone's hands and fingers moved deftly, up and down, back and forth, as though stitching a tear in her cloak, or kneading something deep within its folds.

"Where is my mother?"

"I think you know, child."

A large drop of rain slid from the leafy canopy onto Sibil's head. An overwhelming sadness took hold of her and squeezed. "Am I dreaming? Please tell me I am!"

"Are you? Does it matter?" The woman's black hood swiveled slowly side to side. "Dream or not, you see more than you let on. Just like your mother. Have you still seen nothing of the future, child? No visions that have come to pass? No dreams that have come true? Remember what I said about Euphoria... Just because it courses through your veins doesn't mean it likes you. Small doses when you dare!"

"You speak in riddles," Sibil said, teary-eyed.

"Do I? Have you convinced yourself of that?"

"You only add to my confusion."

A woodpecker with a ponytail of gold fluttered to Sibil's feet.

Ridiculous!

"But you know who I am," the bird chirped.

"I do! You cannot fool me twice... Tristan!"

"Have you read my letter?" The woodpecker hopped back and forth in front of her, its ponytail flopping up and down. The woman's card expanded in Sibil's hand, transforming itself into an envelope.

The words written on its front— "For Sibil, should I not return" —prompted her response. "But it has only been a short while since you left. Would you have me read it now?"

"That is your choice."

"Then I would choose to have you back, Tristan, so that you might read it to me."

"In due time, perhaps. I must first avenge my brother's death."

"But why do so alone? Is that really necessary? The king has declared war on The Guild, has he not?"

"*Pffft!*" The old woman's busy hands stilled. A crooked finger did its best to straighten in the air. "War solves nothing, child!"

"What would you have the king do?" the woodpecker asked. "Sit idly by whilst monsters seek to destroy the realm?"

"It's that simple, is it?" said the woman. "Do you know how many young men I have watched take their last breath on the battlefield? Young men just like you?"

"Oh, stop!" cried Sibil. "What am I to do?"

The woodpecker flew off as a heavy arm encircled her. Comforting. Reassuring. Her father, suddenly beside her, whispered in her ear. "You must do as we have taught you, Sibil. You must follow your heart. It will not lead you astray."

"Your father speaks the truth, my love, even from his grave." Her mother's voice came from behind. "You must do as we have taught you."

Pitter patter, pitter patter, pitter patter.

The now steady rain turned red, spattering Sibil's face and upturned palms. A blur descended past her eyes and splashed into a puddle forming at her feet. The woodpecker lay limp and motionless, its ponytail and feathers drenched in blood.

Sibil woke with a start, out of breath and fully alert. Hushed, excited voices reached her through the dark. It took no time at all to cross her room and enter The Nest's hall, where three whispering figures stood outside her mother's quarters. A lantern held by one illuminated the others, who turned to look at her. She recognized the shortest of them as the attendant who normally kept vigil with her mother through the night.

"We were just coming for you, child." The attendant took one of Sibil's hands in both of hers. "Now would be a good time to pay your last respects."

Sibil's breaths came quicker. "What do you mean?"

"The gods above have granted her admission, love. Your mother's suffering is over."

It seemed only fitting that the sun refused to show itself even after rising, as though it too was in mourning. It could stay hidden forever, for all she cared. Baelon really was a cold and heartless place, steeped in pain and suffering. Why try to mask that with the weather? Or a pleasant disposition? Why pretend one day was any different from another? Evil knew better. It paid no heed to climate, color, or emotion. It did not restrict itself to the dark recesses of places easy to avoid. It visited when and where it wanted. And it did not care who you were, or what lived inside your heart.

It stalked her, taunted her—daring her to do something about it, or give in to despair.

She could not bear it alone.

I know where Rolft is! I can still go to him. He'll be pleased to see me, and he'll want to help. The bond we share transcends the incidents that forged it. No! How selfish would that be? The man's cheated death so many times, and now at last he lives the life he deserves. If you truly honor your bond, you'll leave him be. Keep your troubles to yourself! Sergeant Cogswell? Marshal Carson? Both are as trustworthy as the royal guard, perhaps even better at dispensing murderous advice! But is that what you really need? Father Syrus! A good man with a good heart. His shield-shaped amulet still hangs from my neck. But what would be the point of going there? You know what he would say. Could you resist challenging the very foundation of his faith in response? There is no God of Happiness, no God of Fortune or Good Health. There is no God of Children watching over his flock. There's only Father Syrus, and his convictions won't improve your current plight.

Sibil coaxed Shadow to a hitching post and slid to the ground. Just outside Fostead and off the road to Chalmsworth, The Royal Keep was unimposing yet majestic, humble and impressive all at once. She knew its story better than most. Built of baelonite by her father, it would attract its fair share of visitors by midday, most of whom would be of singular mind and oblivious to architectural details. Those who did notice the trim of crested waves encircling its turrets, or the pair of lovebirds perched on an open windowsill, would likely not appreciate how difficult those were to fashion from royal stone. The four walls of The Keep, low replicas of King Axil's castle, were not intended to impress visitors; they were meant to honor those buried inside.

A short walk down a flagstone path brought her to the structure's entrance. She read the inscription in stone above the iron gate: The Royal Keep of Aranox—A Noble Place to Rest. *Did it occur to you, Father, as you chiseled those words, that you yourself might one day be laid to rest beneath them?*

Sibil swung the gate and traversed the short, arched tunnel leading to The Keep's interior. It did not take long to reach the spot where she had stood to watch her father be lowered into a dark pit. Already, the plot beside him showed signs of preparation for his wife. Sibil tidied the surrounding ground before dropping to her knees beside her father's headstone.

"Ayla, Father. Can you spend some time with me? Has Mother joined you yet? Some say the gods take time to grant spirits entry. I don't believe in the gods anymore, but I trust Mother is with you. She kept one foot in both our worlds for so long that some days I imagined she'd wake and be her old self. Her wounds had closed, and of late, a smile rested on her lips. But I suppose she knew what was coming, and that smile was for you.

"I wonder now... did you know about the Sisters of Systalene? About Mother and Euphoria? I don't want to worry you, but I am left alone now. Do you remember the Godfrey twins? Theos was slain by an assassin, the same as Mother. His brother, Tristan, searches for his killer, and now I fear the worst for him as well. You and Lewen have been gone so long. I feel as though if you were here, none of this would have come to pass. I know that's not right, but still. There is a man I wish you could meet—a royal guard who used to serve Princess Lewen. His name is Rolft, and though he is a soldier, he reminds me much of you. He saved my life and nearly gave his own to avenge Lewen." For a moment, Sibil's eyes searched the fertile fields of the northwest.

"I don't know what to do or where else to go for help. A part of me cannot wait to join you. I know what you would say: follow my heart. I'm trying, Father, but, truth be told, my heart has little left to live for, and so much to escape. I've had strange dreams of late, and you have been there with me. Mother as well."

Sibil withdrew from her tunic the envelope Fereliss had given her outside the palace chapel on the day of Tristan's knighting. Her finger ran across the words on its face: *For Sibil, should I not return.*

"I know it says that, Father, but Tristan told me in a dream that I may read it when I choose. And I would rather you were with me when I do." Her voice softened to a fragile whisper. "I don't think he's coming back, and I don't know if I can bear to learn its message on my own."

Fingers trembling, she opened the envelope and took out a folded piece of paper, which she flattened on her knee before reading aloud:

"Dearest Sibil,

My brother's death consumes me. A part of me is lost forever. In its place, an angry beast has risen. I have tried to banish it, but at best, have kept it hidden. It cries to be unchained. It eats at my soul from the inside out and will not let me rest. I have gone to set it free in remembrance of Theos and Lewen.

Gods willing, you will never read this. Instead, I will return and speak these next words to you. But should I fail, know this:

I have loved you since we first met. Whether or not you would receive it, my heart belongs to you.

Tristan."

Sir Tristan Godfrey

Full sun, dry heat. Not a whisper of a breeze. A large brown lizard with green stripes scurried across the cracked and barren earth. Little else stimulated Tristan's senses, and none of it could steal his thoughts from those who had kept them captive the past half moon: his parents, each grieving the death of his twin brother in their own way. His mother, so overwhelmed by sorrow it seemed she might drown herself in it. Still prone to sudden fits of sobbing, she had gone silent and refused to eat, whilst her husband—Sir Garlan Godfrey—prowled the castle grounds like some caged animal anticipating its release. When the king did strike the Takers Guild, his father would most certainly be at the tip of the first spear. And with him, Marshal Carson, Major Stronghart, Sir Kraven and Sir Garr—all would descend on The GOT with the fury of seven offended gods behind them.

A part of him wished to ride with them—proud son beside his father, aggrieved brother alongside his fellow knights—but the destruction of The Guild of Takers compound might not set all wrongs right. The Guild had members everywhere. Any one of them could have released the arrow that had pierced his brother's chest. Rumors that The League of Assassins had helped to silence the Prince of Quills further complicated matters. He had tried to explain this to his father, but the elder knight was too steeped in his allegiance to the crown to understand.

Tristan swung a leg over his saddle and dropped to the hard-packed ground. He tightened the cord around the ponytail he wore in tribute to his brother. *This is the spot. I'm sure of it. Do you haunt this place, Theos? Can you hear my thoughts? If only we could trade places. Why could that arrow not have found my heart and left you to avenge me? I would have trusted you to do that. You would have been more capable, I'm sure of it. I still cannot believe you took the steward's life! How did you kill him, anyway? Was it quick? Did he fight back?* Tristan grabbed a handful of dirt, letting it sift through his splayed fingers. *How quickly all signs of what happened here have been erased!* Ahead lay The Fekle Forest, where Theos' assassin had laid in wait, and beyond it, the town of Stonybrook, where together with his brother and the royal guard, he had helped to capture the Prince of Quills.

All he knew of Stonybrook he had learned from Fereliss during the hunt for the Prince of Quills. And from what he had seen with his own eyes the night that they had found and captured the hapless printer. Stonybrook was not as heavily or densely populated as Fostead. Shielded from the arid footlands of the Lumax Mountains by the Fekle Forest, and blessed by the Mersal Sea's coastal climate, it responded well to the efforts of farmers. A well-worn route to Waterford transported crops to ships that sailed to both the Southern and Northern Isles.

Everyone knew everyone in the tightly knit community of Stonybrook. Those who did not farm sold wares from carts inside the village square or operated shops on its perimeter.

Tristan entered the establishment where he, along with his brother and the king's royal guard, had learned the exact whereabouts of the Prince of Quills. Behind the bar was the same innkeeper who had told them just which cottage harbored the fugitive.

"What'll it be?" Sparse, graying brown hair framed the man's square face and hung to broad shoulders. His brown eyes took an interest in Tristan before flitting to other places in the bar.

Be honest. Be direct. "I've been here before... in service to King Axil. Last time you told us where to find the Prince of Quills. I'm hoping you can help me once again."

"Don't think I don't recognize you, lad, because I do." The barkeep picked up a glass and began to wipe it clean with a towel draped over his shoulder. "The last time you were here did not end well. I've drink and food if you're in need, but no bed, if that's what's on your mind. You can't stay long, and there's no information for you here. Understand?"

It seemed the innkeeper's words were meant for others as well. Tristan looked at the men standing to either side of him before responding. "Might we speak in private for a moment?"

"No, we might not," said the innkeeper. "And there'll be no whisperin', neither. All I have to say to you is what's just been said, and these men are my witnesses to that." He replenished the drink in front of the man standing closest to Tristan. "You heard what I said to him, Symple?"

"I heard."

"And you, Smithee?"

The man to Tristan's other side nodded slowly, then finished his drink. He stared vacantly at Tristan before exiting the tavern.

The innkeeper placed a bottle on the bar in front of Tristan. "And now all I'm offerin' is drink. You'd best take it with you. You haven't time to eat." His tone wasn't threatening or mean-spirited, but still Tristan took offense.

"Haven't I?" It was far too soon for setbacks, even minor ones. He was not going to be brushed aside so easily. "Keep your drink. And your advice." He turned from the innkeeper and raised his voice above all others. "Listen now! I am Sir Tristan Godfrey, and I seek my brother's killer! This happened not one moon ago, just the other side of Fekle

Forest. Our prisoner was killed, as was my brother. I seek whoever is responsible, and ask for your help in doing so."

An awkward silence hung in the air until broken by a man near the door whose clothes were not intended for laboring in fields. A businessman, perhaps, short and stout, with clean-shaven, ruddy cheeks below his sunken eyes. A mop of dark, wavy hair hung just past his ears.

"Your brother was killed? What was his name?"

"Theos Godfrey. Sir Theos Godfrey."

"Ah! The king's knight. We heard about that. My condolences. The loss of a brother is a heavy load indeed. And your prisoner? What was his name?"

"He was known as the Prince of Quills."

"Not here he wasn't."

What? Tristan cast a wary look toward the barkeep before responding. "Penniluk, then. His name was Penniluk."

"So it was," the man said softly. "Same as mine." *Gods above!* "What will you do, I wonder, when you find your brother's killer?"

"I will grant him passage to Baelon below."

"Ah! A just and fitting ending, to be sure. My brother's killer deserves no less."

Tristan's confidence returned. "Can you help me, then?"

"I can. I know who killed them both."

"Tell me, then! Where will I find them?"

"I don't know their names, but there were five of them." The man's eyes widened. "They came from Castle Aranox, or so they told our friend here."

Tristan stole another glance at the innkeeper. "What are you talking about?"

"Three big, bearded men accompanied by two pups with hair of gold; one tied it back as you do yours."

"What game are you playing? We didn't kill anyone."

"Oh, didn't you? Would my brother not be alive today had you and your friends not come here?" The man took a step toward Tristan.

"We didn't come to kill your brother!"

"Oh no, that's right. You just woke him in the dead of night, dragged him out of bed and threw him on a horse. Shackled and dressed in nothing but his nightshirt. All whilst his poor sister watched! What did he do to deserve that? Tell me, what did he do that was so terrible?"

Go on! Tell him! The truth is not to be feared! "He aided those who tried to kill King Axil!"

"Really! Shaun Penniluk! The Prince of Quills? You're certain of that, are you? It was proven, was it?"

Tristan pictured the pitiful Prince astride his horse in a krep-stained nightgown. The sympathy he had felt for the man that night revisited him.

"No, it wasn't, was it?" Penniluk continued. "And you could not protect your prisoner—which was your duty, was it not? —until he could be judged? And now, you cannot find a killer, though he stands in your own shoes!"

Tristan did not want to further antagonize the man. Nothing he could think to say was going to placate him.

"You've come here by your lonesome this time, have you?" asked the man. "This is not a safe place, as you well know—not even for those escorted by five of the king's men. Imagine how easy it would be for one man on his own to disappear."

"That's enough, Milton," said the innkeeper.

"Shut up, Styles, or I'll burn this place down with you inside it! Haven't you done enough? What have you lost, eh? You've no say in this! Shut up!"

Tristan swallowed. *Stand tall! Assert yourself!* "It would be best if you addressed me as Sir Godfrey, for I am a knight in service to King Axil."

"A knight, you say! My, my! Where is your armor, Sir Whatever-you-said-your-name-is? Your sword and shield? And where are your large friends?" The man stole a quick glance toward the inn's front door, through which two men had just entered in a rush. One of them was the patron who had left the bar a short time back. The other was huskier, a bit older, but with the same crop of dark, wavy hair as the man called Milton.

"Back away, brother," the newcomer said. He stared with an air of superiority at the man accosting Tristan. "Go on! Do as I say! There's no need for this. Can't you see the young man's on our side? Whoever killed our brother killed his as well. If he hunts the bastard who did it, well, he's doing us a favor. Go on, sit down and think on it. I'll take care of this... I promise. Go on!" Everyone waited as Milton begrudgingly stepped aside and sat down.

"My apologies," said the newcomer. "My brother is understandably upset. You're on your own, are you? In that case, and since you represent the king, you'd best have a word with Sharyll Cressen. She lives just down the street. If anyone can help you, it'd be her.

Third house on the right. She's up all night... door knocker in the shape of a bird. Just tell her Maynard Penniluk sent ya."

Another Penniluk! Tristan looked from Maynard to the innkeeper to those standing by the door. "Very well. I'm in your debt." No one moved as he weaved his way past tables and chairs toward the inn's door. He stole a last look at the seated brother before leaving.

He had set only one foot outside the tavern when something thin and hard met him with a violent force. The bones in his right arm cracked sharply before another blow hit his chest. He twisted away and stumbled forward, his cry stifled by another strike to his back. It knocked the wind out of him and drove him to his knees. His left hand fumbled for his knife until something bashed him in the head. He toppled forward, alert but unable to react. He heard shouting and rejoicing.

"Oh, ho!" a voice cried. "Are you watching, Milton?"

Someone kicked Tristan in the back. He curled as best he could into a ball as the beating continued. "Take some of his hair! I'll have it as a souvenir!"

Someone grabbed his ponytail and wrenched his head off the ground.

A boot struck him in the face, and then the darkness took him.

Marshal Erik Carson

Not even a brilliant sun could find the bottom of the castle's shaft. Moisture slicked its walls. A thick, musty scent enveloped it, impossible not to breathe in with the air. Well below ground, and buttressed by three layers of stone, the war room precluded spying or eavesdropping as well as any coffin might. *What better place to contemplate one's enemies' demise?*

The flames of a half dozen lanterns cast a quivering glow upon the faces of Sergeants Perill, Galeran, and Stone; Sir Dreddit, Parrish, and Godfrey.

Carson blew warm air into his cupped hands as he studied each man at the table, his gaze lingering on Sir Godfrey.

Still mourning one son's death. No doubt concerned with the whereabouts of the other. Can you remain objective? The knight returned his stare until Major Stronghart entered the room and closed the door.

Carson stood to place both palms on the table. "The king has declared war on The Guild of Takers for the deaths of Queen Isadora and Princess Lewen, for countless acts of thievery and murder, and for depriving the people of Aranox from the peaceful pursuit of life. Your king will not rest until The Guild is but a bad memory, and you and I—we shall be his hammer and his sword.”

Murmurs of affirmation echoed in the chamber.

“All told, The Guild’s members far outnumber us; they have made themselves a part of every village in Baelon. That said, the king has simplified our planning. We may well pursue its overseers—perhaps even its gatherers and takers at some point—but The High Order must be the first to feel our wrath.

“The king does not care how it comes to pass, but he would have The Guild’s stronghold, the GOT, reduced to rubble, the members of its High Order silenced forever, and the head of its supreme leader, the magister, sitting on a pole outside these castle walls for all to see in one half moon.”

“One half moon?” asked Sergeant Galeran, unable to hide a hint of skepticism.

“The king would have us crush The Guild before it kills another of his subjects. We strike in one half moon, if not before,” said the marshal.

“So... we know who we’re hunting, and we know why,” said Sir Dreddit. “We know where they’re hiding, and the when has been decided. We’re left only to determine how?” His fingers stroked the scar running from his right cheek to his jaw.

“Indeed,” said the marshal. “But that itself is puzzle enough. The GOT lies deep within the Lawless Lands. Taking it presents a special challenge.”

“Is there no hope of striking The High Order on some other ground?” asked Sir Parrish. “Perhaps when its members are on some sort of journey or planned travel?”

“Might we entice them out?” asked Sergeant Perill.

“No. The magister is known to be a fixture there, and regardless, we do not have the luxury of waiting for them to leave. One half moon!” said the marshal.

“They’ll know we’re coming, no doubt. The desert will not hide us, and it’s a full sun’s ride from the Borderlands to the GOT, is it not?” asked Sergeant Stone.

“We can’t use rams or hurlers—their weight won’t travel over sand,” said Sergeant Galeran. “Breaching the GOT won’t be easy.”

“What do we know of The Guild’s army?” asked Sir Godfrey.

“Not much with any certainty,” answered Major Stronghart.

“Do we know their number?” asked Stone.

“We do not, though I hear it’s small,” said the major.

"But growing," added Carson. "They're paying commonfolk to join their ranks, even as we sit here."

"They're what?" asked Sir Dreddit.

"I've heard the same," said Sir Parrish.

"What about the prattlers?" asked Sir Godfrey.

The room went silent until broken by Sergeant Galeran. "I saw them once, you know. They're not a myth. Nor like anything you've seen before."

"Tell us, then," said Stronghart.

"Just before I joined the army, my friends and I went to The Cauldron to celebrate our last days of freedom. This was Validation Night... back when they still practiced that. We stood there as the sun went down and the shadows became one. Forty or fifty of us, I'd say, mostly young men just out of school or coming of age. You can ask Sergeant Vikkars. He was there... he saw them, too. We stood between the desert and The Cauldron. They didn't light the building's lanterns or its candles on the night of validation, not at first. Or the pyres, for that would have spoiled the fun, yeah? You can't really see the prattlers in the pitch black... they blend right in, you know. But you can hear them just fine. Oh yes, the scuttling of their bony legs, the chittering of their jaws, the scraping and rattling of their hard shells crowding one another as they move along.

"The whole idea was to stand our ground as long as we dared, validate our courage, so to speak, knowing that The Cauldron's pyres would be lit just before the prattlers reached us. I remember well how we were laughing when we first marched out to stand in line. Laughing, all of us, a hand on the shoulder of the man to either side. How you hoped they couldn't feel you shaking. How comforting it was to feel their shoulders shivering, too. And how quickly it all stopped when we first heard them coming. We were frozen. I still wake some nights... and I see them just as clearly as I hear them."

He didn't need to say more. Carson knew what everyone around the table was thinking... what they were imagining. Some eight or nine almons ago, something had gone terribly wrong on Validation Night. Some sort of trouble with turning spark to flame beneath the pyres. Twenty-nine men had been killed, and many more severely wounded, before the first fire sprang to life. Several men thought to have been there were never heard from again. They'd simply vanished. It had become known as Evisceration Night, and it had marked the end of validation celebrations at The Cauldron.

"It was a stupid thing to do, of course, but we were young, and it's no longer practiced," said Sergeant Galeran.

"Is there a way to strike the GOT without rousing the prattlers or offending them?" asked Sir Dreddit.

Sergeant Galeran stifled a grim laugh. "The dark wakes them, friend, and everything offends them."

"We cannot reach the GOT and sustain an attack without the dark's company. The distance across the prattler's territory is too great," said Sir Parrish.

Carson's fingers drummed the table slowly.

Major Stronghart looked to the marshal. "We battle them as well, then."

"The prattlers are not our enemy," Carson said, "but should they come between us and those who are, we shall be prepared. Sergeant Galeran, you have one quarter moon to learn all you can about the beasts. Surely there is more to them than what you've shared tonight. Their habits, their strengths and weaknesses. Find someone who has studied them and knows the chinks in their armor."

Sir Dreddit cleared his voice. "We strike in one half moon?"

"Or less. One quarter moon to plan and mobilize," said the marshal. "Another to find our way there and see things through. Whilst we prepare, Sergeant Stone will take three men to measure the size and strength of The Guild's army and its compound—its defenses, and any weaknesses or points of attack. The High Order, Sergeant—confirm its number and its make-up. Names, descriptions, anything to help us identify them." The marshal looked resolutely down the table's length. "We leave when Sergeant Stone returns. One-half moon at best."

Sibil Dunn

It is a worthy venture. A reasoned path. Be patient.

Sibil watched the morning shade, once having carpeted the castle's entire grounds, slowly recede to the bailey's eastern edge. Sunshine bathed the army's barracks long before it ushered warm air down the corridor behind her, jokingly referred to as Staya Way—not because the officers' quarters were off limits, but because a soldier never knew what sort of unpleasant task he might inherit there.

Castle Aranox had turned into a wasp's nest, and someone had kicked the hive. The change in atmosphere was palpable, driven by more than a rapid influx of weapons and warriors, their prevalence accompanied by a marked increase in activity, punctuated by the bark of orders and the hurried movement of palace staff. Even the simplest of tasks seemed tackled with a sense of urgency.

A buzz of animated conversation further energized the swarm. For nearly a half moon, exaggerated stories had swirled about the palace like dry leaves. Sibil could not help but pick up bits and pieces—a word here, a phrase or exclamation there. The monarch's attempted assassination; the murders of a dozen townsfolk; the special powers of a seer that had twice saved the king from certain death; the subsequent beheading of two Guild members; the likelihood of more strikes on the castle, or speculation about how and when the king's army would respond; the untimely death of her mother—all served as additional kindling for those championing the king's declaration of war against the Takers Guild. An occasional surreptitious stare, secretive whisper or finger pointed Sibil's way, reminded her that wild tales about "the daughter of the seer," "The Wisperal," and "the giant killer" had also become commonplace.

Dirt roiled in the bailey's air, kicked up by horses' hooves and soldiers' soles, but one pair of shiny black boots caught her eye... the same boots that had once kicked a servant's door in, enabling the king's marshal to introduce himself and confront the palace steward. It had been a good first impression. She had since come to know the man better, and he had given her no cause to doubt the reputation afforded him by the likes of Rolft and Fereliss: As loyal to the king as any man could be. Trustworthy, capable, and calculating... A thinker with a mind as sharp as the sword hanging by his side.

Marshal Carson and his measured stride. Always so calm and confident! What must that feel like? She had seen him out of sorts only once—the day they had captured the man with the scar on his forehead, and his short sidekick, "the cat." *Good riddance to them both!*

Sergeant Cogswell's words rang in her ears as the marshal neared. *"One task at a time. Do not accept resistance. Barriers are first broken by the mind!"*

The marshal stopped to acknowledge her, his hands coming to rest lightly on his hips. "Miss Dunn. I learned only this morning of your mother's passing. I'm sorry for your loss, and terribly saddened. Truly, I am. She was a remarkable woman."

"Thank you, Marshal. She thought highly of you as well."

The soldier cast a glance at the door to his quarters. "Is there something I or Lady Carson can do for you? Some way that we can help?"

"Indeed there is. I've come to ask a favor."

"Anything."

"I would join your army." *Hold his gaze. Don't falter!*

The marshal's eyelids closed just long enough for him to take a deep breath. "Anything within my power, that is."

"Is it not your army?" *Please, don't shut me out!*

"It is the king's army, Miss Dunn."

"Of course, but surely he does not decide who joins it. Is that not your job, or that of someone you command?"

"It is."

"Well then, why can you not accept me?"

"Truth be told, I could. But I'm afraid it's not to be."

"When my mother and I were first invited here, we were told our lives would be improved."

"That was the king's intention."

"And yet we have suffered just the opposite."

Marshal Carson raked his hair back with his fingers. "Take some time, why don't you? It's not wise to ponder crucial matters under duress."

"What crucial matters do you refer to?"

"Your mother's death, Miss Dunn."

"Does Sir Godfrey not mourn the death of his son, Theos? Will he not ride with you against The Guild? How do his feelings differ from mine? How do his circumstances differ?"

"Sir Godfrey is already sworn to serve the king. I cannot banish him because his son was killed."

"No, but could you not command him to stay here, given his circumstances? While he ponders crucial matters under duress?" A wry smile turned the corners of the marshal's mouth. "What if it were Tristan Godfrey standing here, not already knighted. If he came to you and asked to join your army to avenge his brother, can you say in truth you would deny him?"

"No. Please, I know you hold a soft spot in the Godfreys' hearts. Perhaps you should wait for Tristan's return and speak with him."

"Tristan isn't coming back!" *Mistake! Do not go there!*

The marshal grimaced. "What makes you say that?"

Don't speak to him of dreams or premonitions! "I feel it, just as strongly as the sympathy you feel toward me now."

The marshal studied her before shaking his head slowly, as though trying to convince himself of something. "My apologies, Miss Dunn, but I cannot."

"But why? You've not answered me as yet. How do my circumstances differ? Is it that I'm not a man? Do you think me too young? Too fragile?"

"It's none of that, Miss Dunn, believe me."

"What, then?"

"You no doubt tire of hearing this, but again... conflicting edicts from the king. If you must know the truth, his feelings toward your family prevent me. He does not wish to be responsible for further loss."

"He's said as much to you?"

"No, but I know the way his mind works as well as I know my own, and this much I assure you... if I admit you to the army, neither you nor I will enjoy the king's reaction. I'm sparing both of us the unpleasantness we would suffer on our way back to this same place."

Sibil held his gaze. "Then I thank you for your honesty, and I rescind the favor I have asked of you."

"I am most grateful."

"And replace it with another."

"Which is?"

"To speak with the king directly... and in your presence."

It was the same room into which she had been ushered by Reggie's friend, Bernier, following the steward's advances. She had only a vague recollection of it, but now familiar objects brought her memory back: a globe of Baelon on a pedestal of carmine; a life-sized painting of Queen Isadora and Princess Lewen hanging on the wall; the large smokewood desk with intricate carvings that King Axil sat behind.

The monarch gestured to a chair upholstered in purple cloth—the same chair her mother had been sitting in that day. "Miss Dunn, your presence honors me. Please... sit." He was a big man, somehow regal even without a crown on his large head. Wavy hair with brushstrokes of gray and brown fell to his shoulders, there to rest on a heavy robe of forest green. A full beard concealed much of his expression, but it could not hide his tired blue eyes, or the deep lines of worry that creased his brow and the corners of his eyes.

Or was that sadness? Regardless, his kind face warmed her when he smiled.

"Your Majesty, thank you for seeing me." *Be brave! This is a path you chose to tread.*

"The marshal tells me you wish to join his army."

Definitely sadness.

Sibil stole a glance at Marshal Carson, leaning casually against a fireplace mantel behind the monarch.

"If the army intends to make war on those who killed my mother... yes, Your Majesty."

"He tells me you are quite skilled—more so than most—and with my blessing, he would offer you a contract."

Unexpectedly promising! Sibil shot another look at the marshal, but he remained expressionless.

"Thank the gods that I have better sense," said King Axil.

Wait—what's happening?

"I am indebted to your family," said the king. "Your father died here... on palace grounds, working at my invitation. Your mother saved my life—not once, but twice, mind you—and lost hers in return. Again, on my behalf." He turned in his chair, craning his neck to glare at the marshal. "Now I am supposed to let their daughter... *their daughter*...join the army? As we prepare for war! To what end? To be maimed or killed in service to the realm? Have you gone mad?"

Marshal Carson stood as still as a statue at The House of All Gods.

King Axil's shoulders relaxed, his voice softening. "My apologies, Miss Dunn. You should not think me angry. Not with you, at least. And the marshal, I know, means well. Some days, I must remind him that the realm's continued success relies on more than winning wars. Nonetheless, I am impressed by his account of your talents. Truly. And you have my sympathy."

"I do not require sympathy, Your Majesty."

"Nevertheless, I offer it. I, too, have suffered the terrible loss of loved ones. But the army? What would you have me say to your parents when I pass on? The loss of a child is unspeakable. I will not be party to subjecting them to that."

"My parents are dead, m'lord. If anything, they look forward to the day I rejoin them. I cannot know the pain of losing a child, but can it be much greater than that suffered by a child deprived of both her parents? If you are truly indebted to my family, there is but one of us left to benefit from your good grace. In light of that, is what I ask so unreasonable?"

"I fear it is."

Sibil could not resist. "'Whatever she wishes, whenever she wishes it.' We seem to be falling short of that."

One of the king's eyes twitched. "Revenge is a temptress, Sibil, full of promise and difficult to deny. I can attest to that. But she rarely satisfies, and almost always exacts payment. You must trust me on this."

"Are we not all satisfied differently, m'lord?"

"We are."

"If not for revenge, then why do you pursue The Guild?"

King Axil shifted in his seat, his eyes flitting to the marshal. "The Guild has too long held the entire realm for ransom. I owe it to the people."

Sibil nodded. "My king's reasoning is good enough for me. I am happy to adopt it as my own if it will help my cause."

"Ahhh..." King Axil chuckled, wagging a finger at her. "You see? The scheming temptress, revenge, has already stolen your voice."

"I care not what you call it, Your Majesty. I would join your army. I would slay those who robbed me of my mother, and those who killed Theos Godfrey. The same who killed your daughter and your wife. Lewen was my best friend. I have been robbed of all that I hold dear. My friends, my family... Everything I once hoped for has been taken from me by The Guild."

King Axil folded his hands and rested them on his desktop. "The royal ambassadors would find it difficult to match wits with you, Miss Dunn. Perhaps instead of joining the army, you would do me the favor of joining my staff. The ambassadors could use your help."

"Will they be meeting with The Guild?" asked Sibil.

Marshal Carson's chuckle was his first sign of life. A stern look from King Axil returned him to stone.

The monarch sat forward in his seat. "I knew your father well enough to know he would not want this. No father could. I have been to war, Sibil, and I have seen its horrors naked and exposed. War is so much uglier than you can imagine sitting here. If you could only glimpse it for one moment, you would turn away repulsed and wish never to lay eyes on it again."

"How can you be sure? The marshal has seen war, as have many of his soldiers. And yet I do not see them turning from the prospect of it now."

"That's different."

"Is it?" Sibil tugged at a loose thread on the chair's armrest. "I'm sure you're right, sire."

"Yes. Well then, let's forget this notion, shall we?"

"About my father, I mean. He would not want me going to war. He would spare me from all manner of conflict if he could. But were he alive, m'lord, he would not try to stop me from this. My parents ceased commanding me the day I was released by the God of Children. From that day forth, they helped me sort my options, then left me to chart my own course. My father would no doubt prefer I not go to war, but were he here today, and I told him there were forces trying to bar me from my chosen path, he would not be happy. No matter if they were kings or paupers, sire. My father would stand with me, as you might well imagine." Sibil measured her next words. "As any father who ever truly loved a daughter might imagine."

King Axil winced. Marshal Carson came to life. Sibil could not bear to meet the gaze of either. She regretted her last utterance.

"Well done," the king said softly. "You wield your words as deftly as the marshal does his sword... I yield." He rose to leave. Sibil bowed her head. She watched the hem of the monarch's robe sweep the floor beside her, felt his hand rest lightly on her head in passing. "This battle is yours. And yet my answer is still no. Such is the nature of war, Miss Dunn. Even the victor pays a price."

She counted nine of them before they overtook her. Riders, coming fast across open country. They could easily have skirted her, but instead, they bore directly down on her, as if to boast: *We have some place to be, some purpose to fulfill, and nothing in our way shall keep us from it!* She moved slightly off the beaten path to watch them pass with their grim faces and rough features, an impressive number of weapons on prominent display, either carried on their person or their horses. Several of them looked impassively at her in passing. Then they were gone, as quickly as they had come.

Sibil stroked Shadow's neck. "I'm sorry, boy. Had I been thinking clearly, I would have left you at the castle to live out your days in Reggie's gentle care. I should have chosen some old war horse to join me on this journey." She removed the amulet given to her by Father Syrus from her neck, turning it so she could read its back side. "'Protector of Innocence.' I shall try to do a better job of that, I promise." She pressed her lips to it before draping its leather cord over the pommel of her saddle. The amulet came to rest against Shadow's girth.

She took stock of her meager supplies: a small sack with enough food and water to last a quarter moon if she rationed it. Another satchel with a change of clothes. A bedroll. And what she carried on her person: her daggers—the smallest now strapped to her thigh and hidden by her leggings—and Tristan's letter, tucked inside her shirt, where its words caressed her skin.

The Fekle Forest taunted her as she rode past. There had been a time when thoughts of roaming it with Tristan had kept her entertained on sleepless nights. It was supposed to be enchanted. Lovers who trekked through it hand in hand were bound to one another for eternity, and the spell it cast on those who carved their names into one tree in particular was said to add ten almons to their lives. In the spring, a near-constant shower of pollen mixed with fairy dust promised good health and untold wealth to all it touched. Nothing bad was supposed to happen in The Fekle Forest.

And yet, the fringe of its canopy had harbored an assassin. Somewhere close by, perhaps in that very spot, an arrow unleashed from the tree line had found Theos Godfrey's heart and stopped its beating cold.

What's happened to you, Tristan? Speak to me if you can!

It appeared at first as a narrow slit cut into distant earth, but the closer to it Shadow's plodding gait brought her, the more evident its true length and width became, until a giant crater, blazing white with streaks of blue and gray, revealed itself—a pit large enough to swallow all of Fostead, deep enough to drown five cities piled on top of one another. The floor of the abyss teemed with ox-drawn carts and men swarming over chunks of stone like ants atop dead carcasses. Small puffs of powdered rock billowed from the crater's depths.

By the time she neared the cavity's edge, where an old man stood alone beside his horse, she was completely captivated, enthralled less by the spectacle itself than by the memory it triggered. *The Baelonite Quarry!* She had been there before, at age six or seven, seated beside the smartest and strongest man she had ever known.

"I don't want to go down there. Please don't make me."

"Don't be silly," said her father, flicking the reins to a wagon clearly as frightened as she was. It shuddered and shook, and who could blame it? The prospect of descending that steep, narrow path cut into the side of a giant cliff petrified her. One misstep by the anxious horse, one failing part on a rig designed and built by imperfect men, and they would most certainly find themselves hurtling downward through space toward a most horrific death. "It's entirely safe. You'll see."

Oh, gods above! Does my father have to be the bravest man in the world as well? She clutched her rag doll to her chest, closed her eyes, and prayed the God of Children would watch over her descent.

Despite repeated entreaties and chiding from her father, she had never been back—invariably finding an excuse to avoid tempting fate again.

She fixed her gaze on what she had always recalled as an extremely steep descent. It still appeared to be the only way to access the quarry's bowels—or climb out of them. But the treacherous route she had endured as a child appeared far less fearsome through adult eyes. Wide enough to accommodate at least four wagons side by side, it resembled a broad trough with a healthy earthen berm separating it from the cliff's edge. And its grade was actually quite gentle due to the prevalence of numerous switchbacks.

For one brief moment, she considered circumnavigating the quarry's rim so that she might coax Shadow down the serpentine route that had so haunted her as a child, if only to put the other demons inside of her on notice.

The old man at the quarry's edge slightly startled her when he turned and spoke as though they were the best of friends.

"They fancy 'em young and fit down there; they've no use for the likes of me." Sibil's silence did not dampen the stranger's enthusiasm. "And those wagons don't come this way like they used to. Not since that architect's death. What was his name?"

"Adrian Dunn," said Sibil, still staring at the crater.

"That's right! You know your history, do you? You've studied the Terms of the Two Realms? The pact that governs the quarry and the grove?"

"I know a bit about it." *More than most, I suppose!*

"As do I! The Baelonite Quarry belongs to Aranox, but it hauls stone to Tegan in exchange for Euphoria, the only grove of which is managed by King Tygre's subjects on the other side of those mountains. A trade route called the Exchange connects the two." *Gods above! If my father were here, the two of you would be talking until dark!* "Name's Gradiott. Folks call me Gradi. I'm from Tegan. Summerwinds, to be exact… not far from the Euphoria Grove, you know? I worked inside those woods my entire youth, and still I live right down the road from it. Never have I touched the stuff... not once, if you can believe it! My imagination's wild enough. It doesn't need prodding to go places it probably shouldn't. Anyway, I wish I had the time to see what his hands shaped. Your realm's architect, that is—assuming you're from Aranox. They're works of art, I'm told. Are you?"

"Am I what?"

"From Aranox?"

"I am."

"You've seen them, then? The Dunn buildings?"

"I have. All of them." A bit of melancholy pride warmed Sibil's insides.

The old man's eyes grew even brighter. "Have you really! How many are there, then?"

"Six, if you count Castle Aranox, but the birth of that was well before his time. He did expand it and add a lot of detail. Truth be told, it was a lot more effort than some of the smaller buildings he built from the ground up."

"Such as?"

"Such as The Hold—it's no bigger than a cottage, really."

"Ahh, yes, The Hold... 'All are watched, few are kept.'"

"Few are held," corrected Sibil.

"Thank you, yes; that's right. 'Few are held.' You really do know your history! What were the gods thinking when they took him, your architect? They should at least have let him build one more. It would have been number seven, right? One for each of them!"

Sibil could not help but smile.

He reminded her of Sergeant Cogswell in more ways than one, and not at all in others. She judged him to be the same size, and somewhere near the same age; the same short-cropped silver hair adorned his scalp, though not nearly so thickly as on Cogswell's. His threadbare clothing hung loosely on his gaunt frame. A sword hanging from his saddle appeared to match his age. Too large for its scabbard, a portion of its blade remained exposed, dull and discolored below the hilt. His gray-blue eyes sparkled as he spoke.

"You're headed south, are you? Whatever for?"

Sibil ran a hand along Shadow's neck. "I'm on an errand for a friend."

"An errand, eh? Whatever you say; that's your business. I'm not one to pry, but you should know there's little south of here that cares about your king's law—or my king's, for that matter—or what you might think is right. I hope your friend told you that."

"He did."

"Ah! So it's a he, is it?" Gradi swung into his saddle with surprising ease. "I hope you've not been hoodwinked! You wouldn't catch my daughters here. Not headed south. Not if I could help it. Not even with an escort! I'll tell you what, though... You're welcome to travel with me. I'm not much to look at any more, but I'm still good company." He had the look of a child who longed for approval. "And I know my way around."

Sibil weighed his offer against the prospect of entering the Dark Woods on her own.

"I hardly know you."

"Yes, well, let's see... My eldest daughter would tell you I'm too soft to ever get my due; my youngest would say the same about my head—too soft, that is. And my wife, well, she'd swear to you I lost every bit of my remarkably good sense soon after I married her. Not before, mind you. She'd be very clear about that. But all three would tell you my heart is in the right place."

Sibil's defenses began to fall.

Gradi chuckled as he pointed to the two small satchels slung over Shadow's back. "By the looks of our belongings, I don't think either of us is at risk of being robbed by the other, and if it came to that, you're bigger and probably stronger than me, anyway. What have you to lose?"

Sibil eyed the one small sack hanging from the old man's horse, and the bedroll tied behind his saddle. His only other possessions looked to be the rusty sword and an odd-shaped livestock bell that sang when the man's horse moved.

"All right, then," she said. "Until we reach the Dark Woods, at least."

"Then we're off! I don't mean to be rude, but we should move along—push to reach them before night falls. If we camp outside the woods and rise with the sun, we've a good chance of making it through before it's dark again. We don't want to spend a night beneath those wicked trees if we can help it!"

The thick band of mottled colors that represented the Dark Woods stretched unbroken from one end of the southern horizon to the other. Between its tree line and a darkening sky, a hazy ribbon of sand marked the distant Lawless Lands. The longer the riders were in their saddles, the taller the trees appeared, until they kissed the sky and the Lawless Lands disappeared behind them.

Just as the wood's general shape began to show the outlines of branches, trunks and foliage, the sun dipped into the Mersal Sea.

"Close enough," Gradi said, halting his mount. "The night winds blow mostly south, and the bortok have a keen sense of smell. We'll make camp here."

"Have you ever seen one?" asked Sibil, dismounting.

"A bortok? Never, and I don't care to, either." Gradi joined her on the ground and motioned back the way they had come, drawing Sibil's attention to a number of distant riders. "We need to be a good ways off the trodden path," he said, leading his horse west. "Some of those numbskulls will ride all night, with or without torches. If you're sleeping in their path, they'll trample you and not stop to say they're sorry. They'll ride on as if nothing happened, just you wait and see, right into those dark woods. And they'll keep going, too... until they run into something that hasn't had its supper and doesn't mind the taste of man."

The two went about preparing their bedrolls for the evening.

"Where are they going?" asked Sibil. "Surely not the Lawless Lands."

"You'd be surprised," said Gradi. "The Cauldron lies just outside your king's realm. I'm sure you've heard of it. No doubt some are headed there."

"And the others?"

"Some to The Kindling, I suppose. There may even be a few destined for the GOT. The Guild isn't self-sufficient, you know. People come and go there like the tide. Goods flow in and out as well—mostly in, I suppose."

"How would you know that?"

"How could it be otherwise? This is The Guild of Takers we're talking about. What do you think they're taking? And once they've taken it, where do you think it goes? Where do they store it? Where are their takers trained? Once trained, where do they go? How do they obtain their food and clothing? Candle wax and axle grease, and sundry other things... Weapons for their army. It all has to come from somewhere."

"You seem to know a lot about the GOT." *What else might you share that could help me?*

"Stories, mostly. They say its cornerstones are made of baelonite, and that The Guild stole them from the quarry—took them forcefully, that is—and dragged them all the way across the desert hundreds of almons ago. I've never been to see, of course, so I can't say there's any truth to it, but it would not surprise me. Not in the least."

"The men following us... you really think they might be traveling to the GOT?" *If so, might I fall in behind them?*

"There are many pathways through the Dark Woods. The one we'll take comes to a fork a short way through... Corpse's Choice. Now, if we could watch them ride past that point, I could say with some certainty where they're headed. Go left, and soon after leaving Aranox and the Dark Woods, you'll find yourself at The Cauldron. You can get to the GOT from there, of course, but it's not as direct a route as going right. So, I imagine most, if not all, will go left. In the long run, though, I don't suppose it matters much. As the name suggests, no man with any brain goes either way. The only sensible thing to do at Corpse's Choice is turn around."

Sibil stretched out on her bedroll, face to the sky. "What will you do, then, when that time comes? Which way will you go?"

"At Corpse's Choice? Left, of course. I'll be going left."

"To The Cauldron, then?"

"The Cauldron? Not exactly, no."

"Why left, then?"

The longer the old man took to answer, the more intrigued Sibil became. When he finally spoke, his words only added to the mystery.

"Let's just say... I too am on an errand."

She was stretched out on her stomach, one cheek and both palms flat against the cold ground, when it began to tremble. Softly at first, as though the earth was humming with its lips against her body, then shivering as the sound of horses' hooves rose through the dirt, ever louder, until she could hear it not only in her ear pressed to the ground, but all around her. The earth began to shake more violently, then roll and heave like giant ocean waves; a deafening roar heralded the stampede of a thousand steeds. She covered her ears and tried to shield her body from the relentless pounding of sharp hooves as they engulfed her. She curled into a tight ball until finally the ground stopped moving and the noise subsided. When finally she dared to open her eyes, when the beasts were gone and the dust settled, all that remained beside her was a trampled body wrapped in blood-stained blankets.

The old man, Gradi, had been sleeping in that very spot.

Slowly, she drew the covers back... and screamed.

Tristan!

Sibil sat upright and stared into the night, breathless and apprehensive. She could see nothing but the shadows of shadows cast by a crescent sliver of silver in the sky.

The sound of passing riders carried clearly through the crisp night air, but the beating of hooves came slow and steady, no quicker than her stirred heartbeat, no louder than the sound of several people drumming on their trouser legs. She held her breath the time it took for the sound to fade away, not daring to move, just waiting... waiting for something she could not describe.

Sibil had not slept since imagining the stampede, so she was thankful when the sky began to lighten and Gradi finally stirred. "You're well-rested, are you?" he asked, slowly getting to his feet.

"I am." *What point is there in saying otherwise?*

"That's good. We've a full sun's ride ahead of us."

The two were silent as several riders heading toward the Dark Woods rode past, giving them a wide berth and an appraising look.

Gradi quickly rolled his bed and tied it. Sibil followed suit as the old man collected their hobbled horses. The strange livestock bell hummed as he removed it from his mount. "They'll need food and water before the sun is high," he said. "I know a spot where they can graze a bit and drink their fill. Do you need to eat, or can you chew on something whilst we ride?"

"I'll manage."

"I've plenty of dried bism if you want. Just say the word."

The two were soon in their saddles and at the edge of the Dark Woods. Gradi stopped his mount. "You're sure about this?" he asked.

Sibil stared past him into the thick forest. Aptly named, it hid its holdings from her, and not just because early morning clouds blanketed the sky. She doubted the Dark Woods revealed much more beneath the brightest sun. So many tree trunks, so closely spaced together, their crooked branches interlocking like thick strands of interwoven wood. Something sinister inhabited that place. Even Shadow sensed it. Sibil calmed him with a palm against his neck.

"I'm sure," she said. "But if I'm to continue with you, I would know just where you're going, and why."

"This from someone who's not even told me her name," Gradi said.

"Sibil."

For a moment, the old man appeared to try and read her mind, then sighed. "All right, but you must promise you'll not rush to judgment."

"I promise."

"You didn't hear it from me, but the Takers Guild is paying folk to take up arms against your king."

"What?" She could not have heard him right.

"Yes, indeed. Twenty kingshead just to make your mark, I'm told. Ten more each quarter moon you stay alive."

"You can't be serious."

"Oh, but I am."

"You don't mean to say you're joining The Guild's army!"

"I'm not proud of it, but what else am I to do? Show me a better way to make a living, and I'll follow you instead."

"And you're sure The Guild will take you?"

"Well, that's not very inspiring, is it? But no, I'm not. Still, what have I to lose?"

"Your life, perhaps?"

The old man laughed. "Please. Surely you can see there's not much left of that. I'd gladly give what little remains to help my wife and daughters."

"What about the king? Surely he would match The Guild's offer for those willing to fight on the side of right!"

"I'm sure he would. But his army's got standards higher than The Guild. The king wants fighters in his ranks—men he thinks will make his enemies bow down or suffer. The Guild is a bit different. From what I hear, its army is small but fierce, and it isn't looking to expand. It just wants a sea of bodies to stand between it and the king. To attract His Majesty's arrows and slow his army down, as it were. I can do that much, I'm certain!"

Sibil could only shake her head. "Have you thought to ask the king for help?"

Gradi laughed again. "What... just ride up to the castle and put my hand out? If that would work, child, the line to the palace would reach into the Lawless Lands. No, I'm afraid it doesn't work that way. The king's a good man, so I'm told, but honestly, I can't say he's ever done much for me or mine. Not really."

Sibil's head spun.

"We're wasting precious time," said Gradi. "I still don't know what's driving you. I think you ought to turn around. But if you're bent on going through this place, you're better off with me. I'm no threat to you, Sibil."

And with that, he urged his horse into the Dark Woods.

Sibil followed, checking to ensure the amulet still hung securely from Shadow's saddle.

Gods above, if you do exist, watch over us!

***

THE SEAMSTRESS OF THE NIGHT

"A true bond is forged by the heart, Rolft, not by any calculations of the mind. There is no fire that can burn it, no steel that can cut through it. A true bond lasts forever." Miralda Aerns to her son Rolft, age ten.

Marshal Erik Carson

It took mere moments for the armory's forge to draw the sweat from Carson's brow and neck. Red-hot embers spewed from the Dragon's mouth, then flitted about the hot, oppressive air just outside the giant furnace. The blacksmiths, dressed in little more than leather aprons, seemed not to notice, their smudged and shiny limbs somehow immune to blistering and peeling. The pounding of metal and hiss of steam punctuated the Dragon's roar, drowning most of Baselo's speech despite the lead blacksmith's deep, raised voice. Carson signaled his desire to move further from the raging furnace.

Baselo maneuvered his way to the rear of the armory and waited for the marshal to come close. "Better?" the smith asked. Carson nodded. "I think I know what you're after, Marshal. It shouldn't be a problem."

Carson took the sword from Baselo's hands to help make his point. "It doesn't need to be big or fancy, Baselo. Just some mark to distinguish them as ours. It mustn't require your keen eye, mind you. Something even an aging marshal can identify... without having to search for it. Can you do that?"

"Of course, Marshal. We'll put the mark here, shall we? Where the blade meets the hilt?"

"Yes, that would do nicely."

Carson handed the sword back, his attention captured by a familiar figure slipping through the smoke and shadows of the armory's outer reaches. It disappeared into the weapons' storeroom.

"That'd be Cogswell," Baselo said.

"Indeed. You'll excuse me, will you?"

"Of course, Marshal."

Carson stepped inside the storeroom to discover Sergeant Cogswell mostly hidden by row after row of newly fashioned weapons—lances, swords, cudgels, grappling hooks and armor—some stacked on tables, others leaning against free-standing racks. Stooped over, his back to the marshal, the sergeant occupied himself with the contents of a large wooden bin. A variety of hand implements hung on hooks and nested on shelving beside him.

How long has it been since those hands wielded weapons in actual battle? Longer than I've served as marshal, but the stories are well-known to me. Carson tread lightly, the sawdust floor and the faint roar of the Dragon muffling his footsteps. There had been several rumors of late regarding the sergeant's slowing reflexes and his failing hearing. *None of us live forever!*

"Something I can do for you, Marshal?" Cogswell continued his rummaging in the bin, not bothering to turn around.

Nothing wrong with his awareness! "There is indeed, if you know of Miss Dunn's whereabouts."

The old warrior straightened to inspect a wooden sword more closely. "No more than you, I'm certain."

"Did she speak to you before she left?"

"No, Marshal, not about that. I've not seen her for two suns now... not since her mother's passing. If I knew where she was headed, I'd have told you." Cogswell returned the sword to the bin.

"But you know what she's up to."

"I've my suspicions. Same as you. Do you need me to go after her? I would, you know."

Carson raised his eyebrows. "No. You're needed here, Arthur. Regardless, I suspect she'll be back within a quarter moon. How much trouble can she get into with no food and just one dagger?"

"Not one, Marshal. Three."

"Three!"

"Mm-hmm. She carries her own, of course. That bone-handled beauty with the jewel. And two more of late, gifted to her by Rolft before he went his way."

"Black grips?" Carson pictured them: one sticking out of Rolft's rib cage; the other, much smaller, lying on the ground beside the retired guardsman in Fostead's south end.

Cogswell nodded. "They belonged to the smaller of the two whose heads you took. Fine blades, carmine handles, both easy to conceal. Made an old man blush to learn where she keeps the smallest."

Carson ran his fingers along the shaft of a lance. "And she knows how to use them."

"That she does, Marshal. There's not a squire she hasn't put to shame." Cogswell resumed his fishing. "Even Sir Parrish finds her a handful. With a dagger in her hand, she's as quick as any I've trained. You wouldn't think it to look at her, but to attack is in her nature, and now she knows to defend as well." The sergeant-at-arms raised a creased and weathered finger. "But that's here. Familiar surroundings, friendly foes, no real threat of losing life or limb. I'd not bet against her in a tournament, I'll tell you that. And I think her skills would carry her against a common man of any size, armed or not. But still she struggles with the sword. And in a real battle? Against seasoned fighters? Even with her daggers, I'd not want to see her tested there. Not just yet, anyway. I was relieved to hear the king would not allow her in the army."

Carson used both hands to massage the back of his neck. "It may be she only needs her solitude. Some time to clear her head. Regardless, the fire that burns in her will run its course soon enough, don't you think?"

Cogswell slipped several smokewood training daggers into his waistband. "I wouldn't be so sure, Marshal. Are you certain you don't need me to go after her? It would be a mistake to underestimate the girl's resolve... or your sergeant-at-arms." One of the old warrior's steely gray eyes winked at the marshal. "His hearing and his bite are as strong as ever."

"Gone?" The grizzled king craned his head back, eyes closed, lips parted. "Where?"

Carson shrugged. "She left no word, sire. The kitchen staff prepared light fare for her... dried fruit and nuts. Not enough to travel any distance. The stableboy, Reggie, was the last to see her. Two suns past. She told him she was going home for a spell."

"But she's not there?"

"No, m'lord. The Dunn's cottage remains empty."

"She's sulking, is she?"

"Sulking, m'lord? No. That's not her nature. Simmering, perhaps. Not sulking."

"Simmering! She's not going to put herself in danger, is she? Noggods! Have I condemned the entire family? She's on some sort of crusade of her own, is she? Was I wrong to deny her a commission in your army? What possible good could come of that?"

A rhetorical question, but... "If commissioned, m'lord, she would be under my command. As it is, she does as she pleases."

The monarch pondered the implications. "You could shield her from battle?"

"Soldiers do as they are told, m'lord. They follow orders."

"Mmm. Unlike a king, you mean," grumbled the monarch.

"Not at all, m'lord. But now that you've lifted that scab—"

"I've already given you my word. What more do you want?"

"You agreed to stay behind, m'lord, not keep within the castle walls. The two are not the same. Those who seek your death no doubt wait patiently for another opportunity, and with King Tygre on his way..."

"Now you would command two kings, would you? A bit much, even for you, my friend."

Carson hung his head.

"Nevertheless, I shall humor you and stay imprisoned here until you take the magister's head. Not because I'm bending to your will, mind you, but because King Tygre's presence here will keep me occupied. Otherwise, my patience with your strategy runs thin."

"Understood. And your marshal is most grateful."

"Indebted, you mean."

"Quite, Your Majesty." Carson raised a finger in the air and slowly paced the room. "King Tygre's visit does give one pause to wonder, though, whether he feels Tegan is threatened by The Guild, and if so, what he plans to do about it."

"I know the way your mind works, Erik. The Guild reaches into Tegan the same as Aranox, 'tis true. It's kept me awake as well. I'll find an opportune time to parse the matter with Tygre once our friendship is rekindled. You have my word. But until then, given Isadora and Lewen's deaths, it seems only right that the first strike be delivered from Aranox alone. You understand? This must be by my decree, if not by my hand."

"Yes, m'lord."

"Even with The Guild's High Order crushed, its underlings—takers, gatherers and overseers—all will need sweeping from the shadows of both realms. I'm certain Tygre will do his part whilst we see to ours." The monarch clenched a fist. "But this first blow, we must land ourselves."

Rolft Aerns

Rolft drove the pointed end of a long ironwood pole far beneath the base of a large rock before bringing his full weight to bear on its other end. The boulder would not budge. He tried again, his feet leaving the ground, the ironwood bending until it creaked. He tossed the pole aside and grunted. He glared at a tall pile of loose rocks already extracted from the earth—the fruits of his last moon's labor. Enough stone, perhaps, to lay a small drying shed's foundation.

This monster dwarfed them all. He grabbed a shovel and bent to the task of finding just how much of it remained beneath the soil. Though forced to temper his efforts in deference to his wounds, he considered each thrust of the shovel a celebration of life and strength renewed. By all accounts, he would be dead but for the mysterious magic of a Systalene sister.

His flesh bore several tributes to her skill and his resilience. A ragged mark above his right eye led to one below it, stretching to his cheek. Striated scars bestrewed his left arm. An ugly mass of puckered, congealed skin disfigured his left torso. But the physical effects of his recent encounters in Fostead had largely dissipated. Even his right thigh, stabbed outside The Raven's Nest, seemed nearly recovered. It complained only when he bent his leg too far.

Sweat ran freely down his neck and back, yet he dared not remove his shirt. Midway through Nine Moons, the sun remained capable of blistering skin during the hours of labor. Not until the evening, when the orb slipped beneath the covers of the Lumax Mountains, would the hints of seasonal change make themselves known: a stronger breeze, a heavier mist, a slight chill that lasted through mid-morning. In two moons' time, the ground's moisture would freeze, rendering his fields too hard to work until the coming spring.

His fields! Twenty harcours no less, courtesy of a grateful King Axil. Had he not been rendered speechless, he would have respectfully declined the unexpected gift. Marshal Carson had whispered in his ear: *"There is not a noble or a knight who deserves it more, Rolft. Take it and be at peace. Refuse—embarrass the king—and I shall have no choice but to run you through!"* If he could choose anyone to lead him into battle, it would be Marshal Carson. Or Major Stronghart, of course... The God of Fortune always rode with that one.

Rolft kept an eye on the far edge of his land, where barren dirt met sky. Atop that stark ridge, a lone silhouette moved steadily his way, one arm rising high into the air.

Not caring to disclose the degree to which he struggled, Rolft stopped laboring well before Fereliss brought his horse to stand in front of him. Neither man spoke as the royal guard assessed Rolft's situation. Green eyes beneath long, twisted brows roved the embedded rock and well-trampled ground surrounding it. They evaluated the ironwood pole leaning against it, then the shovel near Rolft's feet. Fereliss prompted his mount to circle the large stone slowly. His eyes came to rest on Rolft.

"You've finally met your match, have you?"

"*Pffft*... Child's play."

"And what will you do with it once you have it out?"

"What do you mean?"

"I mean, it's half-buried now. Once out, it will be twice as big a thorn in your side, will it not? How do you plan to move it once you've captured it? And where will you keep it?" Fereliss surveyed the nearby ground, his gaze drifting to the pile of stones some twenty paces away.

Rolft looked around himself. "Did you come here just to crack my bones regarding something you know nothing about?"

"My apologies, farmer Aerns. Just trying to learn, am I. What will you grow here when you've won this battle, eh? Sweet melba, perhaps? Or stalks of stringy cobble? And who's to cook it all... or sell it once it's grown? You'll need a woman at your side. Every farmer's got one."

"I'll manage."

"You're fully healed now, are you?"

Rolft rubbed his injured side. "I'm not the man I was, but I've no complaints."

"Nor should you have! You were as good as dead. I saw with my own eyes. You've no business standing there, you know. Were it not for that witch from Systalene..."

Rolft let loose a nervous scoff.

Fereliss scratched his beard of tangled vines. "I'm keen to marry one and bring her with me into battle!"

Rolft laughed. "The Sisters of Systalene don't marry, friend."

"Yes, well…" Fereliss chewed the hair below his lower lip.

"What is it?"

"Thistle's gone."

"Gone! Where?"

"No one seems to know. Her mother died three nights ago."

"Madam Dunn's dead?" Rolft stared into his past. Mari Dunn's pleasant countenance smiled back at him.

"And the girl's been missing since."

"Might she have gone home?" asked Rolft.

"No. There's been a soldier posted there the last two suns. No sign of anyone."

"Left without a clue? No word?"

"Well… yes and no. I'll tell you what I think, shall I? Right after Madam Dunn passed, Thistle asked to join the army. Said she wished to be part of any strike against The Guild… you know, on account of her mother, the princess, and Theos Godfrey. The marshal told her no, as did the king. She didn't take to that."

I don't imagine so!

"There's something else as well," said Fereliss. "Tristan Godfrey."

"What about him?"

"The day that he was knighted, you were still laid up. But he's been missing ever since. He too left without a word, but I've no doubt where he's gone."

"To slay his brother's killers."

"Just so. He left an envelope for Thistle at the castle. Gave it to me to give to her outside the chapel the same day he was knighted."

"What was in it?"

"The gods only know, but there's something between those two, believe me… more'n just words in an envelope."

"You're going after her?"

"No. The marshal's tired of people disappearing as he prepares for war. But he cares for the girl, and he knows you well. That's why he sent me here." Fereliss raked the bramble of his beard. "Always thinking, that one."

Overseer Reynard Rascall

Little of the past quarter moon seemed real. Much of it remained a blur. The torture and torment he had suffered at Castle Aranox, and the residual effect of a serum used by The Guild to drug him, had left his body woozy, weak, and bruised from head to toe. He had no idea how many suns had passed since his departure from the castle's dungeon, but three had come and gone since he had woken at the GOT—in Takers Tower, no less!

He had not seen or heard from Ruler Two or the magister subsequent to rousing in their presence, but he remembered well what they had said. Two's tale of a daring rescue from the clutches of the king's men; the magister's recounting of Spiro's death, and the intriguing promise of a proposition.

Three nameless young attendants introduced as 'noms' had nursed him back to health in remarkably short order. Now he followed one of their white robes, his first departure from the room that had hosted his recuperation.

He wiggled his fingers, maintaining a watchful eye on the figure ahead of him. There was little else to look at, really, as they descended the circular staircase at the core of Takers Tower. He had every reason to be mindful of his guide. The soft glow of candlelight spilled from the youth's cupped hands. Every now and then, a captive of the windcatchers high above caused the flame to flicker wildly before calming.

"If the light dies," said the nom, "place one hand on my shoulder and the other on the wall as we descend."

Brilliant!

"If you trip or fall and lose contact with the steps, try to find the rope. It reaches all the way to the bottom."

All the way to the bottom! Just how far might that be?

Reynard could barely make out the thick sisal rope hanging in the black void to his left. He doubted very much whether he could reach it without leaving the safety of the stone steps. And just how many almons had that rope been hanging there? How strong could its fibers be, having been left to rot since the beginning of time?

His knees began to tremble, and not from any lingering injury. The past two suns had left him fully recovered from whatever toxin had been used to render him lifeless in the eyes of King Axil's soldiers. *No, this is the irrational fear of something birthed in your own mind, something that cannot really hurt you. If only you will keep to the edge of the stairs nearest the wall and not lose your footing! Gods above, what am I doing here? What was the point of all that time spent on my back? Did I not resolve to leave this place as soon as possible? Have I not decided to reject the old man's proposition, no matter how enticing it might seem? Why am I not already back in Waterford, lying in my own bed next to some young lass with supple skin?*

Why indeed!

"Because you feel responsible." Spiro's voice! It would not leave him be! *"You live now to avenge me!"*

"Not much further," said the nom.

"Pure rubbish, Spiro! I should not have listened to you in the first place. I should have dragged you from that krephole Fostead when I had the chance, despite your loud objections. I could feel the walls closing in on us there, as surely as I feel the tower's stones beside me now. This is no place for the likes of me—cold, dark, and without a hint of the life I am accustomed to! How I yearn for the comforts of my own feathered nest! Surely the magister does not use this passage himself!"

The nom's forward progress stopped, his candle illuminating the outline of a wooden door below. Reynard took a last step down to join him on a circular landing.

Ah, solid ground!

The candle's flame danced as one of the nom's hands fumbled with the door. It opened slowly, as though feeling its age, to a broad, cave-like opening spotted with flickering wall torches. The pungent scent of an unfamiliar flower assailed Reynard's nostrils well before the sound of creaking hinges stopped. He shivered, reminded of the dungeon in which he and Spiro had spent their last suns together. For the first time since waking from his "death," he regretted the absence of any weapon on his person.

The nom pointed toward the darkest recesses of the cavern as he handed his candle to Reynard. A short distance away, beneath the nearest wall torch, a smaller flame flickered in the midst of three figures standing motionless, next to double doors set in stone.

"The magister awaits," the nom said, slinking away.

Wait! Where are you going? Gods above... surely not to climb those stairs without a light!

Reynard returned his attention to the stationary figures, convinced of one's identity. *The magister awaits!* He shuffled forward, suspecting that the smaller robes concealed attending noms. By the time his feet stopped moving, he knew for certain. The smooth skin of youth glistened beneath two of the three hoods.

"Overseer Rascall." *That scratchy voice! That piece of dried fruit for a nose!* "Your legs are yours again, it would appear."

"Yes, Magister. I am most grateful for their return."

"What I would give to feel as free!"

"To think how close I came to losing what they carry!" joked Reynard. *Was that too much?*

The magister chuckled and wheezed. "All in your past. We're here to celebrate your future." The fingers of his clenched hand slowly unfurled. "Show him what is possible."

One nom brought a candle close while another plucked an object from the old man's palm. A long leather cord tying key to bony wrist unraveled in the process.

The nom inserted the key into a padlock on the double doors. With a turn and a click, he released its shackle and removed it from the clasp. His companion took hold of one of the doors and eased it slowly open.

Burlap sacks stacked on top of one another filled the space behind from floor to ceiling. Reynard could only stare in wonder. This was not a storeroom full of flour, rice, or grain.

The nom returned the key to the magister's palm, coiling the leather cord as he did so.

"Go on," the magister said to Reynard. "Open one."

Reynard hesitated.

"Go on. I insist."

Reynard used both hands to untie one of the sacks at chest height. Its cloth lips freed, it spewed a dozen coins from its overcrowded mouth onto the cavern's floor.

"Marvelous!" said the magister. "You'll find those difficult to stuff back in. Feel free to put them in your pocket." Reynard did not react. "I come now and then just to admire this," the magister said. "There's nothing quite so beautiful as gold, would you not agree?"

Reynard nodded, though the ore in its raw form did little to excite him, nor did he have a taste for it fashioned into jewelry or metalware. A gold goblet or candelabra seemed a waste of precious metal, but gold coins? Something about them had stirred him since early childhood. How easily they tickled his senses. Kingsheads, in particular! The way they jingled in a shaken purse; the sound one made spinning on a tabletop; the way they gleamed in the sunlight; the weight of several nesting in one's hand; the feel of them deep inside someone else's pocket!

This trove is unlike any I've encountered! Is there any use in even trying to estimate its value?

The magister underscored Reynard's thinking. "There are nine other vaults just like this. Each tunnels south beneath the GOT to the very edge of Reception Canyon. Each holds more wealth than even you could steal in one lifetime, Overseer Rascall."

Wait! This vault extends well beyond what I can see? And it is but one of nine? Impossible! Beyond comprehension! But, if true…

"This vault is yours, subject to terms."

What! Reynard's heart began to pound. Chills danced across his chest. His head began to spin. *Terms?*

"I promised you a proposition, did I not?" The magister gestured to the cache of coins. "This is what you stand to gain. This, and a seat on The Guild's High Order. Entertain that notion for an evening. Let it get to know you. On the morrow, we'll discuss what you must do to make it so."

What I must do to make it so? Surely it will be neither easy nor without risk to life and limb!

"You have questions?" asked the magister.

The gold was slow to release its hold on Reynard's imagination.

"Yes, Magister." He bowed his head until his hair dangled against his cheeks. "Is there, perchance, a less adventurous path back to my room?"

He lay awake most of the night, not because the magister had suggested contemplation, but because he was unable to escape it.

"What are you doing?"

"What does it look like, Spiro? I'm cogitating."

"Cogi-what?"

"Thinking, friend, thinking!"

"Not that again."

"It can't be helped. I am of two restless minds."

"Three, you mean, now that I reside here!"

"Hah! Quite right! Shall I tell you what the other two are thinking?"

"Please. What else have I to do, but listen to your ramblings?"

"Very well. One cautions me to leave this place, quickly and without fanfare. You'd like to know why, I suppose. Let me count the reasons: first, I am reminded that I narrowly escaped the executioner's blade just recently! Only a fool would tempt that fate again. Quit whilst I'm ahead… whilst I still have a head, that is, or I shall end up just like you! Second, I don't need what the magister is offering; it's a temptation, to be sure, but I can live quite comfortably the

remainder of my almons without it. And third, my instincts warn me that the magister is not someone to barter with; a man does not reach his position by offering fair deals. These are all compelling arguments for leaving posthaste, would you not agree? And yet... the grounds for staying are equally persuasive."

"I'm listening."

"Do I not owe it to you, Spiro, to see whatever this is through? To place some value on the heavy price you've paid? To lend some meaning to your death? Who am I to doubt the magister's designs? Let us not forget: he saved my life! Surely he did not do so with the intent to fleece me later. You saw all that treasure! It may not be needed, but can one ever have too much? To be courted by the magister himself... To assume a seat on his High Order... Do you know what that would mean to a little boy who struggled to survive the streets of Waterford?"

"I'm waiting," Spiro said.

"Waiting? What for?"

"For what always comes of this, of course: for you to tell me that one mind has silenced the other!"

He had not glimpsed a ray of natural light since arriving at the GOT. His windowless room in Takers Tower would never entertain it, but he had come to recognize several clues to dawn's breaking from the comfort of his bed: the ability to see from one end of his room to the other; the sound of strident voices, muted by at least one wall of stone; and, most evident, the arrival of three nameless noms. This morning, only one came through his door.

"Where are your friends?" Reynard asked.

"They tend to the magister." The nom motioned to the door he had left open. "He joins you shortly."

Reynard rolled out of bed, pulled his nightshirt off and donned his blouse, pleasantly surprised by how well his limbs obeyed him. He stood to snake his legs into his trousers, rushed by noises just outside his room—the murmuring and shuffling of those whose presence sounded imminent.

He tucked his long bangs back behind his ears as the magister came into view, cane in hand, and two noms within arm's reach.

A woman followed closely, her loose-fitting dress sweeping the floor. Shorter than the magister despite the silver bun atop her head, her smooth skin suggested her hair color was not the best clue to her age. She had a small curved nose, taut cheeks, and thin lips. But her most intriguing feature, by far, was her eyes. Were they especially large, or was her face twice as small as most? Either way, her prominent peepers shone like a pair of twin spy glasses.

"Ayla, Master Rascall," croaked the wizened leader. "Allow me to introduce our financier, Ruler Three. As such, she is privy to the terms that you are offered, and shall bear witness to whatever is decided here today."

The woman's fingers flexed and twitched at the ends of her dress sleeves.

One of the magister's hands stilled hers. "Our coffers are so full, she cannot cease counting... not even in her sleep."

Reynard bowed. "Ayla, Magister... Ayla, Ruler Three."

"I trust you had a good night's sleep," said the magister.

"In truth, I did not. Our time together yestersun consumed me through the night."

"Ahhh!" the magister wheezed. "You've thought on it, have you? What you stand to gain by humoring your lord?"

What he is offering is of no use to you! "Untold riches, and a seat on The High Order! I've thought of little else."

"And both rewards within your easy reach," said the magister. "What say you, then? Are we agreed?"

No! Couch it in pleasantries, but commit to that one word! "Forgive me, Magister, but how can I decide? You've yet to say what I must do to earn them." *No matter the proposition or his terms, no matter what he asks of you, say no!*

The magister's thin lips elongated, the creases in them turning to small rivulets. "You're at the GOT, Overseer Rascall. You can abandon caution here. This is as much your house as mine. Trust me when I say what I ask in return—what The Guild asks in return—will be like pinching dires for a man of your talents."

"Beware the flatterer, Reynard!"

"Shut up, Spiro!" Reynard focused on the magister. "You want me to steal something?"

The magister chuckled. "In a manner of speaking. I would have you steal two lives. King Axil's and King Tygre's. Do that, and the vault you were shown is yours."

What? Kill who? Surely I did not hear right. "Kill who?"

"The kings of Aranox and Tegan... King Axil and King Tygre."

Preposterous! What are you waiting for? Say no! A thousand times, say no!

"That's right," said the magister, his glassy eyes searching Reynard's soul. "The man who beheaded your friend, and his counterpart."

Kill both kings of Baelon? Out of the question, and yet... Are you listening to this, Spiro? Why have you gone silent?

"The entire vault? Including its contents?" asked Reynard.

"And a seat on The High Order!" The magister's tongue slithered into view, moistened his lips, then disappeared into its cave.

Reynard sat motionless, maintaining an impassive countenance as he studied the Chalice Room—mostly white, cold, and barren, save for the counter covered in food and drink, which he dared not sample. No one had greeted him, not to say "ayla," or even "what are you doing here?" But the four seated with him at the table—two on either side of it—clearly belonged, each of them dressed similarly in long white robes covering their heads. Only their shadowed facial features disrupted the creepy show of conformity. Reynard could not study those seated on his side of the table without drawing undue attention. The woman, Ruler Three, sat opposite him. Strands of her silver hair lined the interior of her hood. Her eyes, inescapable even beneath that cloak, no doubt saw everything. When she blinked, it seemed as though small curtains were drawn from her forehead to her cheeks.

The man next to her had not moved a muscle. He stared at nothing apparent, his chiseled features reminiscent of something Reynard could not put his finger on. *All business, that one!* His complexion suggested he spent a lot of time outdoors. Lean, muscular... bred by a family of foxes, perhaps.

Reynard waited for one of them to make the first move. It was, after all, their house, claustrophobic and confining, a far cry from the comforts of his den in Waterford, where Spiro had often made himself at home atop a smokewood desk, his short legs swinging freely in the air.

"Tell me again, Reynard, who are these twiddlers dressed in hooded nightgowns? I don't want to make you nervous, but they look a lot like that fellow in the castle dungeon—the one who entertained us with his special tools!"

"Nonsense, Spiro! Get a grip! These are members of The Guild's High Order!"

"The Guild's High Order? Really? Why, then, do I count only four hoods? Everyone knows the High Order numbers five in addition to the magister."

"Patience, Spiro!"

"Patience, you say! What are we still doing here? I thought we had agreed to decline the madman's invitation!"

"Be quiet! I know what I'm doing!"

"Do you? Are you certain?"

"I know a spider's web when I see one! I've spun enough myself! This may be the largest we've encountered, but so long as we tread carefully, we can find our way back out."

"Since when was it a good idea to enter someone else's web?"

"How else are we to earn the spider's trust?"

"Earn his trust! Whatever for?"

"Whatever for, indeed, my friend! Be silent; watch and learn!"

The opening of a door broke the awkward silence. *Ah, the old spider himself, but with a mere six legs this time!* Two cloaked noms guided the magister to his seat at the table's head, then promptly left the room.

"You know what this reminds me of?" asked Spiro. *"It reminds me of our place above the wharf. Only there's no set of back stairs leading to the docks. In the event of an emergency, I doubt you even know which way to run!"*

The supreme leader cleared his voice, and still it sounded like crushed stone. "General business is suspended. Introductions are in order." A bent and bony finger singled Reynard out. "This is Overseer Rascall. The famed Reynard Rascall, who fleeced the Duke of Isles and his entourage; the same overseer who has seen fit to pad our coffers with more than expected each and every moon; the very same to have escaped King Axil's guillotine. Allow me." The magister's sleeve swept the table as he motioned to his right. "This is Ruler One. He keeps the roof above our head and food upon our table." The heavy-set ruler leaned forward, turning his head so Reynard could see his plumpish smiling face.

"Ruler Two, Headmaster of the School of Taking," continued the magister. "You've already met, though I'm sure you don't remember well." The man seated between Reynard and Ruler One turned to acknowledge him without emotion. Reynard vaguely recognized the man who had first woken him and claimed to have saved him from the guillotine. "And Ruler Three, who handles all our finances, and whom you've met as well." The woman across from Reynard smiled wanly as her fingers quivered and flapped above the tabletop as though she were playing some unseen instrument. The others seemed to take it in stride, so Reynard tried not to stare. The magister's fingers drummed the table.

"And Ruler Four. Leader of our army. He keeps us and our treasure safe." And then it hit Reynard. *This one wasn't bred by foxes. Hawks, more like it! "With those eyes and nose, he could pass easily for a distant relative of yours, Spiro!"*

Reynard acknowledged each of them in turn, then all of them at once. "I'm honored," he said, saving his last bow of the eyes for the magister.

"And now, Overseer Rascall further honors The Guild by supporting our plans for Baelon's self-governance. He's going to assist Ruler Two in killing both kings."

This caused a slight stir around the table.

The woman's fingers flitted back and forth spasmodically. Ruler One again leaned over to catch Reynard's attention, his pudgy hands applauding quietly. The army's leader bent forward ever so slightly, nodding appreciatively in Reynard's direction. The woman's fingers became still as the magister's digits drummed the table.

Ruler Two struggled to speak. When he did, his voice wavered. "Is this really necessary, m'lord?"

The magister's glassy, bloodshot eyes sent a message before his lips could underscore it. "It should not have been. Need I say more?" He addressed the others at the table. "Overseer Rascall shall assist Ruler Two in killing the kings of Aranox and Tegan, and by so doing, shall earn a seat at this table and the title of Ruler Five. Feast your eyes upon him, for this shall be the last you see him in my presence without a shabba!"

The old man's gaze again came to rest on Ruler Two. "The watchers tell me that King Tygre plans to visit his old friend at Castle Aranox in the near future." *Wait a tick! The watchers do exist?* "Perhaps you can dispose of both buffoons at the same time. The two of you have much to talk about. And you, Ruler Two, have one moon to show us progress toward 'self-governance' and further prove your value to The Guild. General business will be conducted in your absence. You are excused. Don't come back until both kings are in the ground!"

Sibil Dunn

By mid-morning, they were deep in what Gradi repeatedly referred to as "the wicked woods," surrounded by coniferous evergreens, patches of smokewood, and masses of joining trees so closely knit the sun could not find the forest floor. Overhead, the only visible patch of sky mirrored the trail they followed, like a ribbon of blue framed by the tips of tall trees on either side.

Warm air enveloped them, prompting conservation of movement. Their horses plodded along, side by side, hooves nearly silent on a carpet of duff. The lush forest undergrowth captured other noises, quickly suffocating them. But each snap of a twig, every rustle of dried leaves, reminded Sibil that the bortok thought itself the king of the Dark Woods, and its subjects all fair prey.

There was little in the landscape to spark interest, or to distinguish one stretch of trail from the next, until the sudden appearance of a fork in the road.

"Corpse's Choice?" she asked.

Gradi nodded. "Decision time. You're sure you won't turn back?"

Before she could answer, the old man raised a hand, suggesting she stay silent. What sounded like the faint patter of rain caused her to look back down the trail, her gaze fixed there until three bare-chested riders turned a corner into view.

The biggest of them, a heavy, burly man, sat atop his horse like a large soup kettle. *Or is he half beast?* Thick, dark hair covered his bare arms and chest. A dozen or more coarse braids dangled past his shoulders, a few resting on his untrimmed beard. A string of white shells encircled his neck. Two leaner riders followed, their faces hidden from Sibil's view until Black Braids stopped his mount to gawk at her and Gradi. His companions sidled next to him, one bald with a square, clean-shaven face and sunken eyes; the other was clearly younger than his counterparts, despite his scraggly beard. Even sitting in the saddle doing nothing, he appeared wild-eyed and agitated.

Just the type one might expect to inhabit the Dark Woods!

Wherever they were headed, the leader seemed in little hurry. Black Braids cast a look at Corpse's Choice before cultivating his interest in Sibil. The way he stared reminded her of the king's steward, and she glared back at him. He would have to do or say something especially pleasant in the very near future to change her first impression of him.

He spat into the woods. "Lost, are you?" His bald companion circled slowly behind Gradi. The youngest, all too interested in Sibil, coaxed his mount so close to Shadow the two horse's flanks rubbed against one another. Sibil's hand crept inside her shirt.

"Listen to me, friend." Gradi leaned forward in his saddle to capture Black Braids' attention. "Where we're going is of no concern to you." The words came slowly, as though meant to be digested just as carefully. "But as I can see what's on your mind, I'm going to do you a favor and tell you what you need to know. The young lady is to be received by someone of importance. I'm not at liberty to say just who has sent for her, but given our location and the direction of our travel, I think that you might guess. If she does not arrive when expected, and in sound condition, whoever is to blame for that will live just long enough to regret his actions a thousand times over."

"Is that right?" Black Braids snorted. "Someone special, is she? And yet..." His eyes spent a few moments studying Gradi and his rusted sword. "Whoever waits for her trusts the likes of you to protect her?"

"I'm not here to protect her," Gradi said. "I'm merely her escort, and that should tell you something about the degree of trouble we are expected to encounter from others. You could easily dispense with me, no doubt. Just know that would offend the one who waits for her. She's not to be touched. Not by me. Not by anyone. No one in their right mind would dare."

One of Black Braids' little fingers barely twitched, but its message was as clear to Sibil as it was to its intended audience. The youngest rider removed his hand from Shadow's rump.

Gradi cleared his voice. "You've been warned."

Clearly weighing options, Black Braids tried a different tack. "You don't say. Perhaps whoever's waiting for her would appreciate our joining you. Might they not be grateful for our protection?"

"They would not," came Gradi's curt response. "I'm to report any contact or unpleasantness upon our arrival. I trust I shan't have to mention you, and that we'll not cross paths again." One of Black Braids' nostrils began to twitch. Gradi's expression did not waver. "I'll close my eyes for a silent count of ten, shall I? And when I open them, I'll pretend you were never here."

Sibil's fingers curled around the hilt of her knife. Her heart pounded as Gradi's eyelids lowered.

Black Braids gave her a last look, and she returned it impassively. He spat toward the ground before digging his heels into his horse's ribs. "Hyah!" All three riders took the left fork and trotted out of sight.

Sibil's hand relaxed.

Gradi opened his eyes, and for a long moment, he just stared at her. "We'll stay put for a bit, and let them put some distance between us, shall we?" Sibil nodded. "Though I seriously doubt they'll trouble us further."

"You're shaking," Sibil said.

"Am I?" Gradi held a hand out and watched it tremble. "So I am."

"That was…" Sibil struggled to find the right words.

Gradi gave a nervous laugh. "Yes, it was." He exhaled a heavy breath. "But I know the type."

"Which is to say?" asked Sibil.

The old man smiled. "There are men whose courage is bound to their heart. It's as much a part of them as any limb or bone. You cannot tame it, nor can they, not even in the face of certain death. It's in their blood, you see, and will remain there until the last drop is spilled."

Like Rolft, wounded and unarmed, challenging the knife-wielding "cat" to attack him during the celebration of Six Moons!

"These were a different breed," Gradi said. "Their courage comes and goes like water from their bodies. If they think they hold the high ground or sense a weak opponent, they drink it in and swell like a sponge. But if they sense the slightest threat or danger, their courage leaks from them as easily as sweat or piss until there's nothing left. A baby lamb could be attacking them, but if they're made to believe it is a bortok, if they *see* it as a bortok, they're going to run and hide."

"What told you they were this breed?"

Gradi shrugged. "It was a gamble, to be sure. What I could see without a doubt was their intent. What else was I to do?"

Sibil nodded slowly. "I see."

"You know the kind of man I'm talking about?"

"I do. And now I know the kind you are as well." She tilted her head toward the left fork of Corpse's Choice. "Shall we?"

Sibil pulled gently back on Shadow's reins. The horse slowed, then stopped. To one side of the woodland path, a large swath of bright pink, ankle-high ground cover blanketed the spaces between trees. Its teardrop petals with thin blue veins and purple dots had been described in great detail to every child in Baelon. She recalled the plant's name before Gradi opened his mouth.

"Spotted Spunge," he said, his horse sidling up to Shadow. "Beautiful, but deadly. It's what siplence is made from. A drop or two will kill you."

"So I've been told." *The tip of the arrow that killed my mother was covered in that extract!*

"You know where the word comes from, do you? Siplence?"

"No."

"Sip of silence. It's not the largest patch I've ever seen, but still, this wouldn't be the wisest place to stop for any length of time. It's the bortok's favorite treat, you know. That alone tells you a thing or two about those creatures."

Sibil urged Shadow forward, her motivation to put a dagger in The Guild of Takers' heart reaffirmed. She had decided to follow Gradi well before reaching the fork at Corpse's Choice—as soon as he had told her about The Guild of Takers' efforts to grow the ranks of its army. It had been a primitive thought at first—a simple, unobtrusive way to gain access to The Guild. Far easier and less dangerous than approaching the GOT on horseback unannounced and without any plausible reason for visiting. *"Please open your gates and let me in. I've come to kill your High Order!"* She could only imagine how that would play out. *No. Going right at Corpse's Choice on my own would almost certainly end in frustration. Or disaster. Nonetheless, the notion of joining The Guild's army as a means of getting to The High Order seems far from—*

"*Pssst!*" Gradi reached out to take her reins and bring Shadow to a stop.

"Sorry," she said. "I was daydreaming."

Gradi cocked his head. "Can you hear that?"

Sibil held her breath. Faint voices carried through the thinning woods. "Is that The Cauldron?"

"No. The Cauldron lies inside the Lawless Lands, and we're a ways from that just yet. But we're almost through the woods, so what you're listening to, I think, is our destination."

Sibil's heart beat a little faster. "If that turns out to be true," said Gradi, "well, there's something you should know." The old man ruffled the tips of his close-cropped hair and looked into the distance. "Let's just say you're not likely to see others of your kind there."

"My kind? Women?" Sibil shrugged. "I wasn't expecting to."

"It's not what you're expecting that worries me. It's what they're expecting. Or, more to the point, what they're not."

"What are you trying to say?"

"What we just dealt with back there... I doubt we've seen the end of it. I think it best we stick to the same story."

"All right. I rather fancied that story. Who shall we say is waiting for me?"

Gradi grinned, his gray-blue eyes twinkling. "Ah, therein lies the mystery. And that is what keeps the listener spellbound. Best to keep them guessing, you understand?"

The relief that accompanied surviving the Dark Woods unscathed turned out to be short-lived. The landscape beyond the forest's edge appeared equally foreign and uninviting. An endless scattering of men, hundreds strong all told, stretched across a fairly barren landscape. Some kept to themselves, but most huddled in small groups around makeshift campfires, a few of which had already come to life. The smell of smoke mingled with that of horses and a strange scent Sibil could not place. Gradi's voice found its way to her.

"It's larger than I expected. These are the Borderlands."

He pointed beyond the encampment. "Out there lie the Lawless Lands. And The Cauldron. Were the sun not setting, you could just make out its shape. But come dark, its fires will light the sky. There'll be no mistaking them. Six pyres built of smokewood, all belching different colors. There's nothing like it anywhere. Wait here while I poke around a bit. And remember, once you leave these woods, you're no longer in the Kingdom of Aranox. Your king's law means nothing out there."

Sibil gazed into the distance. The Borderlands were much as the prestigious boarding school, *Quest,* had described—a wide swath of desolate earth. Sparse clumps of struggling grasses beneath twisted spikewood trees. Scattered rocks and stunted shrubs. She scanned the groups of men gathered round their fires. *Might Tristan be among them? Wait! Is that one of those who overtook us at Corpse's Choice? The young one who came so close to me?* She opened her mouth to speak, but the young man in question disappeared behind a cloud of smoke, and anyway, there was no one left to talk to. Gradi had entered the Borderlands. She watched the old man dismount, then lead his horse from one campsite to another, gesturing and conversing with each before moving on. By the time he returned, only the top half of the sun rode the western horizon.

"These are not The Guild's men," he said. "They're all hopefuls, just like me. The Guild and those already chosen to join its ranks are camped further west. I'll head that way tomorrow, and hope that I get picked. You have to prove yourself, I'm told, against another man. No bloodshed, mind you. Just a show of pluck is all they're looking for. A bit of skill on top of that, and apparently you receive a more favorable position, but I'm not in need of that. I'll settle for whatever they offer and be thankful for it." He filled his lungs. "What about you? I've still no idea where your errand's taking you. I'll be leaving at sunrise for The Guild's proving grounds—unless you need me for something, that is. They'll run for the next two suns, so if you do…"

"No. Thank you, Gradi. I've troubled you enough. Though I may come to watch, if you don't mind, before I go my way."

"I'm not sure they'll let you," the old man said. "But I suppose that would be nice. You can help to pick my pieces up when The Guild is through with me!"

"Is that really you, Tristan?" The young knight's shoulder-length blond hair, corded in a ponytail, made him look ever so much like Theos, but the manner in which Sibil's heart skipped beats told her which brother this was.

"They call me Sir Godfrey now." The young man beamed. "But I shall always be Tristan to you."

Thank the gods! She thought she had seen him trampled by stampeding horses, but now he appeared so vibrant and so cheerful!

"Why are you riding Shadow? Where is your own horse?"

"Is it Shadow I'm riding? I really hadn't noticed."

Absurd! "How could you not notice?"

"I don't see much these days," the young knight said. "But I recognize your voice, Sibil, so I believe whatever you say."

"What in Baelon are you talking about?"

"You read my letter? I'm so glad, as I'm not sure waiting for my return would have been a good idea." Tristan's bright blue eyes turned solid white and brimmed with tears.

"Why's that?" Sibil's chest heaved as the color in the young knight's face transformed into a bruised patchwork. "What's happening?"

"You mean, what's happened?" Lewen stood by Shadow's side, a hand on the animal's mane. She let go, tears streaming down her face as Tristan coaxed the horse forward. Not until they passed her did Sibil notice large tears falling from Shadow's eyes as well. "My father warned you. Revenge is a temptress full of promise, but she rarely satisfies.

I love you for trying to avenge me, Sibil, but at what price?" Still weeping softly, the princess gestured in the direction Tristan had ridden, but the young knight had already disappeared.

"Wake up! Wake up!"

Sibil shuddered and jerked away from a rough hand clutching her arm. Her eyes stared blankly into Gradi's steely blue-gray pupils as he continued talking. "Our horses... they're gone!"

"What!" Sibil quickly rose to her feet, certain she was no longer dreaming.

"See for yourself!" Gradi strode the short distance to a long rope tied between two trees at the edge of the Dark Woods. Several horses remained tethered to it, but Shadow and Gradi's mount were indeed missing.

"Are you certain?" Sibil asked. She looked anxiously around. "Might they just have broken free?"

Gradi stooped to pick up two long strands of leather cord before displaying them to Sibil. "Didn't even bother to untie them! Just cut 'em loose!"

"It was those men from Corpse's Choice!" Sibil said, fuming. "I saw one of them just over there last night!" She pointed toward the Borderlands, where smoke and men drifted about the encampment. "What about our saddles?"

"Gone! My sword's still here, but not much else. They look to have taken the rest of our belongings. Remember what I said about your king's law." Gradi sighed.

"King's law or not, it can't be all right to steal another's horse!"

"I'm sure many here agree," said Gradi, "but don't expect their hearts to make them act. We can look around a bit and ask if those nearby saw anything last night, but I wouldn't get my hopes up. In a place like this, most tend not to hear or see beyond themselves."

The entire encampment moved in the same direction. Sibil trudged along, keeping pace with the measured stride of Gradi's shorter legs, her emotions shifting back and forth between anger and anguish. *Poor Shadow! Where are you now? Running free and not suffering at the hands of others, I pray!* "Do you still think we might find our mounts?"

"It's possible," Gradi said. "But more likely, whoever took them is already headed home. Yours will fetch a fine price, and mine still has some spirit left. That's money in their pocket without risk to life or limb." The old man's steely eyes searched Sibil sympathetically. "Look, there's no need for you to follow me further. I came to do this on my own, and I'm still capable of that. Perhaps you'd feel better looking for your horse."

"How far is it to the proving grounds?"

"Not far, I'm told. Take heart. Many of these men had no mount to start with. They've walked all this way, the entire distance here. Through the Dark Woods, mind you. Spent two or three nights beneath those wicked trees, they did. That's pluck right there, if you ask me. The Guild ought to take them just for that!" He brightened suddenly. "Now, there's a thought!"

"What is?"

"Those chosen by The Guild. If you don't have a horse, I'm told the GOT will outfit you. It's just deducted from your pay."

Sibil's shoulders slumped. That would not help Shadow's lot, wherever he might be.

A buzz of conversation, accompanied by animated gestures from the men traveling alongside, drew Sibil's attention to another encampment ahead. At the fringe of the Dark Woods, two long rows of tents stretched out in orderly fashion. In front of them, a neat line of fire pits, still smoldering, freed gray ghosts into the air. Further from the woods, a sea of white cloth stretched across the tops of tall wooden poles, shading the ground and those who walked upon it.

Men moved about with purpose, those in uniform barking orders, others moving materials or supplies. Under one section of shade, fires burned beneath large kettles with steaming contents tended by cooks. The smell of whatever they were brewing wafted its way across the grounds, causing Sibil's stomach to grumble.

"This way! This way! Follow those in front of you!" Two soldiers herded an aimless crowd into a tighter stream along the edge of the shade structures. "Move along! Move along! No stopping!"

Sibil tried her best to see beneath each section of shade, but a moving wall of bodies allowed her only glimpses. Gradi's attempts to do the same met with even less success. The shorter man shot her a look of helplessness as they paraded forward—until they reached the end of the shaded sea. Until those ahead nearly stopped and the walking became shuffling. Until they heard more voices up ahead. "Single file, now! One at a time! Single file!"

The men walking to either side of her funneled into a narrow stream, pressing Gradi's shoulder against hers.

"Single file!" one of the men yelled, before shoving Sibil behind Gradi.

Ahead, the line disappeared beneath a small canopied shelter, from which hopefuls exited in different directions. An eruption of shouts and cries drew Sibil's gaze to an area behind the shelter and close to the Dark Woods, where a formation of men, perhaps a hundred strong, put Sergeant Cogswell's training circle to shame.

"The proving grounds!" whispered Gradi.

Beneath the canopy, a soldier in a black shirt and drab green trousers with black stripes sat behind a counter formed by two axe-hewn planks laid across large barrels. "Next!" he called out on occasion, the line advancing each time. A dark-haired woman wearing the same uniform stood behind him, scowling. Occasionally, she stretched or yawned. Near the shelter's edge, a shirtless man leaned against a support pole, his arms folded across a broad, bronzed chest, biceps bulging beneath his fists. Striped trousers hugged his muscular legs like a second skin. A waterspout of straw-blond hair gushed from his mostly shaved noggin, a few feathers sprouting from the cord that tied it. His oval face presented a tall forehead, curved nose, high cheekbones and square jaw. The pupils of his narrow eyes flitted back and forth.

"Next!"

A young man swaggered to the counter and placed his hands upon it. A few words were exchanged before the appraiser cried out, "Inside!" With the young man escorted away, the line moved forward again.

"What does that mean?" Sibil whispered.

The man in front of Gradi turned unexpectedly to answer. "I think it has to do with where you're placed. Inside's good; outside, not so much. But either way, at least The Guild's accepted you. Some are sent to the proving grounds, where they can get a better look at you, but even that's better than being turned away outright."

"Outside!" The counter man dismissed a beefy gentleman. "Next!"

"Be sure to tell them you're just here to watch," Gradi whispered to Sibil. There were but two people ahead of them now, and she could better hear the words exchanged beneath the canopy.

"You've experience soldiering or fighting?" asked the man behind the counter.

"No, sir. A fistfight or two before I came of age."

"But you're fit?"

"Yes, sir." The hopeful squared his shoulders.

"You have a weapon?"

"No, sir."

"A horse?"

Where are you, Shadow?

"I do."

"You might do inside," said the soldier. "*Might*, I say! Proving grounds!" he shouted, and his guest was whisked away. "Next!"

The middle-aged man in front of Gradi approached the counter.

"You're a fighter?" asked his appraiser.

"I served a year in the king's army."

"You've weapons?"

"Arming sword and short sword, but I can handle a spear or battle axe just as well."

"You've a horse?"

"Yes."

"Inside!"

The man turned to wink at Gradi and Sibil as he was led away.

"Next!"

Sibil's stomach turned as Gradi approached the counter. He appeared to shrink as he walked, growing older with each step. He carried his rusty sword by the scabbard and laid it on the counter's wooden planks before kneading his hands together. The appraiser's eyes flit from Gradi to his sword.

"Move on, old man."

"But I'm..."

"Next!"

Sibil paused to give Gradi time to appeal, but someone grabbed his sword in one hand, latched onto his elbow with the other, and led him forcibly away.

"Next!"

Sibil approached, her eyes on Gradi until he was released just outside the shaded structure.

The man behind the counter glowered at her and waved her off. "Next!"

"But I have my own weapons!"

"No women! Move on!"

The candidate in line behind Sibil took a step forward, but she refused to move.

"How is that possible?" she asked, casting a glance at the woman standing further back beneath the shade.

The man raised his voice. "Move on!"

Sibil withdrew her principal dagger and drove its point into the makeshift counter. "I did not come all this way to be ignored! If I don't fight well enough to join your army, so be it! But I refuse to be turned away out of hand!"

The soldier rose rapidly to his feet. The barrel he had been sitting on toppled backward. "You refuse!" He motioned to his colleagues, but no one reacted. It took Sibil but a moment to realize why. Still relaxed and leaning against his pole, Waterspout's gaze was fixed on her. One of the bronzed warrior's hands moved.

"Your weapon. Let me see it."

A voice as smooth as his skin! How quickly can I withdraw one of the cat's daggers if he uses mine against me? She wrested her knife from the plank and offered its bone handle to the warrior. He turned it over several times, his eyes flitting back and forth between Sibil and the blade.

"You have a horse?" he asked, handing the knife back to her.

"My horse was stolen!"

The warrior showed no emotion. "Proving ground. Follow me."

Sibil glanced at a stunned Gradi as she trailed the warrior, his waterspout glistening in the sunlight, the muscles in his tanned back undulating beneath taut skin.

The proving ground turned out to be nothing more than a huge circle formed by seated hopefuls. Inside its perimeter, two combatants wrestled while another man in uniform—no doubt The Guild's version of Sergeant Cogswell—stood watching. The wrestlers grappled on their knees, arms locked around one another.

"Are you in battle or in love?" shouted the observer. "Show me something!" One of the combatants loosened his hold to swing a fist upward into his opponent's jaw. It snapped the bigger man's head back.

"Ohhh!" yelled the ring of spectators as both fighters fell to earth.

"Outside, the both of you!" shouted the observer.

"What!" The victor gasped for breath as his opponent was dragged from the circle.

"You gave up your weapon... by choice! We need fighters inside the GOT, not scufflers! Be satisfied you're chosen. You'll fight outside!"

Waterspout lead Sibil into the circle as she scanned its perimeter. *Black Braids!* The hairy-chested man appeared to recognize her as well, quickly shuffling something to one of his companions. She caught a glimpse of Gradi's bell before it disappeared.

"Sarul!" the fight observer called out. "What have you brought me?"

The bronze warrior placed a hand on Sibil's shoulder. "This one will prove herself against whoever is sent next."

Sibil pointed to Black Braids as he rose from his seat. "That's who stole our horses!" Though his eyes followed Sibil's finger, Sarul appeared unmoved. Black Braids and his two companions walked away from the circle. "Did you hear what I—" Sibil winced as Sarul's hand dug into her shoulder, his fingers finding a nerve.

"Bring him," the warrior said.

The uniformed observer reacted instantly, shouting "Kairns! Kairns, come here!"

Black Braids stopped walking. He stood still for a moment before turning slowly back toward the circle. "Here!" shouted the assessor, pointing to his feet.

Black Braids made his way into the circle, his two friends stopping at its edge.

Sibil tried to capture Sarul's attention. "He took our horses, I'm sure of—"

She stopped talking as the warrior brought a finger to her lips. He pointed first to her, and then to the man named Kairns. "Prepare to prove yourselves!" He nodded to the assessor, who promptly placed himself between Sibil and Kairns.

"No one dies," he said. "Or you both die, do you understand?" He looked purposefully at Kairns. "Kill her, and I shall send you to the gods myself." He turned his attention to Sibil. "The same goes for you. Understood? The victor is the first to draw blood!" he shouted, as much for those watching from the circle as for the two combatants. *I thought Gradi said no blood was to be shed!* "Prepare yourselves!" The uniformed observer backed away, one arm raised into the air.

Sibil watched as Kairns drew a broad hunting blade. It suited him, large and bulky. The undersides of his hairy upper arms jiggled as he extended his hands in front of him. He half-smiled at her before throwing a nervous glance at Sarul.

You wonder if Waterspout's the one who's been waiting for me! Sibil tossed her ponytail over her shoulder.

Kairns stood with his feet planted solidly a shoulder width apart, his hands spread wide in front of him. He wiggled the point of his knife in Sibil's direction.

"Begin!"

Kairns lumbered toward her, his knife zig-zagging through the air well before he neared. She sprang back, then darted to his side. He pivoted, lurched forward, and hacked at the empty space between them. Something shiny emerged from beneath his vest just below his neck and hung there on his chest. *My amulet!* Kairns shifted his position. *Big, slow, awkward in your movements, and without any sense of space or timing!* Sibil feigned an approach, watched his arm swing past her a third time, then darted toward him before he could react. A guttural growl rose from her throat as she ran her blade across the arm wielding his knife. Her knee rose sharply into his crotch as she slashed his other arm and shoved him backward. He dropped his knife, grunted, and sank to his knees.

"Stop!" the observer cried.

Sibil leaped behind Kairns, grabbed a fistful of braids, and pressed a knee into his back. She lifted the braids until they were straight and taut, then cut them from his head with a single swipe of her blade. "Where's my horse?" she cried, throwing the braids to the ground and grabbing the leather thong around Kairns' neck.

"Stop!" the observer shouted.

"This is mine as well!" Sibil said, drawing back on the leather thong until the metal amulet pressed into Kairns' throat. He raised his bloodied arms to claw at it, gagging until Sibil cut the cord. The amulet slid from the severed thong, falling to the ground by Kairns' knees.

"It's not hers," Kairns said hoarsely as Sarul approached. "It's mine! My father gave me that."

"Liar!" Sibil pointed a rigid arm at Kairns' companions, still watching from the circle. "And they've got something else of ours!" One of them threw the shepherd's bell into the circle. It sang as it cut through the air, turning silent only when it stopped tumbling in the dirt. The man who had tossed it, joined by his companion, was halfway to the Dark Woods.

Sarul placed a leather sole against Kairns' chest and kicked him backward before stooping to retrieve the amulet.

"Ask him what it says!" cried Sibil.

Sarul turned the amulet over, then made a fist around it. "What does it say?"

Kairns shook his braidless head. "I can't remember. Gods above, I can't feel my hands!"

"I'll tell you, shall I?" Sibil said, seething. "Protector of Innocence! That's what it says!"

Sarul handed the amulet to the observer. The smaller man examined its backside before nodding.

Sibil glowered. "And how would I know that?"

A slight tilt of Sarul's head caused the observer to hand the amulet to her. The warrior pointed at the severed leather thong still in her grasp, then summoned it with wiggling fingers.

Sibil parted with it, slowly. *What do you want with it?*

Removing a knife from his waistband, Sarul kneeled beside Kairns. He pressed the tip of his blade against the fallen man's neck as he whispered in his ear.

Kairns muttered a reply.

With a single thrust, Sarul's blade disappeared into Kairns' throat. Sibil looked away.

"We may be thieves," Sarul shouted, loud enough for all in the circle to hear, "but we do not steal from one another!" He held Sibil's leather cord aloft, high enough for most to see, then stuffed it into the broad slit he had made in Kairns' throat, leaving just one severed end exposed.

"What are you doing?" asked Sibil, nearly breathless.

"You did this to him, not me. You made him worthless as a fighter."

"You didn't have to kill him!"

"Worthless as a fighter, but he can still set an example. If it makes you feel better, I'm letting his friends go. They're going to spread my message." Sarul stood. "You'd best hope that his last words were not another lie. He told me your horse is in our pen. Someone will take you there so you can see for yourself."

Sarul addressed the observer. "She's to fight inside. Find her a tent of her own."

Sibil gestured toward Gradi. "The old man comes with me. Gradi comes with me."

"He's of no use to us," said the warrior matter-of-factly.

"How do you know?" asked Sibil. "We're together. We fight as one or not at all." Sarul stared at her for so long she felt compelled to add, "You needn't pay us both. We fight as one... you pay for one. What have you to lose?"

Sarul's eyelids turned to slits. Several moments passed before he nodded to the observer, turned, and walked away.

Sibil felt a jolt, then another. A rough, jarring sensation. *This is no dream!* Something had her by both wrists. It pulled her roughly, dragging her out of the tent and across hard ground, into the cold and dark night air. She squirmed and kicked until her feet were under her, but just as her wrists were freed, an arm encircled her neck and pulled her forcefully backward, pinning her throat in the crook. The blade of a large knife glistened momentarily before coming to rest against her neck.

"Keep your hands where I can see them." *Sarul's silky voice!* She could feel his chest against the back of her head, his lips pressed against her ear.

She held her hands in front of her.

"Lie to me just once, and I'll slit your throat, yeah?"

Sibil did her best to nod.

"Have you heard the story of The Wisperal?" asked the warrior.

Gradi's head emerged from his tent. Sibil returned his wide-eyed stare as she did her best to shake her head.

Sarul's grip tightened around her neck. "What did I say about—"

"I know it!" Gradi's head popped slightly further from the tent. "A spirit with needle and thread—"

"Not that ghost tale!" Sarul squeezed so hard that Sibil found it difficult to breathe. "This story's new. This Wisperal is made of flesh and blood. She slays giants and beheads the enemies of King Axil. You've heard of her?" Sarul pressed the broad side of his blade more firmly against Sibil's neck. "A young woman with raven hair to her backside! She fights like a cragen, they say, and the bone handle of her knife carries a red stone! That's you, is it?" Sarul released his grip on Sibil just enough to let her breathe.

"Yes!" she gasped. "But the story isn't true!"

"Isn't it?"

Sibil felt her neck released. She raised her hands to rub her throat just as the warrior's fist slammed into her temple. The ground rose up to batter her. She lay wide-eyed and dazed, unable to move. The stars in the night sky spun wildly, then faded into black.

What felt like a slap in the face turned out to be a bucket of cold water. Sibil shook her head. She was seated on the ground, her back against a wooden pole to which her hands were tied. Her legs stretched out in front of her, bound together at the ankles.

Her head throbbed, and the sight of Sarul quickly reminded her that the big man's fists were formidable weapons. The warrior squatted in front of her, his forearms resting lightly on his thighs.

"Last chance to speak the truth," he said.

"I can't help what others call me."

"People don't make up stories about little girls killing giants." Sarul flicked a pebble into Sibil's face.

"You think it's true?" Sibil scoffed. "Just how thick are you? So I know my way around a dagger... I told you that. I've proven as much, I should think. I've withheld nothing from you."

"Haven't you?" Sarul picked up another pebble and bounced it off her chest.

"There's no such thing as giants, you dolt! You're the closest thing to it in the real world!"

Sarul grinned. "Big men, then. You've killed big men."

"You're not listening! I haven't killed anyone. Cut me loose, and perhaps you can be my first!"

The warrior's smile spread across his clean-shaven face as a knife appeared in one hand. He made a point of displaying its broad blade to Sibil. "You're of this world, are you?"

Sibil squirmed as Sarul gripped her forearm and drew his blade across the back of it. She winced as a thin streak of blood appeared beneath the blade.

"Have you gone mad?" She did her best to kick him, but the effort was in vain.

"Spirits don't bleed... I'll give you that," said Sarul. "You deny fighting for King Axil?"

Choose your words carefully! "I have never fought on behalf of Castle Aranox! I fight in honor of my friends. Those I fought just happened to be enemies of King Axil. I can fight, it's true... but King Axil will not have me in his army, and I am thus offended. You don't believe me? If not for King Axil, both my mother and my father would still be alive. Both died in service to him. Were you told that? Both! How do you think that makes me feel toward King Axil? Why else would I seek to join your army? You want the truth? There it is... and what have I to show for it?"

Sarul sighed. His brow wrinkled. "Words," he said disdainfully. He looked past Sibil, then stared into her eyes. "Admit you're lying, and I'll spare you."

"I've not lied to you."

"If I find you have, I'm going to strip you naked and leave you for the prattlers and the bortoks to fight over."

"I'm not lying."

Sarul tapped the top of her head with the broad side of his knife before standing to sheath the blade. "We'll see. I'm going to share your story with someone. When I come back, I'll either set you free or kill you both."

The warrior strode away. *Both!* Something writhed against her bound wrists. A hoarse voice startled her. *Gradi! Tied to the same post!*

"Gods above, girl... What kind of boiling kettle have you dropped us into?"

The sweltering Lawless Lands stretched on forever, but crossing them was far preferable to being hogtied to a post awaiting execution. Back astride Shadow, Sibil found even their monotonous sands inspiring. Sarul had given back her knives. Her amulet lay tucked inside a pocket for safekeeping.

"So you're The Wisperal, are you?" Gradi sought her attention.

"I'm not! I don't even know what that means."

"You don't know the story of The Wisperal?"

"I don't. It's just a stupid name given to me by silly boys." *Wisperal! Wisperal!* She could still hear the chanting of the squires' following her first victory in Cogswell's training circle.

"Just a stupid name? Why then, do you think, all of Baelon is talking about her?" Gradi motioned in Sarul's direction. "Why do you think that two-legged ox has taken such an interest in you? He's heard the stories, and all that chatter's in his head, believe you me."

"What chatter? What are people saying?"

"You can't appreciate what's being said if you don't know the tale it's rooted in."

Sibil continued to stare blankly. "I only know the name. I've never heard the story." *And that's the truth!* "Tell me, will you?"

Gradi blew a puff of disbelief into the air. "Where were you raised? The Wisperal's a woman. Well, the spirit of a woman, to be more precise. Legend has it, there once was a young couple betrothed to each other since childhood. Bound not by custom or law, but by true love. Just before they were to wed, the young man was called to war. His bride-to-be begged him not to go. The lad fought well and bravely, but he was mortally wounded. There was no saving him, but he was determined to live to see his true love one last time. She was sent for and he waited, suffering terribly for a half moon, dying only when his lover's lips met his for one last kiss—a final touch that sealed his lips and sent him to Baelon above.

"His bride vowed that nothing else would ever touch her lips again. Thus, she would not eat or drink, and spent her remaining days, which numbered very few, in mourning. It's said her spirit wanders battlefields at night, seeking out the gravely wounded so that she might end their misery. The wind is thought to be her whispering to the dying as she sews their mouths and nostrils shut, hence her name. She is also known by Seamstress of the Night. No one knows the story's origin. Most think it's a fabrication of the Sisters of Systalene."

What? Sibil's heart stopped beating as she pictured the old woman in her dream, sitting at the trunk of a tree with needle and thread in hand.

"It certainly supports their life beliefs," said Gradi. "They reject any justification of war, value life above all else, and are devoted to ending suffering wherever they might find it."

"So The Wisperal's an old wives' tale."

"Yes, except the Sisters don't marry, so..."

"And the latest version? What's being said about me?"

"Ah, yes. Rumor has it The Wisperal's returned to life as a young lass with long, dark hair. As beautiful as her daggers are deadly. Tired of watching good men die and of sewing their lips closed, she's come back to prevent more young men from ever being wounded."

"And just how is she to do that?"

"By killing those who would otherwise do the wounding, of course! This Wisperal singles out the most likely to do so—the most wicked and dangerous among us—and dispatches them to Baelon below. This Wisperal—you, not to put too fine a point on it—is said to have killed six giants already."

"Six!"

Gradi laughed. "Is that not right? Did you have another number in mind, Wisperal? You could have told me who you are, you know. It wouldn't have mattered to me."

"I wasn't lying to Sarul. There's no truth to what you've heard. Not much, anyway."

"Is that right? All of Baelon is spreading lies, eh?

"Do you believe all the stories you hear? I thought you were smarter than that."

"I don't believe in spirits with needle and thread, much as I enjoy the tale. But stories about a young woman killing giants with a knife, a dagger with a red jewel in its bone handle, no less? As has been said, those stories don't just make themselves up. Something breathes life into them, even if some of it's hot air. Add to that what we all saw you do to the cur who took our horses, and let's just say I don't blame our feathered friend there for giving you a hard look."

Mention of the warrior's name caused Sibil to search him out. He was riding a short distance ahead, half hidden by others on horseback, his broad, tanned back glistening in the sunlight, his feathered waterspout shimmering atop his head. She averted her gaze as he turned in his saddle to look her way. A moment later, she dared look at him again, her attention drawn quickly to movement over his shoulder.

The string of riders ahead had concealed two travelers approaching from the opposite direction, presumably from the GOT, until they were nearly opposite her. One of them tilted his head back in passing, using a hand to mop his brow and sweep long dark bangs from his eyes. Something about him distressed her, but she could not look away... and then his eyes met hers.

No! Is it... No! It cannot be! And yet... Gods above! The man with the scar on his forehead! Impossible! The king removed his head, along with that of his little companion, the cat! Am I seeing things? That same dark hair, hanging in the same manner. Impossible! Might he have a twin, like the Godfrey boys?

"Sibil? You all right?"

Gradi! She opened her mouth, at a loss for words. The pair of riders had passed, but a backward glance from one of them further unnerved her.

"Who was that?" she asked. "Did you see them? Those two going the other way... did you see them?"

"I saw them, sure. But I've no idea who they were. Members of The Guild, no doubt. We're halfway to the GOT, I imagine, and there's nothing else out here. Why? What's got into you?"

Sibil looked back again. "It's nothing. It's just... I thought perhaps I recognized one of them."

Gradi shook his head, mumbling. "Now she's friends with a member of The Guild! What's next?"

Sibil peered into his blue-gray eyes. "You're certain there's no such thing as spirits, are you?"

THE PYRES OF THE CAULDRON

"Why do we dwell so on the past? Because it never leaves us! The present never lasts; the future is unknown. But the past... oh, the past. Like a good friend or a worthy enemy, it follows one forever." The palace scribe, Castle Aranox

Overseer Reynard Rascall

Tasked with escorting Reynard to the GOT stables, Ruler One removed his shabba as he waddled. "Not very practical," he said, finally freeing himself from its last sleeve and draping the garment over one arm. "Most oppressive, and during the Moons of Heat, insufferable! Hoods up at all times, mind you! Thank the gods we only wear them in his presence, which isn't all that often." He waved a hand toward an impressive number of stalls and horses standing against what appeared to be the back side of the GOT. "There," he said, pointing to two horses already saddled and separated from the others. "I'm sure you'll find them satisfactory. Ruler Two will join you shortly." The portly ruler squinted as he stared at the overseer's forehead. Reynard pulled his bangs back so the man could better gawk. "Yes, well, good luck to you, then." Ruler One averted his gaze. "Nice to make your acquaintance. We'll see you next moon, I imagine!" He tottered off, raising a limp hand in salutation to an approaching Ruler Two.

Reynard waited until his new partner was nearly upon him before speaking. "I suppose, then, that we'll be—" The man swept past him without so much as making eye contact.

Reynard followed him to the saddled horses and watched the man stuff one small leather pouch after another into his saddlebags. If Ruler Three's earlier count could be trusted, there were forty of them all told, each containing twenty-five kingshead.

"What should I call you?" Reynard asked, checking his own mount's tack. "Do you have a real name?"

"Just call me Two. It's easier that way." The ruler shoved the last of the coin purses into place with more force than necessary.

"You don't seem pleased," said Reynard. "Have I offended you somehow? Something I've said or done?"

"I'm offended by your very presence."

"Ah, is that all? I didn't ask to come here, you know."

"I suppose not, but neither did you ask to leave. I'm told you were given that option."

"True enough. That makes me sour milk, does it?"

Ruler Two gave Reynard his full attention. "In case you couldn't parse the old man's words, my neck is on the line. I have one moon to kill two kings. No easy task, mind you, and you're a liability, not an asset. So no, I'm not at all pleased."

"A liability! What makes you say that?"

"If I may be blunt, you wouldn't be standing here if it weren't for me, would you? You and your clumsy partner were caught red-handed. By the king's sorry soldiers, no less! That's not very reassuring to someone about to engage the same enemy again."

Reynard bristled. "Is that what's troubling you? Get this one thing right: I was tortured to the point I tasted death, and my partner lost his head—all for something we took no part in. My friend and I weren't shackled for anything we'd actually done. No, the king thought we'd had a hand in his wife's and daughter's deaths, which we did not. We'd never even met them! It was all a case of mistaken identity. Pure coincidence, I assure you. The truth is, I've broken nearly all the king's laws more times than you can imagine, and not once have I been caught at it!"

"Is that right? The list of those they shackled you for killing was a lot longer than just the queen and princess. You might be kidding yourself, but you're not fooling me."

"Not to put too fine a point on it, but besides the royal family, we were blamed for killing a shopkeeper and a baron's cook, neither of whom we'd ever laid eyes on. And those we did do away with—a couple of soldiers and some innkeepers... and, oh yes, an apothecary—well, we never would have killed them if half the army wasn't after us for something we hadn't done in the first place. It really was quite a mess."

Ruler Two scoffed. "A nice story. What's the moral?"

"My point is, you're in good hands with me. The magister, at least, believes that. Why else would I be here?"

Ruler Two further tightened the cinch on his saddle. "Good question. When I figure that out, I'll let you know."

Reynard bit his tongue. He waited for Two's snubs to lose their sting before again attempting to engage in conversation. "The magister said I was assisting with 'self-governance.' What's that?"

"He didn't tell you?"

"No. I presume it has something to do with the killing of the kings. That's my only purpose here, so far as I can tell."

"That's right. You're a small piece in a colossal puzzle, and that's all you need to know. I'm sure the magister thought to save you from the bigger picture. Self-governance is complicated. It would take a while to explain ... I'm not sure you'd understand it if I tried."

Another cut! "You've something better to do, have you?"

Ruler Two sighed heavily as he swung into his saddle. "I'll try the simple version for your benefit, shall I? We're going to replace the monarchs with a far larger number of rulers—so many that The Guild will have no trouble finding some whose character allows them to do favors for a price, or look the other way when that's to our advantage."

Reynard climbed his mount. "Self-governance... as in the way the isles operate?"

"Precisely, only on a much grander scale."

What?! Reynard stifled the urge to laugh out loud. *Ludicrous!* "It's brilliant, isn't it?" he said. *Pure madness! What can the magister be thinking?* "It was the magister's idea, was it?"

"No. It was mine." Ruler Two straightened a bit in his saddle.

The first you've said that I've no trouble believing! "Yours! Gods above, I've underestimated you!"

"Spare me your sarcasm. I'm sure you've a bucket full of doubts and reservations to accompany it. Keep them to yourself. Self-governance has already been vetted by superior minds."

"I've no doubt. None at all." Reynard held up a finger. "It makes perfect sense, and the reason for my presence here quite obvious."

"How so?"

"Self-governance for all of Baelon? As you yourself said earlier, it's got to be ever so complicated to pull off. It's going to take almons, is it not?"

"What of it?"

"And yet..."

"And yet what?"

Reynard could not resist. "And yet you've failed to climb even the first step alone. I'm here to make certain you succeed this time around. That's all."

Sand, sand, and more sand... for as far as the eye could see. There was little to do but let his horse plod along behind that of Ruler Two. And as many things to contemplate as there were dunes to stare at.

Reynard closed his eyes to hold court on Ruler Two, who stood accused of hurling unprovoked and rude remarks his way. Especially unforgivable, suggested the prosecution, were those questioning the overseer's competence. *Butt rash!*

A strong and reasoned defense presented its case. *These are, after all, Two's stomping grounds; the man should be allowed some rope. It's not his fault the magister has thrown the two of us together. It's only natural for him to resent my intrusion, is it not? And what better way to give resentment life than through a few quick-witted barbs? Surely he cannot afford to direct those to the magister!*

Having reached a verdict, Reynard opened his eyes. "Listen, I don't think I've ever thanked you for saving my neck from the guillotine."

"No, you've not," came Two's quick reply.

"Ah, well, there's a time and place for everything, I suppose. I've been thinking more about that sun, you know. There in Fostead's town square. It's a shame you couldn't save my partner, too. I suppose that would have been a bit much, even for a man of your talents, eh?"

"Don't be absurd! I could easily have saved you both. And taken every soldier's coin purse in the process. That's not what I was tasked with doing."

"My friend was no more deserving of the blade than I."

"If you say so. But the magister did not value him the same, did he? I was specifically directed not to interfere with his destiny. And, as previously explained to you, his continued presence with the guards helped to feed the illusion we created."

"But you could have saved him?"

Ruler Two snapped his fingers in the air.

Reynard's lips began to curl. "I hope the king enjoyed his show."

"The king? No, no, most assuredly not. Had he shown his face under that sun, we would have killed him, wouldn't we? No, he stayed hidden in his castle and he's been there ever since. I, of course, was marking time with you, but there were several Guild watchers there that day, and more than one assassin. If it's any solace, I'm told your friend drew quite a crowd. Men shouting, women crying—"

"That's enough."

"The executioners removed their hoods, you know, just before they took their heads. As good as my artwork was, I doubt your friend was fooled by your replacement. Imagine his surprise to find a stranger, and not you, standing by his side!"

Reynard fought an involuntary urge to vomit; nonetheless, a bit of what churned in his stomach found its way into his mouth.

Spiro's voice chided him. *What are you going to do about that, Reynard? How does that taste? Is it bad enough to kill for?*

Reynard spat into the Lawless Lands. *"Worse than that, my friend! Much worse than that. It tastes like mutton stew!"*

Specks of pepper in the sand grew closer and larger until they looked as though they might be a trail of ants.

"What is that?" Reynard asked.

"New recruits for The Guild's army. Reinforcements... just in case Aranox or Tegan decides to strike the GOT. King Axil has already threatened war."

"Reinforcements! From where?"

"Ruler Four's grand idea," said Ruler Two. "One of his scavengers, Sarul, is out collecting commoners to join his ranks. You'll see soon enough."

"Commoners! Willing to fight against their king?"

"You sound surprised. They don't care who it is they're fighting. They'd kill each other, for that matter. All they care about is what they're fighting for: money. Don't tell me you're so different, Overseer Rascall."

Reynard ignored the slight. "So you're not enamored by Ruler Four. What do you make of Ruler Three?"

Two scoffed. "The magister favors her, though not overtly. It's most annoying when they're together. He with his finger-tapping; she with hers dancing in the air." He offered a quick, disparaging demonstration. "It's most tiresome. I'm fairly certain they do it just to vex me."

"And I'm certain they do not."

"Is that right?"

"I've witnessed the flying fingers," Reynard said assuredly. "It's most likely nothing to do with you." He lifted a digit of his own. "Most likely, I say."

"Explain yourself."

"The tapping of his nails, the fluttering of her fingers... they're not some nervous habit they've picked up and can't put down. And their purpose is most certainly not to irritate. No, no... not at all. It's their way of talking to each other when they don't care for you to hear."

Two turned to gape at him.

"The real question is," continued Reynard, "what have they been saying? Nothing to do with you? Or everything to do with you. It's really hard to say." He studied Two's face, where seeds of doubt were clearly finding fertile ground. "Why do you think the magister chose to save me and not my friend? Surely he must have known that Spiro was far better equipped than I to kill two kings."

"Your friend was unpredictable, and therefore unreliable."

"Even so, more valuable than I as an assassin."

"I didn't say the magister valued him less. I said he valued him differently."

"What's that supposed to mean?"

"I don't think your friend was used so much as a diversion or illusion as he was a piece of bait."

"Which is to say..."

"Now who's wearing blinders! Which is to say, I think your friend's death was intended to motivate you. Are you not motivated?"

"Are you not?" Spiro's voice! "Are you not!"

"I am," said Reynard aloud. "Most assuredly, I am."

Two stopped his mount and waited for Reynard. "Take a good look, and tell me you still doubt they're commoners."

Reynard focused on the passing riders. *Two hundred strong, if not more!* The lead horseman commanded his attention, muscular and shirtless, a fountain of yellow hair with feathers sprouting from the top of an otherwise shaven head. Perhaps a dozen dressed in drab green trousers and black blouses rode immediately behind him, and in orderly fashion. Another in similar uniform, together with a woman, wrangled a collection of riderless horses to one side.

"They came up short," said Two.

"Does it matter?" Reynard assessed those not in uniform. "Do you really think that scraggly mob can withstand King Axil's army?"

"Let's just say I'm happy to be elsewhere if the king decides to visit. The magister has given us one moon to complete our task. We might be wise to bide our time."

Reynard ran a hand up his forehead, catching sufficient beads of sweat to slick his long locks back. The closest of the passing riders were a hapless lot. Some appeared malnourished, others too well-fed. Lads too young to grow a beard rode next to gaunt old men. A young woman with long raven hair... *another woman! Wait a tick! Is she staring back at me? Is that...? No. It cannot be!*

Reynard reached out to grab Ruler Two's attention. "Do you see that woman?"

"We're halfway to The Cauldron, give or take," Two said, raising a water bag to his lips.

"Never mind that! The woman! Do you see her?"

"What woman?"

Reynard was beside himself. "There!" He pointed to the sea of riders. "Wait! I've lost her!"

"Did she have long, dark hair?"

"Yes! Do you know her?"

"Sarul's pet," said Two, coaxing his horse forward. "The only woman in The Guild's army. Go on, chase after her, why don't you? Or just keep staring! Either way, Sarul will cut your heart out!" He laughed loudly.

Reynard wiped a sleeve across his face before digging his heels gently into his horse's ribs. He glanced back, surprised to catch another glimpse of the woman, her neck craned, her face turned in his direction.

Noggods! It cannot be!

It did not matter where he looked—the woman's face refused to fade. "Sarul's pet. Does she have a name?"

"Raven." The back of Two's head swerved from side to side.

"Could she have been in Fostead this past moon? Have reason to be riding with the king's men?"

Ruler Two reined his horse and mopped his brow. He reached for his waterskin as Reynard drew alongside. "I'm beginning to have serious doubts about you." The ruler sipped from the waterskin. "Sarul was that half-naked savage riding at the front of those who passed. When I say Raven's his pet, I mean that she belongs to him. A half-wit could deduce from that the answer to your question. What does that make you?"

Two's horse resumed its journey toward The Cauldron, now an impressive feature on the horizon.

Reynard released an irritated snort. "You've a plan, have you? For killing the kings?"

"I have the beginnings of one, which is all you need to know of it."

"I'm listening."

"When we reach The Cauldron, we'll split up, each targeting a different king."

Imbecile! "Much as I'd prefer to work alone—no offense intended—I don't think that's wise in this case."

"Why not? I work better without others watching over me. And if forced to take a partner, you're not who I'd choose." Two made a show of parroting Reynard. "No offense intended."

"None taken, but going separate ways is still a terrible idea." *Are you really so blind? Must I assume the role of architect and draw the plans for you?*

"Why's that? With each of us targeting a different king, we can be done in half the time."

Reynard stared at him as though he were a child. "I'll spell the reasons out for you, shall I?" He lifted one finger. "Earlier you said that we should bide our time, and on that point, I agree. Second, splitting up would hardly be fair. One king is bound to be more difficult to kill than the other. Perhaps one of us prevails without losing a wink of sleep; the other, even if he does succeed, is gravely wounded or killed in the process. So the one of us who risks the least and barely breaks a sweat reaps the entire reward. That's fine with me if I happen to draw the right straw, but you've already been at this a while, haven't you, and I suspect by now you know which king will pose the greatest challenge."

"You don't trust me?"

"No, I don't, but even if I did, the issue of fairness remains. Surely you can see this." Reynard held up another finger. "Third, there's the matter of timing and communication. If I kill my king quickly, how am I to know what's happening with you? Are you being tortured? Giving up my location? How long do I wait for you past our appointed time to rendezvous, and where do I go then? Neither of us can return to the GOT without the other. The magister has made that clear."

"Why is it all your 'what ifs' put me in a bad light?"

"I'm merely pointing out the prospect. It is a possibility, is it not?"

"Of course, but it might just as well be you—or both of us—who fails."

"And yet..." Reynard gave Ruler Two a knowing look. "Our past performances suggest otherwise."

Two gnashed his teeth. "Just how many kings have you killed?"

"The same as you, I suspect. But that's really not the question, is it? More like, how many have I tried to kill and failed? This is where our numbers differ. For the record, mine is zero."

Reynard continued before Two could get a word out, another finger rising in the air.

"Fourth, two minds are generally better than one. Granted, you've already given me cause to question the soundness of yours, but I'm accustomed to working alongside slower wits. They still can prove quite useful." *Fifth, how am I to kill you if I don't keep you in sight?*

Ruler Two began to fume, his voice slightly louder. "Need I remind you who you're traveling with? A member of The Guild's High Order... which you are not, by the way. Not yet, at least. Headmaster of the School of Taking, former mastertaker and overseer, and a master of mindal! As such, Overseer Rascall, the terms overseer and underling... they're one and the same to a man in my position. I trust you get my meaning!"

Reynard chuckled. "Patience, friend. Who knows, you may even come to prize our time together."

Two snarled. "You're already growing on me... like some sort of woodland fungus. You remind me a great deal of Ruler Five, who was, by the way, disposed of by the magister."

Ah, did you hear that, Spiro? There's your missing cloak from the Chalice Room! "Disposed of? For what reason?"

"For failing to perform. For his incompetence."

"Ahhh, Five, yes... Ruler Five." Reynard made a show of counting all the fingers on one hand. "I suppose that makes sense."

"Whatever are you on about?"

"The High Order, of course, and its numbering. Based on my observations to this point, I can only assume that the higher the digit, the more skill a ruler is expected to demonstrate; the more faith the magister has placed in him or her. That's why you're lowly number two, is that right? And the reason I'm due to take Five's place!"

Reynard spurred his horse on, a smile spreading from ear to ear.

Reynard's bones complained and rejoiced simultaneously as he struggled to dismount. He sighed as his feet hit the ground, his head resting on his saddle for a brief spell.

He had been inside The Cauldron many times, most often to reward Spiro's exemplary service. It paid to keep one's mind from wandering here, one's eyes and ears attuned to one's surroundings. The building would be full of ill-tempered tosspots crammed so close together they could not help but offend one another.

Reynard tethered his horse to The Cauldron's hitching rail. "I suppose they know you here by name. Or by number, is that right?"

"Hardly," said Two, dismounting. "I've been here but once before."

"But once! You must be joking!"

"I'm a member of The Guild's High Order, Headmaster of the School of Taking. I've better things to do." Two hitched his horse, but could not seem to take his eyes off the rows of fingers rising from the ground on the opposite side of the rail. "I do know what those are, though."

Reynard shrugged. "You have to be both daft and incompetent to be caught pilfering at The Cauldron. It's a fair price for a gaffe."

"A what?"

"A gaffe... a terrible blunder." Reynard recalled gatherer Kasparr's final moments on the Waterford Wharf.

"It's barbaric," said Two.

"Don't tell me you're squeamish. That doesn't bode well for the task ahead of us. And you cannot fault The Cauldron. The Guild's been known to exact an even higher price. What about your friend, Ruler Five? You teach the art of taking. Surely these appendages were not attached to any student of yours. Even your fledglings would know their limitations, would they not? And your graduates... well, I should think their being caught at taking was quite unthinkable."

"What's your point?"

"Those too stupid to know their limitations, or too inept to perform their craft, deserve every malady that finds them. That's true of any profession, if you ask me. I fail to see the problem."

"A singer who misses a few notes or a baker who burns his bread? We should remove their hands as well?"

"Don't be silly. The singer should have his tongue cut out. The baker? That would all depend. Is he baking for himself? Does he like his bread burned to a crisp? That's all well and good. But if I request a loaf, golden brown the way I like it, and he offers me instead a blackened brick, by all means, he should have his hands removed. You'll pardon me, will you?"

Reynard ducked beneath the rail and made a beeline for The Cauldron's porch. A man in business attire leaned languidly against one of its posts, his only acknowledgment of the approaching overseer a slight raise of his eyebrows.

"Ayla, friend!" Reynard took the last stair with a bounce in his step. "You're about to light the evening sky again, are you? Fantastic! I never tire of it!" The businessman issued a quiet snort. "If I wanted to know the type of wood that issues forth those colors, who would I talk to, eh?"

"Smokewood." The man withdrew a tin of snuff from his coat pocket and removed the lid. "The colors come from smokewood."

"Ah, smokewood!" Reynard rubbed his lower lip between thumb and forefinger. "But if I wanted to build one of those monstrosities myself. Procure the proper tools, choose the most suitable trees, knock them down without injury to self, split them into chunks and pile them in fitting fashion... who would I talk to then?" He shook a closed hand, causing the busts of King Axil to sing within. "If only for a short time," he added, disclosing the coins unobtrusively.

By the time a sauntering Two caught up to him, he was two kingshead poorer, and trotting down the porch. He snapped his fingers in Two's face. "And that, my friend, is how it's done! Follow me—we're on the hunt!"

"We're what?!"

Reynard ignored the ruler, setting his sights on a tall brute watching over the preparation of six huge pyres. The man's backside presented a thick mane of dark, wavy hair falling nearly to the middle of his back. His shirtless torso glistened with a coat of sweat and soot so heavy it could not have been donned in one sun. The broad-bladed axe in the man's hand looked to have worked just as hard.

Reynard cleared his voice as he approached. When the woodsman turned to look at him, the overseer held his palms outstretched. "Your boss tells me you're the man to see."

"'Bout what?" The laborer looked past Reynard and Ruler Two to the man leaning on the porch's post. Satisfied by the nod he received, he returned his attention to Reynard.

"I won't waste your time," the overseer said. "We need eight men well-versed in felling trees. Large trees. Larger than any found in the Dark Woods. You know the kind I speak of?"

The woodsman studied him. "The kind of tree, or the kind of men?" he asked.

"Ah, a wordsmith after my own heart! Both. We need men who can make the giants of the forest dance the way they wish, regardless of the wind's direction, or how hard it blows. We need men who know their ropes and knots as well as they do saws and axes. Men with short memories and tight lips."

"What for?" the man asked, his jaw rising slightly in the air.

"For a job that lasts a quarter moon at most, and pays an almon's wages." Even the stoic woodsman flinched at that. "And for the one who finds such men and oversees their work for us, twice that amount. Half now as a show of our good faith. The remainder when the job is done. Might you know such a man?"

The woman lying next to him slept soundly, her body spent. Reynard's eyelids envied hers. The ceiling of The Cauldron's third floor slowly disappeared behind them, leaving his mind to wander freely.

"You've found a new friend in Ruler Two, have you?"

"There are three kinds of people in this world, Spiro: friends, foes and forgettables. As a member of The Guild's High Order, and a key player in saving my neck from the guillotine, Ruler Two is entitled to at least some consideration as a friend, don't you think?"

"If you say so, but he did also donate my head to Castle Aranox."

"A fair point."

"And did you not already open the door of friendship to him? Did he not slam it in your face the moment he first opened his mouth? Was the subsequent drivel pouring from that orifice not increasingly offensive?"

"What's happened to your vocabulary, Spiro? This doesn't sound like you."

"I'm in your head now, friend. I have access to your words!"

"Ahhh, that does make sense. At any rate, you needn't worry. Ruler Two could never replace you—he's not your equal when it comes to company or dialogue. At best, he'll serve as a whetstone, keeping my wits sharp until I decide what to do with him."

"Why not decide now?"

"You'll help me think it through, will you?"

"Of course! He's not your equal, either. I trust you know that."

"I suspect that's true."

"You suspect? Please. Erase all doubt, Reynard! His credentials may be well known, but is there anything he can teach you about the art of taking? No! At best, he is your equal there. And how qualified is he—the headmaster of a school—to kill two kings, eh?"

"Another good point! The very best at one trade is rarely more than passable at any other!"

"You are the exception to that rule, Reynard!"

"Thank you for that, Spiro!"

"You do not need him."

"No, I don't."

"Why not dispose of him now? Where is he, anyway? A man unable to find pleasure on any of The Cauldron's first three floors is not to be trusted, would you not agree? Libations... gambling... lust—to pass on one might be excusable, perhaps two if he were old and difficult to stimulate—but all three? It's unnatural, is it not?"

"It is!"

"Get rid of him!"

"I fear I'm forced to suffer him at least a short while longer, Spiro. The Guild's watchers may have eyes on us."

"I thought you questioned their existence."

"I'm now made to wonder, friend. At any rate, Two's death cannot appear to be by my hand. Not in the magister's eyes. It will need to be carefully done. In the meantime, he's no threat to me."

"You're certain of that, are you?"

"If the magister wanted me dead, he would have let the king take my head, not go to great lengths to save it. Two wouldn't dare undo all that. Regardless, I think he lacks the stomach for it."

"I agree on both counts."

"It does give one cause to ruminate, though, doesn't it?"

"Ruminate what?"

"What the magister is up to. Why send skilled thieves on an errand of butchery when he has better options? Why not Ruler Four, leader of his army, or one of his best soldiers trained to kill?"

"He needs them to defend the GOT?"

"He can't spare one or two to mortally wound his enemies? Please, Spiro..."

"You don't trust him, either."

"No—it's why I've taken to calling him the spider."

"He's decidedly unnerving and unpleasant."

"His very breath smells of manipulation and deceit, Spiro!"

"Just so! Why in Baelon did you accept his offer, then? I begged you not to do that!"

"Three reasons, all of them self-serving. I'll detail them for you, shall I?"

"Please do."

"The first was to avoid death! The spider does not strike me as someone who accepts rejection well, despite his own suggestions to the contrary. Just walk away and call things even? I'm not sure that was ever on the table. I dare say he would have been offended, perhaps deeply, had I refused his offer, and I did not care to learn what retribution looked like. The second reason was to gain his trust, a crucial building block on which reason three relies."

"I'm waiting."

"Reason Three? What else? To turn the tables on him, Spiro! The spider sees in me a fly, and I must humor him whilst plotting to destroy his web! Surely he must pay for allowing you to lose your head! And, oh—this is a minor detail as compared to that—but did you know... there are ten vaults of gold below the GOT, and not just one?"

Sibil Dunn

The closer she neared the GOT, the more of its detail revealed itself, the faster her heart beat. Not even in her nightmares had she imagined it like this—smaller than Castle Aranox, and yet somehow more imposing. Angry and unsettling. Morbid.

There was nothing smooth or symmetrical about it. No curves or flowing lines. An uneven row of metal poles sprang from the battlement, like spears of different lengths, their jagged tips challenging the gods above. Acute angles and rough surfaces, abrupt irregular shapes. Sharp protrusions jutted from its rough face, dark recesses hiding sordid secrets in their shadows.

Half a dozen towers shot high into the darkening sky like spindly fingers reaching from mountainous crags. Dark openings in the tower's pinnacles gaped like empty eye sockets.

But the structure's most conspicuous features were its huge foundation cornerstones. Both their size and color—pure white with streaks of blue and gray—screamed for attention, turning Sibil's stomach with offensive symbolism: this dark place stands despite the laws against it.

Gradi appeared to read her mind. "That's baelonite, all right," he whispered. "I doubt your kingdom's architect would be too pleased."

"Single file! Pass the word! Single File!"

The loose collection of riders converged into a thin stream to pass through staggered, narrow openings in haphazard rows of spikewood barriers—twisted, crooked branches stacked and interlocked to form effective fences with giant thorns.

"Fall into that bramble and you won't be coming out," Gradi said. "Those spikes will pierce your flesh as easily as any lance. You'll bleed to death before you free yourself! The same goes for your horse."

Shadow followed the mount before him, through one barrier, then down the open ground between it and the next until another opening appeared. The long straight line of riders eventually transformed into a tortuous ribbon weaving through a maze of twisted wood. *An exercise in caution even with the benefit of light, and absent real distractions! What would it be like to navigate in the dead of night, with arrows raining down and prattlers on the loose?*

With Shadow safely through the last barrier, Sibil raised her eyes. The GOT loomed, its gates swinging open like a giant's yawning mouth.

Sarul leaped onto the lip of the courtyard's central fountain. "Welcome to the GOT!" He swept a broad arm toward the stronghold's tallest and thickest tower. "Behold His Eminence, the magister!" Half-way up the spire, on a balcony encircling its substantial girth, three hooded figures stood. The tallest raised its arms with palms outstretched, and not until they lowered did Sarul return to life. "Dismount and leave your horses to the handlers!"

Sibil slid from Shadow as the magister's companions escorted him away.

"Be quiet! Listen well!" shouted Sarul. "As soon as I have said my piece, food and water will be rationed! If you are designated 'outside,' gather over there! If you are 'inside,' gather here. Go on! Be quick. We know who you are. Don't try to change your place, or you will not be paid!" The warrior paced the fountain's rim. "Outsiders! This is Raven—henceforth, you will do exactly as she says. Fail to obey her, and you will be left outside at night to entertain the prattlers!" He jumped from the fountain's lip. "Insiders, listen carefully! The spot where you now stand is called Fore Court, where you will greet King Axil should he find his way through our gates. You will train here, but you shall sleep in Back Court. Come with me!"

Sarul traipsed across the courtyard, to where four-story buildings covered its width, arched passageways connecting them at ground level, rooftop breezeways linking them to the GOT's perimeter battlements.

"You shall use this passage and no other. Most lead to Center Court. If you are found there and not killed outright, you shall join the outsiders, which some might consider a worse fate." His laughter grew loud as he entered the enclosed corridor. "Follow me!"

The open space it introduced looked much like Fore Court, absent any fountain or gates. Sarul traversed its uninterrupted length to stand in front of waist-high stalls containing straw, dirt, and—of all things—sand, running half the length of the GOT's back wall. Along the other half, handlers busied themselves leading horses into stables. Sibil could not see Shadow, but it comforted her to know where he was most likely kept.

"Back Court!" said Sarul. "This is where you will gather when you are not training or assigned some other task. You are not to venture elsewhere. Do not enter any building. Do not bother those who live here. Piss and shite in the largest of the straw bins and nowhere else! You are here to fight, and you will train each sun, but you will also do your part to keep this house in order. Rest now. Blankets are there. Food and water will be brought to you. Training starts tomorrow at first light. Welcome to the GOT!"

What is that? Sitting by itself in a field of yellow flowers? No larger than my parent's house. Built of rounded stone, stained glass, and thick straw thatch. Clearly, these are not the Lawless Lands, and that is not the GOT. Yet someone lives behind that door, I know it!

"Wake up! Wake up, you lot! You're wanted in Fore Court!"

Sibil rose onto her elbows. *It cannot be morning. Did I not just close my eyes?* Through a fine gray mist, several uniformed soldiers made their way toward her, kicking those still sleeping. "It's time to earn your pay! Wake up!"

Gradi helped her to stand.

"To Fore Court!" one of the soldiers shouted. "You know the way! Wake up! Move now!"

A low rumble of resentment echoed down the passageway to Fore Court.

"Did you sleep?" asked Gradi.

"I suppose I did. And you?"

"Not a wink! I felt safer in the Dark Woods."

Sibil mustered as much confidence as she could. "We're going to be fine."

Several GOT soldiers corralled their group between the buildings and Fore Court's central fountain, where Sarul and Raven were perched. A round shield with a large splatter of yellow paint on its surface leaned against the fountain's edge near their feet. Dozens more were piled on the ground beside it.

"Welcome, insiders! Wait there!"

The outsiders stood between the warrior and the front gates, separated from the fountain by four more soldiers.

Sarul strode confidently along the fountain's rim, arms raised.

"His Eminence, the magister, graces you again!" The warrior pointed to the breezeway overlooking Fore Court, where several white robes were barely visible through the gray mist of morning.

"As promised, you are paid one moon in advance!" shouted Sarul. The sound of boots pounding the ground heralded a formation of soldiers trotting from the GOT's central passageway. In their midst trundled two large wheelbarrows, each brimming with small leather pouches.

At Sarul's signal, the soldiers below the gates put their backs to them and began to push. Ever so slowly, the panels opened, the crack between them widening little by little. Thick ropes attached to their tops ran through a series of pulleys before wrapping around chiseled grooves in cylindrical rocks the size of a large man. The soldiers pushed, the gates creaked, the pulleys squeaked, and the rocks were pulled into the air. When the panels could open no further, thick poles attached to their bases were released from brackets and allowed to slide into large holes in the ground, effectively holding them in place.

"Outsiders, we salute you! But now your mistress, the desert, calls! You will be paid as you pass through the gates. Train well, and you may sleep tonight with the insiders! Shirk your duty—displease Raven—and you may never sleep again! Go now!"

Raven jumped from the fountain. "Follow me! Collect your pay!"

With the wheelbarrow positioned in front of the gate panels, the outsiders trickled into the Lawless Lands.

"Insiders, form two lines!" bellowed Sarul. "One in front of either gate. When they are closed, you will be paid!" Sibil shifted uneasily as one of the warrior's fingers beckoned her. She left Gradi's side, stopping just shy of the shields piled near the fountain's edge. Sarul grinned down at her. "Not you! Remember our bargain. You and the old man. Two fighters, one purse!"

He dismissed her with a flick of his hand and continued shouting at those forming lines. "Train well and you may earn yourself another pouch! Disappoint me, and tomorrow you train outside!" The soldiers pushed on the gates, lifted the thick poles from their holes, and allowed the stone weights to pull the panels closed. "If the king's army comes through those gates, it shall be greeted by the arrows of our archers on the battlements. You will not attack until their first round has been unleashed! Before this sun goes down, each of you will be assigned to one of three stations. One here, front and center by the fountain. The second and third against the walls, east and west, to collapse from either side on whatever enters!"

Gradi leaned into Sibil and whispered. "Two or three, please. We do not want to be the first thing the king's army lays its eyes on."

"Agreed!"

"You will attack after the first of the archers' arrows have been dispatched!" shouted Sarul.

An insider yelled back. "With those to follow raining down on us?"

"You will learn to fight like this!" Sarul jumped to the ground and grabbed the shield resting by his feet. He hoisted it above his head with one hand. The large hunting knife he withdrew from his waistband looked all too familiar to Sibil. "Like this!" he cried, circling between both lines of onlookers to demonstrate. "The archers will not target your shields!"

"We cannot fight like that!" cried someone from the line opposite Sibil and Gradi.

"Really?" shouted Sarul, locating the speaker with his eyes. "Come here and let us see. Bring a sword!"

Both lines went silent. "Now!" said Sarul. "Come here!" A middle-aged man left the safety of the line to approach Sarul, reluctantly dragging a sword in its scabbard. "Quickly! Withdraw your sword! Prepare yourself for battle!" The man stopped walking. Both legs shook visibly. His limp arms made no attempt to lift the sword from its scabbard.

Sarul continued to hold the shield above his head. "You have a sword. I have a knife. Must I kill you to make my point?"

The man shook his head.

"You will learn to fight like this!" bellowed Sarul. "All of you! Leave your weapons against that wall and take a shield!"

A long, agonizing wait in the dying light of Back Court eventually rewarded Sibil with a few moments of solitude in the straw bins. Much relieved, she made her way to the resting area. Sarul's approach from its other side brought to mind Sergeant Cogswell. *Fail to give your enemies the respect they've earned, and they may take much more than that!*

She would not have thought it possible, but by sun's end, the motley group of untrained fighters under Sarul's tutelage had drilled a simple four-count pattern into something rote. Shields up, advance, retreat, shields down... shields up, advance, retreat, shields down. One unit front and center: shields up, advance; followed by two others from the east and west: shields up, advance. Then all together: retreat, shields down. Again and again, without a weapon drawn. Simple. And yet, when it had come together, the sound of countless shields maneuvered in unison, coupled with the irregular drumming of boots against the ground... well, it conjured the makings of an army.

Sarul dispelled the notion. "Tomorrow we train in earnest!" he shouted at the group sprawled across Back Court. "Most of you are unprepared." He singled out the man who had challenged his shield exercise. "You! Grab your belongings. You sleep tonight in Fore Court and train outside tomorrow. The rest of you, listen carefully to the desert as the sun goes down, and you shall hear what happens to those who do not give the magister their all!"

The warrior strode away, turning before entering the passage to Fore Court. "You will give your all. If not to the magister, then to the prattlers. Think on it!"

Stretched out on the ground, Gradi patted an empty blanket spread beside him. "I've made your bed for you," he said, lightening the mood.

"Thank you, Gradi." Sibil plunked herself down and removed the smallest of her knives, its triangular blade no longer than her little finger. She set to work fixing its sheath to the outside of her thigh.

"What have you got there?" asked Gradi.

Sibil handed the push knife to him. Gradi grasped its irregular handle of black carmine just above the crossguard. He made a fist, and the blade appeared to protrude from his knuckles. "Gods above!"

"Useful in close combat." Sibil finished tying one of the sheath's leather cords around her thigh.

"You're just now getting around to that?" asked Gradi.

"I've been wearing it the whole time. Under my leggings."

"Under your leggings! What good is it there?"

"I was just asking myself that same thing whilst in the straw bins. You remember what you said about the men we met at Corpse's Choice? I suppose it was meant as a surprise for that type. Only it wasn't comfortable at all, and of late, I've been thinking: if a man really deserves such a surprise, why should I wait for my leggings to be removed before delivering it?"

She tied off the second cord, and Gradi handed the blade back to her. She sheathed it, pulled it out, then sheathed it again.

Gradi chuckled. "Be careful, lass. You're not going to change the world's nature with that little thing."

"*Shhh!*"

"Listen!"

A hush spread through the makeshift camp.

"Did you hear—"

"*Shh!*"

A distinct cry for help from outside the compound's wall stiffened Sibil. She held her breath, remaining rigid until the plaintive wail came again, louder, more desperate. A faint clatter followed—a sound she could not place, even as it grew more clear.

A sudden scream of terror startled everyone. It rose in pitch until cut short mid-scream. The clattering continued, then subsided.

"What was that?" she asked breathlessly.

"Someone giving their all to the prattlers, I imagine." A man propped on his elbows just the other side of Gradi offered his grim judgment. "The next sound you hear will no doubt be that of Sarul's laughter!"

Sibil lowered her voice. "What do you know about the magister?" she asked Gradi.

"Only what he wants all of Baelon to know. That he's the most powerful man this side of the Lawless Lands. Perhaps the most powerful in all of Baelon. He's been the magister since I was a child, you know. He's quite old."

"And the others we saw with him today?"

"Hard to say, but by their height, I'd guess those were noms."

"Noms?"

"Short for nominees. Young men and women chosen from the ranks of prospective takers to serve the magister. They accompany him everywhere. See to his every need."

"They live with him in the tower?"

"I've no idea, but it wouldn't surprise me. How else are they to serve His Eminence? He's not cooking or cleaning for himself, I guarantee you that. And I imagine at his age he needs help bathing and dressing, even if that robe is all he ever wears. Why do you care?"

Sibil shrugged. "If you're going to kill for someone—perhaps die for them—it's only right that you know a little something about them, don't you think?" She placed all three of her blades, within easy reach, should she be woken unexpectedly.

"Look around you," whispered Gradi. "These men don't care to know the magister. They're not doing this for him any more than I am. We're doing it for money." He held the single pouch Sarul had offered Sibil. "Or in my case, for loved ones. But you... Remind me, why are you here?"

Sibil stretched out on her blanket. The stars above began to blur. "I told you. I'm on an errand for a friend." She closed her eyes and felt for Tristan's letter beneath her shirt.

King Tygre of Tegan

King Tygre grimaced as the royal coach tipped slightly, one wheel climbing slowly over yet another large impediment—a rock, perhaps—before descending quickly with jarring effect.

"Tree root!" shouted the carriage driver. "Apologies, m'lord!"

The monarch held his tongue. He had known what a journey across the Lumax Mountains meant before he boarded the coach. Peril Pass!

Not the driver's fault! This is the price one pays for ignoring the passage of time. Oh to be that young man once again, fit and fearless, riding this treacherous downhill run on horseback beside Axil!

Tygre glanced out the carriage window. To his left, giant kollum trees blanketed the forest, the closest of them lining the roadside like a row of rigid sentries. They were, no doubt, the same rooted guardians he and his best friend had ridden past so long ago. Now only taller, broader, more magnificent and imposing, their whorls of long, stout limbs so covered in foliage resembling large snowflakes that he could not see the treetops. Not even leaning out the carriage window.

He settled back onto his seat, a sudden swerving of the carriage sharpening his recollection of the tortuous nature of that section of the pass. Scarcely wide enough to accommodate wheeled conveyances, its grade challenged him to keep his buttocks from sliding off the seat. He steadied himself with a hand on the cabin's side wall, then shifted his considerable weight to the opposite bench where gravity pulled his back against the coach's interior, allowing him to relax.

Peril Pass was used far less these days than was the southern route between his and King Axil's realms. When he returned to Tegan, he would put plans in motion to improve the corridor. He intended to make frequent use of it and hoped Axil would do the same.

Marshal Ademar appeared on horseback outside the coach's window.

"This is the worst of it, m'lord. The men are clearing rocks and branches, but the way is laid with ruts and roots as well."

King Tygre snorted dismissively. "I'm not hunting sympathy, Ademar. A sedentary life has made me soft and heavy. I deserve a few reminders."

Marshal Ademar flashed a smile through the carriage door window. "We're going as slowly as we can, m'lord." The smile spread. "You'll let me know if you favor switching places?"

King Tygre scoffed heavily and waved his marshal away.

The carriage continued to shake and shudder over rough terrain.

Endure! It is a small price to pay to see your old friend. What a roguish pair you made! Handsome, charismatic, full of vigor! It's impossible to imagine Axil any other way, but surely time has altered his appearance. No doubt he remembers me the same... I should have better cared for this body! Should have married, sired children... How foolish to have let so many years come between us. Stop! Don't be so cynical. This is a time to celebrate. We have years ahead of us. See to it they aren't wasted. Our shared past binds us forever... Isadora!

The carriage swerved once more, and King Tygre instinctively reached for Isadora's silk kerchief, gifted to him by Axil and now tucked inside his coat.

A prolonged, sharp cracking sound engendered shouting, screaming, a loud, dull thud, and then... silence.

"Whoa!" The carriage slowed, then stopped. A ragged chorus of cries sounded up the road. King Tygre slid his weight to the coach's side and stuck his head out the door's opening. A good distance ahead, a large tree lay across the road, several soldiers and their horses crushed beneath it. With further passage barred, the convoy had broken ranks.

"Turn the coach!" Ademar shouted, coming into view. "Turn the coach!"

"There's not room enough, Marshal! Not here!" shouted the driver.

"Back it up, then!"

"The grade's too—"

A snapping *zi-ing* from the hillside echoed past the carriage, and on its heels another loud *crr-a-ack* sounded. The creaking of wood scraping wood preceded a loud *whoo-ooosh*, this time from behind the coach. The earth beneath the carriage trembled and a gust of dusty air brushed past it.

"Noggods!" cried Marshal Ademar.

"What is it!?" shouted King Tygre, the pit of his stomach rising into his chest.

"They're felling trees, m'lord!" The marshal slid from his horse. "Get out! Get out!" King Tygre moved to the door as Ademar barked orders to his frenzied men. "The woods! Get to the woods!" The marshal flung the carriage door open. "Quickly, m'lord!" One hand on either side of the door frame, King Tygre stood frozen by the terror in Ademar's eyes. *Cr-rack! Crrr-aa-ck! Crr-aaack!*

"Shi-iite!" cried the driver. The monarch felt Ademar's strong hands grasp both his wrists and pull. Isadora's kerchief slipped from his grasp as he landed awkwardly on the road, one leg buckling beneath his weight. His kneecap shattered against a large, flat stone, causing him to roll in agony. Lying on his back, he grabbed the injured knee with both hands and stared up at the carriage in horror. The sky above it was fast disappearing, blocked by two more descending trees. Somewhere behind him, Ademar swore.

The horses reared. The driver jumped. The tree's branches were the first to hit the carriage, and King Tygre closed his eyes a moment before its massive trunk landed with a deafening roar, splintering the coach into a thousand pieces.

THE BLOOD OF BROKEN HEARTS

"What a cruel joke it is to bestow the title king upon mere mortals." King Axil of Aranox, speaking to the seven gods.

King Axil

A broad band of sunlight streamed through his study window, highlighting specks of dust floating like a fine mist in the air. King Axil moved his head to intercept the warming sun—it would be the last to set before his friend arrived.

Have I done all that I should to prepare a proper welcome?

The question haunted him. Could he ever do enough?

He remembered Tygre's favorite meal: roasted squeag bathed in a syrup of bism juice and honey. The kitchen was well-stocked and the cooks eager for a challenge. Whatever Tygre's stomach craved, it would receive. He dared not assume his old friend's physical condition, but he doubted very much the man had lost his appetite. Or his competitive spirit. There were board games ready in the parlor; rolling balls and "kill the straw man" on the grounds. And if Tygre seemed overly ambitious, or was looking to impress his childhood friend, Sergeant Cogswell would be waiting on the training grounds.

King Axil sighed. The details weren't important, really. One firm handshake would bridge their hearts.

A soft knocking on the door surprised him. He was not expecting company. Every palace hand was busy, either preparing for war or for the arrival of King Tygre.

"Enter!"

The door swung slowly open to reveal Marshal Carson.

"What is it?" the monarch asked.

"It's King Tygre, m'lord."

King Axil stood. "So soon! Where is he now? Approaching? At the gates?" The black and gray-striped cragens accompanied him, tails swatting the air, as he rounded his desk.

"No, m'lord." The marshal bowed his head. "There's been an accident."

The monarch had heard that word enough in his lifetime. Uttered with somber gravity, it stopped him in his tracks, causing him to note the marshal's wrinkled brow, hands clasped together at his waist. *And yet, perhaps...* "He's all right, is he?" The king held his breath.

"No, m'lord. Two of his men are at the gates." Carson swallowed. "They say their king is dead."

King Axil steadied himself with a hand on his desk. The room had gone dark and began to spin. He collapsed in the chair nearest him, eyes closed.

"How?" he whispered.

The marshal's voice came from far away. "Descending Peril Pass. Several trees fell across the way. A dozen men were killed... King Tygre among them."

"Several trees! All at once?"

"They were held by ropes, sire. Felled on purpose. Someone was lying in wait."

"I thought you said it was an accident."

"A poor choice of words, m'lord."

"Leave me, Erik."

"M'lord—"

"Be off. You leave for the GOT in two suns' time, do you not? Surely you have things to do."

"Sire... I—"

"Have Caleb ready my horse. I'll be riding with you."

"M'lord."

"Get out! Ready the royal guard! Prepare my armor and my horse!"

"Your Highness..."

"Not another word! Get out! I'd rather die in battle than cower like some child in this place, do you hear? I am the King of Aranox, and this is my war! I shall have the magister's head, and I intend to take it with my own hands. Get out!"

Marshal Erik Carson

Marshal Carson brought the war room to order. "King Axil has decided to join in the attack. No amount of reasoning will sway him. Welcome, Fereliss, to our table." Several grunts bounced off the damp stone walls, acknowledging the royal guardsman's presence. "You'll stay so close to him, he'll think that you're in love. Understood?"

Sir Dreddit chuckled. Fereliss glared at him.

"My apologies for the short notice," the marshal said. "You and the others are ready, are you?"

Fereliss cleared his voice. "I have never been so ready, Marshal, or so proud, to serve my king."

"And the cragens?" asked Sergeant Perill.

The question caught Carson off guard. "Gods above. He wouldn't let them join the Lords and Ladies Feast for fear the noise and excitement would set them off. I can't imagine... No, he wouldn't. I'll make sure they stay behind. For all our sakes."

"Here kitty, kitty," teased Sir Dreddit, eliciting a smattering of nervous laughter.

"Better to worry about the prattlers," the marshal said, quieting the room. "What have we learned?"

Sergeant Galeran sat forward, folding his hands upon the table. "I took Bearman with me," he said, "and now we know more about the prattlers than we do each other." More laughter ensued.

"You trust your source?"

"Yes, Marshal. An ancient naturalist, loyal to his studies and the king. We sat in his home, surrounded by fur and bones, bottles full of insects drowned in liquid. The stench in that place was nearly unbearable, but what we learned was worth the effort. He even offered us a piece of his collection."

From beneath his turncoat, the sergeant withdrew what looked to be an irregular-shaped piece of shiny, thin metal. He handed it to Sir Godfrey, seated next to him.

"It's a piece of prattler shell," said Galeran. "Pass it round and give it a feel. It's not as hard as armor, perhaps, but it would do in a pinch. It can be pierced by sword or battle-axe, but not without great effort."

"Black as coal," said Sir Parrish, receiving the oddity from Sir Godfrey. "I told you... you'll hear them coming long before you see them in the dark."

"The old man gave us this as well." Sergeant Galeran produced a roll of parchment tied with ribbon. "He's half-blind now, but sketched this as a young man." The sergeant untied the parchment and rolled it out for all to see. Sir Parrish and Sir Dreddit stood to get a better look as Sir Galeran tried to bring the drawing to life.

"The prattler's blind as dirt. Those feelers coming out of its head are how it finds its way, so you'll want to stay clear of those. And its sense of smell and hearing are much better than our own. It'll hear you breathing, and smell what last you ate. Its nose looks like a short lance, but if provoked, it can extend it… as quickly as a lightning bolt. Steer clear of that as well."

"We've a better chance against the cragens, is that it?" joked Sir Dreddit.

"How do we battle them?" asked Carson.

"Its keen sense of smell can be turned against it. If you stink of lyla, it wants no part of you. It abhors the scent. No one braves the Lawless Lands without some form of this." Galeran dipped two fingers into a small pouch in front of him and withdrew a pinch of powder.

"We'll need a lot of that," said Stronghart, wrinkling his nose.

"The Cauldron and The Guild keep large stores," said Galeran. "Their demand for it keeps several farmers busy just outside of Stonybrook. We were steered to one whose allegiance to the GOT is strictly monetary. He gifted this to us as a small token of good faith. We'll have no trouble securing what we need as we pass by."

Carson nodded. "Good news, indeed."

"There's more. The prattlers are not fond of the elements. They live in tunnels underground, only to come out at night in search of food. They drink, but they don't like the touch of water, nor will they suffer fire or strong winds. If you do encounter one, attack it from the side or rear; strike its legs where it is weak, or the joints of its segmented body."

"Lovely," said Sir Dreddit.

Carson glanced at Sergeant Stone. "And the GOT? What can you tell us?"

"Only what we learned from one who claimed to have been inside, and those at The Cauldron willing to trade what they knew or what they'd heard from others for free drink and a few kingshead. It's a stronghold, to be sure. Near as old as this castle, and fashioned much the same. Tall walls encircling its perimeter, even taller than ours… Several separate buildings on the inside, most connected by exterior catwalks and a labyrinth of tunnels underground. Rumor has it that's where they keep their spoils."

"Tunnels!" said Sir Parrish. "I thought this was the desert. They've found a way to tunnel into sand, have they? And build a heavy fortress on top, no less? How is that possible? Why doesn't the whole thing collapse on itself?"

"The Lawless Lands *are* mostly sand," said Sergeant Stone, "but the closer one gets to Reception Canyon, the firmer the earth becomes. By the time you've reached the GOT compound, which sits nearly on its edge, the ground beneath your feet will be sturdier than that on which this castle's built."

"That's true," Sergeant Galeran said. "The naturalist told us much the same. The prattlers have been known to roam the breadth of the Lawless Lands, from the canyon to the Borderlands. Places like The Cauldron draw them with its smells and noise. But mostly, they're found along the canyon rim; it's the only ground firm enough to support their tunnels."

"What do we know about the buildings?" Carson asked.

"We thought you might ask. We've brought our own drawing, we have, and ours is much larger and prettier than that of your little prattler." Sergeant Stone unfurled a scroll in front of him, and several other hands helped to lie and keep it flat. One of Stone's weathered fingers moved about the crude map.

"This one here is known as The Hidor, short for The High Order, whose members sleep and operate inside—all but the magister, that is."

"How many are there?" asked the marshal.

"As you thought, Marshal. Five, all told."

"The king has marked each for death," Carson said, "and the men who kill them shall be honored. How will they be recognized?"

Sergeant Stone spread his arms. "We're fairly empty-handed there, Marshal. They don't even go by names. They're known as Ruler One, Ruler Two, and so on. One of them's a woman—she controls the coin. Another leads The Guild's army, and likely wears a uniform. That's all we know, I'm afraid. No descriptions. Nothing."

"Disappointing. What about the other buildings?"

"The one next to The Hidor will be the largest. It's the School of Taking, where young thieves are groomed and brainwashed. Bear in mind, this is only what we're told. For all we know, the entire compound is crawling now with soldiers." His fingers traced the map. "This is mostly open space, here, and these other, smaller buildings we can't be sure of. They probably store supplies or serve basic needs—kitchen, storeroom, whatnot.

"There are several towers, all serving as both windcatcher and lookout. They're going to see us coming from far off; they'll have a lot of warning. No way to avoid that, unless we're traveling at night." He glanced at Sergeant Galeran. "In which case, we risk the company of your friends, the prattlers.

"The tallest of the towers will also be the thickest, and His Majesty may want to visit there, accompanied by his escorts, of course. Most call it Takers Tower, but the magister calls it home."

"He's to be captured, not killed," said the marshal. "This is most important."

Sir Dreddit's brow wrinkled. "I thought his head was to rest on a pole outside the castle, Marshal."

"And so it shall, but taking it is an honor left to His Majesty's blade, do you hear? Make certain your men know. Each and every one." Affirmative murmurs rippled down the table.

"What can you tell us about the inside of the tower?" Carson asked.

"Not much, Marshal. Few have ever been allowed there—it's off limits, even to those living at the GOT. Two things, though: first, it's built like no other tower you've ever seen, with a smaller one inside it. A tower within a tower, as it were. Second, below ground, it holds all The Guild has stolen from Aranox and Tegan."

A soft whistle escaped Sir Parrish's lips.

"I don't understand," said Sergeant Perill. "A tower within a tower. How is that possible?"

"It's like this," said Sergeant Stone, holding out his arms in an imaginary embrace. "The girth of Takers Tower... it's massive—like something my wife, not yours, might recognize."

Marshal Carson closed his eyes as the room erupted in laughter. *Let them have their fun.*

"But here," continued Stone, maintaining his serious countenance, "at its center, rises the likes of which you're more familiar." He raised a pinky finger in the air. "A skinny reed, like so. Surely now you understand?"

Sergeant Perill waited for the chuckling to subside. "I do... I do. I think, in fact, we all do." His eyes grew wide. "Every farmer knows it's the smallest cock who crows the loudest."

Another burst of laughter filled the war room.

"What else?" asked the marshal, raising his voice just loud enough to command attention.

"For what it's worth, Marshal, we did little on our ride back but talk of strategy."

"Go on," Carson said.

"The GOT's location and the habits of the prattlers are most important. It will take the better part of one sun to reach the fortress from the Borderlands, which represents the last known source of water. We either travel in the light, and attack the GOT in darkness, or we travel at night, in the company of the prattlers, and attack at dawn. That seems the better option. With any luck, we'll be inside the fortress by the time the beasts come to life again. Keeping them at bay whilst traveling seems easier than battling them and The Guild's army at the same time.

"We'll need to travel light—no heavy armor or long shields—which will weaken our defenses should we meet a hail of arrows. We can't take bashers or hurlers—their weight is far too heavy for the sand. Though, we stopped a wagon destined for the GOT; it had those wide metal wheels to displace the weight of its load. If we had more time to prepare, and more time to travel, we might fashion something similar for our hurlers."

"But we don't," said Marshal Carson.

"No, Marshal. I mention it because of what we found inside the wagon. Most peculiar. We would not have stopped it if not for those wheels and the direction it was headed. You'll never guess what it was hauling."

"Tell us, then."

"Sand, Marshal. Just sand. Sacks and sacks of it."

"Whatever for?"

"They said they didn't know. Only did as they were told."

Sergeant Stone waited long enough to ensure no one wished to further press the mystery.

"Getting there will be the easy part; getting in will be the trick. Once inside, there's lots of nooks and crannies for their soldiers to hide in. And of course, the longer we're outside, the more likely we'll be visited by the prattlers."

"How do we get in, then?" asked Sir Godfrey.

"Ahh, that's the dilemma, isn't it?" said Stone.

"We could try knocking!" said Sir Dreddit.

"We could, indeed," said Major Stronghart. "Failing that, there's only three ways in, aren't there? We climb over, we crash through, or we crawl under!"

The marshal waited just outside the war room as most others took their leave. A meaningful look from Sergeant Galeran suggested that his difficulty in extinguishing the lanterns was a pretense. Upon succeeding with that task, the stocky soldier joined the marshal.

"What is it, Sergeant?"

"I didn't think it right to mention earlier, Marshal—what Bearman and I heard in Stonybrook. Not a whisper of the Dunn girl, but a young knight with hair of gold was said to have been killed there several suns ago."

"Who told you this?"

"The farmer of Iyla. We asked about them both, but he knew nothing of the girl."

It was wishful thinking, but the marshal voiced it nonetheless. "Perhaps he spoke of Theos. They were ambushed close to Stonybrook."

Sergeant Galeran shook his head. "No. We thought the same, but the farmer knew of that as well. This wasn't about the Prince of Quills, and it was much more recent. This one, he said, was lookin' for his brother."

Carson closed his eyes. "Leave it to me to tell the boy's father." Once Sir Godfrey was informed, no castle gate would hold him.

Carson stopped to review not only his objectives, but the possible approaches he might use to secure victory. *None is more attractive than the others. Not given the king's mood or current state of mind.*

The door to the monarch's dressing room was partially open, the sounds of quiet activity spilling from inside. The marshal knocked with some trepidation before tilting his head into the room. King Axil stood with his arms held to either side, three seamsters with busy hands nearly hiding him from view. Scissors, shears, and scraps of cloth littered the floor surrounding them.

"What is it?" asked King Axil. "This is all your doing, you know. My old armor doesn't fit! Little wonder. This is what happens when you trade your horse for a throne."

Only half listening, Carson nodded. Movement on the room's upper level held his gaze. One of the cragens paced back and forth, its ears laid back, its long, striped tail twitching in the air.

"Don't go back there," said the king. "Sir Black's not allowing visitors. Not even you. If by some miracle you did get past him, Lady Gray would rip you to shreds, as weak as she may be."

"What's wrong?" asked the marshal.

"It's not like that. She's apparently been on the path to motherhood these past three almons, though there would have been no way to tell. A cragen doesn't show until the final quarter moon. She's hidden in all that cloth piled back there behind Sir Black. Why she picked this spot is beyond me, but there's no moving her now."

Carson breathed a sigh of relief. *The God of Fortune continues to watch over me! The cragens clearly won't be traveling. Perhaps...* "Surely you don't plan to miss the birthing, sire."

King Axil scowled. "Surely you did not come here to talk about the cragens."

"No, sire." *Don't poke the bear again just yet. Use your buffer!* "There's a woman at the gates. She claims to be the mother of Pryll Fletcher." *How pleasant it has been here since that rat's demise!*

"The steward's mother? Hismona..." The name crawled from his mouth. "What does she want? Besides money, that is."

"To speak with you, m'lord."

"As if! I've told you the story of that family, have I not?

"You have, sire. I know you thought highly of the father."

"Yes, he was much like you. And Hismona was a beautiful woman, to be sure, but beneath that surface she was as ugly as they come. Both boys suckled venom from her teats too long, I fear, though I had hoped Pryll could be saved. His brother's worse than he was, if you can imagine. A loathsome creature!"

"Shall I let her know you're indisposed, Your Majesty?"

"Have someone unfamiliar with the woman's past say some kind words to her. I am incapable of it. Bring her a basket of food and my condolences, then send her away. She's not to bring her poison inside these walls, do you hear?"

"Yes, sire." Carson stood, unmoving.

"Ow!" King Axil flinched. The artisans all backed away.

"A thousand pardons, sire," one mumbled, two pins clenched between his teeth.

"Nonsense." King Axil summoned the seamsters back, and their trembling hands got busy again.

"That was your doing as well, Erik. Just how long do you intend to stand there? You're making us all nervous."

"Might I have a word, Your Highness? In private?"

The craftsmen's fingers froze. The king gently pushed those nearest him away. "Wait outside, please. As soon as this troublesome meddler leaves, I should like you to continue."

"Yes, sire." The craftsmen scurried off without their tools, closing the door behind them.

King Axil released a deep breath. "You rarely use that term, you know... Your Highness."

"Is that right?"

"Yes. It's almost always Your Majesty, m'lord, or sire. Rarely Your Highness. It's of no consequence, of course, except that I have come to know that you are most troubled when you call me that."

"I had not realized, m'lord."

"Of course not. It's hardly the kind of thing one notices when troubled."

"Are you not troubled, Your Majesty?"

"I have been troubled since I was crowned king, Erik. It cannot be otherwise. Is it so different being marshal?"

"It is not, m'lord, but this... this is—"

"Beyond troubled. Yes. So far beyond, there is no word for it."

"Might I speak freely, sire?

"The times demand it, do they not?"

"Yes, sire. Madness... sheer madness—that is the word for this. As your marshal, I have a duty to protect you. And as your friend, if I might be so bold, I am concerned for your well-being. But even if the rage in you sweeps all of that aside, and who could blame you, there is another voice of higher calling you must listen to."

"And whose voice might that be?"

"The subjects of Baelon, m'lord."

King Axil snorted softly, but Carson carried on. "Not the realm of Aranox or Tegan, but all of Baelon. King Tygre is dead, with no heir apparent. What do you think will come to pass if you follow in his footsteps? No one waits to take your place. If you are killed in battle, what disorder will ensue? Clearly, this is what The Guild plans for. Do you doubt it orchestrated Tygre's death, or that its eyes remain on you? Can you imagine what will befall Baelon if both its realms are kingless?"

"You don't intend to let that happen, do you?"

"Forgive me for saying so, m'lord, but victory will be much easier to grasp if we are not distracted by your presence on the battlefield."

"There's no need to hold my hand or coddle me. I don't need to be watched over."

"I beg to differ, sire. With all that's riding on your continued presence on the throne, what choice do we have?"

King Axil looked away and puffed his chest. "If you choose to cosset me, you do so of your own accord, and not for my benefit."

"Not for you or me, sire, but for all of Baelon."

"We will destroy the GOT, will we not?"

"Of course, but that's not really what's at stake here, is it? Win or not, what's most important is that you remain alive. And that is anything but certain once you leave the shelter of this castle. It isn't just the battlefield, m'lord. The Guild is clearly stalking you. The first arrows may be waiting just outside the castle gates. Tygre's death, in fact, may well have been designed to flush you out. Why play into their hands and rush into a trap that is so obvious? Why please them so, when instead you could frustrate them by staying here inside these walls?"

King Axil collapsed heavily into a nearby chair.

"You're right, of course. Every word of what you say rings true. It's sensible and logical—just what I expect from you. And precisely how a king should govern. Not on what the loudest voices or the deepest pockets clamor for, and not on raw emotion. On what is best for the people. The masses. Every act should be designed to achieve the greatest good for the greatest number. I've always said as much. A king cannot afford to govern on emotion, Erik. Never forget that."

"You'll reconsider, then?

King Axil remained silent for the longest time.

Take your time! Think it through! Come to peace with it.

The monarch stared right through him. "Do you know what happens to the blood spilled from a broken heart, Erik? It cannot escape the body. It pools inside one's head and drowns the brain. And mine is now so steeped in it, I cannot think beyond it. All I see... is blood. What shall befall Baelon should I be killed in battle? I shan't give the notion further thought. Rather, you should ponder that yourself." His eyes focused on the marshal. "Before we leave the castle, I shall pen a declaration and have the clerks and chaplain bear witness to my signature. Should I die in battle, you shall succeed me on the throne."

What?! Have you gone mad?

"And that, my friend, shall be your penance for being a good man who keeps his wits about him at all times. Don't look so shocked, and stop worrying about my welfare. The king you knew and served so well… is already dead."

Rolft Aerns

With Sarah at a standstill just outside the town of Stonybrook, Rolft arched and stretched his back. The morning sun warmed his left shoulder. A white moon stood out against the cloudless southern sky. He pulled a piece of dried meat from his saddlebag and nibbled at its edges. Three suns had set since Fereliss' visit, during which he had double-checked the Dunn's and Godfrey's homes; spoken with staff at The God of Children's House; visited the noble served by the Godfreys, and stopped by The House of All Gods and The Keep. It was all akin to checking one's pockets for a lost item before spending too much time looking elsewhere. He was not surprised to have come up empty-handed.

The arrow that had killed the girl's mother was presumed to have been unleashed by the same gang of thieves who had killed Queen Isadora, Princess Lewen, and Theos Godfrey. Sibil might be seeking to avenge them, or she might be searching for Tristan—a kindred soul to offer her some solace. Either pursuit would likely draw her south, toward the site of Theos Godfrey's death and the stronghold of the Takers Guild. Stonybrook would be a sensible place for her to rest and gather information.

Rolft urged Sarah into town. "Remember why we're here," he murmured. "And if you see that handsome gray from the castle, Shadow, be sure to let me know, yeah?" *This is a sleepy place compared to Fostead. Fewer buildings, more open space and farmlands, no bustling crowds or street hawkers.* The sign above the door to the largest structure in sight read simply "Spirits," a message reinforced by seven empty bottles, one dangling by a cord below each letter.

He tethered Sarah to a rail and made his way inside.

There were but three men at the tables, all too old to be working the fields, each keeping to himself. Two silently nursed drinks; the third appeared to be asleep.

A man wearing a leather apron limped among the tables, stooping awkwardly here and there to pick up small bits of debris from the floor. Long strands of gray-brown hair sprouted from his mostly bald scalp. A weathered face and tired brown eyes could not hide the fact that this had been a bull in its prime.

"I'm looking for a girl," Rolft said by way of introduction.

The barkeep kept to his task. "You've lost a child, have you? Best look in on Mother Downs. She might—"

"Not a child. A young woman."

"Look here." The barkeep stopped working to dispense his thoughts. "If you want one, you've come to the wrong place. If you've lost one, it's the same tune. Not many women set foot in here."

Rolft stepped closer and lowered his voice. "What about a young man? A king's knight, hair of gold, perhaps a quarter moon ago." The man's reaction was fleeting, but Rolft saw the way his pupils danced, and the nervous sideways glance he gave to see if those nearby were listening. "What is it?" Rolft asked. The barkeep hesitated, but Rolft pressed him. "You've as much as told me you know something." Still, the man resisted. "I'm not leaving until I know what that is," Rolft said. "And the longer I stay, the less you're going to enjoy my company." *Whatever the man's harboring cannot be good news.*

"You're probably wondering what's stored out back," the proprietor said suddenly. His eyebrows lifted slightly as he began to wipe the counter. "Behind the building, if you catch my meaning. I'm due there shortly to check on things. You'd best go and see for yourself, don't you think?"

Rolft weighed the proprietor's overture against the prospect of beating the truth out of him. He gave the man a hard look before starting for the door.

But if something unexpected should show itself behind this building...

Rolft reduced the odds of that occurring by positioning himself at one of the establishment's rear corners, where he could see down both the length of its back and the alley he had taken to get there.

But the barkeep emerged alone from the back door. Spotting Rolft to one side, he limped toward him. "Your young knight was much more trusting."

"You've seen him, then."

"He was alive when he walked out my door. I swear it."

"And now?"

The barkeep shook his head and shrugged. "You're asking the wrong man."

"Who, then?"

The man glanced in all directions. "You're from Castle Aranox, yeah?" Rolft did not answer. "Well, let's just say that when your friends first came for the Prince of Quills, they should have taken them all." Rolft's expression conveyed his confusion. "Shaun Penniluk—the Prince of Quills. He has two brothers, Milton and Maynard. Your friends came for Shaun, and I'm sayin' they should have taken all three. Shaun was by far the most decent of the lot. The other two have been in bed with The Guild of Takers since they were young."

"Where are they now?"

"If they were here, you and I wouldn't be talking. The last anyone saw, they were paying their respects to your young knight. Whether they killed him, I don't know—that's the gods' honest truth. But whatever they did to him, they knew they'd pay dearly for it if they stayed here. I'm told they've gone to the GOT. Figured if they have to fight King Axil, they might as well do it with an army on their side—and be paid for it, no less!"

The stout woman outside The Kindling seemed determined to make it down a pathway leading to a thatched shelter without stopping. Sweating profusely, she grunted as she labored, water sloshing above the rims of the buckets hanging from her hands. When she caught sight of Rolft, she set the load down, her sizeable chest rising and falling rhythmically. Her ruddy cheeks nearly matched the fiery red of her hair. She gestured first to Sarah, then toward a crowded hitching rail. "If you're stayin' the night, I'll take 'im. If not, best leave 'im there. The place is hummin' louder than a beehive these past suns."

"Her name's Sarah. She needs a good rest, and food as well."

"I'll take her, then. You'll need ta speak with the man inside about a bed, and good luck with that."

Rolft dismounted. "If it's all the same to you, I'll sleep with the horse."

The woman frowned. "There's not much room in there, not even for the horses. Best take a look before you decide." She grabbed Sarah's reins and bustled off. Rolft picked up her buckets and followed her inside the small, thatched-roof enclosure. "It's frightfully cold at night, and the smell is sumthin' awful."

Rolft's eyebrows shrugged. "I'll make do."

"It's not fer me ta say. Best ask inside." Rolft watched her tackle the saddle with strong, capable hands. "Sumthin' else I kin do fer ya?" she asked.

"Not unless you've seen a young woman these past few suns… traveling alone on a gray stallion?"

"A young woman?" She scoffed loudly. "No. There's just the four of us here. Women, that is. And not ten of us could satisfy that lot inside. You'd best hope whoever you're lookin' for isn't headed this way. There's nuthin' but hurt and misery waitin' for her here. A young woman? And traveling alone? Not likely!" She dropped Rolft's tackle to the ground. "Unless you're talkin' about that dark-skinned creature in there now. I suppose she qualifies, but she's not alone, and she's not like any other woman I've seen. Looks as though she might bite back, that one! I've no business talkin' about appearances, of course." The woman brushed her loose hair back self-consciously. "I've been here so long my skin's as thick as a bortok's hide. No, this ain't no place for women. No place at all." Rolft could find no words. "Don't look at me like that," she said. "I don't need your pity. I stopped bein' any kind of woman almons ago."

"You look just fine." Rolft left the woman to her tasks.

He knew The Kindling by reputation only. Its very name was an admission of its diminutive stature as compared to The Cauldron's towering pyres. Less impressive in appearance and visited by far fewer travelers, it did its best to earn its nickname as the den of debauchery's "wicked little brother."

Common lore suggested there were but two reasons to patronize the place. The first, and most popular: to improve one's standing as an outcast of the realm; the second, to boast that as a follower of the king's law, you had spent time there and survived. A well-worn joke suggested that the latter did their boasting from the grave.

It was an old timber cabin in obvious need of repairs. Its roof, completely hidden beneath a thick mat of dark green moss, sagged like the back of an old horse made to suffer a lifetime of excessive loads. A few members of its stone foundation had succumbed to the passage of time and rested on the ground. Were it nestled in the Fekle Forest, the ancient structure might have seemed mystical or charming—a home to elves, perhaps. But not in the Dark Woods. Here, an aura of degradation and decay surrounded it. The chinks between its logs, some wide enough to slide a hand through, gave passage to rough voices from inside. Visibly weakened by the appetite of bark beetles, the stairs to its front porch groaned and bent beneath Rolft's weight.

He pulled the door open to a pot of boiling oil, frustrated by its containment and looking for a better place to spend its anger.

Always people first.

Men buzzed inside the beehive, hovering over crowded tables tightly crammed together. Too many men to count, none of them in uniform, and one—no, two—women serving them. Most troubling were those few dark spaces he could not see into.

A few patrons near the door gave him a cursory look before returning their attention elsewhere. Apart from that, his presence did not appear to move anyone, so he jostled his way to the bar. His hips nudged the backs of two men arguing at the last table blocking his path.

"Watch your carcass, big man!" All five sitting at the table glared at him.

"Apologies." Rolft squeezed between them and their neighbors to access the bar. Even with his ribs pressed against its counter, his trouser legs brushed the back of one of the men's chairs.

"Noggods!" said its occupant.

"So easily bruised!" said another.

"Like your smellhole!" came the quick response.

"What'll it be?" The skinny barkeep, bald and bearded, sought Rolft's attention. "Beggar's ale?"

Rolft produced a coin from his pocket. "Bism's Blood."

"Bism's Blood it is!" The keeper chose a bottle from an assortment on the floor, and a glass from below the counter. He pulled the bottle's plug, filled the glass and pushed it to rest in front of Rolft.

The argument behind Rolft continued.

"Move on if you don't like it! No one's in your way!"

"Piss off, yourself!"

"That's it, then! Go on! Find somewhere else ta spit your shite! I'll not have it! Go on!" Rolft turned to watch the speaker kick another's chair violently. When the man sitting on it stood, he suffered a boot in his thigh. "Go suckle your mother's teat!" The kicker sloshed his mug's contents toward the target of his ire. "Fargin' twiddler! Gods almighty! How was I ta know The Guild would pack up after two suns?" The words chased the outcast to a different table. "As if you'd have survived the proving grounds, anyway!"

Proving grounds! Was that not where the Stonybrook innkeeper had suggested the Penniluk brothers were headed?

"Sumthin' you need, big man?"

Rolft realized he'd been staring. "No." He turned to resume his conversation with the barkeep. "I aim to stay the night." He brought his glass to his lips and took a healthy swig. The fermented fruit warmed his throat. "Any objections to my sleeping in the shed?"

"No, sir, but you know we've got four women here, yeah?" Rolft took another drink. "Please yourself," said the keep. "You prefer the horses, ain't none o' my business. You mind the rules, though—no rough-housin'. And you keep things quiet out there!" He laughed. "But if you change your mind, you jest let me know. Mae, there, she's a comfort on a night like this to be sure, and she can fit you in. Just not in that shed. I can't do that to her. What d'ya say?"

Rolft watched the woman who had cared for Sarah push her hips between the backs of seated men, wiping spills as she crossed the room.

"No, I—"

"Hey, Mae!" The man who had banished another from his table pounded on its top, causing drinks to spill. "They're talkin' about you over here! Come have a listen, luv!"

"The shed will do," Rolft told the barkeep.

The apparent leader of the group sitting nearest kept on. "Where have you been, Mae? Come see us, yeah? Look here... an empty seat right next to me!" Ignored by Mae, the man waved one of his comrades off to get her. "If you don't want the chair, Mae, we understand. Come warm our laps instead!"

"Leave her be, Garr," said the skinny barkeep. "She's work to do."

Garr's demeanor soured. "Mind your business."

"She is my business."

"She's your whore!" shouted Garr. "We're your business! Shut up and give us another bottle! Beggar's Ale!"

"Leave her be, I said." The barkeep tried to impose his will as Garr's man tracked Mae down.

"More Beggar's Ale, I said!" Garr motioned halfway down the bar. "Hogman, help the useless barman out!"

A beefy, bearded drinker immediately hoisted his torso onto the bar where he floundered, buoyed by his wide girth, until those to either side of him took hold and shoved him forward. He disappeared behind the bar with a loud crash. Garr and his companions burst into laughter.

"Stop!" the barkeep cried.

Too late. You've lost control, friend. This pot of bubbling oil is about to boil over! Rolft briefly eyed the door, but the sight of Mae being forcibly dragged across the room kept him still. *Not your fight. Think of Sibil!*

"You'll pay for what you break!" cried the barkeep. "No one comes behind the bar!"

"Then do your job!" shouted Garr as Mae was brought to his table in tow.

"And no rough housin', neither!" the barkeep shouted back. "You know the rules!"

"Stow your rules, gods dammit! We ain't gonna hurt her. Eh, Kester?"

Kester grinned, tightening his grip on Mae's upper arm. He dropped into his chair and pulled her onto his lap. "No, sir... far from it! You're in fer a good time! Ain't thet right, Mae?" He kissed her on the mouth, then licked her cheek. She recoiled, slapping him across the face. He slapped her back, harder.

"That's enough!" The keep brought both hands to the bartop, one of them clutching a cudgel.

"Oh no you don't!" The man standing next to Rolft grabbed the club with both hands and wrested it from the keep.

Rolft pressed a large palm against the meddler's head and slammed it against the bar. The man crumpled to the floor as the keep regained his cudgel.

Garr calmed those at his table with outstretched arms. "Now you've broken our rules, big man. That was a mistake, that there was."

"Let it rest," Rolft said evenly. "Let the woman go, and I'll buy your drinks for the evening."

"The evening's young, friend. You've that amount of coin, have you?" Garr rubbed his chin. "Perhaps we'll relieve you of that burden." The pub quieted such that even the tinkling of one bottle against glass seemed out of place.

"Think carefully," Rolft said.

"You're going to stop us, are you?"

Rolft placed the back of one hand on the bartop and the keep laid the cudgel across his open palm. "I am if you persist. This is still King Axil's realm."

"King Axil's realm!" said Garr. "You'd best look around, big man. Everyone here belongs to me!" Garr stood. Chair legs scraped across the floor as men throughout the room rose in unison. The man holding Mae released her to draw his knife.

Gods above! More than a handful! Where are you when I need you, Fereliss! Rolft brought the cudgel down with all his might, splintering the chair nearest him.

Garr snarled. "That was your last mistake, big man!"

"Was it?" A female voice, loud and clear, cut through the room. Its owner emerged from the shadows, tall and slender, dressed in supple leather from the neck down. Her sculpted face was smooth, her hair so closely cropped it showed her shiny scalp. She had full lips, high cheekbones, and thin black brows riding large brown eyes. The lower portions of all four limbs exposed her sleek, dark skin. "Not everyone here belongs to you."

Garr spread his hands. "Beg your pardon." He spit a wad of cud in her direction. "I meant everyone who's not a stick of charcoal."

"Hurtful," said the woman. "And ignorant. Is it a woman's company you seek?"

A gold bracelet spiraled like a coiled snake around her wrist and part-way up her forearm.

Garr looked her over. "Is that what you are? A woman? It's rather hard to tell from here." His comrades laughed.

The woman was unmoved. "Is your eyesight really that poor? Even from this distance, I can tell that you're no man, much less a woman. You're just a mouse, and a little one at that. I might toy with you though, little mouse. Because in answer to your question, I'm more woman than you can handle."

The room grew quiet again.

She's put a lid on your pot of boiling oil—not to let things calm, mind you, but to watch the pressure build inside!

Garr seemed not to notice. "Is that right? Are you offering yourself?"

"I'm offering much more than that!" The woman snapped her long fingers, and from the dark behind her three forms emerged, one of them a massive Black man, bald with pendant earrings hanging from both lobes. His arms looked as though they might rip a door from its hinges. Two hatchets hung from his hips. Beside him stood a rail of a man with long dark hair, every inch of his exposed pale skin, including his face, covered with patterned ink. Some sort of blade, strapped behind his back, showed only its sharp tip. Next to him stood a very young woman dressed in long, soft fur, her blond hair pulled back so tightly it turned the corners of her lips into a frown. A leather satchel hung across one shoulder. Her weapon of choice, if she had one, was not visible. Most noteworthy, however, were her bare feet, an oddity under most any circumstance. "These three don't belong to you—or anyone, for that matter," the dark creature said. "But they'll do my bidding, and do you know why? Because they like me. And unfortunately for you, little mouse, I've decided I don't like you at all."

Garr bit his lip and glanced at Rolft. "Friends of yours?" Rolft declined to answer. "There are twenty-six of us," Garr said to him.

"Is that all?" The dark-skinned woman recaptured Garr's attention. The trio behind her were impossible to ignore. The Black man's hatchets were in hand; the pale, skinny man's strange blade, its serrated edges now exposed, rested on a fully tattooed arm. The young woman busied herself with whatever she had withdrawn from her satchel. *Leather straps of some sort?* "Go on, then! Make the big man pay! I dare you!" The girl behind the woman wrapped a strap around each wrist. Shards of pointed metal protruded from the bands. With those in place, she set to binding similar straps just below her knees.

"Let's not be hasty," Garr said.

The young woman applied her last strap while balanced on one leg, the other extended straight in front of her, parallel to the floor. The mark of an assassin on the bottom of her foot sent a clear message to all those watching.

"Stop squeaking, little mouse, and do something! What are you waiting for?" the dark-skinned creature asked. "How many did you say you were? Twenty-six? We are only four! Five if I include the big man! You've made your threat! Don't back down now!"

"Why don't we all just sit a spell and let things simmer down," said Garr.

A fine idea!

"Too late! You've stirred the pot and now must answer for it! I'll tell you what... why don't you teach the big man there a lesson? Just you, alone. Your friends stay put, and mine will do the same. That, or we can all join in the fun! Either way is fine by me. Your choice. What's it going to be?"

Not much of a choice, is it?

Garr shook his head, holding out both hands in surrender.

"You refuse both invitations? I am so disappointed. I should have liked to see you battle the king's champion. I do believe he would have killed you, and deservedly so. Alas, you must still pay a price." Her hands moved swiftly and Garr cried out as the blade of a throwing knife entered his upper chest. He gritted his teeth and blood seeped between his fingers. "If you're thinking that perhaps I missed my mark, let me assure you, I did not!" A quick flick of the creature's wrist dispatched another shiny object from her hand.

Garr swore, slumping clumsily back onto his chair, two blades protruding from his chest.

"What's wrong, little mouse?"

Garr could only sputter.

"We've no quarrel with you," said one of his companions.

"Ah, but I have one with you!"

"We've done nothing to you!"

"On the contrary—these good people have done naught to you. The woman is unwilling. The big man has offered drinks. Where did you learn your manners? They wish simply to be left alone, as do I and my companions. Yet you hound us with your loud, obnoxious voices. Your boorish behavior offends us all. Our evening is now ruined."

"What would you have us do?"

"Put your weapons on the table, apologize, and leave, never to return. If I learn that you've come back, even once, I'm going on a mouse hunt, and you're going to find it painful."

The four men were halfway to the door when the creature called out again, stopping them in their tracks. "Oi! You've something that belongs to me!" It took a mere moment for her meaning to dawn on them, but even then, they could only stare at Garr's chest in disbelief. "They're mine! Leave them with me!"

Garr screamed as the blades exited his chest.

It took some time for all twenty-six to clear The Kindling. The unconscious meddler by Rolft's feet was the last to be dragged out.

The dark-skinned creature left her companions to approach the bar.

"Ayla, big man. If there's ever anything I can do for you…"

"Have you seen a young woman?" Rolft asked. "Traveling alone?"

"Through these dark woods?" The woman grinned.

"Long, black hair. Riding a gray stallion?"

"No, but—" The whites of the creature's eyes grew large. "Ohhh, wait! Would she be from Castle Aranox? The daughter of the seer? The one they call The Wisperal?"

"You've seen her!"

"More's the pity… I have not, big man. But I've heard the whispering. The girl you seek is not alone. She travels with another—an old man twice your age and half your size. They've proven themselves, and now ride with The Guild's army." She moved closer, her eyes searching his. "Makes no sense to you, eh?"

"Proven herself?"

"The Guild's preparing for war, and they're wooing those foolish enough to risk their lives for a few dire. This room was full of such fools. Only, they're too late. The Guild's proving grounds have packed up and returned to the GOT, the girl and her companion with them. They were accepted two suns ago."

"Impossible."

"She fights with a bone-handled blade? A red jewel to help it see? The Wisperal! They say she killed another giant just to prove herself. Made him eat her neck cord before she sent him below!" The woman's large brown eyes dilated. "All I can do is tell you what I've heard, big man. She's alive and with the Takers Guild... by choice!"

The Borderlands really had no independent identity; its nicknames acknowledged its subservience to the lands on either side of it: Edge of the Realms; Gateway to the Lawless Lands. Both desert and forest used it as a dumping ground for those bits of nature they did not want to hold. Even its hard-packed loamy sand was a mixture of material discarded by its neighbors—a welcome mat to scrape one's boots across before entering a more important place. Little wonder everything that lived there seemed downtrodden and neglected: sparse clumps of struggling grasses, stunted shrubs and twisted spikewood trees.

Of greater interest were a host of recently discarded man-made features. A crude pen constructed of dead tree limbs enclosed a stretch of trampled ground littered with horse dung. Scattered rings of scorched earth dotted the landscape where small wooden stakes still buried in the ground suggested tents had been erected. And further down the Borderlands, torn remnants of cloth flapped atop tall poles where larger shelters, or perhaps one long shade structure, had stood. All were signs of a sizable encampment that had been dismantled and abandoned in a hurry.

Rolft had not doubted the Stonybrook innkeeper or the dagger-wielding woman at The Kindling when they spoke about a Guild of Takers 'proving ground.' Now he knew for certain there was at least some truth to it. The details surrounding Sibil's rumored participation, however, remained difficult to swallow. Her other exploits had been widely exaggerated, and this story seemed particularly far-fetched.

Then again, a lot of what had transpired over the past almon would be hard for most folk to believe. And when it came to Madam Dunn and her daughter, well...

Rolft coaxed Sarah toward what had first appeared to be a solitary shelter pole set off from all the rest, rising among a cluster of spikewood trees to the east. The closer he neared, the more its irregular form commanded his attention, until it dawned on him what he was looking at—a barrel-chested man, naked and bound to the pole by leather straps around his neck and lower legs. His feet were missing, as were chunks of flesh from both his thighs. His midsection was laid open, portions of his ribs exposed, and what little was left of his intestines dangled alongside his genitals. Puncture marks and ragged lacerations covered his body.

Most of that is from the claws and teeth of a bortok, whose telltale tracks circle the pole and lead back toward the Dark Woods. Most, but not all.

Both the man's arms bore the marks of a sharp blade—the same instrument, perhaps, that had slit his neck from ear to ear, separating one flap of skin from the other so that his throat looked for all the world like a second pair of gaping lips, between which hung a short, bloody cord. Rolft reached up to pinch the protuberance between his thumb and forefinger. He tugged once, then twice, and a bloody clot popped from the man's throat with a slight sucking sound.

Rolft dribbled a few drops of his waterskin's precious contents onto the congealed clump before rubbing it back and forth between his fingers. Sacrificing a few more drops to further cleanse it, he held the knotted leather cord by its tail and was immediately transported back to Bojun Barr's livery—to the day he had been visited by the young palace groom, Reggie, and a slender girl with raven hair proclaiming to be a friend of Princess Lewen. It was a recollection that would stay with him forever, anchored by the moment the lass had dangled in front of him a familiar amulet by its leather thong.

The tracks from the 'proving grounds' were heading south, directly for the GOT, when they disappeared into shifting sands. Gone too was any expectation of finding Sibil consoled in Tristan Godfrey's arms. Bloody clues were not what Rolft had hoped to find in the Borderlands, but they were clues nonetheless.

Thank the gods for Marshal Carson! Always thinking, that one! Were it not for the way that man's mind worked, Rolft might still have been wrestling field stones, clueless to Sibil's plight.

He craned his neck for another glimpse west, where the horizon suggested a trembling hand with a palette of vivid colors had been confined to horizontal brushstrokes. Higher still, mottled purples, blacks, and blues spread like a large bruise across the sky.

The Mersal Sea sat atop the Lawless Lands like a band of shimmering black glass.

"Storm's coming," he told Sarah softly.

It did not surprise him when The Cauldron's pyres came to life, six bold markers to the east, but he took note when several sparks appeared beside them. They were so small he might not have noticed one or two, but soon there were a dozen, and then so many bunched together, he lost count. They hovered in the dusk, like night flies buzzing 'round a lantern, before dispersing slowly, one or two sparks at a time, until they were no longer grouped but rather stretched into one line, creeping across the Lawless Lands.

Rolft stroked Sarah's neck. "There's only one place for them to go out there." The horse snorted in response. "That's right... the same as where we're headed."

THE TASTE OF EUPHORIA

"It can be difficult–impossible at times–to distinguish reality from fantasy. We all come to know eventually: life itself is an illusion." From the teachings of The Systalene

Marshal Erik Carson

Marshal Carson sat astride his horse, flanked by Major Stronghart, Fereliss, and the royal guards. Behind them, an army five hundred strong waited on horseback for King Axil to deliver his address.

The monarch eased his sturdy mount between them and the castle gates, then simply sat there, as though gathering his thoughts or waiting for some sign. His long hair trembled in the breeze and danced across the breastplate he had agreed to wear.

The marshal second-guessed himself. Such thin armor might deflect an errant sword, but it would not stop an archer's arrow, let alone one freed from a crossbow. It would be insufferable beneath the desert sun, and with an army dressed to travel quickly, it would only call attention to one man.

Just look at him! Even absent armor and in the midst of all these soldiers, what commoner unfamiliar with the royal family would not still pick him out as king?

He felt the flesh below one eye begin to twitch.

Is there any more a skilled assassin might request to help further his own cause? Utter madness!

King Axil's horse pawed the ground. The monarch squared his shoulders.

Not bothering to avert his gaze from the king, Carson muttered, "Once we've left the castle, Fereliss, give him no space at all, and not one moment to himself. When he complains, which he will, you'll lose your hearing. He's to return just as he is. Not a hair out of place, not a scratch on his skin. Understood?"

Fereliss' response was cut short by the monarch's raised voice.

"Once upon a time, there was a little snake in this garden we call Aranox! I saw it on many occasions, but being young and foolish, I thought it harmless. It has since slithered through our land with poisonous intent, its appetite for thievery and murder never quenched. It has grown into a serpent that now makes its presence known in every village in Baelon!

"We are a peaceful people, but we will not be preyed upon, nor suffer unprovoked hostilities! From this day forth, we are at war with The Guild of Takers, and any who would harbor it. We shall suffer it no more! The High Order of The Guild—the serpent's head—hides inside a lair within the Lawless Lands, where it thinks we dare not go. But we do dare! We shall tread so forcefully that the ground beneath its dark den shakes as we descend upon it! This day begins the hunt, which will not cease until we have destroyed the serpent's lair and hold its head! Take heed as you pass through these gates. Just outside, a wooden pole is driven in the ground, waiting to display the head of the one they call the magister. We do not hunt for sport. We do not intend to capture, but to kill!"

The king raised his sword, and a collective roar of approval accompanied the clattering of several hundred spears and swords raised high into the air.

King Axil's stentorian voice rose above the din.

"For your queen and princess!"

"For the queen and princess!" shouted the soldiers.

"For Aranox and Tegan!"

"For Aranox and Tegan!"

Marshal Carson showed no emotion. Major Stronghart and the officers beside him sat solemnly astride their mounts.

Fereliss leaned toward the marshal. "Now, that's the king I swore allegiance to when I was young and beardless! May all seven gods watch over him!"

No longer listening for the sound of falling trees, Marshal Carson turned his energy elsewhere. Relief and worry wrestled for his favor. *Through the Dark Woods without incident! But why is that? The Guild dispatched King Tygre soon after his departure from Tegan. Surely it has not stopped stalking the King of Aranox. Listen to yourself! All the more reason not to dwell on the Dark Woods. Focus on what lies ahead!*

He brought his horse within earshot of the monarch, speaking loud enough for the royal guardsmen to hear as well. "The Cauldron's ties to The Guild are well known, Your

Majesty. You'll fall back as we approach, and let the men surround you. Just until I signal that it's safe."

"Safe! We are at war; don't be absurd!"

Carson took a deep breath, but Fereliss answered for him. "Please, Your Majesty... for my sake. Let us make sure that you remain prepared for battle with the magister. I beg you, do not deny me the greatest honor of my life—to be beside you when you take his head!"

Though slow in coming, the king's heavy exhalation clearly signaled resignation. Carson reined his horse away, further relieved.

The Cauldron was an arrow's flight away when next he brought the army to a halt. Perhaps two dozen horses stood tethered to a rail extending well beyond both sides of the wide four-story building. A small collection of men began to assemble on its front porch.

"They don't appear to be expecting us," said Major Stronghart.

The men on the porch suddenly descended to the ground and moved as one toward the army.

"Shall we?" asked the marshal, urging his horse forward.

"Indeed." Major Stronghart rode beside him. The army stayed behind.

As the small group neared, its leader held out his arms. "Welcome to The Cauldron!" The man flashed snuff-stained teeth while smoothing the wrinkles in his shirt.

Marshal Carson brought his horse to a stop.

"Welcome!" repeated the man. "I don't know that we can serve you all at once, but we'll see what we can do." He placed his hands on his hips.

"We're not your customers," the marshal said. "We're your guests. And we'll be staying just long enough to eat and rest. We'll be gone come nightfall."

"Gone, you say... by nightfall? Well, I suppose that'd be all right." The greeter turned to his companions. "I think we can live with that, can't we?"

"You're not going to like it when we leave, I'm afraid," the marshal warned him.

"Really? Why's that?"

"When we do, we're going to burn your building down."

"What! On whose authority? You can't do that!"

"By the king's decree. It's as good as done."

"King's decree! What do we care about a king's decree?" He looked for support from his cohorts. "Your king has no say here!"

"Do you really want to tell him that? He's in a dark mood, and you'll need to pass five hundred of his soldiers, starting with the two of us, to do so." Marshal Carson withdrew his sword. Major Stronghart followed suit.

"These are the Lawless Lands!" said the man. "You're trespassing!"

"Trespassing?" Carson laughed. "Is there a law against that here? You cannot have it both ways, friend. Either these are lawless lands, or they are not. Which is it?"

"But... but... where's everyone s'posed ta go? Into the Dark Woods this time of night? Out into the desert with the prattlers? There're women here, for gods' sake!"

Marshal Carson lay on his back, staring at The Cauldron's first floor ceiling. Half his soldiers were scattered about him, some sleeping, others resting or speaking in low voices. Several men snored, but none louder than King Axil. On the floor above, the army's other half rested. The third and fourth floors held The Cauldron's staff, with the exception of those pressed into service outside.

Major Stronghart stepped over and around the bodies strewn across the floor. "It's time."

Marshal Carson sat up, rubbing the back of his neck while catching the eye of a stocky soldier seated nearby. "Wake the king, Sergeant. Gently, mind you. Then find the proprietor on the third floor. Bring him outside."

"Yes, sir." The sergeant stepped over two prone soldiers, nudging them to life on his way to wake the king.

Carson followed Major Stronghart outside, where a half sun spread its fiery glow across the western skyline. Shirtless men shouted, cursed and laughed while tossing large logs onto six tall pyres yet to be lit. An occasional roar of approval suggested slinging lumber was as much art as a show of strength.

Two soldiers approached the major. "They seem to know what they're doing, sir. We've pretty much left them to their work. But this..." He pointed to two lines of barrels standing on end, forming a long aisle several paces wide through the dirt. "I hope it's what you had in mind."

"They're all full?" asked Stronghart, striding to the containers.

The soldier looked to his younger companion. "We don't know, but one's as heavy as the next. We were just about to open them."

"Very well." The major rapped his knuckles on the first lid he encountered. "Let's have a look!"

"You there!" The soldier hailed a Cauldron worker with tools in hand. "Come here!" He reached out to relieve the man of his implements, then pried the lid closest to Stronghart.

The major dug his hand into the barrel. Its powdery contents sifted through his fingers.

"That's lyla, all right!" He grimaced, wiping his hand on his trouser legs as he retreated. "Little wonder the prattlers dislike it!"

"Ground nearly to dust," said Carson, shielding his nose. "Right, then. Lids off, and let's get to it! I want a man at every barrel, Major. Have the rest form a line, starting here. Each soldier and his horse is to walk this gauntlet slowly. I want them all covered in the stuff by the time they're through it. A handful down their shirts; another down their trousers. In their horses' manes; wherever it will stick!"

Stronghart nodded. "You heard the man!"

"And gentlemen," added the marshal, "when next I see the king, he's to be so covered in this shite that I don't recognize him!"

Stronghart resumed barking orders. Two dozen soldiers exiting The Cauldron were assigned to the lyla barrels, while the rest gathered horses and formed a single line. The sound of crackling tinder heralded the lighting of the pyres.

Marshal Carson headed for The Cauldron's porch, where its owner stood watching the proceedings in apparent disbelief.

Carson bounded up the steps. "How many torches have you?"

"Four floors; a dozen torches each," the proprietor mumbled.

"And spares?"

"There may be some on the fourth level."

Carson stuck a finger in the man's face. "The king shows you his mercy. You have two suns to get your people out." He pointed to the soldiers who had prepped the lyla barrels, now stationed at the end of the perfumed gauntlet. "Those two will stay behind, and with the rising of the second sun, they'll burn this place to the ground." The owner of The Cauldron did not react. "If any harm comes to them while we're away, I'll see you hang for it!" The owner continued staring off into the night. Carson slapped him lightly on the cheek. "Listen carefully! Don't imagine you can stop it. If this place stands when we return, I'll set it on fire myself. Use your time wisely!"

A faint glow to the southwest served as both a helpful beacon and a source of worry.

Why has the GOT not extinguished those flames to complicate our journey? Surely they can see our torches just as easily as we theirs. What does it matter? Concentrate! All will be for naught if the king is not kept safe upon reaching The Guild's lair! This king who has lost all reason, who no longer values his own welfare! A document signed and witnessed by the clerk and palace chaplain names you his successor should he die in battle. Pure madness! I should have locked him in his chambers, heavily guarded. He might have had my head, but even so, would the realm not be better off? It's not too late for that; he still can be returned. But at what cost? The man will not go quietly. He is still king, beloved and respected. His willingness to die has galvanized five hundred soldiers, each prepared to do the same for him. Removing him will only stir concern amongst the men—something this campaign can ill afford. Think! You don't have long to sort things!

"Halt!" Major Stronghart's harsh command, echoed by a dozen voices down the line, soon brought the entire army to a standstill. Carson peered into the night, searching for the cause.

There! A faint form took shape on the crest of a dune to the northwest, nearly indistinguishable against the black of the Mersal Sea.

Stronghart stood in his stirrups, hands on his pommel, leaning forward. The form began to move, dipping slowly until it disappeared behind the dune in front of them.

"It's coming this way," Stronghart said. "Sergeant Lagos! Take three men. Find out who or what that is."

"Yes, sir!" It did not take long for the quartet to mobilize and make its way to the top of the next dune.

What can they now see that we cannot? Carson looked over his shoulder. *And how long before the king makes his way forward?*

"They're coming back," Stronghart said.

"Indeed." Carson strained to distinguish one rider from another. "Only now they're five."

The group returned at a trot, slowing just before it reached those waiting.

"Look what we found!" Sergeant Lagos bellowed. The soldier holding a torch extended it toward the fifth rider, illuminating his features.

Rolft Aerns! Carson had not seen the man since he was honored by the king for capturing two of those responsible for the queen and princess' deaths.

Rolft brought his horse's muzzle next to that of the marshal's mount. "Going somewhere special?"

"This is unexpected," said Carson. "I thought you were tracking Sibil Dunn."

"That I am, Marshal."

"Explain, please." Carson urged his horse forward, signaling five hundred to gather momentum once again.

"There's no clear trail," Rolft said, falling in between the marshal and the major. "I've not laid eyes on her. But I've reason to believe she's at the GOT."

"At the GOT?" repeated the marshal. *Absurd!* "To what end?"

"Did she not ask to join your army so that she could avenge her mother's death? I should think that was answer enough."

"You think she's waging war on the GOT?"

"I do."

"All by herself!"

"No, Marshal. I'm told she travels with another. An old man."

"An old man! She has company, at least. Seriously, what is she planning, do you think?"

"I'm simply trying to find the lass, Marshal. I'm not inside her head."

"Fair enough. What's going on inside yours? You're headed there yourself, are you?"

"It crossed my mind."

"I'm curious, of course. What would you do once there?"

"Ask to be let in. Find Sibil. Bring her home."

Carson chuckled. "A simple plan! And much easier now to carry out, with an army by your side."

"I was just thinking how much harder it might be."

"How's that?"

"The Guild prepares for war, but its trade is really thievery. I doubt the GOT would be threatened by a poor farmer, all alone, looking for his daughter. I think my odds of being let in were quite good. As things stand now..."

Carson could not fault the guardsman's logic. "What about your odds of making it back out? With Miss Dunn, both of you alive?"

"Yes, well, that's another matter, isn't it?" said Rolft. "I hadn't gotten that far."

Sibil Dunn

Dusk was falling as Sibil collapsed onto her blanket. She watched Gradi, in obvious pain, struggle to lower himself onto his. It had been a long training session, and she had not always been able to keep him in sight.

"Are you hurt?" she asked.

"No. I'm old, and each and every one of my bones reminds me this is a young man's game." Gradi used both hands to massage one knee and then the other.

The envelope containing Tristan's note still pressed against Sibil's skin. She could feel it move as she adjusted her position, even though its crisp edges had been softened by her warmth and sweat.

Will the ink run?

Quickly, she pulled at the hem of her blouse, snaking her hand beneath it to secure the envelope. She plucked the letter from it, relieved to find Tristan's note still legible within its folds. If the God of Fortune did exist, he was watching over her.

Not until the small card given to her by the Sister of Systalene fell from the envelope did Gradi express an interest. "Where'd you get that?"

Sibil picked the card up and blew a bit of dirt from its surface. "The Sisters of Systalene. Do you know of them? It's just a little heart. Like a wax seal."

"Of course. The Sisters still frequent the Euphoria Grove, and I live fairly close to it, so I see them now and then. They're an odd lot, to be sure. I told you when we first met, I spent my youth working in that place. As did all my friends. It's really quite the operation. You know, they use every part of that plant—seeds, leaves, bark; and once processed, it takes on even more forms. Powder, liquid, smoke rolls, ointment, snuff, you name it. And just like baelonite, its use is under strict control in both realms. Most of it goes to physicians, some to the apothecaries. Just how it gets into the Sisters' hands is unknown, but it does, that's for certain. A few of them were always hanging around outside the grove. Once or twice I saw one being ushered through it." He motioned to the card.

"What you're holding, that little heart? It's not a wax seal, Sibil. It's hardened sap from the Euphoria tree. I should know, I was a tapper when I worked the grove; that's all I did. Tap the sap from trees and boil it down 'til it was mostly crystals. Still warm, it could be molded into any shape. Once hardened, it looks just like that. I'd recognize it anywhere. That's their calling card. Why was it given to you?"

Sibil's mind raced too fast to answer.

"They swear by it, of course," Gradi continued. "Worship the stuff. Particularly, its healing powers. But I've seen it used for more than that—outside official channels, of course—and I can tell you firsthand that everyone's affected differently. Some folks seem to drink it in with no adverse effect. I had a friend like that. He could drink the sap, not boiled or concentrated, mind you, so it wasn't very strong, but even so, he could drink a full pint and you'd not know the difference. Others, just one sip, or one puff from a smoke roll, and they're in some other world, crying like a baby or screaming at their loved ones. Others have been known to go completely mad... maybe for one sun, or maybe 'til they die."

"Just because it knows you, doesn't mean it likes you."

Sibil tilted the card a tiny bit, just enough to let the sun's dying rays bounce off the heart's rounded mounds.

"Small doses when you dare!"

She touched the tip of her tongue to it. Lightly. Briefly. Then held it out in front of her.

"Be careful," said Gradi.

Sibil smiled at him. She dropped the card back into the envelope with Tristan's letter, then slipped both beneath her blouse. She felt nothing. She closed her mouth and ran her tongue against the backs of her teeth. A slight tingling tickled the tip of her tongue, then traveled down its length, turning it warm and thick. *Slightly sweet!*

She closed her eyes and let her head roll back.

With a sudden surge, the sensation spread down her arms, sizzling just beneath her skin. Her muscles twitched, as though they had been sleeping all her life and were just now waking.

"How do you feel?" Gradi asked from some distant place.

Alive! And on the edge!

Footsteps!

"So you're The Wisperal, are you?" *A stranger's voice!*

"What do you want?" *Gradi!*

"We want to speak with the girl... The Wisperal!"

Sibil's eyes snapped open. Two men stood in front of her, remarkably similar in appearance. Both had dark, wavy hair to their neckline, blunt noses, and square jaws. A bottle hung loosely by its neck from one of their hands.

"Go away," Gradi said. "She's not to be bothered. Not now."

"Shut up, old man! You're not who—"

It was effortless, yet somehow, she was on her feet, the man's bottle in her grasp.

The intruder's eyes widened, then narrowed, shifting from the stolen bottle to her face. "Word has it you're from Castle Aranox," he said. "What business have you here?"

"My business is none of yours." Sibil turned the bottle upside down, allowing its contents to splatter on the ground.

The man's eyes narrowed further. "So says you. Our brother was Shaun Penniluk. You may have known him as the Prince of Quills. He died in your king's care. Explain yourself. Anyone loyal to King Axil does not belong here."

His hand moved to the hilt of his sheathed knife, drawing Sibil's attention to a thin bundle of gold strands also hanging from his belt. His eyes followed her line of sight. "That's what's left of the last to cross the brothers Penniluk," he said. "A young knight of Aranox, no less."

As quickly as she imagined it, the sheaf of hair found its way into her hands, the man's own fingers grasping at the place where it had hung from his belt.

He grimaced as she brought it to her nose and inhaled deeply. *Tristan!*

"Witch!" The man pulled on the handle of his knife.

The bottle shattered against his lower jaw and sent him reeling.

His brother lurched at her, his blade half withdrawn. Sibil raised his free arm and buried the jagged bottleneck in his armpit. Her dagger slashed his throat, and he staggered backward before dropping to the ground.

Sarul came running across Back Court, followed by several soldiers in uniform. "I warned you about this!"

It was only Gradi's voice that held her back. "It's not her fault! They came at us!"

Sarul stayed the soldiers with a raised hand.

Sibil sheathed her knife, her eyes returning the warrior's glare.

"It's true!" A gruff insider resting next to Gradi spoke up. "The girl and the old man sleep here. This is their spot... beside us. The others started it. That one there tried to pull his knife on her."

"It still rests inside its sheath," Sarul said skeptically. Sibil held the warrior's gaze as she tucked the sheaf of yellow hair inside her blouse.

"Because she was that quick!" said the gruff man. "I don't even know what happened to the other. She moved too fast to see. They both went down at once, or so it seemed."

One of the soldiers kneeled to inspect the fallen. "This one's dead."

"And the other?" asked Sarul.

"Still breathing," said the soldier.

"Take him to Fore Court. He fights outside now. The other's for the prattlers."

Sarul grabbed hold of Sibil's elbow and began to stride away, pulling her behind him. She did not resist.

"Where are you taking her?" *Gradi's voice!*

"We want to be beside her when the fighting starts!" yelled the gruff insider.

Sarul kept hold of her, and she allowed herself to be led roughly out of Back Court. *Take me where you will. I could kill you in the time it takes to imagine such a thing, and with any of three knives, which is to say, no time at all! You no longer pose a threat to me, Sarul!*

Emerging into Center Court, he hauled her down an unfamiliar passageway between GOT buildings. Stopping abruptly, he steered her into a dark opening in the passageway. She stumbled slightly as her feet encountered stone steps.

"Climb!" said Sarul, pushing her from behind.

Despite the dark confines of the enclosed stairwell, Sibil quickly adjusted her stride to match the rise and depth of the stairway's treads. It did not take long to reach a landing spacious enough for her to await further direction. *Am I to enter the door in front of me, or continue up the stairs?*

Sarul shoved her higher. "Keep going!"

She climbed quickly to a second landing. *Another door. More stairs. Third floor?* She vowed to count the steps to the next landing, should Sarul direct her to continue.

"Again!" From somewhere above, a source of light cast shadows against the stairwell walls, allowing Sibil to scamper up another twenty steps. *Fourth floor?* A wall torch illuminated the landing at the top of the next flight.

"Once more!"

Sibil bounded up another flight to be greeted by stone walls and a door. *No more stairs!* Sarul bypassed her as he crossed the landing. "Follow me!" Sibil's hand found the hilt of her push knife as he unlatched the door, pulled it open, and stepped into the night air. She crossed the threshold onto one of the exterior breezeways connecting the GOT's buildings. *The highest of them all, and not so much a breezeway as a wide interior battlement sitting atop the buildings' roofs!* All six of the compound's towers pierced the darkening sky. The tallest and thickest of them, home to the magister, held her gaze.

"Come!" Sarul secured her arm again and, walking briskly, pulled her to a corner of the battlements. "Below is Fore Court!" Despite the fading light, Sibil could make out the central fountain, the GOT's huge gates, and a mass of insiders resting on the ground between. Above it all, a faint line distinguished the sands of the Lawless Lands from a starlit sky. To her right, a narrow catwalk led from the interior battlement to its longer and broader twin tracing the exterior walls of the compound. To her left was a clear path to the base of Takers Tower.

"This way!" Sarul headed back the way they had come, passing the door through which they'd come and continuing down the breezeway's length until they reached the base of one of the shorter towers. "Look, can you see? That's Center Court below. Were we to continue, you'd be looking down on Back Court." He removed one of the battlement's torches from its base and opened a door on the tower's side. "Come!"

He led the way this time, the tower steps steep and narrow, the walls on either side forcing him to turn his broad shoulders as he climbed. A constant breeze with occasional gusts descended from above, prompting Sibil to keep her head down and concentrate on her footing. One step at a time, higher and higher they went, until at last there were no more stairs and she joined Sarul on a landing just below the tower's cap. The wind, rushing in through large opposing catchers, blew fiercely across the floor before swooping down the tower's core. A thin metal railing circled the open shaft, which presumably dropped to the desert floor—perhaps even to the tunnels below that. Sibil kept one hand on the railing as she trailed Sarul around the circular landing. Persistent winds threatened to extinguish the warrior's torch. "It's a long way down," he said, "but the view is worth it." He grabbed her blouse, pulled her roughly from the railing, and pushed her to the edge of a windcatcher. Sibil placed one hand on its sill to prevent herself from falling through. Her other hand found the hilt of her push knife.

"Look!" said Sarul, extending his free arm past her head. "Out there!"

It was indeed a long way down. The GOT compound lay below, a broad view of the surrounding Lawless Lands obstructed only by other towers and the dark. The sun had disappeared completely, and all signs of color with it. Everything appeared as tones of gray, including that area identified by Sarul. Near the edge of Reception Canyon, amorphous shapes gave rise to excited voices, and Sibil realized with a chill why he had brought her to the tower.

The longer she stared, the easier it became to make out the shapes of separate poles protruding from the ground. This was not some solitary sacrifice; there were too many forms for that.

"Listen!" Sarul said as the echoes turned to strident cries for help interspersed with screaming, all largely suffocated by the winds that carried them. "And there!" The warrior grunted with satisfaction, his arm swinging slightly to the east. "Along the canyon's edge!"

Sibil caught her breath. A stream of black beads, shimmering beneath the moon, flowed toward the GOT, swelling and undulating as it neared. The cries of men grew louder and more constant, but the clattering of the oncoming prattlers soon drowned them out. The black stream swept over the captive men and pooled on top of them.

A chorus of cheers sounded from the battlements below; several flaming arrows were dispatched from its crenels toward the sea of black, and the clattering horde of creatures slowly receded.

Sarul stuck his face in front of Sibil's. "The next time you cause me trouble, it will be the cries of your old friend we listen to!"

"If you—" The shrill wail of a warning horn interrupted Sibil. Sarul froze momentarily, then quickly moved to a windcatcher facing north. He swore before turning to thrust his torch into Sibil's hand.

"You know your way back!" Without waiting for an answer, the warrior bounded down the stairwell and into the tower's bowels.

Sibil hefted the torch as she moved to the north-facing catcher. The black of night. A thousand stars she had not noticed with Sarul present. And there... the source of the warrior's curse... barely visible. Little more than a tiny thread of red dots dangling in the dark.

A long ways off, to be sure, but is that Marshal Carson and his army?

The GOT's warning horn sounded again.

Sibil descended the tower stairs slowly. *Returning to Back Court is your safest option. Anything else will be deemed defiance by Sarul, for which Gradi will pay a horrific price. Besides, you're tired, and a night's rest awaits you there. Is that not short-sighted? What will the morning bring if you do not assert yourself? The king's army will be here by then, and mayhem will ensue! You and Gradi will likely die anyway, perhaps at the hands of a king's soldier! You're in the GOT—you did not come here to be safe! Finish what you came for! Now is the time! Kill the magister, and you may crush The Guild's resolve to fight the king!*

She exited the tower, stepping back onto the breezeway. Soldiers scurried up and down its length. Preoccupied perhaps by news of uninvited guests, they gave her little more than sideways glances. She turned the corner where Sarul had pointed out Fore Court and headed straight for Takers Tower, holding her torch aloft—as though she had been charged with a task and knew what she was doing. If stopped and challenged, she would say that she was lost and looking for Sarul. *Mere mention of the warrior's name will carry weight and lend you credibility. Press on!*

She slowed her pace near Takers Tower. A formidable door with multiple locks barred entry to it, but a less imposing iron gate to the west fronted a narrow corridor hugging the tower's exterior. She approached the gate and tried its latch. To her surprise, it lifted freely.

Meaning it leads nowhere of importance. But even so, I've come this far.

Worried that an open flame seen entering the corridor might cause suspicion, she pressed her torch against the tower long enough to deprive it of oxygen, then set it down against the wall.

Fairly confident that no one watched, she pulled the iron gate open and entered the covered passageway. She stepped into a puddle and cursed under her breath as water seeped into her boot. Instinctively, she stepped to one side, found dry ground sloping slightly upward toward the tower wall, and proceeded with one hand against that surface to guide her through the nearly pitch-dark tunnel. Narrow openings in its upper outer walls afforded her glimpses of a starry sky and ushered fresh air into the confines of the passageway.

Do you know what you're doing? Where you're going? No, you don't!

She tried to calm her breathing and bumped into an impediment in the corridor. Her hands felt its surface... *cold metal!* Her fingers ran across round bars and a latch at waist height. *Another iron gate!* Its latch lifted as easily as the first she had encountered.

She withdrew her push knife from its sheath and pulled the gate open. A transparent ceiling and exterior wall allowed the moon to cast an eerie glow upon the contents of what appeared to be a large room filled with... *plants! Am I now inside the tower?*

The unmistakable scent of flowers and moist soil confirmed it was some sort of nursery. She waited a moment, identifying rows of tables and clay pots before stepping inside. She tread softly and carefully, following what seemed to be the widest, least cluttered path around the tables, brushing aside the tendrils of hanging vines that kissed the top of her head and grazed her cheeks. The moon followed her, hiding here and there behind the foliage of plants rising to a glass-paneled ceiling. *Not what I expected to find in Takers Tower, but a good reminder that someone actually lives here!*

A vague outline amidst the far wall begged two questions. *Is that locked? And if not, who or what might I find behind it?* The closer she neared, the more cautious her movements became. She pressed a palm against the wooden door, then brought one ear to rest against it. *No noises on the other side—reassuring, but hardly a guarantee of safety.* Still listening, she grasped the door's pull ring and drew it back. *Gently... slowly...*

Hinges squeaked, and she stopped pulling to squeeze sideways through the narrow opening she'd created. A shaft of dull light spilled across the room, highlighting several rows of long, narrow tables littered with glass containers. Bottles, jars, jugs; orbs, squares and rectangles—some as small as her hand, others as large as a coffin. A few appeared empty, but most looked to be filled with dirt or liquid, and... she stared at the large, wide-mouthed jar nearest her long enough to realize something was staring back. *A dead animal—an eel, perhaps—immersed in some sort of murky pickling juice.*

She tapped the glass. The liquid stirred, startling her, and the eyes disappeared in a flash. *Noggods! Not dead at all!*

She kept her hands to herself as she continued down the aisle, one eye roving the displays. Some appeared empty, but others were inhabited by creatures difficult to ignore. A long, thick snake with iridescent stripes of green and blue patterning its skin; a pair of furry red spiders the size of her hand.

Beyond the tables, an open archway promised to reveal the source of dim light helping her to see. She navigated her way toward it, intrigued by the exhibit of skeletal parts covering a countertop—a collection of craniums peering back at her through empty eye sockets. She could not name the animals they belonged to; one or two looked almost human. *Grotesque!* She stared at one in particular until she backed into something soft against the far wall. She turned and nearly screamed at a hairy beast towering over her, its claws reaching for her head. *Gods above!* Her heart began to thump, even as she realized the creature was not moving. *Stuffed!*

She leaned against one side of the archway leading to the lighted hall, her heart still pounding. She bit her lip while counting a half dozen candles near head height along the corridor's length. *Dimly lit, but not dark enough to conceal movement. What will you do if someone happens upon you here? Not even "I'm lost" will seem a reasonable excuse in this place. Stop! This is the magister's home, is it not?* Sibil adjusted her grip on the push knife. *This is your excuse!*

Wait a tick! Someone lit those candles, and surely not the magister himself! The so-called noms? Do they reside here, too?

She returned the push knife to its sheath and withdrew the blade gifted her by the Godfrey twins. Stepping through the archway, she laid its blade across the first candle's flame. It died for lack of oxygen, and she moved quickly to the second candle to repeat the act. Past a stairwell—*where might that lead?*—and onto the third, fourth and fifth candles. The sixth and last did not react as she wished. It sputtered beneath her dagger, refusing to go out. One swipe of the blade, however, cut through its wax lip and wick, severing the flame, which died on its way to the floor.

The hallway opened to a high-ceilinged semi-circle, its floor extending a good distance before disappearing behind a railing more substantial and ornate than the one to which Sarul had dragged her. A source of light from somewhere below cast a soft glow against what had to be the back end of Takers Tower.

And it carried voices!

Dagger in hand, she left the darkened corridor and headed for the railing.

No more doors. The curved stone wall surrounding her was uninterrupted save for a set of iron stairs that clung to its left side and disappeared into both floor and ceiling.

With every step, the talking from below grew louder, more distinct. And when the words stopped, a loud monotonous humming ensued. "*Nommm.*"

Sibil sank to her knees, then lay on her belly. She snaked her way to the base of the railing and peered into a pit below. A large candelabra at each end of a long table helped illuminate ten hooded figures—four seated on either side, dressed in robes of white; two standing at the table's end, cloaked in darker cream. *Ten noms—young servants of the magister!*

In front of each rested a gold goblet nearly filled with a shimmering substance that reflected the candelabra's light. *Likely that same dark liquid swimming in the large decanter at the table's center.*

"*Nommm.*" The monotonous humming resumed from beneath the hoods of all, and then as quickly, stopped.

The taller of the two standing raised his hands into the air. "Long live the Takers Guild."

"The life that gives us purpose," said the nom standing next to him.

"The life that gives us purpose!" repeated the eight seated.

"From the many, few are chosen," said the leader of the group.

"We are the chosen few," replied his companion.

"We are the chosen few!" chanted the eight.

"Fortunate are the chosen," said the leader.

"Blessed be the magister for choosing us."

"Blessed be the magister for choosing us!"

"Blessed be this life; we want for naught."

"Blessed be the magister for giving us this life!"

"Blessed be the magister for giving us this life!"

"And in return, what do we give?"

"We give ourselves."

"We give ourselves!" chanted the entire group.

"What do we sacrifice?"

"We sacrifice our all."

"We sacrifice our all!"

"Blessed be the magister!" The leader raised his goblet high.

"Blessed be the magister!" His cream-robed companion did the same.

"Blessed be the magister!" In unison, those seated raised their goblets to their lips. When finished drinking, they turned their vessels upside down, returned them to the table, and laid their hooded heads beside them.

Sibil watched, waiting for the ceremony's next phase to begin. One of the hoods began to tremble. A twitching hand knocked over a goblet. It rolled across the table as more robes began to quiver, then convulse. Sibil grimaced as the meeting's purpose became evident.

The two noms standing remained motionless, hands clasped at their waists. "We join you at sunrise," said the leader.

"At sunrise," said the other. Their cream robes glided toward the tower stairs and descended out of view.

Sibil slithered back from the railing to sit, overwhelmed. A goblet hit the floor below, startling her. All went quiet. *What kind of twisted ritual was that? These are young souls, one and all!* Her hand tightened around her dagger's handle. *Where is the old man? Where is the one who most deserves to die?*

She eyed the stairs but discarded the notion of ascending them, given their steep pitch and the magister's age. *His primary living space has to be concentrated on one floor. If not this one, somewhere below as opposed to above. Where is your bedroom, Magister?*

Sibil froze, certain she had heard some sort of clanking. She waited, listening carefully.

There it is again! Metal on metal! From the greenhouse?

She retraced her steps to listen at the entrance to the darkened corridor. *Again the clanking! Louder this time. And definitely from the nursery!*

Sibil imagined someone entering that space from the battlements, crossing its interior, making their way past the collection of creatures, then into the hallway off which she hid. When no one appeared or made another sound, she reimagined the same scenario to be certain she had given enough time for any intruders to reach her.

Nothing.

She stepped into the corridor.

All quiet. No movement.

She peered into the nursery and waited with bated breath.

Nothing.

The moon shone through the glass-paneled ceiling and exterior wall, outlining foliage and flowers.

Sibil sheathed her dagger, withdrew the push knife, and made her way between the potting tables. The absence of intruders reassured her, but an inability to determine the source of clanking was disconcerting. *I'm sure I did not imagine that!* She reached the iron gate leading to the tower's exterior passageway.

Wait a bit! I didn't close that gate, did I? Perhaps it swung shut on its own?

Sibil pushed the gate, but it resisted.

What in Baelon!

She reached for the latch, only to encounter a padlock the size of her fist. The origin of the clanking became obvious as she pulled at the metal fastener in disbelief.

Gods above! This can't be happening! Please tell me I'm not trapped in Takers Tower!

Sibil returned to the spot from which she had spied on the noms. *If I can locate the pair who presided over the ritual, they might lead me to an exit. Or, better yet, to the magister!*

She descended the stairs, hugging the tower's interior wall, and found herself very close to the eight bodies slumped over a table.

Approaching cautiously, she used two trembling fingers to pull back the hood of the nom seated closest to her. Waves of chestnut hair fell across his forehead and closed eyelids. His skin was shiny, taut, and smooth. He had rosy cheeks and long eyelashes. He could not have been more than twelve. A thick white foam clung to his lips and spotted the table beneath them.

Just a boy! What might his life have been like had he been taken in by Father Syrus? How could the God of Children have abandoned him?

Sibil entered the nearby stairwell, certain she was one level below the battlements. *How many more before I reach ground level?* She tried to remember, but could not. *Regardless, Takers Tower rises just west of Center Court, so if I descend to the ground, that's where I should find myself, yeah? One flight at a time!*

Absent any light, she descended the stairs slowly. Flames flickered wildly outside an archway on the next level, but offered no clues as to what lay beyond that opening. *No door? Surely the magister lives on a floor where he can bar all others. Besides, it's too dark and quiet in there.* She considered taking the archway's torch. *No! Too easy to be seen by those you seek.*

The next two landings presented unlocked doors, but the dim view provided by a quick look behind each was less enticing than the sounds that had started floating up the stairwell. She was halfway down another flight of stairs when they turned to voices, suppressed by a soft breeze flowing in the opposite direction. By the time she reached the landing, she could hear them clearly. Two or three separate speakers, not far below. It was an agitated discussion, and she listened as she tried the door beside her. *Locked!*

"I've told you," a male voice said. "He's not to be disturbed. Not under any circumstance. He was quite clear about that."

"We have our orders," said a deeper voice. "Direct from Ruler Four."

"So what? Ours come from the magister himself!" *The noms!*

"The king's army will be here before the night is through!" the deeper voice said.

Ah, the red dots were the marshal and his army, after all!

"The magister is aware."

"Ruler Four wants him protected! Let us in so that we may do our job!"

In from where? Center Court!

"The magister wishes to be left alone. And so he shall be!" *The noms again!*

"Must we force our way inside?"

"We will not stop you, but be advised: The magister will have your head if you disturb him!"

"How old are you?!" said the voice from outside.

"Old enough to know one does not cross the magister. And you?"

No response.

Muffled grumbling.

The sound of departing footsteps.

"What if they return?" a young voice asked from below.

"They're not that foolish. But if they do, this door will still be locked and we will not be here. If they choose to force their way inside, the magister will deal with them himself." *So he is here!* "Come, we've work to do… and a pledge to keep."

Fearing the noms might come her way, Sibil prepared to scamper back up the tower stairs, but their voices quickly faded with their footsteps.

She descended to the next landing. Two flaming torches framed a wooden door in the tower's exterior wall. Beside one hung a large ring bearing several keys. Sibil eyed the door's covered peephole. She brought her face to it, slid the aperture open, and peered outside. A small vestibule partially obscured her view, but it could not hide the chaos engulfing Center Court. Soldiers hustled back and forth across her narrow line of sight, lugging weapons and shouting amongst themselves.

She shut the aperture, her eyes wandering to the key ring.

Might one of those unlock the gate between the greenhouse and the battlements above? Surely one of them unlocks this door to Center Court. But I'm not leaving just yet, am I? The magister is here somewhere! Yes, but what about Gradi? And how long before Marshal Carson and his army arrive? What then?

Sibil picked her way between those resting on the grounds of Back Court.

"Gradi!" she whispered. "Wake up!"

Gradi stirred, rolling over before her hand reached his shoulder. "Gods above, Sibil! No one's sleeping here! Where have you been? Did Sarul hurt you?"

"No. I'm fine, but we—"

"Have you heard? The king's army's on its way!"

"Yes, but—"

"This was a mistake! We never should have come here!" Gradi clutched at the small pouch hanging from his neck. "What good is this if I cannot give it to my wife?"

"You will."

"What have I done? What will become of my daughters?"

"Hey, Wisperal!" the man lying nearest Gradi whispered hoarsely through the dark. It was the gruff man who had defended her actions in front of Sarul. "What's happening out there? We thought Sarul had fed you to the prattlers! When will we move to Fore Court?"

"I don't know any more than you," Sibil said. "But if I don't do as Sarul asks, he's going to kill me!"

"What must you do?" asked the man.

"He wants to see Gradi."

"Me!" Gradi rose to his feet. "Whatever for?"

"He wouldn't say. Only that I was to bring you to him."

"Gods above!"

"With your sword," she added. "Quickly!"

Gradi stooped to retrieve his rusty blade.

Sibil grabbed him by the arm.

"You'll be back, yeah?" the gruff man asked. "We want to fight beside you!"

Sibil dragged Gradi behind her as they entered Center Court. "If we're stopped," she said, her breathing ragged, "don't say a word. Let me do the talking." Gradi remained wide-eyed as they weaved their way across the grounds teeming with agitated soldiers. It was not until they entered the vestibule at the base of Takers Tower that he spoke.

"What is this place? Where did you get that—"

"*Shhh!*" Sibil fumbled with the key before unlocking the vestibule door. Before it could swing fully open, she pushed Gradi through its framework.

"Is this not Takers Tower?" he asked.

Sibil held a finger to her lips as she shut and locked the door. "Be quiet," she whispered. "We're not alone!"

"Where's Sarul?"

Sibil freed one of the torches burning by the door. "I've no idea, but he'll kill us if he finds we've left Back Court."

"I thought you said he wanted to see me! Have you lost your mind?"

Sibil held the torch in front of Gradi's face. "The king's men are on their way. Would you rather die by their hands? Perhaps kill one or two of them before you do?"

"I don't understand. What are we doing here, then? Hiding? I don't think that's—"

"Not hiding! We're going to kill the magister!"

Gradi's eyes nearly popped from his head.

"You and me, together," she said. "It's he who's hiding—somewhere in this tower, I'm sure of it. We're going to find and kill him!" She pointed up the tower's stairs. "We'll start here and work our way up, one level at a time, until we find him. And when the king arrives, we're going to join his forces and help defeat The Guild."

Gradi continued to hold her gaze. "This is the errand you've been on from the start?"

"Yes!" Sibil imagined Lewen watching from Baelon above. "And when we've seen it through, you'll take that pouch hanging from your neck to your wife and daughters, do you hear?" She headed up the stairs, stopping suddenly to spin and hold the torch aloft. She peered past Gradi's head. "Grab that key ring, will you?"

The first floor provided unfettered access to its spaces: A huge library rivaling that of Castle Aranox; a large room full of easels and unfinished artwork; a thickly carpeted music room with a variety of instruments, including a piano and a harp; several smaller spaces storing more books and artists' supplies. Exploring each turned out to be a waste of time.

Fear not! What was it the noms said? "He's not to be disturbed. He wishes to be left alone!"

Sibil's hopes climbed with her to the tower stairwell's next level. *What better place to be alone than behind a locked door such as this?*

"You're prepared to be at this all night, are you?" Gradi asked.

"*Shhh!*" Sibil tried one key and then another while Gradi held the torch. The next to last slid into the door's lock and twisted easily. *Click!* Gradi's bushy eyebrows jumped. He traded the torch for the keys, stuffing their ring down his trousers.

Sibil swung the heavy door and slipped inside, dagger in one hand, torch in the other. Sputtering flames licked at the dark like the tongues of so many snakes. She swept the space surrounding her feet, letting the light linger on a thick shaft of wood propped against the wall near the door. Gradi was quick to set his sword down and lay the wooden bar across iron brackets to either side. *No one else can enter now!*

Sibil raised the torch as high as she could. This space was different from those already explored. It clearly wasn't a neglected or abandoned room; it was lived in, and she steeled herself for whatever might jump from the darkness. The blood vessels in her neck began to throb in rhythm with her heart.

Her nostrils flared as she waited for Gradi to retrieve his sword.

What is that stench? Not sharp or suffocating, but decidedly unpleasant and hanging in the air.

She swung the torch from side to side, and stationary objects appeared to parade across the room. There were several chairs upholstered in plush velvet, an ornate candelabra, a large-wheeled chair, a small dining table with three place settings and the remnants of some dried fruit, a bottle of wine, and a half-eaten loaf of bread.

Another door!

Gradi hefted his sword and nodded. Sibil lifted the latch and eased the barrier open.

That same stench! Only stronger here. Putrid—almost overpowering!

A pair of well-worn slippers rested beside the largest bed she had ever seen. Empty. Its covers were turned down in haphazard fashion. More canes. Two nightstands. A tall dresser, one of its doors open to reveal a collection of nightshirts and robes.

There was a long, low chest against the wall. *Large enough to hide in!* Sibil pointed to it, poised her dagger above it, and Gradi raised its lid. A rag doll, a stuffed bear, a small wooden horse, and sundry other toys stared back at them. *Strange!*

And no magister!

Gradi trailed behind her, the tip of his sword clanking against the stone riser of each step he climbed. Sibil stopped, fairly certain the next landing would lead to the poisoned noms. "Can you pick that up?" she whispered.

Gradi leaned on the rusty weapon as he tried to catch his breath. "I can, but then don't expect too much of me when the time comes to really use it." The old man's chest rose and fell rapidly.

"We can rest ahead," she said. "I've been there already."

"What's up there, then?"

"A greenhouse, a collection of animals... and eight dead noms."

"What! You killed them?" Gradi's breaths came even faster.

"Of course not! They killed themselves."

"Oh, well, that's better, isn't it!" Gradi collapsed on the stairs. "What kind of madness is this? And what use is there in going where you've already been? We should return to Back Court before Sarul discovers we are gone."

"I've been to the next level, but not beyond. Just a bit further, Gradi, please!"

There was no reason to linger with the poisoned noms, or to subject Gradi to that ghastly scene. Sibil passed it hurriedly, hugging the tower wall as she climbed to the semi-circle from which she had witnessed the deathly ritual.

"Madness!" Gradi gasped, peering over the landing railing to the table below.

"Come on. I've already checked this level." Sibil tapped his shoulder and returned to climbing stairs. Higher and higher they went, slowly circling the tapering tower, but there were no more archways. No more doors. Sibil's hopes of finding the magister began to fade.

This can't be right. However would he climb these stairs?

She was the first to reach the tower's last stone step. It spread into a landing barely large enough to accommodate several bodies. A metal staircase sprouted from its rear, a tight spiral leading quickly to a platform of grated metal through which she could see the tower's cap.

"This is the last of it," she said, pointing up the metal staircase as Gradi joined her. "There's nothing left above us but windcatchers."

Gradi leaned on his sword, breathing heavily. "Where is your magister, then? Don't tell me they've hidden him in the dungeon." He motioned to a small wooden door to their left. "And don't tell me he's in there."

Locked from the outside by a sturdy wooden bar, it was unlike any other they had come across.

Sibil reached to lift the bar from its brackets, but Gradi intercepted her.

"Wait!" He ran a hand along the bar. "This is not here to keep us out. You know that, right? It's meant to prevent whatever's in there from escaping."

"He's hiding somewhere," said Sibil, "and we've looked everywhere else."

"What if it's the home of some sort of monster?" Gradi asked.

Sibil eyed the door. "What would the magister be doing with a monster?"

"Your king is said to keep two cragens!"

Sibil stared at him. *That's true!*

"And you think the magister has more sense than that?" Cocking his head toward the door, Gradi lifted his eyebrows and stepped back. "Be my guest."

Sibil hesitated. "We do need to know what's in there, Gradi. And we're running out of time. It's going to be light soon."

"Then one of us should open it whilst the other stands ready to slay whatever comes out."

With one hand still on the bar, Gradi leaned his sword against the wall.

"It can't be a very big room," Sibil said, glancing at the tapering tower walls above her, "and I don't know that we need this anymore." She ignited a sconce on either side of the door before extinguishing her torch.

"Did you want another taste of Euphoria first?" Gradi asked. Sibil scoffed. "I'm serious! Do you even know what you did back there?"

Sibil pulled the larger of her black-handled knives and stood poised, with two blades raised.

Gradi sighed. He freed the wooden bar from its brackets and leaned it quietly against the stone wall. Taking hold of the door pull, he swung it outward as quickly as he could.

Sibil gripped her blades more tightly, but nothing emerged.

It was black inside, and quiet.

Gradi retrieved his sword, then removed one of the sconces from the wall. He held it in front of him and took a tentative step into the room.

Sibil followed. A soft whimper from somewhere close froze them both.

What was that? Animal? Child?

"Please... no more." A young voice joined the whimpering.

Gradi raised the sconce. A portion of the tower flickered into view. A bulky mass quivered against the gray stone wall. The whimpering turned to sobbing.

"Show yourself," Gradi said, taking another step forward.

"Please. Leave us be." *A young girl!* "Tell the magister we're sick."

"We don't serve the magister," Sibil said. "Who are you? What are you doing here?"

She nudged Gradi further forward, shuffling her feet beside him, stopping when the sconce revealed the vague silhouette of several figures. Gradi raised the sconce to show them huddled together against the far wall, shivering beneath a blanket. Three little boys, perhaps six or seven almons old, sheltered beneath the arms of a young girl, all of eleven or twelve.

"We do what the magister demands," the girl said.

"He makes you work?" Gradi asked.

"No. We're made to comfort him. In his bedroom."

That explains the toys!

"I'm hungry, and I want to go home," one of the little boys cried.

"Where is that?" Gradi asked.

"He doesn't really have a home," the girl said. "We live on the streets of Waterford."

"Are you hurt? Can you walk?" Gradi asked.

"Yes! Can you help us?"

Sibil could scarcely contain her rage. *Go on! You know what you must do!*

"Gradi, look at their feet, will you? Make sure they're able."

"What?" Gradi fumbled with the sconce, laid his sword down, and kneeled beside the children.

Sibil backed away, slipped out of the room, shut the door, and slid the wooden bar lock into place.

"Sibil!" Gradi pounded on the door.

Sibil put her lips to the crack of its frame. "Please, Gradi, stop! You'll only draw the wrong attention!"

"What are you doing?" a calmer Gradi asked. "Let me out!"

"You're needed here. Protect them as you would your own children."

"Sibil!"

"I'll be back! I promise!"

THE WEB OF A SPIDER

"Knowing one's limitations is of little use without the discipline to stay within them." From The Guild's Basic Rules of Taking

Overseer Reynard Rascall

Reynard made his way to where Ruler Two sat, trying not to slosh ale on those he passed. Seeing no way to pour from the brimming tankard without spilling, he chose to fill Two's mug while standing. A healthy stream found its way onto the table before heading for Two's lap.

"Damn you!" Two lurched to avoid the liquid, then used his hand to sweep what had puddled on the table to the floor.

"Apologies," said Reynard. "At least we got our money's worth, eh?" He raised the tankard like a prize as he sat opposite Ruler Two. "Don't make a scene. It's just a little ale."

"*Pffft!*" Two looked about impatiently. "Where's our friend?"

"He'll come," Reynard said in a hushed voice. "It was we who told him to wait one sun and let things settle, mind you. What's your rush? It's not even a quarter moon since we left the GOT, and already our task is half done."

"You're certain of that, are you?"

"It's all that's being talked about. 'Squashed' is the most popular description. Apparently, he's going home in pieces. Can you imagine?" Reynard shivered.

"I'd rather be elsewhere, is all. This place is lacking in every respect!"

Reynard licked his lips, the taste of Two's discomfort enhancing the flavor of his drink. Chalmsworth was actually the perfect spot to be. Near enough to Peril Pass for them to have been among the first to receive news of an event of consequence there; close enough to Fostead and King Axil for them to plan their second strike; far enough from anywhere they might be recognized. An easy place to blend in with the locals—far less angry and confused than Fostead's south end. On a bad day, one might have a coin purse lifted there, but it wouldn't be at knife point. It had been a quiet little town until the sun before. News of King Tygre's death had shaken it, and the trembling had yet to stop.

"Ah, there he is now!" Reynard raised his hand to draw the attention of the last to enter The Drinking Den. The man had tidied up well; no forest leaves or needles clinging to his boots, no shavings falling from his garments, no rope or ax hanging from his belt. And, as directed, he had come alone.

The woodsman towered over their table. "It's done," he said, as though he had just dug a hole or cut a cord of wood.

"You'll sit and have a drink with us, will you?" asked Reynard.

"I'll not. I'm needed back where I belong, so I'll be on my way as soon as we're settled."

"So be it." Reynard looked expectantly to Ruler Two. "Pay the man."

Ruler Two leaned closer to Reynard. "How do we know that he's going to give the others what they—"

Reynard caught hold of Two's wrist. "Pay the man!" he whispered. "And be quick about it. He has more important things to do!"

Two wrenched his arm away and pulled a leather pouch from his coat pocket. His eyes held Reynard's captive as he placed it on the table.

"Give me the others," said Reynard.

"What?"

"The others... or I promise you, I'll come across this table and take them myself."

Ruler Two stared venomously at Reynard before slowly retrieving two more pouches. He set them next to the first.

Reynard sat back and smiled at the woodsman. "They're yours. The first is as promised, to be shared with your companions. The second is for your continued silence. The last is to overlook my friend's behavior. There's not enough to make amends for that, I know, but it's all I have to offer. You have my thanks, and my apologies."

The woodsman nodded curtly, picked up the pouches, and left.

Ruler Two was steaming.

"You're welcome," Reynard said.

"And you're insufferable!" spat Two.

"Is that right? You just questioned the integrity of a man who has little else to call his own. He's used to throwing logs around much thicker than your neck, and he's just proven he doesn't mind killing. What's wrong with you?"

"He didn't say a word. He wasn't going to—"

"It's the quiet ones you need to treat with caution," said Reynard. "There's no telling what they're thinking."

Two continued to fume. "You didn't need to give him thrice what he expected!"

"Didn't I? I would have given him four times if you had brought it with you. A pittance, given what he did for it. And how we'll benefit. I hope the magister's watching; he'll know a bargain when he sees one."

Reynard lost all interest in Ruler Two, distracted by a tall woman moving behind him. Her fur vest and cropped leggings, coupled with the way she glided through the room, suggested she might be at least part feline. A good amount of her exposed dark skin glistened with a sheen of sweat. She clearly did not belong in Chalmsworth, but none of the men staring looked inclined to tell her that.

He watched with growing interest as she approached his table, her hands descending to knead Two's shoulders from behind. Reynard could not be sure whether it was her touch that startled the ruler, or that of the serpent's head nibbling on his neck from her bracelet.

Two nearly jumped out of his chair. The woman's hands held him down.

"Charise! What are you doing here?"

Hah! He thought it was the woodsman come back to throttle him! Reynard beamed.

"Ayla, Two." The woman's kneading became a rhythmic, passionate clawing. "Missed me, did you?"

Two shrugged her off, as though she were diseased. "Hardly! I can think of few things less welcome at the moment!"

The woman called Charise frowned. "How disappointing. And here I've been searching for you since the new moon... wasting away, longing to see you again."

"Wasting your time, then. There was naught but business between us, and even that was unpleasant."

"Really? Are you certain? I should have thought our bond was stronger now than ever... now that King Tygre is dead." She looked knowingly from Two to Reynard, capturing the overseer's attention in more ways than one. "But I suppose neither of you know anything about that."

Reynard cleared his voice loudly, turning his palms up on the table.

Two sighed heavily. "This is Charise. Charise, Reynard."

"Ayla, Reynard." The woman's thick brows wriggled like black caterpillars above her big brown eyes.

"Ayla, Charise."

"And just what is it that you do?" asked Charise.

Two overstepped his bounds by answering for Reynard. "He works for The Guild, the same as me."

Reynard shot him a look, but Two did not acknowledge it.

"In what capacity?" asked Charise.

"Not your concern," said Two.

"Overseer," said Reynard, as annoyed with Two as he was intrigued by Charise. "And what is it that you do?"

"She's an assassin," whispered Two angrily. "Though we've seen little evidence of that!"

"Hurtful," said Charise, gliding into a chair beside Two, her eyes lingering on Reynard. She reached across the table and parted his bangs with a finger. Her touch tingled. "Love the scar," she said. "Where'd you get it?"

"Also none of your business!" said Two, speaking out of turn again. He turned to Reynard. "Charise works for The League," he whispered. "We paid her handsomely to put King Axil in the ground. So now you know her worth as well."

"Hmmm." Charise steepled her hands together, resting the tips of her index fingers against her lips. "Some of what you say is true. That last bit, though… not only is it unkind, it presumes too much."

"A failing of my friend, for which I apologize," said Reynard.

Two scoffed loudly.

Reynard reclaimed the assassin's attention. "Are you saying you can kill him?"

"Of course."

"Out of the question!" said Two. "She's had three chances already. Failures, one and all!"

"Three?" asked Charise. "How many fingers am I showing? Does that look like three to you?" Two looked away in obvious disgust. Charise spoke directly to Reynard. "I'll tell this story, shall I? And if I err in the details, Two is free to set me straight. The first attempt on King Axil's life was planned by simpletons." Her eyeballs moved independently of her head, casting Two a sideways glance. "They had no idea what they were up against. They sent three men to do the job, all of whom were skewered by soldiers. All this, during the Feast of Lords and Ladies, if you can imagine. And His Majesty, King Axil? Not a scratch!" She paused, allowing Two an opportunity to object.

"That was before we even sought your help," muttered The Guild ruler.

"My point exactly! The first you asked of me was to kill a man and woman." She again directed herself to Reynard. "Simple. The woman first, they said, as she can see into the future." Charise fluttered her fingers in Two's face. "Easier to kill the other once her eyes were made to close, yeah? Only, they told me she was living in a cottage, when in truth, she was a guest of King Axil's… staying in his castle, no less!" She glared directly at a silent Ruler Two. "These were the same simpletons, mind you, who sent three farmers to kill the king in his own house. Idiots! I killed the man—the Prince of Quills—as promised, but instead of saying 'thank you very much,' your friend here asked for proof of death. Not before I killed the prince, mind you, but after the fact! Can you imagine?"

Reynard shook his head sympathetically.

"It was only then that I was asked to kill the king. Oh, and I killed the woman, too. As promised."

"You wounded her," said Two.

"Is she not dead?" asked Charise.

Thoroughly entertained, Reynard watched the pair square off.

"Are you through? Go on," said Two. "Tell him the rest. What about the king?"

"What about him?" asked Charise.

"He still lives!"

"By no fault of mine," the assassin said. "Five called it off."

"He did no such thing!"

"Oh, didn't he? You were with us, were you, beneath the blankets when he whispered in my ear? I didn't notice you, but then, what would there have been to notice?" Her gaze shifted to the ruler's crotch, her disingenuous smile disappearing quickly. "Ruler Five called it off. Perhaps that's why your magister had him killed." This clearly gave Two pause to think, and the assassin gave him a moment to do so before continuing. "Regardless, I've made good on all I was asked to do. The king's seer may have taken the last arrow meant for him, but even she is gone now."

"We don't need or want your help," said Two. "We've already killed one king ourselves."

Reynard leaned forward slightly. "Hold on, friend. Don't be rash. King Axil will not gift himself to us. If what we've heard is true, he hasn't shown himself since last he escaped death's door. King Tygre's demise is going to make him even less inclined. He isn't going to show himself now. Someone will need to slay him in his own house."

"That's going to be you, is it?" Charise chided Ruler Two with a look of supreme doubt. "You might get inside, perhaps even lay eyes on him. But how will you get past his royal guards? They weren't chosen at random, you know. And if by some miracle you do get past them, I'm told a pair of faithful cragens are always by the regal's side. Do you know how many claws they boast between them, each as sharp as any blade, and twice as quick? I should like to be there when they meet your flesh!"

Gods above, I'm in love!

Ruler Two's mouth twitched. He stabbed the tabletop with his finger. "If we're to further deal with your League, we want to speak with whoever you report to—whoever gives you orders, your assignments."

"That isn't how we work," Charise said flatly.

Two rolled his eyes. "Why's that?"

"No one knows his identity. No one's ever put a name to him, nor seen him in the flesh. We'd like to keep it that way." She held Two's gaze, her eyes boring into him. "You understand?"

Two bristled. "I don't give a piss what you call him! I want to meet with him! This is not some common cur we're asking to be killed. It's the fargin' King of Aranox! Make an exception!"

Reynard waited for Charise's reaction. But for the rise and fall of her smooth breasts, the assassin remained motionless, her expression set in stone. Suddenly, it melted, and she laughed as she broke free of it, her eyebrows rising, her lips parting to expose teeth as white as baelonite. If she was not the most beautiful woman he had ever seen, she was certainly the most alluring.

"Suit yourself," she said, standing to leave. "I'll make the arrangements."

"That's it?" asked Two. "How will we know where and when to meet?"

"You can read, yeah? Guidance shall find its way to you. Soon. And when it does, come alone. Your friend will not be welcome. If we so much as smell another's scent on you, The Guild's relationship with The League will have come to a quick end."

She spoke with apparent sincerity to Reynard. "My apologies, Mr. Overseer. I really don't mean to offend you."

Reynard afforded her a slight nod. "None taken."

"Overseer..." The woman's mouth played with the word before letting it roll off her lips. "You control the efforts of Guild gatherers, then, is that right?"

"As best I can," Reynard said humbly.

Charise's smile broadened. "How exciting!" She left her serious countenance at the table as she glided away, laughing to herself. Reynard exchanged a curious glance with Two. "You shall have to tell me more some day," she called back over her shoulder. "Overseer! Absolutely thrilling!"

Ruler Two

Ruler Two fished a note from his pocket for the third time. It held few words, but he felt compelled to set his eyes on them again.

Brew House. Midnight. Two lanterns.

He read them twice more before tucking the note back into his pocket. This was no time for mistakes. He was going to meet The League of Assassins' overlord.

Charise had regained just a pinhead of his respect. She could have disclosed the meeting's time and place in the presence of Reynard, but to her credit, the assassin had made it clear the irksome overseer was not invited. Moreover, she had the good sense to recognize that he was insufferable enough to attend regardless, if only he knew where and when to go. It was, no doubt, why her messenger had waited for Ruler Two to leave The Drinking Den alone before thrusting the note into his hand, then disappearing.

He had spent enough time as a master thief to feel at home in the dark, to know it well enough, in fact, to call it a friend. He checked over his shoulder before turning down an alley. He had not been able to leave Chalmsworth's only inn without drawing the nosy overseer's attention, and he did not put it past the man to try and follow him. *Perhaps The League will dispose of him as well! Now, there's a thought worth further exploration with the overlord! It would need to appear as though it were an accident, of course, even to the keen eyes of Guild watchers—but then, that should be an easy feat for skilled assassins, should it not?*

He had located The Brew House soon after receiving the note, so that he would later know where he was going, and how long it would take to walk there in the dark. It was a large building, set well away from any other. Shaped more like a ship than a house, two tall masts, fore and aft, the former with a crow's nest at its top. A broad apron of cobblestones surrounded it, allowing for the passage of multiple wagons during its hours of operation. Those he had watched come and go with barrels in their beds now sat empty and horseless against the building's side.

He crossed a short bridge spanning a canal, well aware that two figures had fallen into step behind him. He might have been concerned had they tried to hide their presence, but they carried lanterns and seemed content to keep their distance. Nonetheless, he listened for their footsteps as they followed him up the slight incline leading to The Brew House.

Reaching the top of the knoll, he paused. *No beckoning lights. No welcoming voices. Something's off.* He glanced back. A thick carpet of fog floated through the canal below, blanketing its water and threatening to overflow its banks.

The frames of his pursuers, dark against that gray background, suddenly called out to him. "Have you business on board?"

What in Baelon is that supposed to mean?

"What part of the ship would you visit?" called the other. "Captain's quarters? Crow's nest?"

Ship? Ahhh... what a droll welcome. "Below deck," Two said, reciting from the note he had been given as they approached.

"Of course!" The larger of the two held his lantern up to Ruler Two's face, illuminating his own features in the process. Several shards of polished bone pierced his cheeks and forehead. No doubt the soles of his feet bore the mark of an assassin. "Below deck," he said, heading toward The Brew House. "We've been expecting you."

"Follow us," the other said in passing.

When no better course of action sprang to mind, Two did as he was told, stopping only when his escorts did in front of two empty wagons. Nestled between them was an arched door in the side of The Brew House.

"Give me your weapon!" The larger assassin held out his hand.

Two hesitated, hands tucked inside his trouser pockets. *They cannot know what I have hidden. Why not say that I'm unarmed? But is that wise? What will they do if they discover that I've lied?*

His other escort grew impatient. "If you want to go below deck, you'll hand it over now." Two reluctantly reached behind his back, revealing not only a knife, but the fact that he had hidden it from them. It could have been the flickering lanterns' effect, but he thought he saw a fleeting smile cross the lips of the larger assassin.

"This way." Holding his lantern high, one escort opened the door and started down a flight of wooden stairs.

With a flick of Two's dagger, the man's companion made it clear Two should follow. Not until he complied did the second escort fall in behind him. He heard the door close, and in the tight stairwell, the glow of lanterns seemed somehow brighter. But why were there not sconces on the walls to better light the way? He held on to both railings, his eyes focused on his feet, as they descended in silence. *What might The League's overlord look like? How will his voice sound? More importantly, what might he have to say? Regardless, it will all come down to money. It always does, and I hold the ultimate bargaining chip: "Name your price!"*

Earthen walls, a small landing, a left-hand turn, down another flight of stairs, and then solid ground. *Focus on the here and now!* He took a right-hand turn down a long, narrow corridor, and began to wish he was headed in the opposite direction. *Is the ground still sloping downward? Surely this tunnel's ceiling's getting lower! Dammit, why are there no wall torches?*

The lead escort suddenly stopped, his lantern revealing a gaping hole in the left side of the corridor. He motioned for Two to enter.

What else could he do? Two swallowed and stepped into a large room illuminated by numerous lanterns atop rows of wooden casks neatly stacked on top of one another. Bottles lying on their sides fully lined the visible wall space. So much alcohol—no wonder there were no open flames! The center of the room had been cleared of all but four barrels. Lanterns atop two of them cast a decent amount of light on several figures standing idly, Charise among them, dressed in tight black leggings and a leather top that left bare her midriff and long arms. Delicate chains of gold hung in loops across her chest and hips.

Ruler Two exhaled a nervous breath. He had hoped never to cross paths with her again, but given present circumstances, he was actually relieved to see her.

The others in the room looked all too serious. One of them was massive. Dark-skinned and bald with large earrings hanging from both lobes, he stood with arms thicker than Charise's legs, crossed against his chest. To one side of him was a thinner man who'd done his best to cover every inch of his light skin with nondescript tattoos. To his other side stood a short, young woman, dressed from head to toe in long, soft fur, her light hair pulled tightly back and corded. The two men who had escorted him were somewhere behind him now, but he could picture their faces as well.

Charise, at least, was smiling.

And speaking.

"Ayla, Two. I thought perhaps you wouldn't come." She rested her bottom against one of the barrels and leaned languidly against it.

"Why not? I'm a man of my word, and there's a lot at stake here." *Don't give her the satisfaction!* Two stepped toward her, stopping within arm's reach, one hand in his trouser pocket.

"Agreed. You're certain you won't confide in me? I assure you, the one you wish to speak with is quite comfortable with that." She glanced into the recesses of the room behind her. "In fact, it would be preferred."

Take control! "I think that ground's been covered, don't you? We can't afford more blunders."

The assassin's smile faded. "Just to be clear, then... you'd meet with him alone, would you?"

How can I be more clear? Two wiggled a finger, motioning for her to come closer. When she leaned in, he whispered in her face. "What I have to say... is for the overlord's ears only."

Charise kept her face close to his. "You've not forgotten what I said? No one outside The League knows his identity, thus, no one can finger him or give his name away. Those conditions must remain once you are through here."

Impudent woman! "My memory's intact. He may command your League, but I am a member of The Guild's High Order! This is strictly business, and I want his assurance this time. And for that, he can name his price. I think your overlord will understand what you fail to comprehend. I'm not leaving 'til I speak with him."

"So you insist?"

"I do."

"So be it!" Charise clapped her hands sharply, startling the ruler and causing all but his two escorts to disappear. They moved to stand behind Charise.

"Relax," she said, placing a reassuring hand on Two's knee. "You needn't worry 'til I clap twice!" The larger of the escorts smiled, his eyebrows twitching.

Two hesitated. *Cheap theatrics! Don't say another word until she leaves.*

He stared at her, his resolve strengthening as the silence grew more awkward.

"Well?" she said.

"I'll wait. Where is he?" Two's eyes roved the black recesses behind her.

"I'm here. What is it you wanted to say?"

"What game are you playing? I told you, I'll speak only to the overlord."

"You're looking at her, silly! This is your chance to speak. Get on with it."

No! Impossible! "I don't believe you!"

"That doesn't change a thing."

This has to be a joke! Two searched the expressions of his escorts, but neither of them were laughing.

"You're the overlord?" he said, still in disbelief. "But I thought…"

"You assume too much!"

Her words hit him like a slap in the face. What was it the magister had said to him, having just disposed of Ruler Five? *Ah, yes: "You're blinded by assumptions. You must work on that!"* His predicament began to dawn on him. "My apologies. It's just… I thought…"

"No. It's that you didn't think," Charise said. "Now, was there something you wanted to say to me? For what you're about to give, I owe you that, at least."

"Yes! Yes, The Guild is willing to pay anything. Kill the King of Aranox and you can name your price!"

"There, was that so hard? I accept your offer. The price is all your Guild has stolen and amassed, down to the last dire."

"Don't be absurd! Now I know you're joking. That's preposterous!"

"Is it?" Charise placed both hands on Two's shoulders and squeezed.

He squirmed, but held her gaze. "Of course it is! You know as well as I, it is!"

"Then I've no interest in killing your King Axil. Your offer is declined. But I still want that coin!"

"You're mad!"

"A woman wants what a woman wants. Where is it?"

"It sits beneath the GOT, you crazy, stupid bitch!"

"Five told me otherwise before he died. Are you certain you don't want to change your story?"

What in Baelon is she talking about? That makes no sense! "I don't know anything about—"

Charise silenced him with a finger to his lips.

"Then our business is concluded. Now you know my status, there's only one thing left for you to do. Remember what I said: When we leave, no one can know my name, or what I look like."

"What's that supposed to mean?"

Charise rose, clapping her hands twice sharply as she exited the room. Her voice rang from the dark.

She laughed. "Your time is up!"

Overseer Reynard Rascall

Reynard twisted one way, then the other. A large lump in the bed prevented him from adopting his favorite position. He bent one leg, found that uncomfortable, then straightened it. He rested on his stomach, flipped onto his back, then cursed all seven gods.

Most annoying! He nudged the lump roughly with his knee. It bit him in response.

Reynard threw the covers off in anger, only to find himself staring at Spiro's head. "Noggods!"

"Is that any way to treat a friend?" asked Spiro.

"I thought you'd lost your head!"

"And I thought you had more sense," said Spiro. "Clearly, it's my body I'm missing."

"If you have to live without one or the other, I suppose you've made the right choice."

"Have I? Do you know how damned confining this is?"

"And yet, somehow, you manage to follow me wherever I go. How is that possible?"

"I cannot even shrug without my shoulders!" Spiro said. "How would I know? You're the architect, remember?"

"That's true. I'll think on it, shall I, and see what I can do for you?"

"Please. In the meantime, I've come to warn you."

"Warn me! About what, pray tell?"

"Are you so blind? Were my limbs still working, I would already have put Number Two in the ground for you."

"Ruler Two, you mean."

"Number Two, yes. Does he think he can replace me?"

"I've already told you, Spiro, he cannot. No one will ever take your place."

"A dagger in his heart would reassure me of that. He's not to be trusted, you know."

"I do..."

"And that skeleton in the fancy cloak."

"The magister?"

"I prefer it when you call him the spider. Much more fitting. He's up to no good as well, you realize that."

"Yes. He wants to do more than kill two kings, I'm sure of it."

"I might still be alive were it not for him, and now he spins a web for you!"

"You see that too, do you? This is not like you, Spiro—so cerebral!"

"Yes, well, one learns to use the tools at his disposal, and my brain is all I've got now."

"Then you must know I am one step ahead of that old spider. We're going to beat him at his own game, you and I. He's offered us a vault of gold, but I'll wager we'd be much happier with ten, don't you?"

"I don't, in fact. I told you, I'm here to warn you! I'm the thinker now. You should listen to me. I've a strategy."

"A strategy? What is it?"

"Kill them all, gods damn it! Kill them all, Reynard! Number Two, the spider, that woman you can't seem to take your eyes off of—don't think I haven't noticed! Let's call her the serpent, shall we? Kill them all! And do it now, before it's too late!"

"A bit drastic, don't you think?"

"Drastic? No! Not at all. I'm just getting started. Kill them all! The executioner who took my body, the hooded keeper of the castle dungeon who tortured us, and what about that giant bortok in service to the king? You were right about him. I should have killed him outside The Raven's Nest when I had the chance. Him and his little bitch!"

"I think you need to calm down."

"Calm down? What happened to our grand plans to go back and rob Castle Aranox, eh? Let's start with that, shall we? And while we're there, we can kill half the bastards on my list! Gods below, where are my daggers?! And where is my baby klubandag!"

"I don't mean to be rude, but... um, ah... exactly how do you plan to use those in your current condition?"

Spiro's beady little eyes narrowed to dark slits. "What are you trying to say?"

"I'm not at all sure. What is that sound? Are those your teeth knocking against one another?"

"You're dreaming," Spiro said. "But then, you've always been a dreamer."

"Can you not hear that knocking? Have I gone mad?"

Spiro laughed. "Have you not always been?"

Reynard's eyelids sprang open, as if they could hear, but not another muscle moved. *Was that a knock on the door?* He lay in bed, waiting, listening intently. Ruler Two was still missing from his bed. He had left in the evening, under the pretense of needing some night air. More likely, he had gone to meet the assassin's overlord. Was he only now returning? *No! He would not need to knock!*

More tapping! Soft, but unmistakable. Reynard rose swiftly but quietly, slipping on his trousers before retrieving his dagger from the floor. He crossed the room on the balls of his feet and pressed one ear against the door.

The last time he had entertained an unexpected visitor, it had been one of the king's soldiers, and Spiro had welcomed him with a paper spindle to the head.

"Overseer Rascall?"

It was a woman's voice, followed by a slightly sharper rap on the door.

The assassin?

"It's Charise. May I come in?"

Reynard hesitated. She was a killer, after all. And where was—

"It's about Ruler Two," said Charise.

Reynard concealed his dagger and cracked the door.

The assassin stepped back, displayed her empty hands, and let him take a good look at her. She wore a cream-colored sleeveless robe against her chocolate skin, its flimsy fabric clinging to the contours of her upper body. Slits on either side of the garment extended from her ankles to her upper hips, revealing nothing but skin. "May I come in?" she asked again.

Reynard opened the door wider, allowing her to see his dagger.

Charise glided past him and into the room. She turned to face him.

"What about Two?" asked Reynard.

"I don't think you should wait up for him."

"Why not?"

"Because he's not coming back."

"Really? And why is that?"

Charise shrugged. "The man was careless. He thought too highly of himself. I grew to dislike him." She smiled. "Take your pick. That's three marks against him, all of which are true, any one of which was bound to do him in eventually."

Reynard brushed his bangs back with his free hand. "It's just the last that's got me thinking."

"Mmm. I shouldn't think you need to worry."

"Why's that?"

"It's the first two marks that gave rise to the last. I don't see you as a careless man, and from what I'm told, you're entitled to think highly of yourself even if you don't."

Assassin! Spiro's voice again!

"Besides," continued Charise, "whether or not I like you is of little consequence."

"I'm not sure I follow."

"I need you."

"You need me," Reynard repeated, dubiously.

"I do."

"And here I was thinking we needed you."

"If you continue to insist on killing King Axil, you do. But to be honest, I'm not really interested in that pursuit."

"You're not?"

"No. I've a much bigger prize in mind."

"And what might that be?"

"Do you have any idea how much gold The Guild is hiding?"

She knows about the treasure! "Only that it's more than I could count in one moon's time."

"I want it all."

"You want it all."

"Well, half of it, to be fair. I was thinking you might like the other half."

Reynard's eyes narrowed. *How did you come to know about it, and what exactly are you up to?*

"Did you know Two's friend, Ruler Five?" the assassin asked.

"I never had the pleasure, but I know he's dead. Killed by the magister himself."

"Yes!" said Charise excitedly. "And do you know why?"

"Two told me it was the price he paid for failure to perform."

"It was not! Though Two may well have believed that."

"Why then?"

"Five was killed because he knew too much."

"Too much about what?"

"About The Guild's treasure, silly."

"And you're going to share what he knew with me, are you?"

"I am if you agree to be my partner."

"You've just killed my partner!" Reynard laughed, waving his dagger at her.

"Can you truly say you miss him?" asked Charise.

"Let's just say the manner in which he's gone missing concerns me. How do I know I'll not be next?"

"I've already told you… I need you."

"You'll forgive me if I remain a bit guarded, but there is the matter of your profession to consider."

"That's only fair. But you're the one holding a blade, and as you can see, I've come unarmed." She slid the straps of her gown from her shoulders, and the fabric fell quickly to the floor. She was stark naked and as striking a figure as he had ever seen. "Now, shall I tell you exactly what it is I need from you?" She sat on the edge of his bed. "Or would you rather that I showed you?"

Reynard could only stare. Not even the voice of Spiro had a ready answer.

Charise stretched her slender frame across the straw mattress. "Or can all that wait until the morning?"

Marshal Erik Carson

Marshal Carson sat unmoving. To the west, a level skyline hovered just above the Mersal Sea. To the east, nothing but sand. Behind him rode one tortured king, driven mad by emotion, surrounded by five hundred weary soldiers prepared to die in battle.

What he remained unsure of lay before him.

"What do you make of it, Major?"

Major Stronghart shifted in his saddle. "I'm feeling most unwelcome, Marshal."

"As am I. Which offends you more? The spikewood barriers… or the men waiting for us between them and the gates?"

Stronghart smiled. "Hard to say, Marshal. One is as insulting as the other."

"Indeed."

"They're simply meant to slow us down," Stronghart said. "Both of them. The barriers, so we can't throw our full weight against those gates all at once; the men outside, to hold our attention whilst those archers on the battlements have their fun."

Carson agreed. "The men outside are considered expendable, I'll wager. There's not a uniform among them. Once engaged, we'll know for sure, but I suspect their archers will aim at anything that moves beneath them."

Stronghart pointed to the spikewood barricades. "Their reach is likely marked by the barriers closest to us. But they'll not show that to be true just yet. They'll wait until our men are crammed inside that thorny labyrinth with no quick way to advance or to retreat. That's when they'll unleash their arrows. Our men will panic, as will their horses, and some will fall victim to the spikewood. Those who make it through the barriers will be greeted by that group waiting just outside the front gates. Those trying to retreat will find the way blocked by their own comrades." The major wrinkled his nose. "They know all they need to do is keep us outside until dark. Then they'll sit back and watch the prattlers go to work."

"That's the goal then, isn't it?" said Carson. "Inside before dark! Could we avoid the spikewood altogether? Attack from the rear, or either side?"

"We could, I suppose, but I don't know what we'd gain. It looks as though we might get closer there, but to what end? We'd take losses from their archers, and we'd still somehow need to breach the front gate. We've no way to climb the walls, and the battlements are crawling with men."

"Our best archers—can they scatter that group defending the gate?"

Stronghart pursed his lips. "They can, but they might put themselves in danger doing so."

"They've given us plenty to ponder," said Carson. "We should offer at least a little in return, don't you think? Have two of our best make their way to that first barricade... as fast as they can, mind you. Have them introduce a pair of arrows to that gaggle outside the gates, and then retreat before the GOT has time to think. Let's make our intentions clear, Major. This is not a friendly visit."

A lone soldier on horseback, galloping toward them from the west, held their gaze. He was breathless, and wide-eyed.

"You've seen something?" asked Major Stronghart as the rider's horse skittered to a stop in the sand.

"I've been all around," the scout gasped. He pointed to the east. "On that side... there, can you see? Those poles?"

Major Stronghart squinted. "What are they?"

"Some sort of execution, Major! Looks like men were bound to them, then slaughtered! I don't know how, but there's not much left of them. Just bones, mostly, not yet dry. There are still bits of flesh on them, and lots of blood about. It's horrible."

"Prattlers," muttered Stronghart.

"What else?" Carson prompted the young scout.

"There!" The soldier extended a finger west. "Over that dune. Where the ground rises and turns hard. You can't see from here, but there's two paths, well worn by horses and some strange wheel tracks."

"Where do they lead?"

"That's just it, Major. They sink into the ground, then disappear behind broad doors."

"What?"

"Yes, sir. I traveled down the widest path so far as the doors, but didn't dare go beyond."

"It leads to the GOT?"

"It would appear so, sir, but underground."

"The doors... they're within range of the battlement archers?"

"Yes and no. The path sinks into the ground well before that. So by the time you reach the doors, I'm sure you're within range, but by then you're also well below the dunes and out of sight."

"Easier to break through than the main gates, do you think?" asked Major Stronghart.

"That's the strangest part," said the soldier. "I didn't dare enter, but I tried the doors. We won't need to break through. They're unlocked."

"Unlocked!" said Marshal Carson.

"Yes, Marshal. That's partly what unnerved me. I thought it best to report back straight away."

"They can't lead to the GOT," said the major. "Not if they're unlocked."

"Unless it leads to other doors which are," Carson said.

"Or it's a trap," said Stronghart.

"Or it's a trap," repeated the marshal. "Send ten men. Five to explore, five to remain at the door and watch their backs."

Before the major could ride off, Carson caught him by the sleeve. "Let Sir Godfrey take the lead if he's so inclined. Find Rolft and tell him what we're up to. He may want to make it eleven."

Rolft Aerns

The earth beneath Rolft's boots gradually turned from loose sand to firmer footing. He found the last dune in particular relatively easy to climb. The GOT loomed ahead and to the east on level terrain, firmly planted on hard-packed earth. A few large pock marks dotted the ground. *Are there prattlers sleeping just beneath me?*

He trotted down a wide, well-traversed trough that looked as though it might descend into Baelon below, the earth on either side rising to form walls retained by blocks of stone until even the tops of the GOT towers disappeared from view. He kept one eye on the battle ax strapped to Sir Godfrey's back, the other on the ground before him, lest he trip or sprain an ankle in deep ruts left by some contraption with wide wheels. He did not know the nine soldiers behind him, but Sir Godfrey was battle tested and trustworthy.

The group's pace slowed to a walk just ahead of double doors buried well below ground level. Still a ways from the GOT, Sir Godfrey wasted no time in tugging one open. Nine men waited with weapons drawn as Rolft pulled on the other to expose a tunnel into which the morning's clouded sun penetrated only so far. He stared at a white-robed body lying face down in one of the wide wheel ruts, a tipped gold goblet resting by its outstretched hand.

"What in Baelon!" Sir Godfrey nudged the body with his boot, then turned it over. A young corpse stared up at Rolft, his face framed by a loose-fitting hood, his mouth covered in dirt and the remnants of a white froth.

"Not yet cold," Sir Godfrey said, his fingers pressed against the dead man's neck.

"No blood, no weapon," said Rolft. "Poisoned?" He stared at the goblet Sir Godfrey lifted to his nose.

"Most likely." The knight rose to his feet. "Makes no sense."

No, it doesn't. Rolft's mind began to churn.

"Five to stay behind and watch our backs," Sir Godfrey said, quickly identifying the youngest members of the group.

Those closest in age to your lost sons!

One of them began to protest. Sir Godfrey pressed him against the retaining wall. "You're the fleetest of foot! The Guild can't see us now, but don't think they didn't watch us from the battlements make our way here! Go back; let the marshal know we're inside!" He addressed the other four. "One of you... get back up where you can see what's coming. If it looks to be more than you can handle, one of you—come to warn us. Only one, do you hear? The rest are to rejoin the marshal if at all possible. Understood? In the meantime, make use of that ax you're carrying. When we return, I want these doors off their hinges and out of our way. Go on! Put your backs to it. The rest of you, stay close to me."

Rolft followed Sir Godfrey a few steps into the tunnel's shaft, taking note of several unlit torches before the walls themselves blended with the dark. *Why are they not lit? Why were the doors unlocked? And what was the reason for the robed man's death?*

Sir Godfrey stopped, lowering his voice. "Keep your eyes and your ears open! No unnecessary noise! They may well be waiting for us down this tunnel! If I say turn around, you godsdamn turn around and run like Asperine himself is on your tail! We're here to find the marshal a path to The Guild's heart, not fight its entire army ourselves! And you're not to worry if Rolft separates from us or ignores my commands. He's on his own, understood?" The four veteran soldiers nodded, all eyes shifting momentarily to Rolft. "Right, then, be on your guard, and may all seven gods watch over us!"

Sir Godfrey pressed forward, the sound of steel biting into wood drowning his boot-steps.

"More doors ahead... unlocked," Sir Godfrey whispered. Rolft could just make them out, partially ajar. They gave way to Sir Godfrey's weight, and Rolft followed the knight and four soldiers into a cavernous space extending in two directions. One appeared to grow ever-wider; the other narrowed to a tunnel similar to the one they had just traversed.

Sir Godfrey pointed to the cavern's ceiling. "We're beneath it, yeah?"

He means the GOT! Rolft nodded. They had traveled what seemed an appropriate distance; the doors they had just passed through, the broadened expanse of excavation, an increase in natural light, most likely coming from tower windcatchers or exits to ground level... all suggested that they now stood beneath the GOT's footprint.

"We need to be certain." The knight pointed his sword down the narrower path. "Two of you go that way. Just far enough to find out where it leads, mind you. Then back to the marshal as quick as you can. Don't wait for us, understood?"

Electing himself, the tallest of the soldiers tugged at the sleeve of another. "That's us, Hewitt."

"Lucky us, I suppose," said his chosen partner. "We're off, then."

Sir Godfrey addressed the remaining two soldiers as he slung the battle ax from his back. "You two stay here." The knight nodded at the doors they had just passed through. "The marshal doesn't want to knock, and we need a clear path back, yeah? Off at the hinges!"

One of the soldiers was quick to reach for the ax. "We'll have them off in no time, will we not?" he asked his companion as Sir Godfrey relinquished the ax.

"Six strokes at most, Sir Godfrey!" came the answer. "And as soon as we're done, we'll head back and help the pups with theirs!"

"Then back to the marshal like all the rest. No puttering about." Sir Godfrey locked eyes with Rolft. "And you?"

"With you, of course... until I'm not."

The further they advanced, the more expansive the cavern below the GOT became. Its walls curved slowly in opposite directions, eventually growing so far apart that Rolft could only see the one they used to guide their way.

The rutted ground turned smooth and level. A light breeze stirred his locks.

There's ample room here for a dungeon or most anything. Clearly, it was excavated for some purpose, but what? And so quiet! I can barely hear the blows being dealt to the doors behind us. Why were they unlocked? Their destruction virtually guarantees the eventual arrival of five hundred soldiers to at least this point. If passage to the GOT's interior lies ahead, there will be no stopping the king's army. Why were we allowed to enter in the first place? There's no way we should have come this far without meeting some resistance. We have to have been seen. Perhaps The Guild is waiting for our number to increase before it springs a trap. Is there a way to flood this space? A way to set it on fire? Is an armed horde waiting for us in the dark ahead?

Sir Godfrey pointed to the right, where double doors, their pulls chained and locked together, were set into the stone wall guiding their passage. The knight stopped to heft the lock. "We need another battle ax," he said.

"Some sort of storage, do you think?" asked Rolft.

Sir Godfrey tapped the gold coin hanging from his neck.

Rolft glanced back as the energized knight hurried on. *If he's right... if The Guild's treasure lies behind that door, we're not only below the GOT, we're beneath Takers Tower, home of the magister!* He followed his companion, trying to recall all else Fereliss had shared about the GOT while traversing the Lawless Lands.

Sir Godfrey set the pace, slowing each time they passed another set of locked doors in the wall, and then only long enough to acknowledge them with more coin-tapping. Rolft was grateful, his breathing labored, when the knight came to a standstill near the fifth set, his outstretched arm drawing attention away from both the wall and doors.

Far into the underground interior, a vague stone formation, cylindrical in shape, rose from the cavern floor.

Sir Godfrey made his way toward it. Rolft followed.

Resembling a castle turret, the structure disappeared into the earthen ceiling above.

The two men approached it warily, gathering outside its only distinguishing feature: a single wooden door.

Sir Godfrey opened it with ease and ducked inside.

Rolft leaned his shoulders through the doorway and craned his head around.

A narrow, twisting staircase spiraled upward, hugging the stone walls of a hollow cylinder extending beyond his ability to see. Sir Godfrey stood at its base, the frayed end of a thick rope dangling just above his head.

"Tower, yeah?" asked Rolft in a hushed voice.

"Tower within a tower!" answered Sir Godfrey.

Rolft nodded in agreement. *Tower within a tower! The very center of Takers Tower!*

Sir Godfrey joined him and shut the door. "Later, perhaps," he whispered. "We're looking for a way in, not just up." He cocked his head. "Hear that?"

Both men stood silent.

Rolft's eyebrows rose. *Voices. Faint, but unmistakable!*

They trotted through the cavern, passing three more sets of chained doors, before Sir Godfrey signaled for Rolft to stop. The knight put a finger to his lips.

Ahead, the cave constricted, its curved walls closing in on one another. The only way forward appeared to be a set of stairs in the far wall some fifty strides ahead. The voices they'd been listening to, now mixed with other sounds, seemed to tumble down them.

It was not until they reached the base of the stairs that Rolft could see a landing above, and just the top of a door buffering a harsh, discordant mixture of sounds. He cautiously climbed the steps, Sir Godfrey on his heels. Halfway up, the door came into full view. Rolft breathed a sigh of relief as he climbed to the landing—a bar across the door's midsection would keep those responsible for making all that noise on its other side.

To his left, another set of stairs led higher still. *Takers Tower, no doubt!*

The small peephole in the door was shut.

Sir Godfrey brought his face to it, slid it partway open, then just as quickly closed it.

"Oh, the marshal's smiling now," he whispered to Rolft. "That's our way in, all right!"

"Who's there?" a voice shouted from the other side. "Let us in!"

"For good measure!" Sir Godfrey slid the aperture open, rammed his sword through it, then withdrew it just as quickly.

A scream and several curses erupted before the aperture was closed.

Sir Godfrey slapped Rolft on the back. "Gods' wrath and good fortune!" he cried, swiftly descending the stairs.

What was Sir Godfrey thinking? Why put the enemy on notice? Rolft hefted his sword. *Make up your mind, and quickly! Back with the knight, or up these stairs?*

"Break it down!" a deep voice on the other side of the door commanded.

"But the magister's inside! We've been warned to leave him be."

You cannot help Sibil from outside the GOT. Best find her now. Once the fighting starts, that task will be much harder!

"Break it down, I say!"

"But Sarul—"

"Give me that ax! I'll break it down myself!"

Rolft started up the twisting tower stairwell. *Take heart! If Sibil's elsewhere—if this is your last day—perhaps the God of Fortune will introduce you to the magister before you die. That would be enough!*

Repeated blows on the door below spurred him on. *Two steps at a time! Get out of sight at least!*

He glanced behind, relieved to see nothing but tower stones and stairs.

A loud crash, celebrated by strident voices, energized his legs.

The door is down! Gods above, please let them chase Sir Godfrey!

"Sweep the tower! Every level! Find the magister! Kill the intruders!"

The clattering of bootsoles and the clanking of steel echoed up the stairwell.

Shite! Rolft stumbled onto a flat landing, quickly taking note of a door in the left wall. He pulled the door open, then slammed it shut without entering, hoping the noise would carry to those climbing the stairs below. *Oh, yes! Twice for good measure! Now... as quickly and as quietly as you can...* Rolft attacked the stairs again. By the time he spotted another landing, the one below had disappeared below the tower's curvature.

The noises chasing him had not. The loudest voices were, in fact, gaining on him.

"That's it, Damien! Go on! You've got him now!"

"Stay with him, Karrick! Go, lad, go!"

They'll see me any moment now! Three steps at once if possible! Rolft's thighs complained at once. *Just up to the next landing! No, I cannot manage more than two stairs at a time! Noggods! When did I grow old? It's far too soon to tire!*

His boots hit the landing. *Another door!*

"Trespasser!"

Rolft spun. Two strapping young men bounded up the stairs toward him, as though trying to outdo one another. "Trespasser!" repeated one. "Stay where you are!"

"Death comes for you!" cried the other.

You're not going to outrun them! Go through that door; you'll be giving up the higher ground, but who knows how you may prosper in return. More room to run, perhaps... A place to hide...

Rolft tugged on the door's pull ring. The wood rattled but resisted. He pulled again. *Locked or barred from the inside! Noggods! Don't let them reach the landing!*

He moved quickly to the middle of the stairwell, adopted a short stance, and turned his left side to his attackers. The hilt of his sword, held loosely in both hands and resting on his shoulders, pointed at the two men barreling up the stairs with wild abandon. *The price of throwing caution to the winds is high!* Their swords, held high above their heads, entered Rolft's reach several steps ahead of their bodies. His blade picked up momentum until it clashed with theirs, knocking the first it met into the air and forcing the other to point sideways. Neither impeded the reverse stroke of his blade. It traveled upward, severing the arm of one man before traveling across his companion's chest. The first dropped to his knees, screaming. The other fell backward, down the tower steps, coming to rest just as the stairwell below filled with soldiers climbing three abreast. Those in the lead stopped at the sight of their fallen comrades, but the momentum of those behind pushed them forward.

Rolft turned and ran, the burning in his thighs returning quickly as he climbed the stairs. *Gods above, let there be another landing soon, and let the door there be unlocked!*

"Coward!" came a cry from below.

"Stand and face your enemies!"

The clatter of bootsteps grew louder. *Ever closer!*

He could hear the soldier's grunting and huffing. *They're tired, too! Stay the course!*

There it is! Rolft hit the landing, threw his weight toward the left wall, and came to rest, erect, against the landing's door. His hand found its pull and, as he backed away, the door mercifully came open.

He slipped inside, pulled it shut, and searched frantically for the bar meant to sit inside its brackets. *There!*

It dropped into place just as his pursuers reached the landing. They pounded on the door, but it held fast.

Rolft took a moment to survey his new surroundings as strong voices yelled at him. *What is this place?*

"Coward! Come out and face your death!"

"Bring the ax!"

"Horman, take six to the next level. Once inside the tower, work your way down!"

Shite! There's another stairway inside here? Where?

"Stikkle, go below and do the same. Get inside and work your way back up. Between the two of you, we'll have him trapped. Hurry, or we'll beat you to him! Once this door is down, his fate is sealed. Go on now!"

Rolft plowed through the room, his interest limited to the discovery of stairs, additional weapons, or a place to hide.

No! Hiding is a bad idea. Several men are coming for you from above, several more from below; the rest will eventually break through the tower door behind. How long do you think it will take them to find you, knowing you are here somewhere? Use their plan to your advantage... isolate and eliminate! Divide and conquer! Take your pick—several from above or several from below? No choice at all, really. A child would know the best course! Keep the high ground. Break through the men below, and the path to the tunnels may be clear, perhaps all the way back to the marshal. He and his soldiers could be on their way toward you even now. Close that gap! Find the interior stairs before that door behind you comes crashing down!

The sound of an ax biting wood spurred him on.

Rolft skirted one large chair, then another.

He could not help but notice rich colors and plush fabrics. He knocked a small side table down in his haste to cross the room.

Like a hunted pig, squealing in the woods! Hurry, but be quiet! Find the stairs! Rolft froze. Held his breath to listen. *There are others already inside the tower, and they're coming for you!* He took smaller steps, silently moving to one side of an archway leading to the next room. *Wait for the first one through—one less to deal with right away. No! You cannot afford to wait. Who knows how many will come through the door behind you when it falls? You don't want to be fighting front and rear at the same time!*

Another blow to the stairwell door behind spurred him to action.

He stepped into the archway, shocked to find the next room nearly filled with figures. It took but a moment to realize that the six or seven of flesh and blood were scattered amongst a greater number sculpted from baelonite or clay.

Those living saw him as well.

"There!" cried one.

"Take care; he may not be alone!" said another.

One of the soldiers started toward him, but another called him off. "Hold! Wait until Karrick breaks through. We'll have him trapped!"

More bashing from the room behind suggested they did not have long to wait.

Rolft eyed the open archway behind the men facing him, then forged ahead, kicking a pedestal as he advanced. The sculpted bust it had supported shattered into pieces as it hit the floor.

Unprepared for Rolft's swift advance, the nearest soldier lurched backward, tripping on a chunk of broken stone and falling. Rolft stepped over him, slicing his throat with one blow before running his sword through another soldier's stomach.

He retreated as more uniforms spilled into the room, spreading left and right.

"Together!" cried one, advancing faster than the others.

Rolft sprang toward him. Their blades clashed, but Rolft was heavier and stronger. He pushed the soldier backward, then held the rest at bay with sweeping arcs of his broadsword.

"For Aranox!" he bellowed, preparing to slash his way through the room.

A sculpted piece of baelonite came hurtling through the air. He dodged it, his gaze riveted on those soldiers closest to him.

Another clatter of boots on stone preceded the appearance of more soldiers in the doorway he had hoped to reach. *Ten or more, now! Go, go, go... before they organize!*

Rolft lurched forward, kicking another pedestal to the floor. *Commit, now. Do not stop. There is no going back!*

A piece of baelonite struck his shoulder, another whizzed past his head. Two soldiers rushed at him, one with his sword raised, the other aiming low. Rolft blocked the higher blow with his own sword, twisting to evade the lower blade. The soldier wielding it stumbled past him, and Rolft spun, cleaving the man's head from his shoulders.

For a moment, all that could be heard were the groans of one man wounded, and the heavy breathing of those still standing.

Rolft straddled the bodies of two dead, his eyes glaring at those still standing.

The blood of their comrades dripped from his sword.

This is what awaits you!

A loud crash from the tower stairwell, followed by triumphant cheers, caused Rolft to risk a quick glance back toward the first room he had entered. Battle cries from that direction, and the sound of furniture being overturned, emboldened the men facing him. One rushed at him with a guttural cry as the soldiers from the stairwell poured into the room.

Rolft stepped back, parrying the attack with an upward intercept, recovering, then lunging forward, thrusting his sword into the man's mid-section.

The room closed in on him as several bodies rushed toward him all at once. He parried one blow, blocked another, but a blade slashed his outer thigh, causing his right leg to buckle.

A primal, high-pitched scream from the midst of the chaos curdled Rolft's blood as he rose unsteadily. He parried yet another blow, then watched as his attacker fell, blood spraying from his neck for no apparent reason. A second man dropped next to him, empty hands clutching at his stomach.

Rolft stepped back, tripped over a prostrate body, and righted himself just in time to challenge the advance of two more soldiers. His right leg complained, and he cried out as he assumed a short stance and high guard position, blocking two blades traveling downward at the same time. He twisted away, using his momentum to give life to his sword. It sliced through the air horizontally, decapitating one of the men and carving through the shoulder of the other. The wounded man stood frozen as a short blade pierced his neck two times in rapid succession. He crumpled to the floor, and Rolft gaped at the figure standing over him, a dagger clenched in each hand. *Sibil Dunn!*

She whirled to face the remaining soldiers scattered among the sculptures. Rolft quickly counted eight, all hesitant to attack. She hissed at them, adopted a wide stance, and put her daggers on display for all to see. For a moment, no one moved. But when she screamed and rushed toward them, the eight came to life again.

Rolft hobbled after her, attempting to ignore the pain in his right leg. He watched as Sibil weaved between the sculptures. One of them exploded as she ducked beneath a blade intended for her head. She deflected her assailant's arm with one hand, driving her dagger up into his armpit with the other even as she slipped behind him. An upward thrust, a horizontal slash, a downward slice, and she moved on—swiftly, smoothly, dodging statues and carving flesh.

Rolft lost sight of her as two soldiers stepped in front of him, one with both hands wrapped around the hilt of a broadsword pointed at his chest. The other was a tall warrior wielding a battle ax. The soldier's blade circled up and then came thundering down, narrowly missing Rolft and ringing against the stone floor. Rolft brought his own sword down on it with all his might, dislodging the weapon from his assailant's hands. He refrained from counter attacking, knowing it would leave him vulnerable to the battle ax, now raised overhead and ready to strike.

With another scream, Sibil leaped onto the ax-wielder's back. Clenching his torso between her legs, she used both hands to drive her dagger into the base of his neck. Still riding him, she left it there, and as the man slumped to the floor, she relieved him of his upraised ax and brought it down on the swordsman, cleaving his head in two.

Wild-eyed and panting, she glared at a trio of remaining soldiers as she handed Rolft the ax. She stepped on the man who had wielded it and wrested her dagger from his neck.

"Gods above," one of the remaining soldiers muttered.

Rolft drove his sword into the prostrate body of their comrade, lifted the ax high overhead and hurled it at them. It smashed a statue standing next to them, and they bolted through the nearest archway toward the tower stairwell.

Rolft exchanged a glance with Sibil.

"You're wounded!" she said, staring at his leg.

"I'll be all right, though it would be wise to stop the bleeding." He bent to remove the belt from a fallen soldier's waist. "May I?" He reached for Sibil's dagger and she handed it to him. He wrapped the belt around his thigh, cinched it tight, then used her blade to make a new hole for its catch. "There," he said, grimacing. "Good as new!"

"What are you doing here?" asked Sibil, accepting her knife back.

"One might ask the same of you!"

Sibil was silent for a moment, her breathing returning to near normal. "You've given up on farming, have you?"

"Given up?" Rolft jerked his sword from the soldier's body. "What does that even mean? I'm pacing myself. You've never seen so many rocks!"

Sibil laughed.

"What are you doing here, really?" asked Rolft.

"I came to kill the magister!"

"And? How goes the work?"

Sibil shrugged. "I'm pacing myself as well."

"Ah." Rolft looked about the room, strewn with shattered artwork and dead bodies. There were several she must have slain in the brief time he'd been preoccupied. "You may want to rein things in. Just a bit, mind you."

Sibil grinned. "Truth be told, I'm tired." She took a deep breath, her shoulders relaxing. She wiped a dark clot from her face, smearing blood across her cheek.

"I dare say."

"And you? What are you doing here, truly?"

"I came to help a friend I thought in need."

"Did you?" Sibil beamed. "Really?"

"Are you injured?" Rolft looked at her more closely.

"No. Just exhausted."

"Where did you come from?" asked Rolft.

Sibil jerked her head. "Much higher in the tower."

"We should go," said Rolft. "Before more soldiers come."

Sibil moved toward the stairwell. "I can't leave just yet. I've unfinished business to attend to."

THE SECRETS OF A LABYRINTH

"Why do you care? Nothing matters. All your world is made of dust... and my hands are on the broom!" From the Scriptures of All Gods, attributed to the God of Fortune's nemesis, Kallamus.

Marshal Erik Carson

A handful of the king's men chased a dozen Guild defenders on foot through the spikewood barriers and into the Lawless Lands. Marshal Carson watched from the front gates just long enough to ensure they steered clear of a small contingent on horseback: King Axil, his royal guard, six healers, and one scribe—all waiting well beyond the spikewood for word that it was safe to enter.

By all accounts, the battle was well in hand. Even the smallest pockets of resistance seemed to have been quelled. War cries within the GOT had turned to shouting and exuberant cheers sprinkled with a smattering of nervous laughter.

"I'm feeling much more welcome now, but it's not home, is it?" called Major Stronghart. The manner in which the empty-handed soldier swayed from side to side, arms loose and hanging by his thighs, suggested he bore good news.

Marshal Carson sheathed his sword. "No. It's hardly that."

"You're standing in what they call Fore Court, by the way." The major pointed past a courtyard fountain and into the GOT's interior. "Through there, between those buildings, is Center Court, where we made our entry from below. Further back lies... can you guess?"

"Back court?"

"Ah, you see? They may be good at thievery, but I can't say much for their imagination." The major resumed his pointing. "That there's The Hidor, home of The High Order. To its right, on the other side of the passage leading to center court, is the School of Taking, and that beauty rising there, of course, is Takers Tower!"

Carson acknowledged the approach of Sergeant Galeran. "Our losses, Sergeant?"

"Twenty-three dead, Marshal, including Sergeants Vikkers and Mayhew. Most fell to their archers before we took the battlements."

"And the wounded?"

"At least twice that number, Marshal."

"And The Guild?"

"Their dead and wounded?" The sergeant scratched his beard, jerking his head toward the GOT's interior. "I'm happy to say we're still counting, sir."

"Very well. The best place for our wounded? Those who can be moved?"

"I'd say that building, sir." The sergeant pointed to The Hidor. "It looks to be the cleanest, and it's quite roomy. More than enough space for those who just need rest. The building beside is even larger, but not nearly so open. Lots of rooms and walls... and it's crawlin' with children, Marshal."

"Children!"

"Students of The Guild. The School of Taking," said Major Stronghart.

"We've got 'em penned on the upper floor, Marshal, but they're like kid goats—some are frightened, some are frisky. There's no tellin' what they'll do next. The ground level's empty and open. I think that's a better place for your war room. Leave the peace and quiet to the healers and those suffering."

"Very well. It's safe enough, you think, to bring the healers in?"

"I think so, Marshal, and there are some who really need them."

"Have them brought in under guard, Major. The king and scribe as well, but don't let them wander. Tell the king he's needed in the war room, where he can find some shade."

Carson jerked a thumb toward those being chased into the Lawless Lands. "And let those stragglers go. They're as good as dead out there. Bring our men back. Gather our horses and close these gates."

The School of Taking matched Sergeant Galeran's description, its foyer far brighter and more spacious than any of the smaller rooms it served to introduce. A dozen officers accepted information and imparted orders to soldiers streaming in and out.

The palace scribe sat at a table in one corner, his quill furiously scratching out the story of what had come to pass. The king, encouraged to assist with those details, refused to sit. Instead, he prowled the area in front of the scribe, exhibiting his impatience.

Across the room, Carson raked his hair back with both hands, his lips parting to release a mixture of weariness and frustration. It grew late. "We've scoured all the buildings?" he asked Major Stronghart.

"From top to bottom, Marshal. More than once."

Carson shook his head in refusal. "They're here somewhere. They have to be. Hidden passageways? Secret chambers?"

"It's a big compound. We're still looking. A different set of eyes each time. All the men know to come here if they find anything at all." The monarch's frustration was not lost on the major. "Perhaps we could occupy his majesty outside. Parade him around the grounds and let him have a look at things."

"No. We can't find the magister or his High Order... an old man and his friends. What makes you think we've flushed out all their soldiers?"

A commotion near the front doors drew the marshal's attention.

Unbelievable! It was Rolft, accompanied by Sibil Dunn, an old man with short, gray hair, and four disheveled children in nightclothes—a young girl and three little boys, all holding hands. Rolft walked with a pronounced limp, a leather belt cinched around one leg. Miss Dunn, covered in dirt and blood, otherwise appeared no worse for wear. A small group of officers joined the king in trailing them across the foyer.

"Miss Dunn! I don't suppose there's any point in asking what you're doing here."

"I should think that was obvious." The young woman turned to King Axil. "You would not let me join your army, so I joined The Guild's instead."

"You joined The Guild's army," repeated the marshal in disbelief.

"How else was I to get close to the magister?"

"You've seen him!" said King Axil. "He's here?"

"I arrived two suns ago. This is the first time I've not seen him standing on the balcony of his tower. But he's here somewhere."

Another noisy burst of activity at the school's entrance caused all to watch Sergeant Galeran approach, roughly prodding a rotund man ahead of him.

"Who's this?" Carson asked.

"He calls himself Ruler One, Marshal! We found him hiding on the fifth level of The Hidor. Inside a giant laundry basket."

"Please, please, have mercy. I'm not a threat to you." Ruler One kneaded his hands nervously.

"But that's not the question, is it?" said Carson.

"What is the question?" sputtered Ruler One.

"The question is, are you of any use to us?" Carson grabbed the man by the back of his shirt collar and roughly repositioned him. "This is your king! King Axil of Aranox! And he would have your head for your offenses!" He buckled the man's knees with a bootsole to their backs. "Where are your friends?"

"My what?"

"Don't play with me!"

"I'm not! I'm not!"

"Your friends! Your fellow rulers! How many of you are there?"

"There are five of us. Yes, five! Five rulers and the magister make up The Guild's High Order."

"Where are they?"

"Here! Inside The Hidor. We all live here! This is our home. We make our beds on the second floor."

"Where are they hiding, then?"

"I don't know. I swear it!"

Carson released his hold on the man in disgust. "He's useless, Your Majesty. We may as well take his head, here and now!"

"No! Let me think. I can help! I can help! You're not going to find Ruler Five. He's dead! The magister had him killed. His bones are lying at the bottom of Reception Canyon. I can show you where, if you like! And Ruler Two—he's gone."

"Gone where?" asked Marshal Carson.

"To... To..." The kneeling ruler clasped both hands, as though in prayer. "Forgive me, Your Majesty... he's gone to kill you and King Tygre!"

Carson lowered his face to Ruler One's level. "That accounts for numbers one, two and five. What about three and four?"

"Four leads our army. That's his job. Surely you have killed or captured him already. You see, I can help! I can identify him for you!"

"And number three?"

"Here! Hiding just as I was, no doubt. I can help you find her, too. I'm sure of it. That's my job, you see. No one knows more about the GOT than me. That's all I do—I take care of all its needs. I know its every nook and cranny."

"What about the magister?" asked Carson.

King Axil leaned forward.

"He resides in Takers Tower. I can take you there!"

"I've been in the tower, top to bottom. I saw no sign of him," said Miss Dunn.

"What about his noms?" asked Ruler One, looking to Miss Dunn. "If you were in Takers Tower, surely you saw them."

"Noms?" Carson asked.

"His aides," said the ruler. "Young men and women, all dressed in white robes."

"The noms are dead," said Miss Dunn.

"You killed them?!" said Ruler One. "The noms? They're children, really! What harm could they have—"

"They killed themselves," said Sibil. "With poisoned drink."

"What?" The ruler's mouth hung open. "That makes no sense."

"I watched them do it with my own eyes," said Miss Dunn.

"But why would they do that?"

"Because they knew the king was coming," the marshal said. "They knew the end was near. Might the magister have done the same?"

"I've no idea, but I can take you through the tower. I know it rather well. I can show you where he sleeps. Where he eats. Where he might be hiding."

Carson glanced at Miss Dunn.

"It's very big," she said, meeting his gaze. "He could easily be tucked away in there."

"Yes, yes!" said Ruler One. "I can think of several places he might hide. He's old and doesn't move well on his own. He can't have gotten far without his noms. He has to be there somewhere!"

Carson took a moment to think things through. "We've only a few hours left before dark falls. I'm not so worried about the woman. If she's hiding in The Hidor, she's not going anywhere without our knowledge."

"If I might," said Ruler One. "There's an egress on the fifth level. All the towers and the buildings allow access to the breezeway there. It runs across the GOT and connects to the battlements on the perimeter."

Carson eyed him steadily.

"You see? I can be helpful," said Ruler One.

"Major!" Carson said. "Take as many men as needed. Station guards on the battlements, and at every door on that breezeway. I want anyone trying to get in or out brought here. Have the floors above the wounded swept again. Find the woman... Ruler Three!"

Carson addressed King Axil. "It looks as though the time has come for you to join the hunt, sire!" He grabbed Ruler One by the scruff of the neck and lifted him to his feet. "You'll take His Majesty floor by floor, room by room, until you find the magister."

"Yes, yes, of course! I know just where to look on every floor!"

"Where's Fereliss!" shouted the marshal. "Sergeant Galeran, you're to accompany the king and royal guard. You have but one job, do you hear? To watch this wretch. If he tries to run, if he fails to do just as you ask or makes one move out of turn, you're to take his head and bring it back to me. Do you hear?"

"It would be my pleasure, Marshal." Sergeant Galeran helped the kneeling ruler to his feet.

"I'm going, too," said Miss Dunn. "If someone will watch the children."

Carson eyed her keenly.

"As am I," said Rolft.

"You're hurt," said the marshal.

"Just try to stop me," advised Rolft.

A bad feeling kept stride with Marshal Carson. There was something he had left unattended. Some sign that he had missed. Something he should have been doing.

He stared briefly at Sir Godfrey across the room. There had been no word from those stationed on the battlements or breezeway; no report from Major Stronghart, searching The Hidor for Ruler Three; the royal guard and king had not returned.

Where is everyone? How long does it take to search one building? One tower?

There were twenty-seven strides between one end of the school's foyer and the other. It had been hot when he'd first counted them. Now the heat looked to escape, and the scribe bent his head ever lower to better guide his quill across a sheet of shaded parchment.

The sun sets regardless.

Carson stopped in his tracks. *That's it!* "Sergeant Stone!"

"Marshal?"

"We've secured the GOT for the evening, I trust? The gates are closed?"

"Yes, sir."

"What about those doors Sir Godfrey broke through to let us in? We can't have the prattlers coming through those tunnels!"

"They've been barricaded, Marshal. Crude, but effective. I can't see anything getting through there."

Carson's frame relaxed. *That was it, was it not? The prattlers?*

The sudden appearance of Sergeant Galeran, with Ruler One by his side, renewed the marshal's misgivings.

"Where's the king and royal guard?" he asked.

"Still searching, m'lord," said Sir Galeran. "The king didn't want to give up. But this one—he seems to have exhausted his ideas."

"Then he's of little further use!"

"No! No!" The terrified ruler held out his hands in protest. "That's not true. I can show you where the money's kept!"

Carson scoffed. "It's directly beneath us, is it not? Within the tunnels? Behind locked doors? We knew that before we came. And we've since seen the doors."

"But have you seen all ten? I can show you! And I know where Ruler Three keeps all her records."

All ten? Carson exchanged a glance with Sir Godfrey.

"I've had my fill of your false promises," he said to Ruler One. "If this turns out to be another, I'll kill you myself!"

"Follow me, gentlemen." Ruler One waddled rather proudly out of the School of Taking. "This is the quickest way below ground from here. The best way, really. The only other entrances are from the core of Takers Tower, and from outside the GOT. You'll see."

Marshal Carson followed closely with Sir Godfrey. "If you really want to prove your worth, you'll tell us what your fellow rulers look like. How will we know them when we see them?"

"All right, of course! Easily done, although I still hope to help you find them myself. I'm not at all friendly with any of them, you know. Not really. In fact, most of them act as though I don't exist. Absurd, really, because if I didn't, they'd soon come to realize how much they depend on me, a fact I'm sure you've already—"

"Ruler One."

"Ah, yes, well, let's work backward, shall we?" Ruler One waved a pudgy hand at the limp bodies of two Guild soldiers being dragged away from Fore Court. "Ruler Five's as dead as those men there. No doubt about it. I can show you where they threw his body if you like. Into Reception Canyon! Who knows how much of him is left down there, though, what with all the—"

"Ruler Four," pressed Marshal Carson.

"Sorry. Ruler Four, leader of our army. Well, he's rarely out of uniform, for starters. He loves to strut around in that old thing. And he most always carries a rider's stick. You'll tell him by that alone, I'll wager. There's no one else who carries one here. And it has a gold knob with tassels on its end. But even absent that, you'd know him. His expression rarely changes. You need only imagine a chunk of spikewood with angry features carved into it. Dead or alive, he's going to look the same. That's Ruler Four. Straight hair, slicked back, much like yours, Marshal, only that's where the resemblance ends."

"Next."

"I don't mean to state the obvious, but Ruler Three is a woman, so she should be the easiest to recognize—at least here at the GOT. There are very few others with her anatomy here. Two of the cooks, the chambermaids, one wildcat in the army. You won't mistake Ruler Three for any of them. Her long silver hair sits in a braided pile on top of her head. Ruler Two calls her 'the owl,' and for good reason. She doesn't need to turn her head to watch you. Those big eyes of hers see everything."

Ruler One wound his way through Center Court, where bound prisoners were detained and made to sit in rows.

"And Ruler Two? What does he look like? How will we know him?"

"He may be your biggest challenge," said Ruler One. "Average height, average build. Dark hair of common length. There's really nothing special about him. Unless you feel someone's hand inside your pocket or your purse. That would be him—but you won't feel it, because he's good at it. As far as what he looks like, no, you're better off searching for the man he's with. He'll be much easier to find."

"What man is that?"

"Ah, yes, how would you know? Again, you see, this is why you need me. Alive, I might add. Ruler Two has an accomplice to help him destroy your kings. You didn't know that, did you? How could you? I saw him but once, and still his face lingers here." Ruler One tapped his head. "He'll be much easier for you to find than Ruler Two. Much easier to pick out of a crowd. Black hair like a horse's mane, falling straight to touch his shoulders."

"That's hardly noteworthy," Carson said. "I can think of several men who fit that description."

"As can I, Marshal—may I call you that? It's not his hair that makes him stand out, but rather what it hides. He has an ugly scar—here—in the middle of his forehead."

"What?" Carson stopped in his tracks. *Impossible! Coincidence! Or is there a group that marks its members this way? Why not? Assassins for The League ink the soles of their feet. Why not?*

"What's his name?"

"Honestly, I don't remember. Was it Raymond? Rickert? It started with an R, I'm fairly certain. But he's an overseer for The Guild, that much I know."

"An overseer! Do they all wear that mark? Your overseers?"

"Not that I know, Marshal. Why would they do that? And it didn't look intentional by any means. More like his forehead met the wrong end of a blade."

Impossible!

Ruler One paused at the base of Takers Tower to stare and shake his head in disapproval. "Oh my, look at that... someone's broke the door down. That was your men, I suppose."

"No," said Sir Godfrey. "That was yours, chasing after me."

"And look, no harm done," said Ruler One. "Not to you, nor to the door... not really. I'll have that replaced in no time! That's how handy I can be. You wait and see. I'm not just a wealth of knowledge, no sir. Always at the ready! This way, gentlemen. Watch your step!"

Marshal Carson and Sir Godfrey exchanged a quick look before following Ruler One down the stairs and into the ground below Takers Tower.

"I've always said that we should pave this earthen floor. Why not, I ask? Surer footing makes for safer travel, especially when the lighting's poor, would you not agree? And it would feel so much more inviting, less like your dungeon, I imagine. Not that I want to know what that's like. I don't. And why should I, really? What have I done to deserve that? I merely maintain this complex. It keeps me busy, day and night. There's no rest for me. I've no time for other pursuits. I don't know anything about The Guild's external affairs, not really. Nor do I care to. No."

"Ruler One."

"Yes?"

"Shut up!"

The portly ruler reached to fiddle with small objects sitting on a barrel near the foot of the stairs.

"What are you doing?" asked Carson.

"Just wait. Just wait," said Ruler One. "The belly will be dark soon. That's what I call this place... the belly. We're going to need some light. But you see how well prepared I am. Here, just watch. I'll have this going in no time." A few strikes of flint against a ball of tinder turned some of the dried fibers bright red. A few puffs from Ruler One's full jowls turned them into flame.

"There! You see? Always prepared, am I." He carefully picked up the flaming ball and turned toward the wall. "Noggods!" he cried, staring at an empty torch bracket. He dropped the flaming tinder to the ground and stepped on it. "That's strange." He brushed his hands against his trousers. "Wait a tick." He sniffed the air. "Something's not right."

"Where are you going?" Carson followed as Ruler One walked further into the GOT's belly.

"He's stalling," said Sir Godfrey.

"I'm not!" said Ruler One, setting a brisk pace.

"Then show us the treasure," said Sir Godfrey, as they passed a set of chained doors in the wall. "That's what we came here for. Stop and unlock one of these."

"Unlock them?" Ruler One hurried on. "I never said I could do that. I said I'd show you where they are. Only the magister has keys to these."

"Scoundrel!" said Sir Godfrey.

"Forget about the treasure! Where are all my barrels?" Ruler One asked, growing more agitated. "And why are there no torches on the wall?"

"What's the problem?" Carson asked.

"My barrels filled with lyla! They're missing—all of them!" The portly ruler's face suddenly contorted as he waddled quickly down the tunnel. "This place should reek of lyla! This isn't right. I check their levels every sun! What have you done with them?"

"We've done nothing with your barrels." Carson looked to Sir Godfrey for confirmation.

"No, Marshal. Never saw them," said the knight.

"Two hundred barrels!" screamed Ruler One. "They didn't vanish on their own! They're what repels the prattlers! The soil all around us... it's full of creatures!"

"Surely they can't tunnel through these walls," Carson said.

"Oh, can't they? Of course they can! It's only rock and soil! What do you think they live in? They'll dig through that much quicker than your army could."

Ruler One continued down the belly of the GOT, passing several more doors as if they were not there.

"Stop!" shouted Marshal Carson. "Where are you going?"

But the ruler kept on.

"Take him," Carson said.

Sir Godfrey's long strides quickly brought him alongside the stout man. One hand grabbed the ruler's collar, pulling him backward and nearly off his feet a short distance from where the cavern narrowed, forking into two tines. He pressed cold steel against the man's throat.

"Listen carefully," the ruler said, choking. "The prattlers won't need to tunnel if these passages are not secure. Look at those doors!" He motioned toward a pair splintered from their hinges. "Is that your work?"

"Calm down," Sir Godfrey said, tightening his grip and shaking Ruler One. "This is the way we entered when we first attacked. The doors at the other end of that tunnel—the ones leading to the Lawless Lands—they've been barricaded. Nothing's getting through there."

"And the others?" asked Ruler One. "What about the others?"

"What others?" Carson asked.

"There are several passages leading to the outside world! This one to the left opens to the canyon's side. The rest, including the one that you crashed through, lead to the Lawless Lands. Doors chained and locked every night—that's all that keeps the prattlers from visiting us, do you hear? One hundred torches and two hundred barrels of lyla are just added precautions should they somehow stumble in while tunneling. They're guided by their senses! Do you understand? Repelled by heat and the scent of lyla! Attracted by sweat and blood! And what do they smell now? Only what you've spilled inside the GOT!" Ruler One was beside himself. "We need to get some lyla down here, now!"

"But they were not," Sir Godfrey said, lowering his sword.

"Not what?" said Ruler One.

"Locked." The knight pointed down the narrower tunnel with his sword, past the doors torn from their hinges. "This is the passage we came through, and we found the doors unlocked."

"Impossible!"

"They were unlocked, I say, with a dead man just inside the door! One of yours, wearing a white robe."

"A nom?"

"I don't know what that is," said Sir Godfrey.

"What about the other doors?" asked Ruler One, wringing his hands together.

"Other doors?"

"Yes! Have you not been listening? I'm telling you… there's more than one set that leads into the desert. If those your men came through were unlocked, what makes you think— *Shhh!* Listen!"

Carson held his breath. A faint scuffling from some far-off place swept briefly down the wider passageway.

Complete silence ensued until Sir Godfrey whispered. "What was that?"

Ruler One held up a hand, his head cocked.

The scuffling resumed, grew louder, and did not stop.

The sound of many, not one!

"Too late!" whispered Ruler One. "Turn around!" He pushed Sir Godfrey roughly. "Turn around!"

The scuffling turned quickly to a clattering, like the sound of countless pebbles being dropped into a bucket.

Far down the wider fork, a dark object spilled into the passageway, followed by a steady stream of others.

"Run!" cried Ruler One. "Run!"

Carson bolted back into the belly, Sir Godfrey at his side. They quickly pulled away from Ruler One, whose labored breathing was soon masked by the sound of gaining prattlers.

Carson glanced back to see them overtake the pudgy man.

"Gods, no! *Ahhh!*"

The cry was cut short, and when Carson next dared to look back, the ruler was gone, hidden somewhere beneath an undulating mound of black.

We're not going to make it! Center Court's too far away! Even if we reach it, there's no door to seal the prattlers out!

"There!" Sir Godfrey suddenly veered left, forcing Carson with his shoulder to do the same.

It loomed out of the belly's dark midst, the same solitary column of stone the knight had pointed out during the initial attack on the GOT. With a burst of speed, Sir Godfrey raced ahead of him, slamming into the stone column and fumbling at its surface. A door swung open. Carson rushed inside, Sir Godfrey's weight shoving him forward. He fell onto the ground as the door slammed shut. Sir Godfrey stood with both hands on the door pull, leaning backward.

Carson could barely see the outline of a staircase spiraling upward. The end of a thick rope dangled above his head. He rose to join Sir Godfrey.

"They can't get in, can they?"

"Listen," the knight said. The sound of hard-shelled bodies crashing against the door had stopped abruptly. "I think they've lost interest in us."

"Are they going back?"

"No." Sir Godfrey cracked the door to peer into the belly. "They're headed for Center Court!"

Carson swore. He could hear them scuttling across the cavern's floor. "How many do you think?"

"Hundreds... if not thousands," answered the knight.

The marshal swore again. "We've got to warn the others."

"Too late for that," said Sir Godfrey. "Help them, perhaps, but the prattlers are inside by now!"

"Tower within a tower; skinny reed; it's the smallest cock who crows the loudest," recalled Carson. "We're in the center of Takers Tower, yeah?"

Sir Godfrey nodded. "The king may be above us, still searching for the magister."

Marshal Carson started up the narrow stairs as quickly as he dared.

Sibil Dunn

It was growing ever darker. Sibil stepped over a lifeless soldier she had earlier slain defending Rolft. They were once more two floors from the top of Takers Tower, and in the company of sculptures.

Someone needs to say something! We cannot hunt all night!

She watched Fereliss spark a tuft of tinder. "Did you want to go again, Sire? Sweep the floors once more on our way down?" The royal guard blew embers into flames, then dropped them on the torch held out by Yurik. Its oil-soaked rags blazed orange and yellow.

"No." King Axil sighed as Yurik's torch brought to life another held by Garth. The monarch looked reluctantly at his surroundings. "What do you think, Miss Dunn?"

You're asking me? Surely you see the same as I, which is to say, not much. "The magister may still be here, Your Majesty, but if we could not find him in the light... what hope might we have now? Perhaps renew our search at dawn?"

"Yes, quite. Which is the way down, then?"

"Here, Your Highness." Rolft offered the monarch a hand.

"Step carefully, sire," said Fereliss. "There are bodies everywhere. This is what happens when Rolft and Thistle get together!"

"Who?" King Axil asked.

"Thistle, sire. It's what we call Miss—"

"*Shhh!*"

"What was that?" asked Garth.

"Listen!" said Yurik.

Sibil's heart began to race. *Could it be the magister?*

All five of her companions stood motionless, listening to the sound of torch flames licking oxygen.

Distant shouting rose above it, then screaming and more shouting, louder still.

"Is the battle on again?" asked Yurik.

"We need to see the grounds below," said Fereliss.

"The windcatcher!" said Sibil. "To the stairs, and up!"

The sound of bedlam below resounded through the tower's stairwell. The shouting and screaming had become constant, now somewhat muffled by a noise Sibil likened to a room full of cutlery dancing on plates absent food.

"Soldiers on the march!" said Yurik, his torch leading the group.

"Coming this way!" said Garth, his torch lighting the group's rear. Sibil moved in tandem with Rolft. *We could move faster, but your leg... and the king tires!*

"Up the stairs, and quickly!" shouted Garth.

"Not soldiers!" shouted Fereliss, pushing King Axil from behind. "Prattlers! Run, Your Majesty!"

Prattlers! Gods above! Sibil glanced back down the stairwell, its curvature and the shroud of night hiding most of its substantial length.

"We need to leave the stairs!" shouted Rolft.

"The last landing!" Sibil cried. "There should be a small room!" *Where the children were kept!*

"Run, Your Majesty!" A familiar voice, shouting from the dark below, had the opposite effect, causing all to stop and look back. Garth held his torch aloft as two shadowy figures rounded the lower stairwell's bend. "They're right behind us! Run, gods dammit! Run!"

Marshal Carson! Coming fast with someone else!

Sibil turned and ran, her small group gathering momentum once again.

King Axil grunted as he stepped onto the landing. His boot toe caught its lip, and he stumbled, taking Fereliss with him to the stone floor. Yurik turned to give them light. Rolft scrambled to assist the king.

"What are you waiting for!" yelled Marshal Carson, now just a dozen steps below them, Sir Godfrey by his side. "*Ru-u-un!*" Behind them, a black mound appeared, clattering as it shifted shape.

Garth raised his torch, and Sibil screamed. The undulating mound was a collection of shiny, black-shelled beasts, each twice the size of a cragen. Their segmented bodies clambered over one another on spindly legs as they clattered up the stairs.

Garth waved his torch in sweeping arcs, trying to ward them off as the marshal and Sir Godfrey passed him by. "They don't like fire!" he cried. *Whoosh!* The torch blustered as it moved from side to side. *Whoo-oosh!*

Sibil watched, mesmerized, until Rolft and Fereliss yanked her back across the landing, past Sir Godfrey, to where Yurik stood, his torch held high above an open doorway. Fereliss and Marshal Carson ushered King Axil inside the room.

"Garth!" Yurik said. "Leave it!"

Whoooo-ooosh! Garth threw his torch at the chittering heap of prattlers. Those it hit screeched and jumped; the torch's flames sputtered and died beneath a wave of clattering shells, and the mound of prattlers surged forward. Garth turned and ran, stumbled, and fell to one knee. Sir Godfrey helped him up, shoved him toward the door, and cleaved the head from an oncoming prattler. Several others scuttled over its body and enveloped the knight. Sir Godfrey's sword clattered on the stone floor, and he went down beneath a cluster of scrabbling shells.

"Sir Godfrey!" said Garth, turning back to help him.

"Leave him, Garth!" yelled Yurik.

But the young warrior was already knee deep in prattlers, his sword raised high above his head. One of the beasts butted him, its nose suddenly extending like a lance, piercing his stomach. Impaled, Garth issued a loud battle cry, brought his sword down hard into the prattlers back, then slumped on top of it. He disappeared beneath another wave of prattlers, and Yurik pulled the door shut.

Fereliss and Yurik took turns holding the door fast. It was bumped, scratched and banged relentlessly, but it could not be barred from inside. Loud chittering and the scrabbling of sharp claws against wood and stone served as constant reminders of what wanted to break through. Until the terrifying noises receded. Quickly, and without warning.

The quiet became insufferable.

"It's safe, do you think?" Sibil asked.

No answer came.

"Let me out," she said, shouldering her way to the door. "There's a windcatcher just above us. I'll go and have a look."

Someone grasped her arm. "Not so far you can't get back in time, yeah?" *Marshal Carson's voice.*

"Gods' speed," whispered Rolft. The door opened and Sibil stepped outside, one dagger at the ready. She glanced quickly down the dimly lit stairwell before scurrying up a spiral set of metal stairs to peer out the closest windcatcher.

A steady stream of torches flowed from the east, across the Lawless Lands, before spilling through the GOT's main gates and dispersing amidst rivulets of ebony, men, and more torches. Swords clashed. Shouting mixed with screaming.

She scurried down the stairs and nearly fell into Rolft's arms. He pulled her back into the little room and shut the door.

"Someone's broken through the gates!" she said. "I don't know if it's The Guild, or what it calls 'outsiders,' but there are lots of them! Hundreds! There's still fighting below—prattlers, too—but it looks as though Front Court's been captured!"

No one responded as the sound of footsteps echoed up the stairwell, stopping just outside the door.

A sudden rapping on its slats ensued.

Prattlers do not knock!

Sibil positioned herself to help create a barrier between the king and the door. With Yurik holding it closed, Fereliss withdrew his sword.

"Who's there!" he shouted.

A gravelly voice cleared itself before responding. "It's Marshal Ademar of Tegan, sir, in service to King Tygre—may all seven gods watch over him. And who might I be speaking with?"

Marshal Erik Carson

Carson's mind churned as he entered the School of Taking accompanied by Marshal Ademar. It had been a sleepless night, but with the rising of the sun had come a bit of clarity. Thirteen chairs were configured in a circle, and all but two had occupants. His bleary eyes roved those seated, confirming the attendance of all he had requested be present: Major Stronghart, Sir Parrish, Sir Dreddit; Sergeants Perill, Galeran and Stone; Fereliss and Yurik, Rolft, and Sibil Dunn.

As intended, King Axil sat outside its perimeter, not to exclude him from the discussion that would follow, but to prevent him from feeling out of place or inadequate, and because it was important to remind all present—including the king himself—of his stature. The chair prepared for him was not unlike the others, except it rested on a platform consisting of a table with its legs cut off, its top draped by a blanket, creating a crude throne of sorts.

"With your blessing, Your Majesty." The marshal assumed his place in the circle, gesturing to Ademar to take the empty seat beside him. King Axil spread his palms, signaling his permission to proceed.

"You'll please all welcome Marshal Ademar of Castle Tegan. Without him, we might none of us be here today." A chorus of appreciation followed, during which Carson collected his thoughts.

"We have much to do before we leave the GOT, and little time to do it. Seven tasks have come to mind. Each of you is asked to take the point on one and see it through. Should you encounter potholes, Major Stronghart and I shall help you to navigate them. Right, then: Sergeant Stone and Sir Parrish. What are we to do with the dead and wounded? You'll need to speak with the healers. How many can be moved? How long can the others survive here? Food, water, medicine. How much of what they need is already here? We need a plan. As for our dead, can we transport them back? If that is not feasible, their keepsakes are to be recovered for their loved ones, their bodies burned so that they are not feasted on by prattlers.

"Sergeant Galeran, the prattlers are old friends of yours, and therefore, your responsibility. Most of us will leave the GOT today, but I imagine the most gravely wounded will need to stay behind. You'll stay with them. Let Major Stronghart know how many men you'll need. Work with Sergeant Stone, Sir Parrish and the healers to determine how many wounded will remain, and where they'll stay. I want to know with certainty that they will not be bothered by the prattlers come evening.

"Miss Dunn, Rolft... you're under no obligation, but the next task is yours if you would have it. The children. And not just those few you found in Takers Tower, but the many now held above us. Most are still watched over by the God of Children. Do we take them with us when we leave today, or leave someone to watch over them until we can come back? Again, we need a plan. Can you shoulder that?" The two in question looked at one another and nodded. "Very good," Carson continued. "There are a dozen or so inside the school who are no longer children, which brings me to our next task: prisoners. With your approval, sire, any adult living within the GOT, or fighting on the GOT's behalf, shall be treated as such."

King Axil gave a slight nod.

Miss Dunn opened her mouth to speak, but the marshal cleared his voice, preempting her with a stern stare. *I'm one step ahead of you!*

"Very good, sire. What shall be their fate? Are The Guild's soldiers to be executed here? Transported back to Castle Aranox? What would you have us do with them, m'lord? And will there be exceptions?"

King Axil raised his eyebrows in question.

"The commoners fighting for The Guild," Carson said. "Most are poor, and were enticed with coin. We now know it was twenty kingshead to start. A handsome wage for most. And some are known to have turned their backs on The Guild and to have risked their lives for the realm once the fighting started. Some gave their all to fight beside your soldiers. Are we to provide them any dispensation for their change of heart? What about those not wearing The Guild's colors? House staff, stable hands, and the like?"

King Axil stroked his beard, then gestured to his scribe, who dipped his quill into fresh ink.

"We came to take a serpent's head," the monarch said, "not chase cooks and chambermaids. And certainly not children. Let it be known that the King of Aranox is just and merciful. Those under age shall be returned to their homes or to The God of Children's House. All others not in uniform—be they students of The Guild, GOT staff, or misguided subjects of the realm—are by right, prisoners one and all. But those willing to express remorse are hereby pardoned. They are to be set free and left to fend for themselves. It's a long journey back to Aranox or Tegan. Let the gods decide their fate."

"So be it, m'lord. And those unwilling to repent?"

"Shall share the fate of The Guild's soldiers. They are to be shackled and escorted to the quarry, where they can make amends for their remaining time among the living. And be useful whilst they do so."

"There is one, at least, undeserving of your mercy, sire." All heads turned to Miss Dunn.

Rolft placed a hand on her knee.

Carson held his tongue.

"Go on," the monarch said.

"A man called Penniluk, who, with his brother, beat Sir Tristan Godfrey to death, then boasted of that act."

Penniluk!

"He boasted, too, of his desire to fight against the realm," Miss Dunn continued. "I killed his brother myself, but one Penniluk left is one too many, sire."

"Penniluk," said the king. "Where have I heard that name before?"

"Shaun Penniluk, Your Majesty—the Prince of Quills," Carson said. "The man who penned the invitations to the Lords and Ladies Feast."

"Ah, yes. Killed by an assassin. He had brothers, did he?"

Rolft lent his voice to Sibil's. "Two, Your Majesty. I too heard the story of how they beat the Godfrey boy."

"My men as well," Carson said. "You can identify him?" he asked Miss Dunn.

"I can."

"Very well," said King Axil. "He is to be shackled and returned to Castle Aranox to answer for his crime."

Marshal Carson placed a hand on his counterpart's shoulder. "Marshal Ademar has offered to assist us with the prisoners. Sir Dreddit, you'll share the task with him." A smile spread across Sir Dreddit's face, intersecting with an old scar that ran from cheek to jawline.

"Sergeant Perill, you'll deal with the treasure. Ten vaults beneath us, each extending to the canyon, according to Ruler One. You'll need to break the locks to see, but how are we to move all that? We cannot leave it here for long. Not unguarded, anyway."

"There are wagons with wide wheels behind the GOT," said Sir Parrish. "I've seen them."

"So I'm told," said Carson. "No doubt how the treasure got here. But you'll need to speak amongst yourselves. Those wagons may be needed to transport the wounded or the children. Our last task, Your Majesty, will be assumed by Major Stronghart and myself. We have yet to find the magister, or Rulers Three and Four. They may still be hiding here; we may yet find their dead bodies. They may have escaped our net. Nevertheless, we shall not rest until they stand or lie before you."

"I don't doubt that," said the monarch. "Not for the time it takes one grain of sand to pass the hourglass. May all seven gods watch over you."

Sibil Dunn

Sibil stood in the middle of Center Court, her eyes roving rows of seated prisoners tethered to one another. She paid little heed to those wearing the drab green uniform of The Guild's army, separated to one side. What she was looking for would not be found among them.

Dark wavy hair to his neckline... blunt nose... square jaw. He isn't here! Look again—he has to be!

"No?" Rolft asked.

Sibil shook her head. *Disappointing!*

"Sergeant Stone and Sir Parrish are handling the dead," Rolft said. "We should search among them as well."

"It's possible the prattlers took him," said Sir Dreddit, a glint in his dark eyes.

"That would be a fitting end," Sibil said. She started back toward The Hidor and the School of Taking. *Wait a tick! Was that...?* She stopped and turned around.

"What is it?" Rolft asked. "Do you see him?"

Sarul! Sibil marched across the grounds, sidestepping some prisoners, stepping over others, until she reached a string of uniformed men sitting with their knees raised, hands bound to their feet, their backs against the rear courtyard wall.

Sarul's eyes were closed, his face and chest smeared with blood and dirt, his cheek cut, and his trousers torn. His waterspout stood erect, shining in the sun, but its feathers were all missing.

Sibil sat on her haunches in front of him and waited.

When he did not stir, she searched the ground, picked up a pebble and flicked it at his face.

Sarul's eyelids fluttered open.

A disdainful snort flared his nostrils. "Wisperal!"

"An old wives' tale," Sibil said.

"I knew I should have killed you!"

"Tell us where the magister is hiding, and the king may let you live."

Sarul sneered. "Let me live? Shackled in his quarry, cutting stone? I'd rather die!" The sneer turned to a smile. "Just the same, I'll tell you where the old man is. Not to court the king's mercy, but because it pleases me to do so." The warrior leaned forward the best he could, a broad grin exposing his white teeth. "He lives inside your heart, Wisperal! Look there, why don't you?" Sarul sat back, chuckling to himself.

"Words." Sibil picked up a larger stone and bounced it off the warrior's chest. "You know my other name, do you?"

"I don't care what your name is," Sarul said, still chuckling. "The magister lives in you!"

"Shut up!" Sir Dreddit pressed a bootsole against Sarul's chest and shoved him back against the wall.

"Seamstress of the night." Sibil rose to her feet. "That's my other name. Keep talking, and I'll be back tonight to sew your mouth shut!"

Marshal Erik Carson

A small gathering of soldiers loitered inside the belly of the GOT.

The splintered doors to the first treasure vault exposed a wall of burlap sacks, filled and neatly stacked on top of one another. If Ruler One had told the truth, the trove of treasure extended all the way to Reception Canyon. A large number of the sacks had already been removed and piled on the ground.

"What is it, Sergeant? What's wrong?" Carson asked.

Sergeant Perill gestured toward the bags piled near the soldiers. "This was but the first layer, Marshal." He kicked the lumpy pile, and it jingled. "They're full of coin, as one might expect. But those behind…" He approached the open doors, withdrew his knife, and jabbed it into the remaining wall of burlap. As the blade wriggled free, a stream of sand escaped the sack and cascaded to the ground. The sandfall slowly stopped, but not before the sergeant had created several more in different places on the wall.

"Nothing but sand!" he said. "The whole lot of them!"

THE TALE OF A DOG

"Hasten not another's death whose grip on you is firm."
Sergeant Arthur Cogswell

Overseer Reynard Rascall

Reynard woke to the sound of creaking carriage wheels and muted voices in the street. A band of sunlight brightened Ruler Two's still empty bed. The saddle bags, presumably still full of kingsheads, were propped against the wall.

The overseer rolled over, the sight of Charise's smooth, bare backside helping him recall the previous evening.

He lightly touched her shoulder, and she stirred.

"Are you ready to tell me why you need me?" he asked.

"Last night wasn't evidence enough?" One of Charise's hands reached back to grope his stomach.

"I'm talking about The Guild's treasure."

"Of course you are." The assassin's hand strayed lower.

Reynard writhed. "I'll make you a deal. Help me kill King Axil and I'll help you get your gold."

"*Our* gold. We're as good as partners now. But I told you, I've no interest in killing the king. Besides, I wouldn't worry about him if I were you."

"Really. Why's that?" Reynard closed his eyes as her fingers became active again.

"Didn't I tell you? He's on his way to the GOT, together with his army. If the magister's soldiers don't kill him, the prattlers may."

Reynard scoffed.

"You don't believe me?" Her hand stilled.

"Oh, I believe you. It's just that..." Reynard chuckled. "Are you listening to yourself? If the king's army is on its way to the GOT, then we haven't a prayer of getting our hands on that treasure."

"Why would you say that?" Charise nuzzled him, nibbling his shoulder.

"Are you serious? We might have taken it from those vaults a moon ago. But now? Do you really think the magister and his soldiers can withstand the king's army? I'd not bet on that. And if the king secures the treasure, it will be a trick to take it from him."

"Mmm. But that's the beauty of it all, you see? It doesn't really matter who wins this war."

"On that much, we agree. Because if by some miracle the magister finds a way to keep his plunder, by the time we come up with a plan, he'll have fortified those vaults and doubled his guard."

"I'll let you in on a little secret, shall I?" Charise rolled over and draped an arm across Reynard's chest.

"Let me guess... you're a raving lunatic?"

"Hurtful. But I see how things might look to you. No, that's not it at all. Guess again." She twirled his chest hair with one finger.

"I'd rather not," Reynard said.

"Fine. It's not there."

"What? What's not where?"

"The treasure, silly. The Takers' gold. It isn't at the GOT."

Reynard laughed and, escaping her embrace, swung his legs until he was sitting on the bed's edge, his back to her. "Now I know you're mad! Or grossly misinformed by our friend, Two. Trust me, the gold is there."

"It's not."

"Stop! I've seen it, Charise! Seen it with my own eyes. Do you understand?"

"You thought you saw it."

"No! Gods dammit, woman! You're not listening! I was taken to the tunnels by the magister himself, do you hear? I watched as one of ten vaults was opened for my viewing, and I gazed upon the treasure locked inside the same way I'm looking at you now. Shall I describe what I saw for you? The height of the doors? The shimmer of gold? I know what I saw!"

"Really? What did you see when I dropped my dress last night?"

"What?"

"Did it relieve you? What did you see? An assassin who could kill you just as easily naked and unarmed? Or did you see what you wanted to—a woman willing to pleasure you? Wooden doors—meaningless, would you not agree? A wall of gold behind them? Just how much treasure did you lay eyes on, really?"

Reynard was silent.

"I'm told those vaults are tunnels themselves, and that they extend all the way to the edge of Reception Canyon," Charise said.

"That's right."

"And that they're filled with treasure, all ten of them."

"Yes. I was told the same."

"You saw the entire length of the vault you were shown, did you? All the way to Reception Canyon?"

"Of course not. How could I? It's so full of gold you can't get past the door!"

"Then how much treasure did you really see?"

"What are you getting at?"

"And who did you say showed it to you? The magister? The master of illusion himself?"

Reynard considered the possibilities. "But it does exist."

"Of course it does. You yourself have been contributing to the magister's wealth for almons, have you not?"

"All right, I'll bite, if only out of curiosity. If it's not buried beneath the GOT, where is it?"

"Ahhh, therein lies the mystery. If I knew that, I wouldn't need you as my partner, would I?" Charise sat up and scooted next to him.

"Five didn't know?" asked Reynard.

"No. He'd only just discovered the magister's charade himself. He was fairly certain Two was in the dark, but wasn't sure about the other so-called rulers. One of them designed the tunnels. Another runs the army and oversees all that enters and leaves the GOT. Yet another maintains its finances. Any or all of them may know, but it was clearly not the magister's intention to share his wealth with all. Five sought payment for his continued silence, but the magister secured it the old-fashioned way."

"So you've no idea where the money is?"

"No, but I've a very good idea as to who can help me find it." She retraced Reynard's scar with her finger.

"Do tell."

"Five was fairly certain the money never made it to the GOT. A trickle found its way there, to be sure. An occasional display of wealth entering the compound helped maintain the desired illusion; just a wagon-load now and then to fill the fronts of all ten vaults, to pay the soldiers and the staff, and to maintain the appearance of unlimited wealth available for any purpose at any time."

"But that means…"

"Yes! Most of what The Guild has taken—the riches amassed from your takers and your gatherers, from you and every other overseer—has never been destined for the GOT. It's all been siphoned off to somewhere else!"

"And that's why you need me."

"That's right! You see it now, don't you? The key to finding The Guild's treasure lies in what happens soon after the money leaves your hands! If your offerings aren't headed to the GOT when you kiss them farewell, just where are they bound?"

Reynard could not think straight. "I've no idea."

"And if you did, why tell an assassin breathing down your neck, eh?" Charise expelled a puff of warm air just below his earlobe.

"That's not it. Honestly, until just now, I would have said the GOT. But…" Reynard held a finger up. "That doesn't mean there's not a trail to follow, and a clear one at that."

"Ahhh!" Charise sighed, leaning her warm body into his. "Spectacular! Where do we begin?"

There was something warm and welcoming about Waterford, even on a cold night. A friendly moon. The outlines of familiar buildings against a starry sky. Reynard walked briskly, keeping to the center of the street lest he turn an ankle in narrow ruts carved by countless carriages and wagons. Spiro would have had to trot to keep up, but Charise strolled casually alongside him. *Gods above, her legs are longer than mine!*

Without giving notice, he stopped at the mouth of an alley and removed his coat. Handing it to Charise, he rolled one shirtsleeve up to his elbow before plunging his arm into a rain barrel beneath the eaves of a small shop.

"What are you doing?" Charise watched in amusement as he groped inside the barrel.

"Fishing," he said, soon withdrawing a key from the watery depths.

"It's a rather small haul, is it not?" Charise handed him his jacket.

"I'm not a big fish eater. This way."

"But I am," she said, trailing him down the cobblestones.

"Are you? Then you're going to love my place of work. It's on the docks, and it's literally swimming with the creatures. You can find any size you like there."

"You're going to cook one for me, are you?"

"I'm not. I hate the smell. I'll not have it in my house."

"That's not very romantic."

"Romantic! You want romantic? I'll take you to dine aboard *The Gusto*, shall I? The cook is from the Northern Isles, and you've never tasted better. You can have your fish cooked any way you like while I digest my chops. We'll drink the finest spirits and watch the mermaids dance beneath the moon until we're drunk. How's that?"

"Delicious!"

Reynard stopped in front of a low stone wall fronting a large masonry building. An opening in the wall served as a gateway to the path he began to tread.

Charise shadowed him as he ambled to the building's front door.

"Do you always fish your key out of that barrel?" she asked. "Wouldn't it make more sense to hide it somewhere closer?"

"Don't be silly. I normally carry one on my person. But when you're dragged to the king's dungeon to be tortured, they take everything that wasn't yours when you were born. And then they start taking that which was. It's quite uncivilized, really."

He placed the key into the front door lock. "This one's for emergencies." He fumbled a bit with the key. "And no, you don't want to hide it too close to the keyhole, lest someone find it and match the pair."

"You were tortured at Castle Aranox?"

"To the edge of Baelon below. It's not something I'd recommend." Reynard pushed the door open and stepped inside. It did not matter that he could not see. The dark reached out to greet him like an old friend, and he found his way into the study.

"What was that like?" He could hear Charise feeling her way behind him.

"There's nothing to compare it to, and thank the gods for that. Here." He found her hand. "Sit and I'll make a fire." He guided Charise onto a chaise lounge, then felt for the timber mantel upon which he kept his tinderbox.

The sharp rapping of firesteel against flint sent sparks flying. Those landing on a tuft of dried grass fibers caused it to smolder before bursting into flame. The burning tinder lived long enough to light a candle that Reynard used to ignite the fireplace.

"Sorry," he said. "It won't be long now. This room heats quickly."

He joined Charise, already stretched out on the chaise, and she made room for him.

"I'm still curious about this, you know." She lightly traced the scar on Reynard's forehead with a fingertip. "How ever did you come by it?"

Reynard brushed his bangs back. "It was a gift, I suppose. Given to me by several hoodlums on the docks."

Charise grinned. "A gift, you say!"

"That's how I've come to think of it, yes."

"Well, now I really am intrigued. There's a story, is there?" She snuggled closer to him.

"It's an old tale now. Nearly fifteen almons old. It was late, and I was headed home along the waterfront, listening to the lapping of the waves upon the shore, mindful of three men striding after me, intrigued by the young boy chasing after them, screaming at the top of his lungs. A steady, strident stream of insults, threats, obscenities. It wasn't something easily ignored, believe you me, but the three men didn't seem to care. Preoccupied, they sped past me and barred my way, demanding my purse. And when I refused, they gave me this." Reynard massaged his forehead, as though to relieve some pain. "They would have done far worse, I'm sure... perhaps killed me. But by now the boy has caught up to us, you see, and he's in an awful mood. He doesn't stop his screaming, and he's carrying a pocket knife. You know, the kind you use for whittling, or cutting string? And these three large thugs with their daggers meant for cutting flesh attack him like a butcher might a carcass. But he's much too quick for them, and quite adept at using his small knife. He doesn't stop his screaming until he's stabbed them all to death and he's standing over them."

"They'd robbed him too, had they?"

"No."

"Hurt him, then?"

"No. Turns out they'd kicked his dog."

Charise tightened her embrace. "They killed his dog?"

"No. Just kicked it. Once, for fun."

Charise laughed. "He killed them... three men... for kicking his dog?"

"Yes."

"Touching. But you've not explained why you consider the scar a gift."

"Ah, yes, well, I took pity on him... the boy, that is. It's not every day a street urchin saves your life, you know. I took him in. Him and his dog. The dog was old and died soon after. But the boy became a man under my tutelage. He was a steadfast companion, and despite all our adventures, I never once feared for my life when he was near. I never would have met him were it not for those three hoodlums." Reynard tapped his forehead. "That's why I consider this a gift."

"Steadfast companion? Where is he now?"

"Dead, by King Axil's decree."

"Ahhh. I did wonder what your motivation was. A Guild overseer hunting down a king—it made little sense to me. Did you ask to be involved, or was it the magister who requested your assistance?"

"He sought my help. Saved me, in fact, so that I could do his bidding."

"Stranger still, don't you think, given all his options? Especially now you know the fate of Ruler Five? The magister's using you, you know. But why?"

"Yes, but no more than I'm using him. What do I care, so long as it all ends with the king dying?"

"Is avenging your friend more important to you than the money? If so, and this assumes, of course, that the king survives his journey to the GOT, I'll kill him for you… for just half your rightful share of the treasure."

"Help me kill two others and you have a deal."

"Tempting! Two others? You've already killed King Tygre. We're running out of royalty. Who else would you see die?"

"One of King Axil's royal guardsman, and a young woman who befriends him."

"The one they call The Wisperal?"

"The Wisperal! I've no idea. I only know she's friends with a royal guardsman who goes by the name of Rolft. I could have sworn I saw her just the other day!"

"I wouldn't be surprised. The one I'm speaking of, the one they call The Wisperal, she rides with The Guild's army now."

"What? I knew it! I did see her, then! Traveling to the GOT with a horde of well-armed men. And yet that makes no sense! None at all! Is she not a servant of King Axil?"

"If you can believe the stories… which I'm not sure you can. This much I know: one of the king's men is looking for her. A big man, not without a certain set of skills. Why he's seeking her, I didn't ask—to kill her, perhaps?"

Reynard's head began to spin. It took a while for it to stop, at which point he realized Charise had gone silent as well. "You're all right, are you?" he asked.

"What? Oh. Yes, I'm fine. I was just thinking, is all." Her large brown eyes widened. "You've a plan, have you? For finding our gold?"

"I do. It's simple, really. I operate three territories for The Guild: north, south and inland. A percentage of what I collect from them is due to the magister each moon. I make that payment rain or shine, feast or famine. No excuses. The Guild collects regardless of my circumstances, and the next payment is due two suns hence."

"They come here to collect?"

"No. Never here. Always at my place of work. On the docks."

"And where does it go from there?"

"Well, that's the question, isn't it? I've always assumed it traveled to the GOT. If, as you suggest, that's not the case, discovering where it does go should be a simple exercise, don't you think?"

"We follow it?"

"That's the plan." Reynard adjusted the position of his legs, laying one across Charise. "We follow it."

Reynard sat alone on the edge of the wooden table on which he had killed gatherer Kasparr. His legs dangled freely beneath him in silent tribute to Spiro. The glow of a single candle provided little light as he surveyed the bleak surroundings of his rented space: two large bags of coins resting by his side; a well-used door leading to a worn, exterior staircase; three desks, a few chairs he rarely used; useless shelving; some pulleys draped over ceiling rafters; and the windows overlooking Waterford's wharf.

The pervasive stench of rotting fish.

It was all so familiar.

And yet, without Spiro present, somehow not the same at all.

Reynard ran a finger along a deep scratch in the table's surface.

Spiro's voice could stay silent no longer. *"You know, don't you—my absence can be traced to this very room!"*

"Ah, your ghost now haunts this place as well, does it?"

"There isn't a place we've been together that it does not."

"I'm beginning to realize that."

"But this is where the end began, Reynard... you realize that?"

"A disturbing truth. Yes! "

"And it had little to do with my own penchant for violence."

"Must you rub my nose in it?"

"Ah, well, at least now you know the difference between gaff and gaffe, eh? That's something!"

The hand Reynard had used to embed a large steel hook in Kasparr's throat began to tremble. *"A colossal blunder indeed! My apologies, friend!"*

The dull thud of bootsoles on old wood joined a jaunty whistling. A creaking stair preceded a moment's silence. A soft knock on the door sent Spiro away.

"Come in," said Reynard.

A solitary figure in dark clothes and a heavy cloak soon blocked the opened doorway.

"Overseer Rascall? Evenin', sir."

Reynard had heard that gruff voice once a moon for the past several almons. He pictured the man it belonged to before he moved into the candle's light. Square jaw, short, well-cropped hair and beard sprouting like the stiff bristles on a new push broom. Reynard's legs remained dangling as the man removed his gloves.

"Good evening to you." Reynard shook the proffered hand.

"You're all alone tonight, are ya?" asked the courier. "Where's your friend? Spiro, is it?"

"Indisposed, I'm afraid."

"Ah, well, I'll not keep you, sir. It's nasty soup out there tonight, so we're making haste." He nodded toward the candle. "You'd do well to find yourself a bigger fire. And somethin' warm ta drink!"

"I'll do that, thank you." Reynard lifted the satchels of coins and handed them to the courier. "And these are for you." He offered the man two kingshead.

"Thank you, sir. Most generous!"

"Until next moon," Reynard said out of habit.

"It's been a pleasure, sir, but you'll not see me next moon. This is my last run."

Reynard's eyebrows jumped. "And why is that?"

"Not my doing, sir. I do wonder the same. Perhaps I'm being replaced."

"Surely you asked why."

"I did, sir."

"And?"

"Well, I don't suppose there's any harm in telling you, but I was asked to accept a rather handsome sum in lieu of hearing any proper answer to that question."

"I see."

"Yes, well, I'd best be off."

"Yes. Fare well." Reynard watched the courier's cloak billow and twirl before it disappeared through the door. The man's whistling resumed, as did the drumming of his boots on the stairs.

Reynard pinched the candle's wick, lowered his feet to the floor, and counted slowly to twenty before moving to a narrow window overlooking nothing but gray. *Nasty soup out there tonight!*

"Noggods!" Reynard located his turncoat on a peg beside the door, then listened to ensure that all was quiet before exiting the building. Greeted by a thick cloud, he scurried down slick stairs with too light a grip on the handrail. He slipped and stumbled near the bottom. Cursing, he regained his balance as his feet hit solid ground.

Charise appeared from nowhere to help steady him.

"Hurry!" she whispered. "He's already disappeared into the fog!"

"Hurry, you say! I nearly killed myself just now! Where are the horses?"

"Exactly where we left them, of course."

Reynard peered in the direction he presumed the courier had gone, but the fog only grew thicker. Were it not for the sound of water lapping against ship hulls, and the abhorrent stench of fish, he might have been standing most anywhere.

"There's no rush. He and his partner always come and go by wagon," he said, reassuring himself, if not Charise. "Trust me, they're headed back this way."

Reynard halted his plodding horse as the couriers' wagon rolled to a stop near the far end of a street well east of the wharf.

Charise sidled her mount close to his. "They're picking up another payment to The Guild, are they?"

"Not possible," said Reynard, watching the couriers leave the wagon and disappear into a building. "My gatherers collect from all who owe The Guild in these parts. There's naught but taverns down there. They've probably stopped to float their corks. We'll wait a tick."

It did not take long for Charise to begin squirming in her saddle. "Who leaves a wagon full of gold coins unattended?" she asked. "In the middle of the night, no less?"

"Most peculiar, indeed," muttered Reynard, urging his horse forward.

"Might they be trying to give us the slip?"

"Without the coin?" Reynard scoffed. *Still, something's not right!*

The clip-clop of their horses' hooves went silent as they came upon the wagon. The couriers were nowhere to be seen.

"Curiously careless," said Reynard, dismounting. He drew back the leather tarp, leaned over the wagon's sideboards and jabbed his dagger into one of the sacks furthest from him. A stream of dry material skittered out the incision and onto his hand. "What in Baelon?" he whispered.

"What is it?" asked Charise, still astride her horse.

Reynard drew his knife hand back and rubbed it with the other. *Sand?* He glanced quickly toward the tavern's door before slicing the side of a closer sack. A gritty stream flowed from it as well. He groped and kneaded the other sacks within reach.

"Wait here!" He pulled the tarp back into place and sheathed his dagger. "Don't let this wagon out of your sight. I'll be back posthaste."

He brushed all evidence of sand from his hands and clothes before pulling the door to the tavern open. There were, not surprisingly, few patrons inside. Both relieved and confused, he found his way to the table occupied by the couriers.

"Mister Rascall!" The man who had received the satchels of coin from him put his drink down. "What is it? Have you been following us, sir?" The man's partner looked on with minimal interest.

Think! Think! "Yes. Yes, I'm afraid so. It's just, well... I fear I may have handed you the wrong satchels, you see, and in so doing, short-changed The Guild."

"*What?*"

"Inadvertently, of course. I'd never do so on purpose."

"No, sir, I don't believe you would. The Guild doesn't take kindly to being short-changed."

"Just so," said Reynard, sighing. "I was hoping to catch you and make things right, but your wagon—I didn't want to go rummaging through it without you."

"Ah, yes. In any case, I'm not sure I can help you. That's not the wagon you want, sir."

"It isn't?"

"No, sir. You'll want the wagon we left at the docks."

"What?"

"Yes, sir. That's how it works. You're always our last stop. We leave everything we've collected in that wagon there at the docks. Quite a ways from your place. We trade it for another waiting for us there. The one sitting just outside now. I suppose I can tell you—this being our last run, and you being an overseer and all—it's full of sand, sir. Otherwise, we'd not abandon it like this! No, sir, we wouldn't!"

"Sand!" Reynard feigned ignorance.

"Yes, sir. You're free to look, if you like. Once or twice each almon, we're told to take what we've collected back to the Borderlands, but most moons we go there with what I've just mentioned."

"Do tell."

"Yes, sir."

"My coin's still on the docks, then?"

"Just so, sir. Along with all the rest that we collected."

"Where does it go from there? In case I need to follow it."

"Oh, that I couldn't say, sir. That's the whole point, isn't it... to stop it being followed? It doesn't move until we're gone."

Noggods! Reynard stared off. *What are the odds of finding a wagon The Guild wants to stay hidden? In the clutter of the docks, no less, in the dark and heavy fog?*

"You'd best hurry, sir. I doubt that wagon stays there very long."

"I'll pay you," said Reynard.

"What's that?" The man returned his drink to the table.

"I'll pay you to show me where you left it."

"Oh, I dunno about that," said the man. "We've got to be getting on."

"Surely your partner can manage without you for a bit? It shouldn't take long. You can catch him up."

The man's companion rolled his eyes and spat on the floor.

"How am I going to do that, sir? I've no horse to travel either way. No, I don't think that—"

"You can take my associate's," said Reynard. "It's right outside. And once we've parted ways, you can keep the horse."

The seated courier adopted an apologetic expression, spreading his hands wide. "I'm sorry, Mr. Rascall, really I am." His partner shook his head and rose to leave.

"Fifty kingshead," said Reynard.

"Fifty kingshead!" The seated courier turned to his companion for approval.

"And fifty for your partner, to mitigate the inconvenience he will suffer," added Reynard, quickly withdrawing from his pocket a small leather pouch. *This looks familiar, yes? You know I'm good for it!*

The partner's eyes grew wide. His beefy rump returned to his chair with a loud thud.

He raised his glass in a salute, first to his friend, then to Reynard, before bringing it slowly to his lips. "Bide your time."

"There!" The courier pointed to a half-dozen wagons positioned beside a barn-like building set back from the wharf.

Reynard stopped counting. *Eleven docks north of my place.*

"That's where we left it," said the courier.

Reynard's misgivings mounted. There wasn't another soul or horse in sight. The wagons were all empty.

"You're quite sure?" he asked, making his way through the mist to stand beside them.

"As sure as the sun sets, Mister Rascall. I know they all look much the same to you, but if all you did in life was drive them, well..." He ran a calloused hand along the wagon's sideboard as he circled the contraption.

"This is the gal you're after, no doubt about it. I can tell you without looking that her toeboard's got a hole in it. Her rein hitch has been sheared off, and on the side you're on right now, if you look closely, you'll find there's a pin missing from one of its cleats."

Reynard did not bother asking what a cleat pin was. The courier could be taken at his word, a fact the man seemed eager to prove. By the time Reynard arrived at the wagon's front, the driver's little finger was wriggling around in a knothole in the toeboard. "You see?" he said. "And no rein hitch, neither. It's gone missing... just like your coin, I'm afraid."

Reynard rested his forearms on the wagon's sideboard, allowing his head to hang between them.

A light breeze stirred the stench of fish.

"Well..." The courier coughed awkwardly. "I'd best be off, sir."

"Yes, quite." Reynard straightened, brushing his long bangs back out of his eyes. He tossed a leather pouch onto the toeboard, its contents clinking as they settled.

"I'm much obliged, Mr. Rascall." The courier gathered the pouch and mounted Charise's rented horse. "I do hope you'll set things straight with The Guild."

"You can count on it," muttered Reynard, watching him ride off.

The street where he had left Charise was empty, the fog lifting to reveal dark shadows and glistening masonry. The couriers' wagon load of sand was gone. No doubt, Charise had sought shelter from the cold. Reynard hitched his horse to a rail and went inside.

The place was empty, save for the keeper, Charise, and two others with whom she was engaged in lively conversation. Even seated, one appeared to be—quite possibly—the largest man Reynard had ever seen. Black and bald, a pair of silver earrings dangling near his cheeks, he sat a short ways from the table, his knees too tall to fit below it. His huge frame hid his chair, but not the hatchets hanging from his hips. *Assassin! And that little thing whispering in Charise's ear, all dressed in fur and frowns... is that a child? Clearly, he—no, she—is too young to be in the business of killing. Gods above, she's barefoot! And staring at me!*

The odd couple stood, their conversation with Charise clearly terminated prematurely by Reynard's arrival.

Both appeared to judge him in passing, the girl's frown unaffected by her findings, the giant bumping Reynard's chest with his hip. *Was that on purpose? Some sort of message? Definitely the biggest man I've ever seen!* Reynard regretted even a brief exchange with the giant's eyes.

The tavern emptied as Charise came to his side.

"Friends," she said, as though it explained everything.

"What did they want?" asked Reynard.

"They came bearing news."

"Do tell."

"Perhaps we should retire to your place." Charise glanced toward the barkeep. "Where we can speak more freely." She draped a slender arm across his shoulder and guided him toward the pub's door. "Did you at least find what we were looking for?"

Reynard half expected the gold serpent wrapped around her wrist to come alive.

Delicately removing her arm, he encouraged her to precede him out the tavern. "I'll share my news when you share yours, shall I?" Still inside the doorway, he took a long look down both ends of the street.

Charise laughed. "They're long gone. And I told you, they're friends. If anything, they're looking out for you."

"Like a pair of hawks looking out for their next meal, perhaps." Reynard climbed into the saddle.

He offered Charise his hand and the use of one stirrup. She swung effortlessly into position behind him, her long arms encircling his torso.

"Come now," she whispered. "If I wanted you dead, I could have killed you a hundred times over by now." She nibbled on his ear, pulling at it gently with her teeth.

A most reassuring thought, indeed! Gods above!

Reynard gave life to a candle, set it on his study's smokewood desk, and started pacing the room. "I'm listening. What kind of news? Your friends did not look happy."

"Nor will you be," said Charise. "Our friend, Two. He's not dead, after all."

"What!" Reynard stopped moving altogether. "How can that be? You said you killed him!"

"I said that he would not be coming back. To be fair, I did say that to mean that he was dead." Charise tried the desk chair out for size.

"And?" Reynard held his hands out in disbelief.

"He got away." She opened the desk drawer to inspect its contents.

"He got away?" Reynard's hands moved to his aching head. "He got away? That can only mean you held him captive at some point! Is that right? You had him in your clutches? And he managed to escape?" Charise let him rant. "How is that possible? Where were you when all this happened? How is it that you're learning this just now?"

"Two came to see me that night, when you and I first met. We spoke. I sent him off with one of my assassins... to be killed. I left."

"And?"

Charise closed the desk drawer. "We should have bound his hands."

Reynard threw his own into the air. "You think? A man who teaches trickery? A master of illusion? What were you thinking?"

"Clearly, I was not. But even you called him a buffoon."

"In comparison to me, perhaps, but he is still a member of The Guild's High Order, and he didn't get there fumbling and bumbling about."

"It would appear that we both misjudged him."

"Even so, one might think a trained assassin could keep the upper hand once given it. Who did you send to kill him? That little girl?"

"Perhaps I should have. She's more reliable and skilled than most."

"Two escaped one of your assassins! Gods above, that's rich! However did he manage?"

"Inkollar. He must have had a pocketful." Charise held a palm level to her mouth and blew upon it. "One breath of it and you can breathe no more. It's quite rare, and its nickname is well-earned: hangman's noose."

"Are you telling me Two killed him? What did you say your group was called? The League of Asses?"

"Be careful, Reynard. I can't say I'm any more impressed by you to date. You promised gold, but all we've chased so far is sand."

Reynard slumped into a chair. "That's fair. Point taken." He thought for a moment. "Where is Two now?"

"If I knew that, we wouldn't be having this conversation."

"Perhaps he's still in Chalmsworth. Perhaps he's headed back to see the magister," said Reynard.

"Without having killed King Axil? Knowing that the GOT is under siege? Please. Does he know you live here?"

"What? No, I don't believe so. You don't think he's coming here, do you?"

"Why not? As far as he knows, the two of you still share a common goal. It's me he won't be pleased with."

Reynard put a finger to his lips. "Those two in the tavern. Why did they come to warn you, if you've turned your back on them?"

"I told you, we're friends. I haven't turned my back on them, just The League."

"You can do that?"

"Asks the overseer who's turned his back on The Guild of Takers."

"Another point well made. The girl... Seriously, she looked to be a child."

"You needn't worry about her. She's not as young as she appears, and it's her life, not yours. It's what she knows. The work suits her."

"But not you."

"I've had enough. I'm leaving it behind. And you're helping me, presumably. What happened on the waterfront?"

Reynard drew in a long breath. "The wagon was there, but in the time it took to find, someone had unloaded it."

"Empty?"

"Just so."

"So we wait until next moon. Enlist one or two lookouts to help us watch the docks. Follow your courier more closely. We won't make the same mistake again."

Reynard shook his head. "I'm not sure we'll get another chance. He said it was his last run."

"So what? We wait for his replacement."

"It didn't sound like that. More like The Guild has changed its plans."

"We can still find it," Charise said hopefully. "It can't have gotten far. Are there buildings near the wagon? We can go back. You can pick the locks, can you not?"

Reynard cradled his head in both hands, his fingers massaging his scalp. "I've already been inside the one closest. As soon as the courier left me, I gave it a quick look. Nothing. Do you know how many buildings front the wharf? How easy it would be to hide the coin inside them? It may be on a ship by now, for all we know. Or on its way to Summerfield or Chalmsworth."

"I suppose anything is possible." Charise pursed her lips.

"Unbelievable," Reynard muttered. "I've been doing this for so many almons, and not once did it occur to me to follow the couriers."

"Why would it?"

"At least you were right about it not going to the GOT."

"Did you doubt me?"

"Are you serious?"

"That's so unfair, Reynard! Assassins are among the most trustworthy people you will meet. We've little to fear from the truth. Or anything else, for that matter. Whereas a thief, it seems to me, might have a lot to gain from telling falsehoods. Would he not?"

"Are you saying you don't trust me?"

"Are you saying that I can?"

"Most assuredly! We're as good as partners in this now."

"What, like you and Two?" Charise scoffed.

"He never earned that honor, and I've never stiffed a partner. Not only can you trust me, you can count on me."

"For what?"

"For most anything, I suppose."

"You'll befriend me and my dog, will you?" she asked sarcastically.

"I would. Do you have a dog?"

"I'll get one if you like."

"Please don't. Not on my account. They're far too much work."

"What will you do if Two shows on your doorstep?"

"Hold my breath and watch his hands, for starters. I don't think he has a clue about the money, but I shall ask him nonetheless."

"And then?"

"Kill him, of course. I can only hold my breath so long!"

A sleepless night had drained Reynard. The Waterford Wharf appeared sympathetic to his plight. As though out of respect, it hung thick banks of fog over land and water, obscuring anything not clinging to those surfaces. The hulls of ships faded into white, their decks and masts invisible. Sailors, dockworkers, travelers, and fishermen; tradespeople, businessmen, street hawkers, and shoppers—all bustled about their business more quietly than usual. Though crowded and alive, the entire place seemed subdued and lost in thought.

Were you not strolling this very wharf a mere two moons ago with Spiro, planning to catch and kill a taker thought to have stolen a few kingshead from The Guild? Now, here you are—an overseer, no less—plotting to relieve The Guild of its entire treasury yourself!

The irony of it all was not lost on him. When had everything gone sideways? How had it come to this?

A dusty, bumpy trip to fargin Fostead! Godsdamn Kasparr and his worthless bookkeeper! If only they had kept a better handle on taker Raggett Grymes! A royal guard and his pet bitch! That creepy spider from the GOT and the gold web he's been weaving! And now, an assassin by your side? What next!

Reynard raked his hair back and stared into Baelon above. *Listen to the voice of reason: Pack it in. Cut your losses. Walk away!*

"Ah, but we don't tuck our tails between our legs! We don't leave loose ends untied!"

"Are you mocking me, Spiro?"

Several seagulls laughed while circling above.

Charise chimed in between vicious bites of bright red bism. "I'm trying to decide which is more sour—this piece of fruit, or you." She gnawed another chunk, made a face, and tossed the pome across the wharf. "Definitely you."

"Kill her!"

"Enough, Spiro! She's not nearly as obnoxious as you were! And she's far more pleasing to the eye!"

Charise kept on. "We're wasting time, you know."

"You've a better plan, have you? What would you have me do? I'm all ears."

"Visit another overseer? Ask what they might know about the path their money takes once it leaves their hands?"

Reynard sighed heavily. "Is this the way your mind works? They don't know any more than me, and even if they did, they wouldn't talk."

"How can you be sure?"

"Because I know The Guild, Charise! Because that's the way this business runs. Because if another overseer came asking me that sort of question, I'd think it very queer, and my answer would be ambiguous at best. It would arouse my curiosity… make me wonder what he was up to. In fact, I might follow him and start asking questions of my own. And we don't need that, do we?"

"No. One moody overseer's quite enough."

"Is that right? You're no prize yourself, today. The whole idea was to blend in. Wander up and down the wharf as if we both belong. Why couldn't you have worn a dress?"

"I don't see any dresses here! Not a single one. Besides, I told you. I've never worn a dress. I never will. And that's the end of it!"

"You should've borrowed some of my clothes, then."

Charise compared the length of her arm to one of Reynard's. "You can't be serious. It's almons since I fit in little boys' clothes."

"Ha-hah! Suit yourself. But that fur of yours is going to smell like fish forever more. Don't say I didn't warn you! You'll be turning heads and noses wherever you go now."

Before Charise could respond, Reynard hailed a man fiddling with a wagon's tongue outside the building he had broken into the previous evening.

"Good day to you, sir! Would this be the place to rent a wagon?" He could not help but look to see whether the toeboard of the vehicle being worked on had a knothole. It did not.

"It might be," said the man. "For what purpose, and how long would you be needing one?"

"That depends. But if, let's say, it was to carry sacks of silver buttons from the Isles, could you store my wares for me a sun or two whilst I bargained with my tailors?"

"No, sir. We don't store nuthin' here. Just rent the wagons, is all. You want storage, you see Kannard three docks down."

Reynard tipped an imaginary cap. "Much obliged, sir. Good day to you." He spun to smirk at Charise. "And that," he said, triumphantly walking away, "is how it's done!"

"As if you've actually accomplished something!" Charise strode after him.

"Oh, my..." Reynard stopped suddenly, his attention fully diverted.

"What is it?"

"Hang on!" Reynard gripped her wrist and pulled.

"What is it? Reynard!" Despite her protestation, the assassin allowed herself to be dragged behind tall stacks of crated produce.

"There! Look! The woman in that wagon!"

"Which wagon? Where?"

"There, godsdammit! The woman with the busy hands!"

Reynard used his own to swivel Charise's head toward the ocean and moored ships. Two wagons rested dockside, both near the water's edge. Only one carried a passenger with animated hands.

"How do you know that's a woman?" asked the assassin. "Three hooded robes, that's all I see."

"Her hands! Watch her hands! Yes, it's a woman. That's Ruler Three!"

Charise squinted. "What's she doing?"

"Speaking, I dare say!"

"With her hands? What's she saying, then?"

"I haven't a clue, but does it really matter? Does the hound care what the fox it's hunting says?"

"We're the hound, I take it?"

"We are, indeed, no longer chasing our own tails or a mere scent." Careful to conceal his face behind a crate of leafy greens, Reynard pointed toward the wagon. "The fox has shown itself! I'll wager anything the magister's beneath one of those two other cloaks. We are the hound, our nose is off the ground, and now we run in earnest!" He positioned Charise a bit further behind the crates. "Stay put! Keep a watch on them. I'll find you if need be!"

"What? Where are you going?"

"Don't let them out of your sight!" Reynard strode away, head down, his back angled to the docks. "I'll be back directly!"

Two or three alleys down from here... It's early. They should still be— Aha! Reynard quickened his pace, skirting several men repairing fishing nets, his gaze riveted on three boys loitering in the narrow space between two buildings. By the time he grew close, he could see down the alley's mouth. A half dozen youths were gathered there with buckets. Against the buildings' walls leaned a collection of long-handled tools. Those seated stood as Reynard entered the alley.

"You've a ship whose hull needs scraping?" asked the tallest of the boys, squaring his shoulders. He snapped his dirty fingers and one of his younger companions grabbed a shovel-like instrument with a narrow, rectangular blade from among several leaning against the wall. Another grasped a stiff-bristled broom, its head no wider than his feet were long.

"I do not," said Reynard. "But I do have a task for someone who knows the ships docked here, and the men who sail them." He dangled a pouch of coins at arm's length. "A task for which I'm willing to pay handsomely. Interested?"

Reynard watched as Charise perused those items adorning a small table in his study. She picked up the small glass orb holding his most prized possession—the first dire he had ever captured as a pickpocket.

"How much money do you think The Guild is holding, truly?" She turned the orb one way, then the other.

"I've absolutely no idea, other than to say, *a lot.*"

"But if you had to guess..."

"I needn't guess, Charise. The Guild has so much money the number doesn't matter. So much you'll tire of counting just your half of it and cease to worry about numbers. So much you couldn't spend it in your lifetime, no matter how you tried. Will that suffice?"

Charise returned the glass orb to its resting place. "It will, indeed. And we are so very close now!"

"Are we?"

"Aren't we?"

"We've located the magister and his friends, but it's not as though they're carrying the treasure in their pockets. We still don't know where they're hiding it."

"Are you doubting what the boy was able to discover?"

"Not at all. I asked him only to find out where the robes were going, and to do so without asking them directly. He's an alley rat, and as such, he knows his way around the docks. I've no doubt that what he told us is the truth."

"They've booked passage to the Southern Isles, then."

"On *The Fair Winds*, yes."

"She sets sail in three suns' time, Reynard. What shall we do?"

"What would you do?"

"We know where they're staying while the ship prepares to sail. Take one hostage, I suppose. Torture him or her until they tell us where the money is."

"And if they take their secret to the grave?"

"Doubtful, given my techniques." Charise inspected her hands carefully.

"And if they're not informed? What if only one knows, as a means of keeping the rest honest, and you take the wrong one prisoner?"

"Take them all, then. Torture all of them!"

"Ah, you're starting to remind me of someone." *Don't tell me she's not growing on you, Spiro!* "Still, I think, too risky, for having come this far. What if only the magister knows, and his weak heart gives out whilst you're tickling him? What if all are schooled in the ancient art of mindal, and can separate what they feel from what they think? Our friend, Two, boasted of that very skill, mind you—where do you think he learned it?"

"What are you thinking, then?"

"I'm of two minds, Charise. One of them agrees with you, though I fear it is unduly influenced by my distaste for traveling."

"You don't like to travel?"

"A short trip to the theater in a fine coach with cushioned seats is one thing; it's quite another to suffer an entire sun in some wheeled contraption built to bruise you to the bone. To say nothing of heat or dust or bugs."

"We're talking about a ship, Reynard, not some flimsy carriage."

"Quite! Even worse! A bowl made out of wooden pieces, bound together how? With bedsheets strapped to skinny sticks, reliant on fair winds to help it move, but just as likely to meet heavy gales or be rocked by angry seas, or both? Floating in an endless soup you could never swim across—if you could swim, mind you—a soup seasoned with the stench of fish and the vomit of sea travelers; a soup so deep you cannot see the bottom, or the rocks just below its surface, waiting to crack the little wooden bowl in two! All this to say nothing of the creatures living in that soup, just waiting for the ship to sink so that they might get to know you better…"

"You can't swim?"

"I'm really not sure. I've never tried."

Charise laughed. "No, then."

"Do you know how long it takes a ship to find its way to the Southern Isles? A quarter moon, give or take!"

"You're fond of your analogies, Reynard. As am I. But this one troubles me."

"Why's that?"

"It's a bit off, don't you think? A wooden bowl bobbing around on a sea of soup? The soup should be inside the bowl, for it to make any sense."

"And still," said Reynard with a sigh, "our best odds of laying hands on The Guild's treasure would see us follow those three robes. They're sure to lead us to it."

"I could go alone. They don't know who I am or what I look like. You stay here and wait for me."

Reynard eyed her steadily. *Tempting, touching, and trap-worthy, all at once!* "Nonsense. We're partners now. In the bowl, or in the soup—we suffer and prosper together as one—that's the way this works."

"You're sure about this?" Charise laughed. She cut the air adjacent to Reynard's ear with a pair of sharpened shears. *Clackety-clack! Clackety-clack!*

He flinched. "Need I remind you?" he asked. "They know what I look like. I'm sure they've never seen the likes of you before, but one as handsome as I? Impossible to forget. I cannot board that ship without altering my appearance. Cut away!"

"Not what I meant," said Charise. "I meant, are you certain you can trust me? You're quite vulnerable now, you know. The things I could do to you with these!" *Clackety-clack!*

"Ahh. Yes, quite sure, thank you, as I know what it is you see in me."

"Really? Do tell!" *Clackety-clack!* A shock of Reynard's hair fell to the floor.

"Aside from my good looks, you mean?" *Clackety-clack!*

"Of course!" A row of bangs slid past his eyes.

Reynard could hear the assassin smiling.

"You see a man of ways and means," he said. "A man of the world, sophisticated and cultured, but without airs, and quite comfortable in the company of the common man. A philosopher and muse. An artist in his own right. A man who speaks three tongues. You see a man confident in his skills, which are many. A man capable of taking most anything from anyone, without their ever knowing it. All of which is to say, you see in me your ticket to untold wealth and ever-lasting happiness, an end to all your worries, an answer to all your prayers."

"Three languages? Really?"

"If I'm being modest."

Charise put the scissors down and cupped Reynard's cheeks. "Adorable! But given our circumstances, whatever are you going to do with this?" She tapped the scar on his forehead, now more visible than ever.

A soft rapping on the front door silenced them both. They held each other's gaze for only a moment. Charise picked up the shears in her left hand, a dagger appearing in her right. Reynard found his own and moved to the door. He pulled a hat from a wall peg and pulled its brim below his scar. "Who is it?" he asked. Charise positioned herself to the side of the door.

"It's me, sir. The boy from the wharf." Reynard pictured him. The lad had done a good job, not only gleaning the magister's travel plans from ship workers, but trailing the spider to The Seaside Inn before introducing Reynard to *The Fair Winds* cargomaster.

Reynard cracked the door, tightening his grip on the hilt of his dagger.

"What brings you here?"

"The cargomaster, sir. He said to tell you he wants double what you offered."

"Double!" Reynard was dumbfounded. "To travel in the ship's hold? In the company of spice and livestock? And for that, did I not offer far more than the going rate for passage in the best berths? Has he lost his mind?"

"He wants his payment now, sir."

"All the more offensive! We were to settle our account tomorrow before we board. You were there—that was the arrangement, was it not?"

The boy shrugged. "I'll tell him that, shall I?"

Reynard looked down the street. *Something's not right.* "How did you know to find me here?"

"I recognized you, sir. You work upstairs on the wharf's south end. I've seen you many times. I live not far from here. I often see you come and go."

Plausible... and yet...

"I'd best go and tell him." The boy stepped back into the street. "He said he wouldn't wait long, and tomorrow he can't be bothered."

"No, wait." Reynard's eyes consulted Charise.

"In the soup or in the bowl," she said, opening the door wider. "Let's go!"

The act of stuffing small leather pouches into pockets was still fresh in Reynard's mind, and yet he felt compelled to pat the bulges in his turncoat, then confirm the presence of the dagger in his waistband. It was a long walk to the wharf. The lantern he carried illuminated little more than his immediate surroundings. A moist, gray sponge engulfed all else. Anyone with any sense was safe behind barred doors and tucked beneath warm bed covers at this time of night.

"Can you not smell that, Reynard?"

"Yes, Spiro! Please, not now!"

"That's not the stink of rotting fish wrinkling your nose. That's the smell of danger, friend! It's not like you to bring it on yourself!"

"You think we have a choice? The cargomaster might not know it—all the more annoying—but he has us over a barrel. We cannot afford to force his hand or call his bluff; we must set sail with the magister tomorrow, or let the spider's trail go cold, perhaps never to find it again!"

"Even so, to come out here alone like this..."

"I'm not alone!"

"Aren't you? Do you really trust that serpent by your side? Is it not possible she arranged all this? Are you certain she's not playing you?"

"Is this how you normally walk to the docks?" asked Charise. She looked from Reynard to the boy.

"It's the most direct route, yes," said Reynard. "Another hundred paces and you'll sink or swim. Why?"

"We have company," Charise said.

Reynard glanced back. It was difficult to make out shapes, but four, perhaps five, men were stretched across the street behind, keeping pace with them. Or gaining.

"And they have friends," said Charise.

Reynard's feet stopped moving as five figures appeared in the street ahead. Their stationary silhouettes were spread across its narrow width, outlined against the foggy backdrop of the wharf. All were armed with weapons much longer than his dagger. One of them dragged a sword as he walked, the tip of its blade scratching dirt.

The boy began to run toward the wharf. "Apologies!" he called back to Reynard, sprinting past the armed men and out of sight.

The central figure took two additional steps forward.

"Ayla, Reynard... Charise."

"Two!" Reynard feigned surprise. "Where have you been?" *Think, dammit!*

"Concerned for my welfare, were you?" asked Two. "Is that why you left Chalmsworth so quickly? With all our money and your new mistress? I hope, for your sake, she's a better lover than assassin. She can't kill a member of The Guild's High Order, let alone a king!"

"Listen, Two, the magister won't be pleased if you—"

"Spare me, overseer! If the magister finds out what you've been up to, if his watchers are doing their job, he'll thank me for what comes next!" Ruler Two began stepping backward. "And it gives me great pleasure to bear witness! I've disliked you from the start!" He froze, his last words punctuated by the sound of a galloping horse.

What in Baelon? Reynard withdrew his dagger, lifting the lantern as though that might help him see better into the distance.

"Stay close to me," Charise said, the glint of steel in both her hands. "Not so close we can touch, but not so far away I cannot help you."

"*Haieee!*" A shrill, high-pitched cry caused a thousand pinpricks to needle Reynard's skin. A steed burst through the line of men standing with Ruler Two. *Cra-aack!* One of them collapsed to the ground before the rider galloped past Reynard and Charise, scattering the line of men behind them. A small form leaped from the horse into the startled men's midst. It sprang from the ground and attacked the lumbering men with swift and vicious purpose.

"Maki!" said Charise, returning her attention to the five men fronting the wharf. "Oh-h-h, it's blood pudding in the making now, Reynard! Stay where you are!"

She cocked her arm and snapped it forward like a whip. The man closest clutched his chest and gasped. Before he even hit the ground, Charise released another blade. A second assailant toppled to the dirt, his hands wrapped around the hilt protruding from his torso. Ruler Two turned and ran, leaving only one of his companions to face Charise.

She bounded forward, retrieved one of the fallen men's weapons, and sliced the mist repeatedly with criss-cross swipes.

"Bloody bysh!" the lone man shouted, slapping his sword awkwardly in her direction.

"Bloody death!" said Charise, sidestepping his blows and bringing him to his knees with one well-placed thrust.

A sudden burst of energy sent Reynard chasing after Two. He passed Charise as she removed her borrowed sword with a flourish from the kneeling man's midriff.

"Kill him!" she shouted.

Two's dark silhouette bobbed up and down against the wharf's gray background, like a malformed mast on a small boat riding the waves.

Reynard inhaled a mouthful of cool mist as Charise drew abreast of him. He kept his legs churning. *Faster! We're gaining!* Two's entire frame was visible now, wobbling slightly as it ran, shoulders dipping and rising, side to side. *That's it... close the distance! We've got him now!*

The pounding of hooves drowned their footsteps. In a flash, the beast sped past them and alongside Two. Club in hand, Maki left her saddle, wrapping one arm around Two's neck and riding him to the ground. By the time Ruler Two got to his hands and knees, the lithe assassin had adopted a wide stance in front of him, an odd club raised overhead. She brought it down with both hands and a vengeance, its pointed end plunging into Two's head like an axe biting into dense, green wood.

The ruler's body went limp, his limbs splayed out on the wharf's wet promenade.

Maki planted a bare foot squarely on Two's cheek, pinning his bloodied head to the ground. She leaned her weight against the weapon's handle and tried to wrest it free. When it would not budge, she strode to her horse, grabbed a shorter-handled club hanging from its saddle, and returned to bash Two's skull in with one blow. The longer club popped free, a chunk of Two's cranium still impaled on its spiked end.

"Gods above!" said Reynard, still catching his breath. *Are you seeing what I'm seeing, Spiro? It's a godsdamn klubandag!*

"We'd best make ourselves scarce," Charise said, embracing the shorter assassin. "Stay well, sister, and may all seven gods ride with you!"

It was not the most direct route back, but it was more discreet, and safer under the circumstances. Even so, Reynard did not breathe easy until his home came into view.

"I should have asked the lad more questions," he said, seeking Charise's forgiveness.

"And miss out on all that fun? Nonsense!"

"You're really sisters, are you?"

"Not by blood, no, but in every other way imaginable. I wouldn't recognize my birth sister. Maki's closer kin than she will ever be. We're bonded."

"I understand completely." Reynard retrieved a key from his pocket as he preceded Charise through the opening in the stone wall fronting his building. "It's rather like my rela—"

He stopped moving and Charise nearly collided with him.

"What is it?" she asked.

Reynard moved slowly to the front door, reaching out to touch a feathered arrow shaft protruding from its center. He looked nervously back down the street. "What's this! Not one of them carried a bow, did they?"

Charise examined the shaft, gripped it firmly, and broke it free from the door. "It's not what you think," she said. "This has nothing to do with Two. Or you."

"Please explain." Reynard slid his key into the lock, and they both slipped inside the house.

He bolted the door, and eyed the pointed arrow tip that had pierced its thick, dense kollumwood. "That's not just any arrow," he said.

"It's not an arrow." Charise held up the shaft. "It's a bolt from a crossbow. And not just any crossbow, mind you."

"Do tell."

"And I'm not your common assassin."

"I dare say. You're going to elaborate, are you?"

He followed Charise closely as she felt her way into the study.

"Last night, when we tracked the couriers to that pub, and you saw me with Maki and Geralt—"

"Geralt. The big brute with the hatchets?"

"Just so. I told you, they came to warn me."

"I recall. Regarding Two's escape in Chalmsworth."

"Yes. But the warning was two-fold."

"And you didn't think to share them both?"

"I did consider it, and opted not to trouble you. The other's not your concern."

"In the soup or in the boat, Charise, we prosper and suffer as one. Sound familiar? And that's my entryway that's just been ruined, not yours."

"Fair enough. But if this comes back to bite you, don't say I didn't warn you."

"Fair enough."

"And promise you won't overreact."

"I swear it."

Charise placed both hands on his shoulders, one still holding the bolt she had removed from the door. "I am—or was—The League of Assassins' overlord."

A puff of air exploded from Reynard. He stared hard into Charise's eyes.

"I wasn't going to bother you with that detail," said the assassin, "but now it helps to explain."

"Explain what?" Reynard continued to hold her gaze.

"Before I left The League, I named my successor. It was, as one might imagine, a coveted position. Some of the hopeful were not pleased with my decision. One in particular." She ran a finger down the feathered shaft. "Teebald."

"And this is how he voices his displeasure?"

"In a manner of speaking, yes. Teebald's a good assassin. His favorite weapon is the crossbow, and he likes to let his marks know that he's coming. He thinks it only sporting, and that somehow it enhances his prowess."

Reynard cocked his head. "I must say, that does seem rather sporting."

"Ah, but it's not a sport, is it? It's a business, and when it comes to the business of killing, there's no room for bravado or taking unnecessary chances. There's just getting the job done."

"You'll pardon me for saying so, but you did seem to enjoy yourself this evening."

"Indeed! But that wasn't business, was it? No contract. No payment. No client expectations. No League of Assassins counting on me to keep the business afloat. I'm no longer the overlord, or an assassin by trade. It doesn't mean I can't still kill, or that I can't enjoy that pastime. In fact, I'm freer now to do so than I have been in quite some time."

She thrust the bolt's shaft in front of him.

"Take a good look near the feathered end and you'll see it bears Teebald's mark: two stripes painted black. It's his way of saying, 'Death comes for you!' The one to follow looks quite the same, only it finds a different target, and its stripes are red, to say: 'Death has arrived!'"

"So, this was for your benefit? Lovely. How long before the next message, do you think?"

"Let's just say our trip to the Southern Isles is well-timed. I need to think and plan. We board at dawn?"

"Yes."

"Our bags are packed, our kits laid out?"

"Yes. Anything else?"

Charise placed a palm against his cheek and kissed his forehead lightly. "Do you have a back door, perchance?"

"How do I look?" Reynard adjusted the black kerchief wrapped tightly around his scarred forehead. "Like I was born to sail, eh?"

"Best hang on to that smile," Charise said. "Lose it, and people will wonder whether the bottom of your soles are inked."

"You're going to be warm in those, are you?" Reynard appraised the black leather togs reaching to Charise's calves. A matching leather turncoat covered her upper torso.

"There's nothing warmer," she said. "It's the hide of the woodland hopper, turned inside out, so its fur is brushing my skin."

They slipped out the back and down an alley, each with a large kit akin to a sailor's bag slung over one shoulder. The morning air nipped at Reynard's cheeks and hands. A cool breeze carried a familiar coastal fog down the alley, reminding him he had shorn most of his hair. *At least the Southern Isles will be warm! Gods above, just get us there in one piece and I'll be thankful!*

The alley dumped them onto the same street they had traversed the night before, well before they reached the mouth of the wharf. Already, lights were glowing inside buildings. Men criss-crossed the foggy street, shouting to one another near the spot where Ruler Two had first waylaid them.

The bodies of those killed had been moved to one side and covered with tarps. A few men loitered near them, perhaps to keep those gathering outside adjacent homes and shops at bay.

Reynard could not resist. Conscious of his appearance, he bypassed several women to tap the arm of a man who looked as though he might work on the docks.

"What's happened?" he asked.

The bearded man did not even glance at him. "No one knows," he muttered. "Ten dead! Murdered, they say! Some sort of gang war, I suppose. This is what happens when—"

Reynard pressed on, shadowed by Charise, down the same street they had chased Ruler Two. Screeching gulls and street hawkers welcomed them to the wharf's promenade, already teeming with sailors, dockworkers, travelers, and shoppers. In the cloudy background, ships large and small, moored to the piers and anchored in the shallows, bobbed gently on a calm sea.

It all appeared to him quite normal, but for one noteworthy blemish: a small, but somewhat frenzied, group gathered round another tarp-covered body on the promenade. *How much larger would that crowd be, and how much more excited, if it knew a member of The Guild's High Order lay beneath that tarp!*

"Move along, folks! Move along!" said a stout man.

Reynard complied, keeping to the buildings set off from the sea. His shouldered kit concealed his face from the waterfront until he reached the pier to which *The Fair Winds* was moored. There he waited until he spotted the ship's cargomaster standing with two others near the bottom of the ship's gangway. "Let's go," he said, leading Charise across the wharf's promenade and onto the pier's wooden planks.

He hailed the cargomaster by name as they neared the gangplank.

"Eh?" The cargomaster cocked his round head. His creased eyelids narrowed to slits. Suddenly, they sprang open, his head righting itself. "Ah! It's you, sir! I didn't recognize you, what without your hair and all that... that..." He waved a hand in the air, grasping for words. He laughed, pointing at Reynard's head. "*The Fair Winds* is not a pirate ship, ya know! You have your fare, have you?"

"Four kingshead each, as agreed." Reynard withdrew his coin purse.

"Yes, yes..." The cargomaster held his hand out. "That's it. Mmm-hmm. Three... four..." He poked each coin with a finger as it landed on his palm. "I thought perhaps you wouldn't show, ya know. There's ten dead on the wharf, I'm told! All killed last night. No idea jest yet who they might be."

Reynard grinned. "Not us, thank the gods."

"No, not you, but if any turn out to be passengers of ours, I can give you their berth at no extra charge."

"Very kind of you, but we're quite happy in the hold. To be honest, we prefer it."

The cargomaster snorted. "Suit yourself." He craned his neck toward the ship's deck. "Piper! Come 'ere!" He waited for a skinny lad to scamper down the gangway. "Show these two good folk the hold, and give them each three blankets and a chamber pot. Off ya go, now!"

THE ANSWER TO A RIDDLE

"What is it, if not magic, that makes even absurd dreams seem so real in slumber?" Lady Carson to her husband

Marshal Erik Carson

Deep in the Lumax Mountains and surrounded by vegetation that mostly blocked the sky, Carson struggled to get his bearings. Somewhere to the north lay Peril Pass, where King Tygre had met his untimely end. Much further south, The Exchange connected the Baelonite Quarry to the Euphoria Grove in Tegan. He had traveled both routes many times, but never the vast and mountainous wilderness in between.

A trip into the unknown! How fitting, given the jumble inside my head right now! Nothing is as it appears. Where is the magister, if not buried in the rubble of the GOT? Where are the missing members of his High Order? At least one is said to be stalking King Axil—where is he right now? It's a bit much to believe the others were taken by the prattlers. And where is the trove of loot stolen from the realm? Why leave so very little at the GOT? Why were the tunnel doors left unlocked? And what about the dead noms just inside those doors? Why did the GOT leave its torches burning, knowing our army was advancing? This puzzle has no borders! Its pieces are missing and misshapen!

The marshal kept a watchful eye on the forest floor as his horse climbed ever-steeper terrain. On occasion, a loose rock or branch hidden by leaves caused the animal to lose its footing. He could hear Miss Dunn behind, reassuring Shadow.

Start with something simpler, why don't you? Something more pleasant. The rest will come to you.

"What did you say your friend's name was?" he asked. "The old man with the ancient sword?"

"Gradi," Miss Dunn said. "Gradiott, from Summerwinds. I never learned his surname."

"From Summerwinds! It would appear Tegan is full of helpful souls!"

"You've yet to tell me where we're going. We're not lost, are we?"

Carson turned in his saddle just enough to bring the young woman into view. "Not at all, Miss Dunn. Lost is a three-legged stool. You don't know where you are, you're not sure just where you're going, and—most importantly—you can't find your way back to your beginnings. To be completely honest, I don't know where we are, and I'm not sure just how to get where I'd like to go. But we're not lost. The path we're on leads back to where we left Kings Road."

"We're sitting on a one-legged stool, then. That feels about right."

Carson laughed. *Sharp-witted lass!* "It's not for everyone, to be sure. A superior sense of balance is required, which is why I chose you to join me. Have I misjudged you?"

"You may have, though not in the manner you think."

"You might be surprised, Miss Dunn. For what it's worth, I hold you in rather high regard. So I'll give you this much: we're looking for a spot to shed some light on things. A place no army would be welcome; where no doors would open for a marshal, even traveling alone. I'm hoping your presence will change all that."

The ground gradually grew more level, the air cooler, crisper, and easier to breathe. A grove of giant kollum trees slipped slowly by, a shower of snowflake-shaped leaves suspended from their whorled branches high above. Carson grimaced. Despite their stately stalks and graceful crowns, he would never look at them the same again.

"You don't believe he's dead, do you—the ruler sent to kill both kings?"

Don't tell me she reads minds! Mari Dunn's daughter! The marshal dismissed the notion with a light scoff. "Ruler Two? No, I don't."

"Did you watch the executions in town square? Following the celebration of Six Moons?"

Why bring that up now? "I did. Why do you ask?"

"I could have sworn I saw one of them on my way across the Lawless Lands. It could not have been, yeah? You saw them die?"

A prickly sensation tickled the marshal's spine. "I gave the signal to proceed, Miss Dunn. I watched the blades take their heads. Of that, at least, I'm certain. Which one did you imagine?"

"The tall one with the scar on his head."

The same description given by Ruler One of a man tasked with helping to assassinate both kings: an ugly scar where his forehead met someone's blade!

Carson half-heartedly swatted at a winged insect circling his neck, most of his attention captured by a sudden change in scenery. The forest abruptly gave way to an open glen, its far side framed by an impenetrable thicket of vines nearly smothering the face of an immense stone wall. He rode into the glen and dismounted, his eyes coming to rest on a wooden portal at the base of the wall, conspicuously clear of any vegetation. No sooner had his boots hit the ground than the door swung open and a short, hooded figure emerged. It shuffled toward him, its black robe sweeping a wide and well-worn path amidst tall grasses.

"Are you lost, child?" A wry smile nearly disappeared in the mass of creases surrounding it.

Carson displayed a cheerful visage, relieved not only to have reached his destination, but to have encountered a familiar face so soon. It struck him that he knew her only as the Sister of Systalene who had tended Mari Dunn. She had never offered her name, and he had never asked. She wasn't what he'd call a friend, but neither were they strangers.

"No longer," he said.

"Fair enough. Not lost, then. At least, not to your thinking." The old woman smirked. "So serious and haggard! You look as though you need a respite from your worries. A sojourn to the Southern Isles, perhaps."

"Some day... perhaps." Carson mopped his brow with a sweaty palm.

"I wonder, then, what could have drawn you here?" With the slightest nod of her head, the old woman motioned to the wall behind her. "The sanctuary is hardly a place to conduct a soldier's normal follies. You're looking for your mother, are you? Some much-needed maternal guidance?"

Carson accepted the chiding good-naturedly. "My mother's here, is she?"

"Like to come inside and look for yourself, would you?" The Sister of Systalene moved to within arm's reach of him, lowering her voice as if to impart some wisdom. "It is I who shall decide whether or not you enter, child, and that is all that should concern you." She raised her eyebrows, as though questioning him. "How does that feel?"

"Embarrassingly familiar."

"I should hope so. And to think, when I first journeyed to your castle, it was to offer my assistance. Is that the purpose of your visit? To offer assistance?"

"I like to think so. I come in service to King Axil, who rules in service to his subjects, including you and your sisters."

The woman cackled. "It must be nice to know the needs of an entire realm, though that seems a bit presumptuous, don't you think? And we don't consider ourselves 'subjects.'"

Carson eyed her steadily. "I meant no offense, Sister."

"Then none is taken. But you've come a long way. Why, if not to give offense?"

"I was once told that you are given passage to places others are denied. People talk and the Systalene listen. A wise woman once told me this. I took her at her word."

"One mark for your good memory, child. One mark offset by blatant flattery, to which I am immune."

"We come seeking information, nothing more."

"You could have come alone for that." The crone shifted her gaze to Miss Dunn, still sitting astride Shadow. "We've been expecting you."

"Expecting us?" asked Carson.

"Not you. Her." The old woman shuffled closer to Shadow. "Our paths cross again, Miss Dunn. What brings you here, I wonder?"

Carson sought to intervene. "She—"

"You haunt my dreams," Miss Dunn said, her eyes fixed on the crone.

"And you, mine, child. So what? That's not why you're here."

"Isn't it?" asked Miss Dunn.

The crone stared hard at her. "Oh, my. You're not sure!" Looking back at the sanctuary, she waved her cane in the air. "What else have you been dreaming?" she asked. The small door creaked again, opening to discharge another figure draped in black. It shuffled toward the crone, several inches of its robe dragging on the ground.

"You speak in riddles," said Miss Dunn.

The crone laughed. "In your dreams?"

"And now. Can you not just speak your mind directly?"

"Can you not be honest with yourself?" said the crone.

"I don't know what you're talking about."

"Don't you?" The crone took the hand of the shuffling form. "Have you made use of the card I gifted you?"

Miss Dunn did not answer.

"Ahhh, you have! What did I tell you—small doses! Come down from there, child. You know you want to. We're not going to bite. Quite the contrary. It's you who is invited inside."

Miss Dunn dismounted.

Carson placed himself between her and the sisters.

The old crone poked him in the chest with her cane. "I know what you've come for. If you want that information, you'd best let her pass."

Carson hesitated.

"It's all right," Miss Dunn said. She brushed past him and accepted the hand of the smaller figure, transferred to her by the old crone.

"It's why you brought her, isn't it?" asked the crone, watching them walk toward the compound. "To use as your bargaining chip? It's a little late to be second-guessing that, isn't it?"

Carson watched Miss Dunn disappear into the sanctuary.

She prodded him again with her cane, regaining his attention. "What's the matter? She's safer in there than out here, I can assure you of that."

Carson's expression let her know he was not convinced.

"You're worried that we'll keep her, is that it?" The woman cackled. "Tell you what... I'll stay here with you 'til she returns." She held his gaze. "And I'll answer questions while we wait. How's that?"

Carson glanced again toward the sanctuary. "What do you know of The Guild of Takers?"

"The question is too broad, child. I don't intend to stand here blathering all day."

"Very well. What might you know about The Guild's High Order, and the where-abouts of its members?"

"Why ask me? Weren't you just knocking on their door with your instruments of death?"

Carson sighed. *You call these answers?* "Our visit seems to have scattered them."

"Shocking! My sisters would have been there to tend the wounded and help clean up your mess, but the prattlers don't discriminate. And we're not fond of being eaten."

Press on! "The High Order numbers six, is that right? The magister and five others?"

"It did, yes. Five men, including their version of your king—the magister—and one woman. But they are six no more."

"You're certain?" *More detail, please!*

The old woman's eyes begged his to dance with hers. "Much as you might like to, you can't claim credit. The magister killed one for his disloyalty. The prattlers dined on another. But it wasn't you who scattered the rest. They left on their own terms, well aware of your plans."

Now we're getting somewhere! "He's one step ahead of us, is he? The magister's that shrewd?"

"The magister!" The old crone scoffed. "Your narrowmindedness continues to lead you astray, child. Have you not been listening? You're looking under the wrong rock!"

Carson took a deep breath. "Where has he gone? Do you know?"

"I once told you, did I not: we won't embroil ourselves in your petty politics or wars. Besides, where the magister goes is of little consequence." *More riddles!* "What about all they stole from your subjects?" The old woman's voice teased him. "Did you find their buried treasure?"

"I'm sure you know that we did not. A taste of it at best."

"Perhaps you're better off chasing the remainder. It doesn't move so easily, you know. And The Guild cannot profit from what it cannot touch. Find the treasure, and you'll find The Guild's High Order, or what's left of it."

"You're going to tell me where it's hidden, are you? The treasure?"

The sister tapped the ground impatiently with her cane. "I already have, child. Don't let your feet get wet!"

Sibil Dunn

The sister's hand, small and soft, warmed Sibil's fingers as it guided her across the sanctuary's threshold. The sheltered entryway consisted of an arbor of large timbers smothered by creeping vines, their variegated foliage left to hang like drapes shimmering in the breeze.

"My name is Sister Rae. You needn't be so guarded. You can breathe freely here." She disengaged from Sibil, shut the sanctuary door, and peeled the hood back from her head.

Freed curls of auburn fell across her smooth brow and danced about her rosy cheeks. Large blue eyes beneath long lashes disappeared momentarily as she lifted the robe over her shoulders. Smiling, the young girl rolled the garment into a ball and tucked it under one arm.

"I thought you wore those always," Sibil said.

"Always outside," the girl advised her. "For me, that's a rather rare occurrence."

Ah, so you borrowed one that doesn't fit!

"Two more almons and I will join the sojourners." Sister Rae took Sibil's hand again. "Until then, there is no better place to pass the time. Come."

Crushed stones grated beneath their feet as they walked. Sturdy arbor posts framed a wide pathway leading through a mix of landscaping and structures. The creeping vine remained above, sheltering them from the sun, but to either side, its shoots and leaves were cropped to allow a clear line of sight.

"Are there no children here?" asked Sibil.

"No. We've all been released by the God of Children." Sister Rae flashed another smile. "We all entered here by choice, if that's what you're wondering."

"What does the sanctuary want with me?"

"Nothing. Your presence here was not requested or required, was it?"

"No. And yet..."

Sister Rae nodded knowingly. "And yet you have reason to be here."

"Yes."

"Sister Omenn was right."

"Sister Omenn—the old woman who greeted us?"

"Yes. She's been expecting you."

Sibil's brow wrinkled. *Surely that is not her given name!*

"You really don't know why you're here?" asked the girl. She left the shade of the arbor to lead Sibil down a narrow path bordered on both sides by masses of tall, yellow flowers. At its end sat a squat cottage made of rounded stone.

Sibil raised a palm to her chest. The quaint building's thick thatched roof and stained-glass windows seemed all too familiar. "Someone lives here?" she asked.

"That is well put."

Well put?

Her young escort lifted the latch and ushered Sibil inside. "See for yourself."

The tidy room, drenched in white, was empty save for a bed encased in sheer mesh fabric hanging from the rafters.

"To keep the bugs away," said Sister Rae, releasing Sibil's hand.

The room grew suddenly warm, its air thick and hard to breathe. Sibil's feet began to move.

An image of her mother, laid to rest inside The Nest, assailed her as she neared the flimsy canopy.

But there was no question who this was.

"He's alive?" she dared to ask.

"You said yourself: 'Someone lives here.'"

"What's wrong with him?"

"He was beaten. Badly."

Sibil felt the envelope beneath her shirt. It contained not only Tristan's letter, but the lock of hair that she had stolen from his attackers. *That's what's left of the last to cross the brothers Penniluk. A young king's knight, no less!*

"But he'll survive," she said breathlessly. "You can save him?"

"The body, yes. He doesn't yet move, but his heart beats ever stronger. Healing's what we do. But the mind... it's hard to say. You can tell that it's at work, though. His eyes shudder beneath their lids. See for yourself."

Sibil crossed the tile floor, quickly dropping to her knees beside the mesh screen. "Tristan?"

"He means something to you," said Sister Rae. "To your heart."

What? "How could you know?" asked Sibil.

"Know what?"

"That we're connected. How could you possibly know that?"

"Ah. You're wondering what mystic powers we possess."

She's been expecting you! Sibil swallowed. "Yes."

The young woman smiled. "The truth is much more bland. Your friend speaks at times, even though unconscious. 'Sibil' is one of very few words to have passed his lips. It meant nothing to most of us, of course, but to Sister Omenn, your name held great meaning. Not so mysterious, you see. What's much more deserving of wonder"—she paused to lay a hand on Sibil's shoulder—"is how you knew to come here."

Marshal Erik Carson

Though his presence had been requested, Carson knew to hold his tongue. He would wait at least until the king's eyes acknowledged him, if not until the monarch spoke. A royal finger rose in the quiet of the library, requesting the marshal's patience before slowly returning to piles of parchment strewn across a table designed for perusing maps. King Axil's bowed head followed the digit slowly back and forth until it stopped. He looked up and over the brim of his spectacles. "The scribe's recounting of our adventure south," he said, quickly returning his attention to the parchment, murmuring to himself as he read. A snort broke free of his nose, chased by a chuckle and a shake of his long locks.

"Listen to this, Erik: 'It was the twenty-third sun of the ninth moon, the first in a new chapter for Baelon, the last to warm the backs of many who would give their all to make it so.'" The cautionary finger rose again. "Wait... wait, you must hear one more passage. It's my favorite thus far!" A shuffling of the scribbled notes ensued. "Wherever did that go? Oh, yes, here." King Axil cleared his voice. "'The giants of the Takers Guild were legion, their teeth sharpened by an appetite for bones, their hearts darkened by a thirst for thievery. Their pets from Baelon below, the prattlers, shielded in black armor, joined them on the battlements, screeching, 'Come and tame us, if you dare!' With the blessing of King Axil, Marshal Carson led the charge against them all, his bright sword gleaming with the righteous light of truth and justice! The enemy fell swiftly, blinded by its brilliance and unable to withstand its mighty blows. Neither man nor beast could stay the heavy hand of Aranox, and the black blood of the Takers Guild flowed freely in the GOT.'" The king removed his spectacles. "A bit understated with regard to your prowess, but he does have a way with words."

"You have to give him that," Carson said.

The king gestured to the reams of parchment scattered across the table. "And this is not the half of it! I'm supposed to read it all, you know. Every word! It's not official 'til I do. I would just let it go, but it will be recited by every orator in both realms, and there are few who will not hang on every word. It should at least have a shred of truth to it, don't you think?"

"Nothing about Ademar and his men?" asked the marshal.

"Oh yes! There was one line. Something like: 'By the time the fist of Tegan joined the battle, the enemy was on its knees.' Not to worry... I'll see to it the final record shows that without Tegan's assistance, victory was anything but certain."

"As it should, m'lord."

"It's been two suns since you visited the Systalene. Three since our return from the GOT. I'm curious what your next move will be."

"We learned little from the Systalene we did not already know. Our most important discovery was, in fact, quite by accident and not what we were searching for."

"Young Godfrey, yes. I've been meaning to ask: does he know about his father's death?"

"No, sire. He's not aware of much, I'm afraid. But still, it's good news for Lady Godfrey at this point. He couldn't be in better hands, really. But our next move... To be honest, my head has been in somewhat of a muddle. Not all is lost, and I've not given up, mind you. We do occupy The Guild's lair. We know rulers one and five are dead. The magister is somewhere, as are the other members of his High Order. A small group continues to explore the GOT, inch by inch—they may yet uncover something... clues, if not dead bodies. I've been thinking... I may go myself, or send Major Stronghart, to further question those prisoners sent to labor in the quarry. Might we offer something in return for information leading to the magister? Some sort of carrot, as it were?"

"Of course. You have free rein. The gods have made it clear that I have yet to pay enough for a life too full, too rich, too free of pain to date. Offer what you will. Perhaps the gods will credit me and consider my debt paid. In the meantime, I too have been thinking. Perhaps we should remove the pole outside the castle gates. Absent the magister's head, it serves only to remind me of my most recent failure."

"I would not, Your Majesty. Not yet, anyway. Removing it would surely send that same message to the people. We should leave it, I think, and use the palace gossipers to spread the word beyond these castle walls: the pole remains as a reminder of King Axil's will, of his sworn task yet to be completed—a symbol of his intent and perseverance."

King Axil's bearded cheeks expanded. "That's quite good, Erik. Your head is not so muddled as you think. It's your king who's lost his way. What was I thinking, going off to war? Those days are further behind me than I realized. Thank you, by the way, for all your efforts to make me look as though I belonged amidst your soldiers; not easy, but much appreciated."

"Nonsense, m'lord. But there are those in addition to Marshal Ademar and our dead who we should honor. There were those not obligated by position who nevertheless lent their hand to our cause and who helped to secure our victory: Miss Dunn and her companion from Tegan; those commoners who fought by our mens' sides; and once more, Rolft Aerns."

"There you go again, deflecting praise due you. Make a list, and I'll see to it."

"If you really want to thank me, m'lord, destroying that declaration of succession will suffice. All that rubbish about who should succeed you on the throne should you die in battle. I confess it caused me to lose sleep. I presume it can be burned now."

"What? No! Think of something else, my friend. And while you're at it, go back and read that document more carefully. It speaks to my dying, of course, but it says nothing about battle or how else that certainty might come to pass! Honestly, it's the most sensible thing I've done in quite some time. Off you go now!"

Sibil Dunn

Sibil moved as stealthily as she could—so silently she could not hear her own footsteps. She watched the back of Cogswell's head as she made her way down the slope behind the barracks, across the training grounds and to the edge of the shade structure where the old man sat applying pressure to a blade against a whetstone.

She stopped moving when he spoke. "I thought perhaps these eyes had seen the last of you." The old man's hands stayed busy. His salt and pepper hair appeared a bit thinner on his crown.

Sibil stepped into the shade. "You'll not be rid of me so easily."

The Sergeant's hands stilled. He swiveled on his stool to look her over. "And in one piece, no less!" He grinned and rose to embrace her. She hugged him hard in return.

"When did you last sharpen your blades?" he asked when she released him.

Sibil's eyes rolled in embarrassment.

"Too busy wielding them, eh?" Cogswell held a rough hand out. "Let's have them, then."

Sibil produced all three, placing them on the table by the whetstone.

"I can't stay long, I'm afraid. I have to meet someone. But I'll come back, shall I? I do so want to spend some time with you!"

"Your friend, Rolft, stopped by," Cogswell said, returning to his stool. He leaned far to his side, grabbed another by one leg, and slid it next to him. He patted the seat, and Sibil sat beside him. He took hold of her white-handled weapon, set its blade at an angle on the whetstone and started to make passes, one smooth stroke after another.

"Did he?" she asked.

"He did. A good man, that one. In all respects. You can't say that about many."

"I could name a few, but as many are dead as are alive, I'm afraid." *My father, Theos, Sir Godfrey, Garth...* "Those living—it's a short list, to be sure."

"It's the same with women, of course. Just look at your mother. But that's the way of things, isn't it? Death's not very particular about those it dances with." Cogswell held the blade up to inspect it. Clearly satisfied, he traded it for the longer of her black-handled knives.

"I s'pose not."

"I'm told you've refused her several times of late, choosing instead to introduce her to a different partner." The old warrior began sharpening the thinner blade. "You know, when you left here, I worried for you. I told the Marshal as much when you first disappeared. You were skilled, but you weren't battle-tested, and facing true death—well, that's a different world entirely from these training grounds. But you know that now, yeah?"

"I'm not the same person I was, if that's what you mean."

Cogswell nodded. "I don't imagine so."

"Nor the same fighter, for that matter. I've learned a lot."

"Have you now?" Cogswell inspected the sharpened blade, then turned his attention to the push knife. "This one's fairly sharp still." He gave the short blade a few strokes across the whetstone before turning it. "I've heard quite a few stories to that effect." He moved the hilt of the white-handled blade into the sun. "Including the one about this dagger with the jewel that helps you see!" He chuckled as the red stone sparkled. "The Godfreys chose the right color for its angry eye, I'll give them that!"

He finished sharpening the push dagger and set it down.

"C'mon." The old man rose from his stool, plucking two daggers from a jumble of wooden weapons on a counter. He tossed one of them to Sibil and headed for the grounds. "Let's see just what you've learned!"

Sibil pressed the wooden blade against Cogswell's throat, just long enough to let him know. When she released it, he stepped back, eyeing her with new regard.

"Not the same, is right," he said, rubbing his neck between fingers and thumb. "Not the same at all."

Sibil handed him the training tool and retrieved her knives from the shade.

Cogswell stood his ground.

"Well?" she asked. "What do you think?"

"Honestly? I was just thinking I wouldn't want to tangle with The Wisperal outside these training grounds." He rubbed his neck again.

Sibil pecked his cheek and started off. "You needn't worry, Sergeant. You're on my short list, you are!"

Marshal Carson

"Erik! Are you coming to bed?" called Lady Carson.

"In a moment," the marshal said. "Do you want some bread?" He withdrew from his pocket the chunk he had ripped from a fresh-baked loaf in the castle's kitchen. No longer soft or warm, it would still be very tasty.

"At this hour? Come to bed!"

"Shortly!" shouted Carson, tearing at the bread with his teeth.

A soft knock on the door caused him to groan. He finished chewing, set the bread down and swallowed, wiping a few crumbs from his lips.

"Who is it?" shouted Lady Carson.

The marshal opened the door. "It's Major Stronghart... and Sergeant Stone," he called back to his wife.

"Beggin' your pardon, Marshal," the major said, "but that old woman's back. She—"

"The steward's mother?" Carson found it impossible to hide his irritation. "The king has made it clear she is not welcome here. Is she at the gates? Send her away. Tell her she—"

"Not that woman, Marshal. The ancient Systalene that tended Rolft and Madam Dunn. She has Sir Godfrey's boy with her. Tristan."

"Why didn't you say so?" Carson hesitated. "Is he...?"

"He's alive, Marshal. But they won't keep him at the sanctuary any longer."

Carson shouted to his wife. "I'll be back as soon as possible!"

He stepped into the night air, shut the door behind him, and started for the gates. "Did she say why?"

Stronghart stood his ground. "Not that way, Marshal. She's outside the infirmary. And she won't talk to anyone but you."

Carson reversed direction with a sigh. "Send for Lady Godfrey. Quickly. I don't want the first she hears of this to be from gossipers. Have her escorted to the castle for as long as she would stay."

A perfunctory nod from Major Stronghart sent the sergeant on his way.

Nearing the infirmary, the marshal sought to identify those gathered between the building and a wagon with its bed hidden by soft cloth.

"The boy's beneath that cover," said Stronghart. "The physician tried to take him, but the old lady wouldn't have it. She let him know so with her cane. I left Sergeant Perill in charge, as much to stay the physician as to protect him from the woman."

Carson recalled the prodding Sister Omenn had given him during his visit to the sanctuary. He skirted the wagon and spoke directly to the physician, a short man with coarse brown hair and spectacles.

"Doctor Kelce. Wait inside, please. With your staff."

The flickering light made it difficult to read the physician's facial tics.

Sister Omenn, standing by the wagon, underscored the man's dismissal with short backhand strokes in the air.

"My, my," she said to Carson as the infirmary staff retreated. "Three words and all the world moves as you ask. I may have to stop calling you 'child.'"

"Sister Omenn," said Carson.

"Marshal Carson."

He peered at the shroud of fabric covering the wagon.

"Sleeping," said the sister, her eyes wandering over Major Stronghart.

"He's better, is he?" asked the marshal.

"Than what?" asked Sister Omenn.

Carson frowned in frustration.

"He's better than we found him," said the sister. "Not well enough to travel on his own."

"Why bring him here, then? Why won't you care for him?"

"Is that what you were told?" The old woman gave the major a look of disapproval. "I said we can't keep him any longer. Not that we wouldn't care for him."

"What's that supposed to mean?" asked Carson. "You prefer to care for him here?"

The woman cackled loudly. "Surely you jest!"

"What then?"

"We can't keep him. Twice now he's left us in the middle of the night, trying to make his way here."

"He can walk?"

"Walk, stumble, wobble... call it what you will. He hasn't made it very far. Both times we found him face down in the woods, a short distance from the sanctuary."

"He has to have known he couldn't travel this far... especially on foot."

"An exaggerated sense of one's own capabilities; a reluctance to acknowledge pain or suffering; a refusal to seek or accept help when needed. These are hallmarks of your species, not mine."

"Why didn't you tie him to his bed or lock the sanctuary doors?"

"We don't hold people captive, Marshal."

"Not even for their own good?"

"Who are you or I to say what's best for him? We tend to people's bodies, not their minds or spirits. All three work in concert. Focusing too hard on one is bound to leave the others lacking. We've done all we can for his physical well-being. I don't think his midnight treks have been in search of your physician."

"I've already sent for his mother."

"Have you? I'm impressed. That may, in fact, prove helpful. What about the other woman in his life?"

"Miss Dunn?"

"If you truly care for him, you'll send for her as well."

Carson nodded at Major Stronghart, who quickly motioned to Sergeant Perill.

"One more thing you should know about the boy," said Sister Omenn, watching the sergeant's departure until he was well out of earshot.

"And that is?"

The old woman's watery eyes lingered on Major Stronghart. A bony finger beckoned Carson closer.

"For your ears only, child."

Sibil Dunn

The back of Sister Omenn's robe was so long that Sibil could not help but tread on it as she followed the woman down a long, dark tunnel. She tried to avoid it repeatedly, but the woman kept hold of her hand, so she could not distance herself enough. "You should visit me more often!" The crone's cackle sounded sickly.

"Where are we going?" Sibil asked.

"Just to the point where we can no longer turn around. To where there is no going back!"

"No!" Sibil cried, twisting her hand away. She commanded her legs to stop, but the robe beneath her stilled feet glided on, carrying her with it.

"Here we go!" said Sister Omenn. The tunnel dropped so precipitously that Sibil lost her footing. She fell onto her back and started sliding ever faster, captive on the robe.

"Sibil!"

Sibil clutched her bedcover to her neck, her heart racing. All was dark inside The Nest.

Loud whispering stirred her. "Are you awake? Sibil!"

She slipped out of bed and listened at the door, breathless.

"It's Reggie! Can you hear me?"

Reggie! "I hear you," said Sibil, her cheek pressed against the door. "What do you want?" She opened and closed her eyes several times. *Is this really happening? What was I dreaming?*

"It's your friend, Tristan."

What? Oh no, please don't tell me... "Where is he? What's wrong? Is he all right?"

"I'm not sure. Better, I suppose, though he seems weak to me. He's waiting for you in the stables."

"The stables! He's out of bed? And walking?"

"Yes. He's dressed and waiting for you in the barn. He asked that you wear riding clothes."

"Riding clothes! What's going on, Reggie?"

"That's all I know. He asked that you make haste."

Riding clothes! What in Baelon? "All right! Tell him I'm coming... just as soon as I'm dressed."

"I'll let him know!" whispered Reggie.

"Reggie? Reggie!" No answer.

Sibil pulled her nightgown over her head and began rummaging for clothes in the dark.

Her heart was still pounding as she left The Nest.

None of this makes sense! I thought it might be early morning, but it's the dead of night! Just one sun ago, Tristan was proclaimed to be too weak to leave his sickbed, let alone venture outside. Or go riding!

The soft glow of a lantern guided her toward the livery.

Make haste? In the middle of the night? What am I to make of that?

The evening air was cool and crisp. She wrung her hands together as she walked. A lantern's light began to move well before she reached the barn. Back and forth it gently swayed... a horse's chest... a man's torso. Tristan's horse was saddled, and he seemed to lean upon it for support. The lantern's glow illuminated the young knight's upper body, casting shadows on one side of his face. A veil of fine gold hair hung loosely to his jawline.

"Your bandages! They've been removed!"

Tristan lowered the lantern. "Yes. They're no longer necessary."

"But just one sun ago—"

"Do you trust me?"

"Of course!"

"We're going for a ride."

Reggie appeared from the livery, leading Shadow by his reins.

"A ride!" *Preposterous!* "What does the physician say?"

"That I should embrace life, not hide from it."

She could hear him grinning.

"What does that mean? I thought that—"

"Here. I need you to wear this." Tristan held the lantern just above his open hand, across which a length of black cloth was draped.

Sibil reached for it instinctively.

"What's this?" she asked, plucking it from his hand.

"A blindfold," Tristan said.

"A blindfold!" A nervous laugh escaped her lips. "Whatever for?"

"It's a surprise."

"I'm not putting on a blindfold in the middle of the night! Not whilst on a horse. Not even for you, Sir Godfrey."

"Please, don't call me that."

"Not even for you, Tristan."

"I thought you said you trusted me."

"I do trust you. There's no one I trust more."

"I promise you'll be safe. Reggie's going to tether our mounts together. I'll be right by your side and we'll go slow. Please."

So serious!

"You should be okay," Reggie said. "I've seen it done before. So long as you ride slow, like Tristan says." But the young groom stood fast, clearly waiting for her to bless his actions.

In a strange sort of way, that increased her comfort.

"Very well." She sighed. "Because it's you, Tristan Godfrey." She gave Shadow a kiss on his muzzle. "And because it's you, Shadow. You'll keep an eye out for me, will you?"

What's the worst that can happen, after all? These aren't the Lawless Lands. How adventurous! How mysterious!

It was the tail end of Nine Moons. Soon Ten would take its place, accompanied by even colder weather. What would she have done without the heavy blanket draped across her shoulders? Thank goodness Tristan was a planner, and a thoughtful one at that!

It was impossible to tell just where they were. The young knight had spun Shadow round and round at the bottom of the palace road purposely to disorient her, then kept her in the saddle far longer than necessary to reach familiar haunts. She had ticked them off as likely destinations: his or her family's house... *Quest,* where she and he had schooled with Theos and Lewen... The God of Children's House... The House of All Gods... The Royal Keep. Unless, of course, he was toying with her. It would be just like him to keep her in suspense all morning long, only to unmask her back inside the castle! If that was not the case, they could be most anywhere by then. *Gods above, tell me we are not destined for The Sisters' sanctuary!*

Periodically, she sniffed the air or cocked her head, such that she might hear or smell something to lend a clue, but she had no idea in which direction they were headed until she felt the sun rise to her left.

The blindfold tied by Reggie had done its job, narrow gaps between its bottom edge and her cheeks little help in distinguishing black cloth from night air. It had been most comfortable to simply keep her eyes closed through the evening. But now, the morning sun's teasing was more than she could stand.

"Tristan, the blanket is a bit much now. Can we not stop to rest? Perhaps remove the blindfold for a spell? I promise not to peek."

"It's not much further. Trust me." The words were reassuring, but the quiver in his voice troubled her.

"Are you certain you're all right? You don't sound well."

"I'm fine. Just tired."

"Then we should stop. You're in no condition to be traveling like this."

"We're nearly there, Sib. I can see our destination. We'll rest soon."

And on they rode.

"Did the Sisters of Systalene tell you that I visited you there?" Sibil asked.

"They didn't have to. I knew," Tristan said.

Even blindfolded, Sibil could not help but smile. "Is that so? You heard me speak to you as well, did you?"

"Yes. Every word. I remember most everything you've ever said to me."

Sweet talker! As do I!

Shadow plodded to a full stop.

"We've arrived," Tristan said. She heard the young knight dismount, and the next thing she knew, his hands were on her waist and she was sliding to the ground. He helped to remove her blindfold. "Don't open your eyes too quickly. It's quite bright out. Just a little at a time. There! Can you see?"

"It's The Fekle Forest!" For a moment, Sibil found it hard to breathe. The blindfold slipped from her hand.

Tristan took a deep breath. "Theos died not far from here, you know."

Sibil nodded, her racing heart bridled by the memory of how Theos had met his end.

"It should have been me who was killed that day," Tristan said.

"What? Why would you say that? It should have been no one, surely."

"If someone had to die, I mean. It really isn't fair. He was so much stronger than me."

"Tristan, don't. That isn't true."

"Isn't it? It was Theos who killed the king's steward. Did you know that?"

"What!" A vision of Pryll Fletcher chilled her, but imagining his death at the hands of Theos hit her hard.

"It's true. The steward was known to force himself on castle staff. One of them was the young lady Theos planned to marry."

"What!"

"Emily Beckridge. One of the palace servant girls."

Sibil closed her eyes. *Emily! The girl with Tristan outside the chapel that day. Beautiful... long blond hair.*

"I met her once," she said.

"Theos would have killed him for that alone, I'm sure, but when Reggie told us what happened to you... oil on a fire already raging."

That night we met inside the royal coach! The same night the steward was killed! No wonder Theos seemed so serious!

"I feel his presence now," Tristan said. "That's how strong he is."

"We've come to honor Theos?"

"In part, I suppose. He's smiling down on us right now, I guarantee you that. And prodding me in my sore ribs. But mostly we are here because of questions I must ask you, and two truths that I must share. And much as I love Castle Aranox, it would not do them justice."

Sibil swallowed, her heart racing once again.

"Did you read my letter?" the young knight asked.

Sibil's lips parted. *He cannot know one way or the other. Would it not be easier on both of us to say that I did not? It was to be unopened until his return. How awkward the truth will be if he has had a change of heart!*

"Yes," she whispered, unable to lie.

"Then you already know one of my truths. Will you walk with me, through the Fekle Forest, hand in hand?"

Lovers who pass through it hand in hand are bound to one another for eternity! "Yes!" she said, a warmth unlike any other she had ever felt coursing through her.

Tristan offered her his hand. "It's supposed to be enchanted, you know."

Sibil interlocked her fingers with the young knight's, and they stepped into the shade of Fekle Forest side by side.

"You said that you had questions," said Sibil.

"Have I not been asking questions?" said Tristan. "Have you read my letter? Will you walk hand in hand with me?"

Sibil laughed. "You're right, of course. I was so happy hearing them, I suppose I wanted more."

Tristan smiled. "There are, in fact, two more. Do you love me, Sibil Dunn?"

She squeezed his hand. "I do! You know I do. I've loved you for so long now!"

"Then would you marry me? Not will you, mind you... would you?"

"Why do you ask like that? Of course I would! Of course!"

"There are two truths I still must tell you. The first you already know, but I must say it out loud and look into your eyes whilst saying it: "I love you, Sibil Dunn. More than you will ever know."

"And I you!"

The two embraced, then kissed. Tristan wiped the tears from Sibil's cheeks. "And now, Theos, you can stop haunting me," he said. They continued walking, hand in hand, until they reached a grove of friendship trees, one of its members much larger than the rest. Its massive trunk branched quickly into several large limbs hovering above the ground. Exposed roots criss-crossed the soil beneath its canopy like so many knotted ropes of different length and girth.

The two young lovers picked their way across them until they reached the base of the ancient plant. Tristan leaned heavily against it, his eyes closed.

"What's wrong?" Sibil asked. "You're not well, are you?"

Tristan opened his eyes and smiled. "Nothing new, I'm afraid. It's constant now. My head hurts all the time. As though they are still kicking me."

"Why have we come, then? You should be at rest!"

Tristan chuckled softly. "We've come this far. You know what we must do." He ran an open palm across the friendship tree's scarred surface. "Here. Help me, would you?" Tristan produced a small blade. He handed it to Sibil, first wrapping her fingers around its hilt, then clasping both of his hands around hers.

"You pick the spot," he said.

Sibil searched the tree's scarred trunk for an unmarked section large enough to hold their initials. "Here," she said. "This will do nicely, don't you think?"

"It's perfect," he whispered. "Will you do the honors?" His hands were trembling so.

It took her quite some time, but she wanted it to look just right, and to last forever. Tristan eased himself to the ground as she worked. She carved deeply, and as smoothly as the knife's limitations would allow.

"There!" she said. "A spell is hereby cast upon us, adding ten almons to both our lives! All we need now is fairy dust to fall upon us!"

"Fairy dust," Tristan whispered. "A lovely legend, and this..." The tips of his fingers reached up to pass slowly over their carving, lingering on Sibil's initials. "This is a thing of beauty. But I've one more truth to tell."

Sibil sat next to him and searched his eyes. Tristan reclined further, until he was supine on the forest floor.

"Lay with me, will you?"

She did, and he reached to find her hand. "I've told you but one truth. There is one more to tell." The young knight held her gaze, tears welling in his eyes. "I'm dying."

Sibil could not speak. Could not breathe. Could not think.

"I've known for quite some time, as have the Systalene. They've done all they can for me."

Sibil found her voice, but it wavered. "No... that can't possibly be true!"

"I haven't any strength left, Sib. It's why we're here, together. So that I can tell you in my own words what I've held captive in my heart for so long. Lie next to me, would you, so that I may bid you a proper farewell?"

He pulled her close, and she allowed her body to complement the contours of his.

"I love you, Sibil Dunn."

Sibil sobbed. "And I you, Tristan Godfrey."

"This is how I always hoped that we would be," Tristan whispered. "I am most content here in your arms. I pray Baelon above feels much the same."

Please, please... just a bit further!

Sibil urged Shadow up the last stretch of palace road to Castle Aranox, one outstretched arm helping keep Tristan's body, slung belly down across his horse's saddle, from slipping to the ground. Dusk had long since fallen, turning even the bastion of baelonite into a streaky gray.

"Help!" she cried, her eyes fixed on blazing torches blurring outside the gates. "Help me! Please!"

A dark form atop the battlements challenged her.

"Who goes there?"

"It's Sibil Dunn and Tristan Godfrey! Sir Tristan Godfrey!" she shouted. "Help us, please!"

One voice behind the castle walls quickly turned to several.

When the creaking of the gates added to the clamor, a wave of relief and emotion swept over her. Lanterns swayed as several figures poured from the castle's mouth.

"Be careful!" she said. A group of men surrounded both mounts before heading back toward the castle with hands stabilizing Tristan.

"Here, Shadow." *Reggie's voice!* The young groom's hands took Shadow's reins from hers, and she surrendered to exhaustion in the saddle.

Inside the castle gates, a small crowd was gathering, lanterns held high to help illuminate the two horses while maintaining a respectful distance. Sibil was relieved to see Marshal Carson emerge from it.

"He's not moving, and he hasn't said a word since we left The Fekle Forest," she sobbed. "I'm not sure he's breathing."

The marshal approached as Lady Godfrey joined the group behind him, a light shawl pulled tightly over her shoulders. She stood next to Major Stronghart, one hand resting lightly on his forearm, the other clenched over her heart.

Marshal Carson placed two fingers on Tristan's neck and closed his eyes in concentration. Sibil held her breath. Repositioning his fingers, the marshal spoke softly. "If it's there, it's too faint to feel."

A loud wail escaped Lady Godfrey. Her head lolled back, her eyelids closing as her body collapsed.

Sibil slid from Shadow, sobbing.

Major Stronghart's hands lifted Lady Godfrey from the ground. He hefted her once to gain a better hold, then strode away with her limp body cradled in his arms.

Marshal Erik Carson

Marshal Carson motioned for the servant girl to wait. He knocked lightly on Lady Godfrey's door. When there came no answer, he knocked again, slightly louder. "Lady Godfrey?"

He turned to the servant girl and nodded, stepping back to allow her ingress. She knocked, lifted the latch, and entered the room timidly.

Carson waited.

"Lady Godfrey?" he heard the young girl query.

Her ensuing scream caused him to rush into the room, where he found her shaking, staring at the bed.

"Take your leave," he said. "Summon the chaplain."

The girl left hastily.

Carson approached the bed. Lady Godfrey lay fully dressed on top of its neat covers, her head resting on a pillow. One arm was dangling down the bedside, her lifeblood pooled on the floor below. The dagger she had used to slit her wrist had fallen to the floor. Her other arm rested on her chest, a piece of parchment held to her heart.

He held his fingers to her throat, but found no pulse.

He picked the note up and read to himself:

Dearest mother and father,

Please forgive me this awkward farewell.

I do not know how to say goodbye.

Even if I knew the words, I could not bear to say them in the flesh.

I am so weak, and in constant pain.

I know these are my final days.

If you had not already guessed, I am in love with Sibil Dunn.

Please do not blame her for what I have planned next.

I am not long for this world, regardless.

How fortunate I was to be born a Godfrey, and to have been raised by both of you!

I now join Theos, and we await you in the next life.

Forever your loving son,

Tristan

A prattler with a human face scuttled toward Erik Carson, snickering.

Noggods, it's the magister!

"Hah!" the creature cried. "This is why you could not find me! Come closer, why don't you?"

Carson advanced warily, his sword drawn and pointed at the beast.

"Closer still," the magister said. "How else are you to capture me? Closer... closer. That's it!" The magister's pointed nose suddenly shot forward, extending to a lance's length. "Is this what you've been looking for?"

Carson dodged the lance, swiping at it with his sword and cleaving it in half. The magister melted into water.

Carson turned to the sound of clapping.

Marshal Ademar and Sister Omenn, buried in beach sand to their waists, applauded him.

"What's wrong with you?" asked Carson. "Something is not right. You both look so strange!"

"You don't look so well yourself!" said Sister Omenn. "Have you not yet taken a respite from your worries? Foolish boy! What did I recommend to you? A sojourn to the Southern Isles! Don't let your feet get wet!"

"Nothing is as it appears, my friend," said Marshal Ademar. "You, of all people, should know that."

Marshal Carson looked down at his boots, suddenly half-buried in beach sand and coins of gold. A receding wave left shallow water circling his ankles, depositing more sand up to his calves.

"Don't let your feet get wet!" the sister screamed at him.

Marshal Carson sat bolt upright.

"What is it, Erik?" his wife mumbled, her lips pressed into her pillow.

"I know where it is," the marshal said, his breathing fast and ragged. "The Guild's treasure! I know where it's hidden!"

Sibil Dunn

It was the same room in which her mother had taken her last breaths.

Sibil closed the door silently behind her. *Hurry, the marshal has already left!* Her eyes were drawn to the only light in the room. Wisps of smoke rose from a small bowl next to a bedside candle, filling the chamber with a scent she could not place. *Meant to heal, or meant to mask the scent of death? Impossible to say!* Dressed in nothing but a nightshirt, Tristan was positioned on his back atop the bed, hands folded on his stomach. Sibil tip-toed to him, watching for the rise or fall of his chest, a twitch in his throat, a throbbing in his neck... the slightest movement of any kind. *Please tell me it's the lighting that makes you look this way! So ghastly gaunt and pale, as though all blood has drained from you! Is that really even you, Tristan?*

Soft snoring drew her attention to the candlelight's furthest reach. It spread just far enough to reveal the curved feet of a rocking chair. Between them, the scuffed tips of two black shoes protruded from beneath the dark folds of a hem. The rocking chair was still.

Hurry! You're needed elsewhere!

She brought her mouth to Tristan's ear and whispered what she could recall of Gradi's telling of an old wives' tale: "He suffered terribly until she was sent for. A final kiss sealed his lips, assuring passage to Baelon above." She touched her lips to Tristan's. "Goodbye, my love!"

She was halfway to the door when Sister Omenn's voice caught up to her. "So you do know the tale!" Sibil's feet stopped moving. "You must take care, Wisperal!" The rocking chair began to creak. "That's not how the story ends, you know."

THE PAYMENT OF DEBTS

"Be mindful of the weight you ask your heart to carry; it will not be easy to shrug off." From the Scriptures of All Gods, attributed to the God of Happiness, Ekstata

Marshal Erik Carson

They had traveled south throughout the night, quietly bypassing Chalmsworth before winding their way west, toward the Mersal Sea. Riding behind him and the major were twenty-five men roused from sleep, six of them prepared to sail. A red banner embellished with the crest of Aranox—a gold half sun rising—flapped in the early morning breeze above them.

And all set in motion by an old woman's riddles!

Carson only wished he had been quicker to construe her cryptic message.

The road widened and swung south along the seacoast, dirt turning to cobblestones well before introducing Waterford's wharf. It had been almons since his last journey there, but it looked much the same as he remembered.

A long row of two-story buildings stretched from one end to the other, separated from the sea by a wide, stone promenade from which a dozen piers extended, wooden fingers reaching out above the water. Multiple ships of different shapes and sizes wobbled on the ocean's waves, bound to its floor by anchor, or tethered to the piers by rope.

The marshal's approach had not gone unnoticed. A group of four men trotted toward him, waving frantically as he and his party neared the first dock.

Do not allow distractions. Locate the harbormaster. Search the wharf! All twenty-five men know to watch for the same quarries: an old man known as the magister, perhaps dressed in a white robe and slow afoot; a short woman with large eyes and long gray hair, perhaps piled in a bun atop her head, known as Ruler Three; the leader of The Guild's army, distinguishable by his sharp facial features and a riding crop topped with a gold knob and tassels; a third man of average height and build, thought to consort with another bearing a large scar on his forehead. And any sizable cache of gold, whether stored inside a building, on the docks or aboard a ship.

"Welcome! Welcome to Waterford!" said one of the four men. "Harbormaster Foley, at your disposal."

Carson brought his men to a halt with an upraised palm. *Harbormaster! The God of Fortune smiles on us!* "Marshal Erik Carson. In service to His Majesty, King Axil."

"We weren't expecting you, Marshal! But thank the gods you're here! How did you know to come so quickly? And with so many soldiers! Follow me! The bodies are this way!"

"Bodies!"

"Ten of them, Marshal! All murdered last night. One of them right here... on the docks. The other nine lie down a side street just ahead."

"We'll need to view them. Major..."

Major Stronghart turned in his saddle. "Sergeant Perill! Front and center!"

Harbormaster Foley nodded. "Of course, Marshal, of course! Jamison—escort the sergeant, would you? Make sure he sees all ten."

"And everything they had in their possession," said Stronghart. "Take two men with you, Sergeant. And take your time. Make certain."

"Yes, Major." Sergeant Perill called back into the ranks. "Parsons, Arliss! With me!"

"We'll need to search the wharf as well," Carson said to the harbormaster. "Every building, one at a time... no exceptions."

"Whatever you need, Marshal. Just say the word!"

"Your logs... I need to know those ships familiar with The Southern Isles, and when they come and go."

"You're welcome to the books, of course. I'll show you them myself. They tell a story true when it comes to the past, but they can't be relied on for the future."

"How's that?"

"They're full of hopes and promises, Marshal, but the sea's a moody creature, and her currents don't consult us. Nevertheless, I don't need the books to say this much: there are but seven ships that call the Southern Isles home. It takes a quarter moon to sail there; a half moon back and forth. A quarter moon in either port to empty a ship's bowels and then refill them. That's a full moon, give or take, between visits here."

"Understood. When is the next ship due?"

"I don't need the books for that either, Marshal. *The Blessed Bride* should make port in two suns. The only one with us now—the next to leave these docks for the Southern Isles—would be *The Fair Winds*. She's been here a quarter moon already. She sails this sun. As soon as the fog lifts."

"No! Not until we've searched her! You must hold her! And I've six men who need to travel with her to the isles."

The harbormaster showed his first signs of doubt. "Well, that'll be a trick, Marshal. We'd best move quickly. I'm sure she's set to cast off any time now. And no doubt she's fully loaded—to add cargo or passengers this late in the game... well—"

"Split the men, Major! Half with you to search the docks. Half with me to *The Fair Winds*, including those six made ready to sail! Harbormaster Foley, lead on!"

"Cargomaster Munson!" The harbormaster's voice boomed down the pier, catching the attention of everyone who had not already been alerted by the sound of a dozen soldiers' footsteps. A portly man directing traffic at the bottom of *The Fair Winds'* gangway responded. "What now?"

"Where's your captain?" asked the harbormaster.

"Already on board, of course. What's all this?"

"Hold fast. You can't cast off until the ship's been searched. And you've six more passengers to board."

"Six! Impossible! We're overweight as it is! And we've no time for silly searches. We're just about to push off!"

"In this fog? And who are you to say when you push off?" said Foley.

"I'm the *Fair Winds'* cargomaster, as you well know!"

"And I'm the harbormaster!" said Foley. "As long as you're docked here, you'll do as I say! Don't mess with me, Munson. Not this sun! There's ten men dead out there! Are all your crew accounted for?"

"You think we didn't check? Of course they are!"

"And can they all account for where they were last night?"

Munson's chest deflated. "Our cargo's accounted for, that much I know." He directed his next words to the marshal, clearly annoyed. "What is it you're looking for, anyway?"

Foley put his ruddy face in front of the cargomaster's. "Don't bother the good marshal, Munson. He isn't your concern. If you've something else to bark about, take it up with me—whilst his soldiers search your ship."

"Under different circumstances, perhaps," said Munson. "And with more notice. But not now. We're late as it is!"

"You don't have a choice," said the harbormaster.

"The fargin' bysh, I don't!" said Munson. "Our stay here is done. Your services are no longer required."

"But the marshal—"

"Has no jurisdiction aboard *The Fair Winds*!" the cargomaster shouted. "The seas belong to no realm!"

"What's going on here? What's happening, Munson?" A large man, well-groomed with a bushy beard and steer horn mustache, appeared at the top of *The Fair Wind's* gangway. He buttoned a thick wool coat with large gold buttons as he awaited a reply.

An officer, if not the captain himself!

Munson gestured toward the soldiers. "They want to search the ship, Captain! And six want passage to the isles!"

The captain nodded toward Carson. "And you are…?"

"Marshal Erik Carson, Captain, in service to King Axil."

"Captain Bixby Abrahms, at your service, sir. I take it this has to do with last night's murders?"

Carson cocked his head. "Time will tell, Captain. At the moment, we're looking for three men, one woman, and property belonging to the realm. They wouldn't be members of your crew, if that's any comfort."

"It is, indeed." The captain tugged at his jacket. "The cargomaster is correct, of course; you have no jurisdiction on *The Fair Winds*." He stared directly at Munson. "When she's on open water, that is. But as he should also know, so long as she's attached to land, be that by rope or gangplank, she's governed by the king's law, and is subject to your search." He made a sweeping gesture with his arm. "Please, Marshal, you and your men are welcome aboard. My apologies for the misunderstanding. Mister Munson, a word, if you will!"

Overseer Reynard Rascall

"Aside from the fact that we are now deep in the belly of a death trap, this is perfect," said Reynard.

"You think?" Charise eyed *The Fair Winds* hold with obvious misgivings.

"I do. Close enough to the magister and his friends to account for them, but absent their prying eyes. Left to ourselves in the company of a small portion of his treasure, no doubt."

"Promises, promises. Where should we begin the hunt?" The assassin nudged a tall coil of rope with her foot.

"At the bow or stern—take your pick," said Reynard. "I don't think it matters, so long as we work our way from one end to the other. But that can wait. We have a quarter moon all to ourselves to manage that. In the meantime, we've more important things to do."

"Such as?"

"Such as make this krephole home. A quarter moon will seem a lifetime if we don't. Foremost, we need a place to sleep and to relax. Comfortably, mind you. Let's work on that while it's still light."

"Agreed." Charise looked from one end of the hold to the other. "Why don't we—"

"Hallo, down there!" A male voice froze them both.

Reynard's raised hand cautioned Charise against further dialogue.

Footsteps rattled the stairs, heralding black boots and red trousers with a yellow stripe down their length.

Reynard's hand found the hilt of a dagger tucked into his waistband.

"I thought I heard voices." A young man wearing the colors of Aranox scampered down the hold's last stairs. "You'd best get a move-on. The rest of your crew is already disembarking. Passengers are being held on deck."

Several more boots clattered down the stairs, and the young man was suddenly joined by two fellow soldiers.

Reynard relaxed his grip on the dagger. "What's happening?"

"We're searching the ship, that's what. You need to leave."

"Searching for what?" asked Reynard.

"You need to leave!" the largest of the soldiers said. "Ask your captain!"

"Very well. No need to shout. We're going." Reynard urged Charise to precede him up the stairs. *What in Baelon? Soldiers searching for what? For the gold? For the magister? Ahhh... for those who murdered Two and his newfound friends last evening!*

Charise hesitated on the lower deck above the hold. Reynard glanced right and left. According to the young man who had escorted them on board, the crew's quarters were through the door to his right; passengers' quarters to its twin on the left. Both were left wide open, revealing flashes of red and gold down their corridors.

"Keep going!" he said, pressing his palms against Charise's buttocks. "The ship's crawling with soldiers!"

He followed her up another flight of stairs and onto *The Fair Winds'* main deck. A morning mist chilled the fresh, crisp air. On the raised stern deck, a half dozen soldiers, swords drawn, guarded a group of men and women. *Passengers! Don't stare, but is the magister among them? Ruler Three or Four?* "We don't want to mix with that crowd," he said, unable to make out any helpful details.

Near the bow, two men conferred together, occasionally pointing to other places on board. One wore the king's colors; the other, a dark blue jacket with gold buttons.

Reynard steered Charise toward the gangplank. "Don't speak," he whispered. "Just smile and keep walking. Remember, we're part of the crew. If all goes well, we're back on board after the soldiers' search, with no harm done. If things go wrong, we can at least make a run for it on land."

A lone soldier at the top of the gangway eyed them as they approached.

"We're with the crew," Reynard said, stepping to the deck's edge. He took a moment to survey the pier below. Two soldiers watched over a group crowding its wooden surface, presumably *The Fair Winds'* crew. Beside them... *Noggods! The giant royal guardsman with the—*

Whizzzz-thunk! Something sped past Reynard and hit the ship's main spar below its bottom sail.

"Reynard!" Charise gasped, clutching her chest and reaching for him. Blood poured from her leather coat and between her fingers as she crumpled to the ship's deck. For an instant, all went still and silent.

The soldier at the top of the gangplank ducked behind the ship's railing, crying, "Crossbow!"

Reynard staggered back onto the deck. The two uniformed men near the bow started toward him. "Get down!" one shouted. "Get down!" Reynard could only stare. *That voice! Those shiny boots! That head of auburn hair! Gods above...* He ran.

"Stop that man!" the familiar voice shouted.

Reynard sprinted across the deck and to the opposite railing, two soldiers heading from the stern toward him. He grabbed hold of a rope ladder connected to the main mast and hoisted himself onto the railing. *If you climb up, you're trapped and certain death awaits!*

"Stop!" shouted one of the soldiers. "Stay where you are!"

Reynard glanced back toward the gangway, but all he could see of Charise was a lifeless arm protruding from the group that had surrounded her.

He let go of the rigging and jumped.

Nothing but gray air! A stiff breeze blew up his trouser legs. His arms rose to his sides. His turncoat lifted to his chest as he let go his knife and closed his eyes, knowing what was coming. *Ker-splushhhh!* Cold water crashed around him, pushed him down, and tried to smother him. He flailed his arms and legs, but nothing gave and he could find no purchase. He kicked and pawed and thought he might have broken the water's surface, but water poured into his mouth. *I need to breathe!* He flailed his arms again, hit something hard, and gulped for air, swallowing salt water as he sank.

Something in the water bumped or bit him, and he clawed frantically at it, managing to grab it with one hand. He pulled and his head broke the water's surface. Still flailing, he inhaled until he felt his lungs might burst. Something exploded on the top of his head, his body surrendered, and black water swallowed him again.

Marshal Erik Carson

Carson watched in disbelief as the man jumped from the ship's railing. "Noggods!" He peered into the fog below, slapped the railing with his palm, then traipsed quickly across the deck. Those gathered near the top of the ship's gangplank, including the ship's captain, stepped back as he approached, allowing him access to the prostate body of a woman.

"She's dead, Marshal," said one of the soldiers kneeling at her side.

"One of yours?" Carson asked Captain Abrahms.

"No, Marshal. Never seen her before. Must be a passenger."

"A passenger… why wasn't she with the others?"

Captain Abrahms shrugged.

"Where'd that come from?" Carson directed a soldiers' attention to a feathered shaft protruding from the ship's main mast.

"From the next pier over, Marshal. One man with a crossbow! He ran toward the wharf!"

Priorities! "Take Skorr and Cheswick. Find the major on the docks. Tell him to call off the search. Have all our men come aboard. Be careful! And have this woman's friend fished from the drink!"

"My pleasure, Marshal." The soldier sped off, nearly running into Rolft Aerns, coming up the gangway.

"Marshal." The retired royal guard peered down at the dead woman.

"Sibil's here?" asked Marshal Carson.

"We only just arrived," Rolft said. "She'll wait on the docks until you send for her." The warrior kneeled by the woman, his brow deeply furrowed as he reached to touch her face.

"What is it, Rolft?"

"I know this one!"

"What!"

"I met her at The Kindling. She helped me to find Sibil."

"I don't understand. Helped you how? Who is she? What's she doing here?" *Another piece to the wrong puzzle!*

Rolft shook his shaggy head. "What business she has here, I've no idea. But that someone would be hunting her does not surprise me."

"Why's that?"

"Unless I'm off my mark…" Rolft took hold of one of the woman's ankles and removed the sandal from her foot. He cocked his head at an angle and sighed, lowering her foot to the deck. "Her soles are inked, Marshal."

"She's an assassin?" asked Captain Abrahms.

"And she helped you to find Sibil?" The marshal scratched his head. "I'm lost. What was she—"

"Marshal Carson! Marshal Carson!" It was Sergeant Galeran, lumbering across the deck from the stern. The stocky soldier placed a hand upon his chest as he slowed to catch his breath. His cheeks were red, his eyes wide with excitement.

"What is it, Sergeant?" Carson rose to his feet.

Sergeant Galeran pointed back toward the raised stern deck, where two remaining soldiers kept watch over the passengers.

"It's the passengers, Marshal. I only just noticed, but one of them's got a stick... like the riding crop you're lookin' for! Short and black! He keeps it tucked in tight behind his legs, and his hand's mostly coverin' its knob, but it's gold, all right, with tassels, just like you said!"

"Which one? What does he look like?" Carson tried to pick out individuals in the group, but it was too great a distance for that.

"To the right side, Marshal. He fits the description. And he's twitchy... can't stand still."

"Very well. Let's see if we can't help him sort things out." Carson addressed the lone soldier guarding the gangway. "No one on or off the ship except the captain, Rolft, and our men, understood?" To Rolft he said, "You'd best get back to Sibil. And watch for that crossbow! I'll send for you both if needed."

Carson took stock of his men. He had brought a dozen onto the pier. *Three in the hold, searching for Guild plunder. Two on the pier below, watching over the captain's crew. Three more now headed back to the wharf for Stronghart. One guarding the ship's gangplank. That leaves Sergeant Galeran and two others still guarding passengers on the stern.*

The marshal started across the ship's deck, Sergeant Galeran beside him.

"Does he know you've taken an interest in him?"

"I don't think so, sir. I've tried not to be obvious."

"Very good. What about the woman and the old man?"

"Hard to say, Marshal. We've not spoken to any of them. There's thirty-six, all told. Several women and five old men among them, but none are wearing robes, of course."

Two sets of stairs led from the main deck to the upper stern. Carson headed for the ones furthest away.

"Take the other side, Sergeant, and keep the passengers from using the stairs. No one leaves."

"Yes, sir."

Carson bounded onto the stern's raised deck. With the passengers loosely assembled near its broad rear, he quickly identified the man Sergeant Galeran had taken an interest in. Average height, lean and tanned. His narrow eyes followed the marshal's every move, one hand surreptitiously held behind his legs.

"His Majesty apologizes for this inconvenience!" the marshal shouted. The passengers all went silent. "We'll try to keep it short. Women to that side, please, in front of Sergeant Galeran. Men to this side, facing me!"

The passengers began to move as requested, muttering and murmuring amongst themselves. Many of the women had their hair covered by a bonnet or scarf. Carson took note of five old men. The two soldiers already on deck separated, one joining the marshal, the other staying with Sergeant Galeran. When the male passengers were gathered together, the marshal spoke again. "You there, in the back, in the black turncoat. Step forward, please!" The man responded slowly, his eyes flitting between the marshal and his surroundings. One hand remained behind his legs. "Front and center, sir!"

The man sidestepped out of the group and began to shuffle forward. When he stopped midway, the soldier standing next to Carson exhaled heavily and strode toward him.

"No, wait!" the marshal shouted. *Too late!*

The passenger's hand swung from behind his leg, revealing the black riding crop. *Ruler Four!* With one hand on its top and the other grasping its bottom, he pulled the two lengths apart—one, a cylindrical scabbard; the other, a needle-like blade the length of the man's forearm. With a single thrust, the needle pierced the soldier's torso, its tip appearing out his back.

As quickly, Ruler Four withdrew the blade and shoved the soldier backward into Carson. A woman screamed. The marshal wrapped both arms around the soldier. Ruler Four leaped forward, shoving the soldier yet again. Carson stumbled backward, into the stern's deck railing, the weight of the soldier pinning him momentarily. Ruler Four sped past him and down the stairs. Sergeant Galeran and the soldier with him gave chase. "Stop him!" Carson shouted, laying the dead soldier on the deck. "Don't let him leave the ship!" He shot a look of worry toward the gangway, pleased to see several soldiers running up its length to join the one already stationed there.

Ruler Four changed course and headed for the midship cabin. Flinging wide its door, he disappeared into the ship's hull.

"Stop!" Carson shouted, trailing his men. "Sergeant Galeran, stop!" Sword in hand, the marshal reached the door through which Ruler Four had disappeared.

"We've got him now, Marshal!" the sergeant said.

Carson shouted to Captain Abrahams. "Is there another way out from below?"

The captain pointed between the two sets of stairs leading to the stern's upper deck. "That hatch in the deck, there!"

"Position four men above it," Carson commanded Galeran. "The rest should gather here with you. Once I'm through this door, you'll close it and put your weight to it, do you hear? Don't let anyone in or out until you hear me or one of our soldiers on the other side."

"You're not going in after him!" said Sergeant Galeran.

"Three of ours are in the hold, and they don't know he's coming! Listen, wait here for Major Stronghart and the others. If this bastard somehow makes his way back onto the main deck, I want a royal welcome ready. Understood?"

"Yes, sir! May the gods be with you, sir!"

Sword in hand, Carson ducked into the midship cabin and started down the stairs. He heard the door behind him close.

He waited for his breathing to normalize, his eyes to adjust to the dark, before descending. The deck at the bottom of the stairs presented several options. He could go left or right down narrow passageways, presumably leading to the crew's quarters and the passengers' berths. The hallways leading ahead and to behind appeared to open wider some ten or twenty paces away, perhaps into a galley or a map room. Directly below, another set of stairs introduced the hold.

"Hallo, down there!" he shouted. "In the hold, can you hear me? This is Marshal Carson!"

"Aye, Marshal!" came a quick, albeit somewhat muffled reply. "This is Wicks, sir! Arnett and Baskill here as well!" The sound of boots scraping wood was soon followed by the appearance of Wicks' face as he climbed the stairs from the hold. "What is it, sir?"

"Are you armed?" asked the marshal, his eyes roving the avenues surrounding him.

"Of course, sir!" Wicks looked back down the stairs. "You're all armed, are you not?"

Affirmative replies echoed up the stairs. "Come up, then, and draw your weapons," called the marshal. When all three men had joined him, he cautioned them.

"There's a man hiding on this deck. Don't take him lightly. He's already killed one of your comrades. There's only two ways out of here. One is up these stairs, which you're to guard. Don't go looking for him. Stay here. Major Stronghart and the others will be on the main deck soon. If you see the slightest sign of anyone, call out to me. Look lively!" Carson entered the passageway to his left. A shaft of light near its end disclosed the presence of the vented hatch referenced by the captain. *The only other way out of here!* But there were a half dozen doors on either side of the corridor leading to it, some open, others closed.

Clear the rooms one at a time—and carefully, lest one become your coffin!

He pushed the first door slowly inward with his sword, then peered through the crack created between its hinges. *No one standing there!* He scanned the room's interior before entering. *Bunk beds, floor to ceiling, covering every wall. Little room for much else. Keep a watch behind you, and move on!*

Across the hall and a short way further down the hallway, the next door hung partially open. He looked between its hinges, pushed them to their limit, and stepped inside. *More bunk beds. Nothing else.* Back into the hallway, and up to the next door, fully open. *Still nothing!*

He cleared the next three rooms in similar fashion, stopping in front of a closed door before moving on. *More than halfway now!* His gaze settled on the corridor's dead end, beneath the vented hatch. *Only it's not a dead end, is it? That's a door, and it no doubt leads to the captain's quarters, spacious beneath the wide and raised stern deck. A good place in which to hide! Don't get ahead of yourself! There are several doors before you reach that one!*

Carson pushed the door before him open with his sword and peered inside. *But wouldn't the captain lock his d—* He turned just in time to see a straw mattress, standing on its end, barreling toward him from the door across the way. It slammed into his chest and sent him reeling backward through the opened doorway. He managed to land upright, a tight grip on his sword. But the weight of his assailant, pressed against the mattress, pinned him against the bunk beds. A large needle pierced the mattress, dangerously close to his chest. He leveraged his own weight against the bunk beds, pushed hard against the mattress, and repelled it.

The mattress fell to one side, exposing his assailant. The man stood motionless a few paces away, brandishing his weapon. *Half the reach of my sword—a fact that clearly has him thinking twice about advancing!*

"Marshal Carson of Aranox, I presume?" the man said, his chest rising and falling quickly.

Carson adjusted his footing and winced, a sharp pain reminding him of where his spine had met the bunk bed's framing. "And you're Ruler Four of The High Order."

"The honor is all mine," said Ruler Four. "Your reputation as a swordsman and a leader are well-known to me."

"Surrender, then," said Carson. "It was a mistake to come down here. You know that now, yeah? You would have been better off taking your chances with the sea, like your friend."

"That was no friend of mine, Marshal. I haven't any. Unless you'd like to call me yours..."

"It's a little late for that, I'm afraid."

Ruler Four half smiled. "You have me at a disadvantage, that's true. And yet... I'm going to kill you! And then I'm going to kill your men, one at a time, without worrying about you breathing down my neck. How many are there, by the way?"

High marks for bravado! "Twenty-five, and by now, they're all on board above you, just waiting. You should reconsider."

"Twenty-five," said Ruler Four. "A challenge, but one I'll savor when it's over. Why haven't you already called to them? I'll tell you why, shall I? I heard you give their orders. Because you know I'll kill whoever first comes through that door, that's why."

"If you don't surrender, you're going to die, either by my hand or theirs."

Ruler Four laughed. "Surrender! So you can parade me down your streets in shackles? To be stoned before you torture me and take my head? I don't think so."

"Identify your fellow rulers and the magister for me. Perhaps the king will have mercy on you."

"I've just killed one of the king's men. And I dare say, in his eyes, that's not my worst offense."

Carson watched the ruler's hands intently. "I cannot say what the king—"

"Please!" said the ruler. "We both know what awaits me at Castle Aranox."

"Regardless... you've little choice. Right here, right now... it's shackles or death for you. You're not leaving any other way."

"You're quite sure of that, are you?"

"Quite sure."

"That's not much of a choice, is it... when shackles lead to certain death?" Ruler Four pointed his weapon at the marshal's heart. "What would you do in my place, I wonder?" The man hung his head, as though in thought. "No... not really, I don't."

He suddenly lunged forward, his pointed steel needle thrust in front of him. It glanced off Carson's upraised blade and into the marshal's shoulder. Carson grabbed the ruler's lapels and shoved the smaller man aside. The edge of his sword sank into skin and tissue as it glided across the ruler's neck.

Carson pushed away from the bunk beds as Ruler Four crashed to the floor. The point of the marshal's sword quickly came to rest on the man's chest. Blood pulsed from a long gash across the ruler's neck, streaming through the fingers of a hand that could not stem it. "Is it not possible," Ruler Four asked, choking on his own blood, "to serve with honor... despite serving a most... dishonorable cause?"

The fingers gripping the black hilt of his blade began to relax, revealing its tasseled gold knob. His eyes stared up at the marshal. Carson kicked the needle away. Leaning back against the beds, he propped his sword against them, pressed a hand against his injured shoulder, and watched Ruler Four take his last breaths.

"You're hurt!" Major Stronghart offered his assistance, but Carson waved him off. In no time, the marshal was surrounded by his men on the main deck.

"It's nothing. I'm fine." He looked past his soldiers to the raised stern. "What's happened? Where are the passengers?"

"Beggin' your pardon, Marshal," said Sergeant Galeran, "but there was no one left to guard them. When all the shouting and killing started, the passengers got skittish and tried to disembark. Can't say I blame them, really."

My fault! "Tell me they were not allowed to leave the ship."

"By the time I noticed, a few may have, Marshal."

"Noggods!"

"We'll take a count, shall we?" said the sergeant. "There were thirty-six to start. At least the old men are still accounted for—I did manage to move all five of them as far from the gangway as possible." He pointed toward the ship's bow.

"That's something, all right." Carson grimaced as he walked. The hand pressed against his wound did little to relieve the pain.

"Major! Send for Rolft and Miss Dunn. You'll find them waiting on the docks."

Carson returned the stares of five older men who had stopped their milling near the bow to watch his approach. Four wore hats. Two carried canes, one of whom leaned against the ship's railing, his complexion suggesting he rarely saw the sun. Carson tried not to stare. "Gentlemen," he said, "again, my apologies for keeping you waiting."

"What's this all about?" asked the hatless, most active one. "What's it got to do with us?"

"Nothing, I suspect. This will all be over shortly. Then you can go about your business. Now, please, face the gangway and put some distance between you and the next man." The five did as told, all joining the pale man at the railing until they were an arm's length from their neighbors. "That's it. Now just stay put, and keep quiet unless you're asked to speak. The rest will take care of itself."

Carson turned to watch Rolft's hulking frame rise slowly up the gangway. Behind and to his side, Miss Dunn took smaller steps, occasionally looking down and back to something or someone she was leading. It was only as the pair boarded and cut a wider path that he could somewhat see between them. Flashes of a crown of dark brown hair no taller than Sibil's chest. Thin legs beneath a faded blue dress. One arm linked to Sibil's hand, another gripping Rolft's blouse at his waist.

As the trio crossed midship, the old man with the pale skin set his cane down and shifted his weight against the railing. "What's the meaning of this?" he asked in a low, raspy voice.

"Did I not tell you to be quiet?" The marshal drew his sword. The old man licked his lips and pulled the brim of his hat lower.

Carson held his free hand up, stopping Rolft's and Miss Dunn's progress some twenty paces away. Though largely hidden behind them, the young girl's presence was now obvious. She peered through the gap between her escorts. Miss Dunn drew the child close, one arm encircling her protectively as she whispered in her ear. The girl nodded. Miss Dunn pointed toward the marshal, and the young girl's head moved slowly side to side. Miss Dunn's arm moved ever so slightly before she spoke again. The girl's head moved side to side, and without further prompting, one of her thin arms rose to point a finger. Something Miss Dunn said caused the child's gesturing to become more animated. Miss Dunn placed both hands on the distraught child's shoulders and spoke at length. The girl nodded, shook her head, then responded, pointing once again.

The marshal waited as Miss Dunn approached, leaving the young girl under Rolft's wing. When she was close enough to speak confidentially, she turned her back to the old men.

"It's him!" she whispered, her eyes wide with excitement. "The magister is the tall one, nearest us!"

Carson kept his eyes on her. "The girl's certain?"

Miss Dunn nodded, glancing toward the line of old men, her gaze lingering on one. "As am I."

"How can that be? Perhaps she should come closer."

"No! She's scared to death, and there's no need."

"We cannot guess at this, Miss Dunn. There is too much at stake for all concerned."

"She's young, Marshal, but very bright. She understands. I told her much the same, and do you know what she said to me?"

Carson's eyebrows rose.

"She said she can't forget his face, much as she would like to. She sees it every night before she falls asleep. She swears that's him!"

"Even so—"

"And she said that when the magister undressed them, his breath smelled of rotting food and his voice was like a frog's!" Sibil's eyes burned into the marshal. "But what frightened her the most, what made her close her eyes whenever he came near, were his clacking fingernails. Long and yellow, like a bird of prey. She can't even see his hands from there, Marshal! But she won't come any closer. 'Go see for yourself!' she said to me!"

Carson took a deep breath, exhaling through his nose. He turned and closed the distance to the old men.

"Show me your hands. All of you."

Four of the five extended their arms, palms exposed.

The pale-skinned man resisted. "For what purpose?"

Not quite a frog's voice, but then, what would one call that? "To satisfy my curiosity, and to secure your freedom."

The heavy creases in the old man's pale face deepened and turned downwards, but he reluctantly unfolded his arms to display both palms.

"Turn them over, please. All of you."

It took no time at all to inspect them. "You're free to go," the marshal told the first man. "As are you." He nodded to the second. "As are the two of you." He excused the third and fourth. "Your king is most grateful for your cooperation."

He paused in front of the remaining man. *Long fingernails! Thick, hard, mostly yellow with black borders extending all the way to curved and pointed tips. Like a bird of prey!*

"Take your hands away before I cut them off." Carson used the tip of his sword to lift the brim of the old man's hat slowly until it fell backward, revealing a misshapen crown of pink, wrinkled skin devoid of any hair. "Your king looks forward to making your acquaintance... magister!"

"I don't know what you're talking about," wheezed the old man. "I'm traveling with my sister to the Southern Isles. She'll vouch for me!"

"Your sister!" *Ruler Three!* "Where is she, pray tell? Point her out and I'll discuss the matter with her."

"You've chased her off the ship!" said the old man. "There's no telling where she is now!"

"More's the pity," Carson said. "Major Stronghart!"

Sibil Dunn

Two flaming torches showed the way, like the nostrils of some fire-breathing beast unleashed upon the dead of night. Marshal Carson and the major rode between them, pursued by the body of the beast—a wagon surrounded by soldiers on horseback. A wagon laden with precious cargo, including the wrapped bodies of a soldier killed in service to King Axil; the corpse of Ruler Four, slain by none other than Marshal Carson; two barrels discovered in *The Fair Winds'* hold, said to be filled with gold coins stolen by The Guild of Takers; and a wicked old man, gagged, trussed, and blindfolded: the magister!

She had stared for so long at those beacons in the dark that now, even when she looked away, two small red orbs appeared to burn in front of her. But she no longer needed them to know just where she was. Somewhere off that road, in the woods to her right, lay the house where stablemaster Bohun Barr had met his untimely end.

Shadow plodded onto Fostead's main street. Past the livery where she and Reggie had caught up with Rolft. Past The Hold, where Sergeant Fields had lost his life, and the apothecary's shop where old Master Simpkins had been murdered. Past The King's Inn and to The God of Children's House, where Sibil brought Shadow to a halt. Rolft stopped there as well, the young girl nestled between him and his saddle's pommel. The wagon rolled noisily on toward Castle Aranox, garbling the faint murmurs of its uniformed escorts.

Sibil slipped from Shadow, relieved to feel the ground beneath her feet. Without speaking, she moved to Sarah's side and reached up to support the child's weight as Rolft lowered her from the saddle. The girl half woke and yawned, leaning heavily against Sibil.

Rolft dismounted, and scooping the child into his arms, climbed the building's steps alongside Sibil, who knocked three times on the door.

It took little time for it to open. The same brother who had joined Father Syrus in seeing them off now welcomed them back, candelabra in hand. He had to have been waiting, seated in the chair just inside the doorway. "How did it go?" he asked, rubbing his eyes with his free hand and stifling a yawn. "Everything's all right?"

"Everything is fine, Brother Kane," Sibil said in a hushed voice. "Please tell Father Syrus we're most grateful, and that I'll return to tell him all about it. What she needs now is rest."

"Of course." Brother Kane stared up at Rolft. "If you wouldn't mind, can you carry her? I'll show you to her bed."

As they reached the bottom of the palace road, Rolft reined Sarah in. High above, the gates of Castle Aranox were open wide, its battlements ablaze with fiery torches.

"This is where we part ways," the grizzled guardsman said.

"You'll not be staying at the castle?" Sibil asked. "Not even for one night?"

"No." Rolft tilted his beard to the stars. "The shedding moons are on their way. The fields don't work themselves, you know."

"Oh." Sibil hung her head. "It was selfish of me to take you from them."

Rolft laughed. "Nonsense! Had you not, I never would have forgiven you. Truly! Don't ever run off without me again, do you hear? Give my regards to Fereliss and Yurik, will you? Tell them I'll return to watch the magister receive his due." He clicked his tongue, and Sarah ambled off. "And you!" he called out. "Be well! Take care!"

"And you as well!" Sibil called out after him. "Thank you, Rolft!"

She eased Shadow up the palace road, too tired to think about much other than the feathered bed awaiting her. One of the guards stationed at the gates tipped his cap to her as she rode through. "Welcome home, Miss Dunn."

"Thank you," she murmured, purposely skirting the soldiers gathered round the wagon stopped inside. She caught sight of Marshal Carson but continued on, thankful not to be in his boots. The marshal could not simply disengage from the wagon's extraordinary cargo.

But she could.

Not even an enthusiastic Reggie could stay her. She handed him Shadow's reins and walked away.

The Nest's silhouette enthralled her. She approached the darkened structure, hoping against hope. But Sister Omenn's wagon no longer waited near its steps. The windows to the room where the Systalene had tended Tristan—portals to the same room her mother died in—were as dark as the rest. The candle that had made them flicker and shimmer throughout the sister's vigil had been extinguished.

Sibil climbed the stairs and plodded down the hallway, her hand running along its wall until she came to Tristan's room, its door ajar. She paused, then stepped into the black void, shuffling her feet until her shins touched the bed where he had lain. Her hand dropped to the blanket, her palm gliding across its smooth, taut surface. She did not bother to undress. She stretched out on the bed, found the pillow at its head, and buried her face in it. The scent of Tristan's hair unleashed her tears, and she sobbed until she slept.

Lewen, dressed all in white, held Tristan's hand. A long, wide scarf of white mesh wrapped itself around her neck, its two long tails riding on the winds above the sand. The pair walked hand in hand toward her.

"You found your horse," said Lewen.

"It's Shadow." Sibil stroked the stallion's muzzle. "Your horse, Lewen, not mine."

"I don't need him anymore," the princess said. "But he needs you. Shadow's yours now. As is this one," she said, letting go of Tristan's hand. "He's been visiting a spell, but he's yours, too."

Sibil's eyes popped open to the pitch dark.

She lay frozen, listening to her own breathing, until something crawled upon her shoulder. She brushed it with her hand, twisting violently away.

"Sibil!" The face of Tristan's ghost appeared, and she screamed. "Sibil! It's me!" Tristan's hand covered her mouth gently, then retreated. "You were having a nightmare," he said. "Wake up!"

"Tristan?" Sibil sat. "Is that really you?"

"Yes, of course it's me. Who else would it be?"

She grabbed his arm and kneaded it. "Am I not dreaming? I thought that you were—"

"What? Dead?!"

"Where is Sister Omenn?"

"Sleeping down the hall. At least she was until you started screaming."

"And you? Where were you?"

"Sleeping in your bed. I went to find you as soon as I awoke. I must've fallen asleep there." His hands felt the mattress. "This one's so much lumpier, don't you think?" He stretched out next to her. "It will be light soon. Here, go back to sleep. You must be exhausted."

Sibil reclined, still in disbelief. She scooted her body next to his. "Yes, I am so very tired! But I don't think that I can sleep. I never want to close my eyes again!"

His arm encircled her and drew her close. "Are you crying, Sib?"

"Yes, but I've never been so happy in all my life!"

For a long while, neither spoke.

"Sibil."

"Yes?"

"I should go."

"What! Why?"

"I left a note for my parents. They must be worried sick. I should let them know I'm well."

What!? Terror strangled Sibil's happiness. *He doesn't know? Not about his father's death, nor his mother's suicide! Gods above, of course! How could he—unconscious but for the short time he spent with me! How am I to tell him?*

Marshal Erik Carson

"Erik!"

The king's voice! Just outside the gates leading to the dungeon, Marshal Carson's response registered his surprise. "Your Majesty!"

King Axil waved a hand through the air dismissively. "I know we were to meet in the study, but honestly, I cannot bear it any longer. The scribe has just brought two more piles of his writing, and my head is too addled to digest them. Walk with me, will you? I need fresh air, and lots of it!"

"Of course, Your Majesty. I was just headed your way."

"A stroll through the gardens, perhaps." The monarch headed toward the castle's rear.

The marshal followed. "Lady Carson would approve. I've not been in quite some time."

"You've been visiting our prisoner?" King Axil set a rhythmic stride across the grounds.

"Several times now, Your Majesty."

"You've spoken with him?"

"I have."

"And?"

"He's frightened, sire. Stripped of all he hid behind, he is exposed for what he truly is: a wretched old man who has committed grievous sins. Still, his character shines through. He remains, above all else, self-serving. He knows the end is near, and is resigned to his fate. But in the meantime, he'll do anything to avoid torture, and he's been singing like a bird."

"Any tunes worth hearing?"

"Some. We now know why we could not find him at the GOT. He, along with his financier and leader of their army—Rulers Three and Four—left the GOT in the dead of night the very same evening we crossed the Lawless Lands. A prattler sacrifice was used as a diversion; they left the tunnels open beneath the GOT on purpose, hoping we would access them. He led his young disciples, the so-called noms, to believe the end was near, and that he was locked within his chambers to commit suicide. He convinced them to do the same, but only after they removed all the lyla from the belly of the GOT, leaving its tunnel doors open to receive us. He knew we would find that access point, and hoped the prattlers would feast on whoever was not killed in battle, regardless of whose side they fought on. No one was expected to survive. It would be assumed by all of Baelon that the magister and his High Order were also killed during the carnage."

"And the treasure?"

"Never there, Your Majesty. A pittance kept locked away for appearances, and to promote the farce, but most of it remains tucked away somewhere in the Southern Isles."

"He's told you where?"

"He says he doesn't know, and I believe him. The financier, Ruler Three, controlled that aspect of their plan. She made the arrangements, and he trusted her."

"Now what?"

"Six of our men are on their way there, m'lord. The isles are not large. They'll find it. And hopefully, Ruler Three as well."

"And the man who killed King Tygre? Ruler Two, was it?"

"Most interesting, sire. There were but three members of The Guild who conspired to keep all the treasure for themselves. The magister, and Rulers Three and Four—those seeking to escape to the Southern Isles. Ruler Five caught on, and the magister had him killed. Ruler One, the portly man who maintained the GOT, was clueless, and you know what happened to him. That leaves Ruler Two, who apparently concocted his own plan to kill you and King Tygre so that Baelon would be thrown into turmoil, allowing The Guild to take control. The magister humored him as a means of keeping him preoccupied. With two's nose out of his business, there was little else to fear from inside the GOT. The magister thought it most likely Two would be killed pursuing his ambition, but if by some miracle he succeeded, it would only help the magister's cause. With both kings in the ground and all of Baelon in turmoil, who would care about the magister, dead or alive? The rest is mostly confirmation of what we already knew or suspected."

"Where is he, then—Ruler Two? He must pay for Tygre's death."

"Bad news, I'm afraid. I thought perhaps it was a man we saw aboard *The Fair Winds*. He was, after all, in the company of an assassin. But he drowned, and we did not recover his body. The magister believes he's still at large, and that he likely is still stalking you. Either way, you cannot afford to leave the castle, m'lord. Not until we find him, or we're sure he's dead."

"Enough with that, Erik. That ship is lost to sea and isn't coming back. Time for you to let it go."

"But sire—"

"No! I'm serious. I've been outside the castle, have I not? Across the Lawless Lands and back with you! And look—here I stand! Do your job. Do your best, that's all I ask. Let the gods decide the rest. None of us are here forever."

"Do you still insist on executing the magister yourself?"

"Of course. On that I've never wavered."

"Then you'll do so here? Within the castle walls?"

"Most certainly not! That was never the plan. I appreciate what you're trying to do, but that simply won't work. Anyway, it's not as though this place guarantees my safety. We entertained a much smaller number for the Lords and Ladies Feast, and look what happened there. How would you intend to keep the cutthroats out?"

"We will be that much more attentive and particular about who enters, Your Majesty."

"But that defeats the whole point, Erik. It is important that this be a public spectacle. The people must see for themselves to feel at peace. The castle's far too small."

"Anywhere else puts your life at stake, m'lord. Please reconsider."

"I don't care if it kills me. I really don't. Besides, we have a backup plan in the event of my death, remember?

"And if we're both killed, sire? You standing on the scaffolds, me trying to protect you? What then?"

"Can you not, just this once, be more agreeable with your king? Listen to me carefully: the people must be allowed to witness the magister's demise. And it must be by my hand. The details, I leave to you. Do as you will."

Carson sighed.

King Axil laid a heavy hand on his shoulder. "And lest you think we're bargaining, let me assure you, we are not. I won't say it again—these things are non-negotiable."

"Very well, sire. As you wish." *But I do have a notion!*

Sibil Dunn

Marshal Carson led her down a passage on the castle's lower level, halting at a door just shy of the kitchen. "You don't have to do this," he said. "Just say the word."

"No. I want to. She saved Rolft's life. Nearly spared my mother from siplence. And now, Tristan. It's the least I can do. Besides, I'm more curious than fearful now."

"Nor would we have the magister," said Carson. "Not without her help. I'll be right behind this door should you have second thoughts."

"I really don't need you to stay."

"Ah, but I'm compelled. When you're through, I'm to escort you to the king. He'd like a word as well." And with that, Marshal Carson opened the door.

Sibil stepped inside, recalling before the latch clicked behind her that she had been there once before. *Was that my very first trip to the palace? My second? Lewen was giving me a tour, and the history of this room was especially intriguing.* Conveniently located adjacent to the kitchen, it served as a modest banquet room, intimate and ornate, well-suited for entertaining small groups and visiting dignitaries. Sibil remembered the story. Lewen's father had given her mother free rein to decorate, and the queen had immediately replaced all symbols of aggression with creative works of art. A coat of arms, a wall covered with weapons of war, and several hunting trophies—all had been relocated to the Great Hall. Colorful tapestries and paintings were hung in their place. Commissioned sculptures, carvings, and metalwork adorned side tables. Thick rugs from the Northern Isles covered the floors.

"Come closer, child. I'm not going to bite you." The ancient Sister of the Systalene sat in a plush armchair, well away from the main banquet table.

"Sister Omenn."

"Miss Dunn."

"I thought you'd left."

"Not without first mining your brain, child."

"But your wagon—"

"Is being repaired. A boy from your livery noticed a large crack in one of its axles whilst passing by."

"Reggie! That would be just like him."

"A useful boy, no doubt in training to become a useless man."

"He's not at all! Why must you be so heartless?"

"Am I?"

"Aren't you? Toward men, especially? Why do you dislike them so?"

"I don't dislike men, Miss Dunn."

"Then why disparage them at every opportunity? You do, you know. And then you turn about and tend their wounds. It makes no sense!"

"Most men are generally useless, if not dangerous, save for one fundamental function. The same is true of the bortok, and any number of other wild beasts. Stating that fact doesn't constitute disparagement. I don't dislike men any more than I dislike the bortok or the cragen. They can be pleasing to the eye, in fact. Every living thing deserves to live its life. And no animal deserves to suffer. But they can't be counted on. They're unpredictable. One simply needs to be careful in their presence."

"That's ridiculous! Not all men are like that."

"I said *most*, Miss Dunn, not all."

"The same could be said of women, you know."

"Of course, but saying something doesn't make it so."

There's no reasoning with this woman! "What is it that you want from me?"

"Only to get to know you better, child. Or should I call you Wisperal?"

"I've told you. That's just a silly—"

"Poppycock! You clearly know the story. A young man, mortally wounded, holds on for one last kiss from his betrothed, then dies. In mourning, she starves herself to death, only to return in spirit form to ease the suffering of others by sewing their lips closed."

"What of it? A fairytale, and nothing to do with me."

"You've been doing a lot of sewing lately, only not to ease anyone's suffering."

"You're certain of that, are you? How do you count the number they would have made to suffer if left to live themselves? How can you know the amount of future suffering their deaths prevented?"

"How can you?" The old woman seemed to ask in earnest.

Sibil had no ready answer. "Listen, I'm not sure what you think of me, but I am most grateful for all you've done. You saved Rolft's life, helped tend to my mother, and now Tristan. You've saved his life as well."

"Oh, no, child. We brought him here to die... so that he could leave this world in the arms of those he loves. There was no hope for him. None. His spirit lingered to say farewell to you, but his body had already left. He was as good as dead. No one can tell me otherwise."

"And yet he lives."

"Just so! Why is that, I wonder? What did you do for him?"

"Me? Nothing."

"Healing's what we do, Miss Dunn. I've lived eighty-six almons, and never seen the likes of it. What did you give him?"

"What do you mean? I gave him nothing."

"Please. No food? No broth? Nothing on your lips when you last kissed him?"

"No... I..."

"Think, child! This is most important!"

Sibil could only shake her head.

"All right." Sister Omenn took one of Sibil's hands in hers, patting them reassuringly. "All right. But you did taste Euphoria?"

"I did," Sibil whispered.

"It's not the only drug we use, you know, but it's by far the most versatile and powerful. What happened when you tried it? How long did it take for you to feel its effects?"

"Not long at all. It tasted sweet and tingly. And I... I felt I could do most anything."

"How much of it did you ingest? Where did you get the rest?"

"What do you mean?"

"I gave you but a hardened drop of sap, child. Where did you get the rest?"

"The rest?"

"Surely you savored more than one drop! Where did you get it?"

"But I didn't. I didn't even use all that you gave me."

"Nonsense!"

Sibil produced the card from beneath her tunic. "You see? Most of it remains. I licked it, but once."

"Licked it!" Sister Omenn chortled, her baggy eyelids quivering. "Oh, my! Perhaps it does like you. It comes in other forms, you know. Powder you can snort; extract from its sap. Sucked on, even its bark has power. The leaves can be processed many ways. They can be smoked or turned to snuff. But its seeds... those are the most powerful." The old woman dug into her pouch, her fingers rummaging inside. "Here." She handed Sibil a small tin no larger than a kingshead. "Licking's fine. All well and good. But try your teeth next time, and let me know how that goes!"

Sibil did not know what to say, except "Thank you, Sister."

"You should come to stay with us. What do you think?"

"What?" *Completely unexpected, and out of the question!* "A most generous offer, Sister. But I couldn't."

"Couldn't you? Hmmmpf. Think on it, will you? My time is up. I'm told the king awaits you, and we wouldn't want to poke that bear, would we?"

Sibil helped her rise, and together they shuffled to the banquet room's door. Sister Omenn rapped on it with her cane, and Marshal Carson opened it.

The old crone gave him a hard stare. "Turns out you're good at riddles, child. Let me know when you solve this one!" She turned her watery eyes on Sibil one last time. "Sweet dreams, Wisperal!"

Marshal Carson led her through The Great Hall and into the arched tunnelway she knew to be King Axil's private domain. On a day the king had been traveling, Lewen once pulled her down that passageway. Two giggling schoolgirls, excited by their own daring and boldness. But they had only explored so far, retreating before they'd reached the monarch's bedchambers, scared off by some innocuous noise, never to return.

Sibil knew as the marshal passed the hallway's third door that she was in uncharted territory. "Under the circumstances, you might let his highness do most of the talking." It was most politely phrased, but she knew what he meant. Her eyes searched the floor. She did not need to be reminded that she had overstepped her bounds the last time. *"As any father who ever truly loved a daughter might imagine." What was I thinking?*

The marshal stopped in front of the fourth door, one hand glued to its latch. He raised the other with a finger to his lips, speaking softly. "The king's dressing room. You'll need to keep your voice down."

Quiet in the dressing room? How peculiar! She did not dwell on it, as Marshal Carson opened the door to a chamber much smaller and more cluttered than she expected. Standing at its curtained rear, the king greeted her in a velvet robe of purple with black trim. "I trust you'll turn a blind eye to the muddle," he said. "Please... sit." He motioned to the room's only vacant chair; all others were buried by mounds of clothing. Piles of garments littered the floor, some neatly stacked, others in disarray.

Sibil skirted them to climb into the empty chair. "Your Highness."

He was indeed a big man, taller even than the marshal, but he had somehow aged in just a quarter moon. The deep lines of anger and frustration she had witnessed at the GOT now creased his brow with weariness. His shoulders sagged in sorrow. Still, his blue eyes sparkled as he spoke.

"My daughter would have been the first to tell you how often I am wrong. My wife would not have contradicted her. The marshal might well join their chorus, but he's not at liberty to sing to anyone but me. You understand? Turns out, even kings can make mistakes."

I don't understand at all.

"Who would have known?" the king continued. "At any rate, if you still wish to join the army, I'll not stand in your way."

Ahhh. "Thank you, Your Majesty, but I am no longer so inclined."

"Really? I must say, I'm relieved."

"My reasons for doing so are gone."

"Regardless, and despite my best efforts to keep you from harm's doorstep, your recent exploits have managed to increase the realm's indebtedness to your family. If you won't join the army, how else can I repay you?"

"On behalf of my entire lineage, sire, I absolve the realm's debt."

The king shifted his weight uncomfortably. "Yes, well..." He made eye contact with the marshal, his head twitching just slightly toward Sibil.

Carson stepped next to her, then leaned to whisper in her ear. "You cannot relieve the king of his obligation to you."

She whispered back. "Why not?"

"I'll explain later. For now, you must allow him to pay the debt."

King Axil met her gaze, one bushy eyebrow rising above the other for a moment.

"What I meant to say, sire, is that your most generous offer to join the army is acknowledged. The opportunity it represents cannot be diminished, and is considered payment of your debt, whether or not I act on it."

King Axil's beard could not hide his smile. "Well stated. We'll consider that partial payment, shall we? The offer to join the ranks of my ambassadors remains as well."

"Another most gracious offer, sire, whether or not I accept it. I consider your debt paid."

Sibil looked anxiously to Marshal Carson, but the soldier's head was already half bowed and shaking side to side.

"Not yet," the king said kindly. "I'm only half serious about the ambassadors. They could use you, to be sure, but I've come to know it's not a proper fit for you. I'll not be offended if you refuse the offer. The marshal tells me you've been riding Shadow, Lewen's stallion."

Sibil was caught off guard. "'Tis true, m'lord, but at first, I did not ask to ride him. I asked only for a horse, and I was given Shadow." *Gods above, don't get Reggie and Caleb in trouble!* "Since then, I suppose... What I mean is... I think they felt he needed riding."

"I'm sure he does. You like him, do you?"

"I love him, sire!"

"He needs someone to ride and care for him besides the stable hands. Lewen would want that to be you. On behalf of my daughter, I gift him to you."

Sibil's chest heaved. "Thank you, Your Majesty." Her response was barely audible. Her mouth hung open as the image of Lewen, all dressed in white upon the desert sands, reappeared to her. *"He's yours now."*

King Axil was still speaking. "...your love for animals."

I've no idea what you just said! "M'lord?"

"Come. Join me." King Axil held out a welcoming hand. Sibil slid from the chair, crossed the room, and accepted it. "Shhh," the monarch said, his fingers parting two sections of the floor-to-ceiling curtain behind him. "Just enough to see."

Sibil peered through the gap, her eyes widening at the sight of the two cragens, Sir Black and Lady Gray. The male sat on his haunches a mere five strides away, staring back at her while Lady Gray paced the full width of the floor behind him. And just beyond her, near the back of the dressing room, small puffs of striped fur lay nuzzling one another to form one fluffy ball.

"Oh!" Sibil whispered. "She's had babies. Look at them! They're beautiful, Your Majesty."

"I thought you might like that." King Axil closed the curtain. "We can't get closer yet. Lady Gray would kill us, mark my words."

"Of course she would," Sibil whispered. "Oh, but they're so cute and cuddly looking."

"Quite." The king ushered her away from the curtain. "You'd like one, would you?"

"What?" Sibil stared at him in disbelief. "Surely you're not serious!"

"Oh, but I am."

"But... no..." Sibil stammered. "I couldn't be so cruel. I mean, you're not going to take them from her, are you?"

"Yes. And save them in the process. It's anything but cruel, Sibil."

"I don't understand."

"They're everything to her now. She won't let them out of her sight. But, in another moon, she won't have anything to do with them. That's just the way it is with cragens. She'll suckle them until they're old enough to forage on their own. But then she'll turn her back on them, and those that continue to depend on her... Sir Black will make quick work of them."

"Kill them, you mean?"

"Yes. They can't stay kittens forever. Sir Black and Lady Gray have lives to lead."

"That's horrible!"

"No... no, it's not. In the wild, it works quite well. It's the cragens' way of preparing their young for what they're bound to encounter. The strong survive; the others, well... they don't stand a chance. But here, even the weak are cared for. We'll find homes for all of them, trust me. Without Lady Gray's attention, which by nature, she won't give beyond that time, they'll die most certainly. We could release them, but the Forgotten Lands are their only remaining habitat, and they'd die quickly there as well. They won't have learned how to survive in that environment.

"So we can't blame Lady Gray, you see—she's only doing her job. But we're not the villain for taking them from her, either. Whoever adopts them will be saving their lives and will become their surrogate parents. I've a long list of nobles who have been waiting almons for her to give birth. Trust me—those who don't have the right temperament will be waiting forever. I'm offering you first pick. Think on it, why don't you? But I'll need an answer within the next half moon." He nodded toward the marshal, who made it clear to Sibil that it was time to leave.

The king's voice stopped her half-way to the door. "Oh. One more thing, Sibil. A reminder only, really, but I do want to stress how welcome you are here, and how pleased I would be if you would choose to make Castle Aranox your home."

"Thank you, sire. You've been most generous."

"What was it your father liked to say? 'A humble home of stone is laid...' No, that's not it..."

Sibil closed her eyes. "'Where stones are laid with caring hands, a humble home forever stands,' Your Majesty."

"Yes! That's it, of course." The king chuckled to himself. "Your father was much more than just a brilliant architect."

"Thank you, sire."

It was not until they stepped onto the bailey, and the sunlight kissed her cheeks, that Sibil asked, "Why could I not dissolve the king's perceived debt to me?" The sound of hammering interrupted her. "Does he not, on occasion, dissolve the debt of those who owe the realm?"

The hammering continued.

"He does indeed," said the marshal. "To those of lower station in life. When someone with more power and wealth forgives your debt, it's clearly a magnanimous gesture. But when someone of lower status attempts the same, it's considered rude."

"How so?"

"It's thought to imply the debtor cannot pay his debt... to a man of lower status, no less."

"Absurd!"

"I quite agree, but it can also be seen as a disingenuous act designed to curry even greater favor."

Sibil thought it through. "So no one can forgive a king his debt?"

"Another king, I imagine. A god. Under certain circumstances, a priest, perhaps."

"Ridiculous!"

Marshal Carson smiled at her. "I don't create Baelon's conventions or its customs, Sibil. This is the world we live in."

They both listened as the hammering grew louder.

"Is that...?" Sibil waited for the marshal to finish her thought.

"Yes. They've been told to take their time, and to make as much noise as possible."

So much fuss and fanfare! "And all for one old man," she said aloud.

"On the contrary, Sibil. The message they're sending will spread across both realms. It will be heard by every man, woman, and child in Baelon."

"He can hear it from the dungeon, then?"

Marshal Carson smiled. "If his hearing's near as good as mine, he can. The doors leading to the dungeon are purposely left open. It's funny how sound carries down those passages!"

Sibil watched with mixed emotions from the battlement.

For a quarter moon, saws and hammers had stayed busy just outside the castle walls. The first time she had ridden past, on her way to Father Syrus, there was little to see save four large posts driven deep into the ground. Stacks of lumber lay beside them, watched over by the severed head of Ruler Four, impaled atop a tall pole. "Oi!" one worker had yelled to another. "Tell your skinny friend there to eat something! He doesn't look so good!"

By the time she had returned from The God of Children's House, a few inquisitive townsfolk had traipsed up the palace road to watch spindly sticks of wood connect the sturdy posts.

Before another sun had set, the scaffolding had started to take shape, and a string of soldiers had been dispatched to keep a growing crowd from disrupting the worksite.

Now, one would find it difficult to navigate the palace road without an army escort, for it was lost beneath a loud throng, restless with anticipation.

A muscular man disguised by a black mask stood at the bottom of the scaffold's stairs, his arms folded across his chest. *Executioner!*

Also on the battlement: King Axil, positioned above the gates, Marshal Carson, Major Stronghart, and the soldiers who had ridden with them to Waterford's wharf, the loved ones of those who had been killed there, the members of the royal guard, and Rolft.

Below, two columns of armed guards fenced the crowd from a wide clearing encompassing the castle gates and the grounds surrounding the scaffold. The remains of Ruler Four's head, prominently displayed atop a pole within that clearing, no longer observed anything. His eyes had been pecked out by birds, his skin shriveled beneath the sun.

Rolft leaned closer to her. "Where's young Godfrey, Sibil? I thought to see him here with you. I'm told that he's recovered."

"Yes, but he mourns his family. I'll tell you later, shall I?" *I cannot bear to speak about it now.*

"You wouldn't want to be the magister today," Rolft said to her, mercifully changing the subject.

"Not ever."

Drums began to beat at the far end of the bailey. *Ba-rum, bum, bum... ba-rum, bum, bum.*

Sibil followed Rolft to the other side of the battlement, from where the drummers could be seen marching across the castle grounds, six soldiers in lock step behind them. Four more uniforms surrounded a small, hand-drawn cart, in which rode the magister, wearing nothing but a nightgown, shackles, and a black hood. Six more soldiers brought up the rear.

A murmur rippled through the crowd outside, and as the castle gates swung slowly open, the murmuring turned to loud, unintelligible conversation. When the magister rolled into the crowd's view, their collective shouts and cries erupted in a roar.

The edges of the throng closest to the castle surged forward, only to be pressed back by two columns of armed guards.

The cart came to rest near the scaffold stairs, and the executioner took control. The masked man lifted the magister from the wagon as though he were a child and carried him up the scaffold's stairs. There, he lowered him to his feet and turned him to the crowd. It was the first sighting of the magister for many of those standing further down the palace road, and another roar erupted.

King Axil raised his hands. The people quieted, and the drumming stopped.

A black raptor landed on the head of Ruler Four, causing some to "oooh" and "ahhh," as though it were an omen or a message from the gods. A few vicious pecks into rotting flesh spawned sufficient laughter to scare the bird away, and there was utter silence.

Beside King Axil, a barrel-chested man beneath a feathered hat and dressed in purple velvet unfurled a scroll and held it level with his eyes. His thunderous voice shattered the still air.

"Hear ye, hear ye, demons of the dark! Listen carefully, this message is for you! On this, the third sun of the tenth moon, in the thirty-first almon of the reign of His Majesty, King Axil of Aranox, his lordship sends a message. Let it be known, you are not welcome here; not your dark hearts, nor the hands that do their bidding. Baelon will suffer you no longer. Behold one of your subjects—the magister, leader of the Takers' Guild!"

The executioner placed his hands on the magister's shoulders and squared them to the crowd. He removed the old man's hood. Name-calling, boos, and hisses greeted the old man's unveiling. A brief shower of rocks, eggs, and fruit rained down on the scaffold decking.

It was an ugly scene in all regards, and Sibil wished for it to come to a quick end.

"Magister! Behold the King of Aranox!" bellowed the orator. The executioner spun his captive to face the king. The magister jerked, squinched his face and closed his eyes, attempting to avoid the brilliant sun above the monarch. "It is by his decree you die today! By his hand, and his alone! You are hereby banished from this world. May all seven gods pass judgment on you, and may your soul be trapped forever more in the darkness of Baelon below!"

The executioner took hold of the magister and led him forcibly to the guillotine. The old man was made to kneel. His shackles were removed, and he was strapped to the bascule, his head poised over a basket.

Sibil could not bear to watch. She shifted her gaze to the giant blade above the magister's head.

King Axil's hand fell to his side.

The executioner pulled the lever; the blade whistled down its track and thudded to a stop. A deafening roar resounded from the crowd, punctuated by shrieks and gasps. The executioner stooped over the basket and reached inside. There was no hair to grasp, and so he picked up the severed head with both hands before holding it aloft for all to see.

Sibil descended the battlement stairs in silence. It was a lot to take in.

"Miss Dunn!"

She glanced back to see Marshal Carson, several steps behind a small group following her. At the bottom of the stairway, she moved to one side and waited.

"Miss Dunn! Would you join for a moment?"

Sibil did not know what to say. It felt like a good time to be alone.

"Please, I think it will do you good." The marshal signaled the guards at the gates. "Wait here, would you?"

Too numb to respond, Sibil remained as the marshal walked away. When he returned, he had a visitor in tow.

"Gradi!" Sibil rushed forward, and the old man met her halfway to embrace her. "What are you doing here?"

Gradi held her at arm's length to display a large red card with gold trim and a gold half sun rising embossed in its center. "I'm here by special invitation!" he said. "Look at this!" He handed her the colorful correspondence, and she read from its backside:

Gradiott Gamble of Summerwinds

The honor of your presence is requested at Castle Aranox on the third sun of the tenth moon, in the almon 1006.

Upon your arrival, please present this card and make yourself known to the guards at the gates.

With Warm Regards,

His Majesty, King Axil of Aranox

"Gamble!" Sibil handed the card back to him. "Your name is Gamble?"

"We had to send a man to Summerwinds to sort that out, Miss Dunn." Marshal Carson joined them, his hands behind his back.

"Dunn!" Gradi said. "No, it can't be! Your surname's Dunn?" Sibil grinned. "All this time! Adrian Dunn, the architect... you're his offspring, are you? And you let me go on about him for so long!"

"This is for you." Marshal Carson revealed his hands to present Gradi with a box, wrapped in bright red cloth and bound with wide, gold ribbon.

Gradi accepted it tentatively. "What's this?"

"From the king," Carson said. "See for yourself, why don't you? I'm needed elsewhere, I'm afraid, but I expect to see you both this evening. You've been invited to sup with the king, and he asks that you come as you are. Sunset. Lady Carson and I shall meet you outside our chambers. It's good to see you again, Gradi Gamble. Miss Dunn."

After the marshal took his leave, Gradi looked from Sibil to the gift box, then back again to Sibil.

"Well?" she asked. "Open it, why don't you?"

Gradi moved beneath the battlement stairs, away from the bailey's bustle and din.

Sibil followed to watch him untie the ribbon, then peel the cloth away. "My daughters will be as impressed with these as anything inside this box," he said, stuffing both down his shirt. Sibil eyed the wooden container. "It's got some weight to it," said Gradi, giving it a heft. Holding it with one hand caused his arm to shake. He lifted the unhinged lid carefully.

"Oh, my!" he said. The interior of the box was lined with purple velvet and partitioned into two square halves, each brimming with neat stacks of shiny gold coins. "Kingsheads!"

"Look!" Sibil said. "King Axil on one side, King Tygre on the other!"

Gradi shook his head in obvious wonder, his blue-gray eyes starting to glisten. "What did I do to deserve all this?"

Rolft Aerns

Most visitors to The House of All Gods had either left or sought shelter within the confines of the cathedral. Strong winds whipped through the grounds, sweeping sheets of fine mist across the cemetery. The last worshipers to leave might have mistaken the odd pair left sitting on a stone bench atop the royal's graveyard for sculptures—neither the large figure cloaked beneath a bortok's hide nor its lithe companion had stirred in quite some time.

Sibil tilted her face to a darkening sky before breaking the silence. "What will you do now?"

"Go back to farming, I suppose."

"It gives you pleasure, does it?"

Rolft shrugged. "Fereliss and Marshal Carson have asked me much the same. Why is everyone so interested in farming?"

"We're not, silly. We're asking about you. It's what friends do. So... does it give you pleasure?"

"Farming?" Rolft shrugged. "Truth be told, I've not been at it long enough to judge fairly."

"I'm allowed to visit, am I?"

"I shall be very sad if you do not."

"But you're happy now, Rolft?"

Rolft took his time in answering. "Happy? What does that really mean?"

Sibil sighed. "I suppose it means that you are not."

"And you? You're happy, are you?"

"I am, but there's sadness in me still. It's possible to be both at the same time, don't you think?"

"Not just possible. Quite normal, I should think."

Sibil motioned toward Lewen's gravesite. "I don't like to think of her down there. Buried in the dirt. Lying in the dark, alone."

"She is not," Rolft said assuredly. "Her bones rest there, of course, safe from wild animals, but they cannot see the dark or feel the cold. That part of her you cherish most is not imprisoned in her body. It lives among us, and will be with you forever."

Sibil nudged a small rock with the toe of her boot. "Do you really believe that?"

"What else is there to think?"

"I wish I could be sure of it."

Rolft shrugged. "If my arm is severed and buried, does it miss the light or suffer pain?"

Sibil's face wrinkled in disgust. "No."

"Just so. And if I travel to some far-off land? Whilst you stay here, what then? Is the bond between us broken by the distance?"

"Of course not."

"Some say it would grow stronger still." Rolft gestured toward one of two large headstones. "What lies there in the ground, lass... her flesh and bones... have naught to do with it. Does she not make her presence known to you?"

"Yes, now and then, she does."

"What more proof do you require? Lewen is with you now, and always will be—no matter where you go." Rolft placed a heavy hand on Sibil's shoulder. "And when my bones are in the ground, so shall I be—make no mistake."

"Why must you talk like that? You are forbidden to die!"

"Am I!" Rolft chuckled, and for a moment, there was silence between them.

"I've been seeing things," she said.

"What kind of things?"

"Do you believe in ghosts?"

"Ghosts! Gods, no! Spirits, yes. Like the spirit of Lewen, or your parents. I do think they live on in us. But ghosts—walking and talking among us? No. Either you are dead or you are not. There is no in between—no before or after."

"I believe the same, so I'll not use that word, but I am seeing things I cannot put a name to."

"Such as?"

She hesitated once more. "The man with the scar on his forehead. You remember?"

Rolft leaned back to study her. "The one we captured during Six Moons?"

"Yes, the very same! I've seen him, Rolft. In the flesh!"

"Not possible. He was put to death, Sibil. He and his wee partner, both."

"I know! So what am I to think, if there's no such thing as ghosts?"

"You thought you saw him, but you did not."

"But I did! I'm sure of it! I've tried convincing myself otherwise, but I know what I saw. It was him, unless he has a twin!"

"And where was this?"

"On my way to the GOT. In the Lawless Lands. He was going the other way... riding with another man."

Rolft could only shake his head. "I was busy dying at the time, but Fereliss watched him lose his head. Garth and Yurik, too."

"Of course they did! As did I! Why do you think I'm so upset?"

"Have you told the marshal?"

"Yes. You both think that I've gone mad."

"I think you're troubled. For good reason, mind you."

"I am troubled. And confused. But I know what I saw."

Rolft drew in a heavy breath, then let it slowly out.

"That's not the sum of it," Sibil said. "There's more. I won't call them dreams because my mother used to hate it when I called hers that. But I've been seeing things inside my head as well."

"Sibil—"

"I don't know what to call them. Visions. Premonitions. Sometimes while I'm sleeping, I see things that might have happened, or that might be forthcoming. Tristan... Lewen... but also..."

"Go on. Tell me."

"I tried Euphoria!"

"Euphoria! When? Why?"

"That old lady! Sister Omenn of the Systalene. The woman who brought you back from certain death. Did you know she delivered my mother? It's true! My grandmother was a slave to Euphoria, and she died giving birth to my mother. Now it runs through my blood, Rolft. Less of it, I'm sure, but still. The sister said it might affect me differently, and I think perhaps it does, and yet... She gave me a drop of it, hardened like wax. She told me, 'small doses when you dare.' I tasted it! Just licked it, mind you, and oh—it's in me. I could feel it... almost instantly. It started with a tingle on my tongue, but then it washed throughout my body, and—this is going to sound impossible, I know, but—it awakened something else already in me. As though it were a spark, igniting something waiting to be burned. I could see everything. It was as though I stood in two places at once. And everything around me moved so slowly, as though everyone but me was moving through water."

"That's how you felt. But what happened? Were you awake, or did you sleep? Did you speak? What happened?"

"I killed a man!"

"You what!"

"Yes! One of those who beat Tristan so badly in Stonybrook. He was at the GOT, and boasting about it, and I had just tasted the Euphoria, and he had a knife, but he was so, so slow in using it, and I could see how black his heart was, and I was beside myself with anger, and the movements came so swiftly and easily and... it was like nothing I've ever felt before. And now I need to know. Was that the Euphoria? I barely touched it with my tongue! But I'm so scared to try again, for fear of what I might do without even knowing it. And so I thought... I thought perhaps... you would watch over me."

"Watch over you?"

"Yes."

"While you taste it, you mean?"

"Yes."

"Here? Now?"

"Yes."

"I'm not sure that's wise, Sibil. What if you take ill? There's no physician here."

"I didn't suffer any ill effect the first time. I doubt such a small amount can harm me. It's why the sister cautioned me to take small doses. She'd know if it could hurt me."

"You've only tried it once, yeah? Who's to say it will have the same effect? You can't know. That's the whole point, is it not? The reason you want to try again—because you can't be sure what it will do to you?"

"Yes, but I'm only going to touch my tongue to it. I'm not concerned with my welfare. I'm more worried about what I might do to others."

"Are you saying you might try to harm me?"

"I don't think so. I felt in complete control the first time. But it's why I thought to do it here... out in the open, with no one else around."

Rolft heaved a heavy sigh.

Sibil reached for the stubby punch dagger tucked into a low exterior pocket on her trogs. "Here," she said, quickly producing a second, longer blade with a matching carmine handle. "You can hold my daggers." It was impossible to look at them without recalling the moment he had first been introduced to them. "Old friends of yours," she said, "and this..."

She handed him the white-handled blade gifted to her by the Godfrey twins.

Rolft accepted all three half-heartedly, and Sibil withdrew a small, rectangular piece of parchment from her turncoat.

"That's Euphoria?" Rolft had heard a lot about the substance, no doubt much of it untrue, but he had never laid eyes on it.

"Just this part... here." Sibil turned the parchment so that he could see the small bump protruding from one side, like a white heart the size of a thumbnail in the center of the parchment.

"You're sure about this?" he asked.

"Yes. Are you ready?"

Rolft tucked Sibil's daggers into his waistband and stepped back to give her room. The life-sized statues encircling the plateau stared back at him. "May all seven gods watch over you."

"Over us, you mean." Sibil winked at him as she licked the surface of the parchment. She slipped the card down her blouse and closed her eyes.

Rolft waited anxiously. Expectantly. The wind tore at Sibil's hair and rippled her clothes, but her limbs remained motionless, her expression unchanged. *I should have asked her how long it takes to work its magic! Might she be dreaming, even now?*

Sibil's eyes opened suddenly to stare through him.

He looked for signs of anger or aggression, ready for the slightest twitch of a hand or leg.

"That's it," she said, smiling.

"That's it? That's all there is? Did it do anything at all?"

Sibil covered the ground between them, extending her arms, then wrapping them around his waist. "It's happening," she said. "But it's not controlling me; I'm controlling it." She tightened her embrace. "You needn't worry further."

"What's that supposed to mean?"

"I see you, Rolft Aerns. For who you really are."

Sibil Dunn

Where Have You Been?

The words above the iron gates to *Quest* welcomed Sibil back, but a padlock barred her entry to the school grounds. It would remain, no doubt, for the duration of the tenth moon, while teachers and students alike enjoyed a respite from each other.

She clambered up the rough stone wall adjacent, finding toe and finger holds along the way to its top. There she rested momentarily. On the other side, the ground sloped quickly away, so it appeared an even longer drop to where Tristan stood waiting beneath tall trees. Her feet found a substantial ledge halfway down to him, and when the young knight reached up to assist in her descent, she jumped past his arms and landed in the leaves.

She sought his hand, and together they skittered down the steep wooded slope. At its bottom, the trees gave way to a sprawling stretch of open ground, dotted by a half dozen buildings. They passed in front of the largest, its facade's inscription giving voice to the institution's founding fathers:

Where Are You Going?

Sibil followed Tristan behind the structure and back into the woods. Down another slope and past an amphitheater. Across a narrow stream, and up a gentle knoll to where tall grasses browned and shimmered in the sunlight.

Sibil gave Tristan's hand a little squeeze before letting go of it to sit.

So many fond memories of this place!

It was the very spot where Theos and Lewen had sat with her and Tristan so often, the four friends convening whenever possible outside the confines of their classrooms to compare notes on the mysteries of life. Their own private retreat—a place of comfort and support.

She did not feel the need to speak, and the two sat silent for the longest time amidst the swaying grasses.

"I like it when you tie your hair back," Tristan said eventually. "It shows your face, yeah?"

Sibil tucked an errant wisp behind her ear. "You were cording yours too, for a while. Don't think I didn't notice."

"After Theos died. To honor him, I s'pose. But since Stonybrook... well, it's not very becoming. Look." Tristan pulled back the curtain of gold hanging down the left side of his face to expose a bald patch just above and behind his ear. A long, raised scar highlighted the puckered skin there.

"It's not as bad as you think," she said. "I quite like it, actually. It says that you're a fighter, and a survivor at that. I would show it off, were I you! It will strike fear into your enemies and endear you to those you fight for." Tristan scoffed, but could not hide the beginning of a smile. "Just look at Sir Dreddit's face. He's a handsome man, you know, all the more so for that scar of his."

"Be serious, Sib. Really?"

"I am serious! He's not for me, to be clear—too cocky, too cavalier—but if you doubt how women see him, ask any at the castle what they think. There aren't many who'll say they'd refuse his advances—not if they're being honest."

"Cocky and cavalier are not for you, eh? What is, then?"

"I should think that's obvious." Sibil brushed the bangs from Tristan's eyes. "Is it not?" She kissed him on the cheek.

Tristan plucked a slender blade of the browned grass and twirled it round his finger. "I'm sorry I ran off the other night. It was all too much to bear. It still is, really. None of it seems real. I don't know what to think or do. My head is so... so full of sharp clutter. The pain doesn't go away."

"No, it doesn't," said Sibil.

"I have no family left." Tristan tossed the grass aside.

"Nor I. But we have each other, Tristan."

The young knight leaned his forehead against hers, and they kissed.

Epilogue

"It's difficult to grasp the meaning of life when one's hands are covered in blood." From the teachings of the Systalene

Maynard Penniluk

With his back to the Lawless Lands, Maynard vowed never to set foot on their godsforsaken sands again. Though pleasant by comparison, the scrappy Borderlands would also be deprived of future visits. Since early morning, the Dark Woods had welcomed him with cool shade and the musty scent of decomposing leaves. *Could Baelon above be any more hospitable?*

A root rudely introduced itself. Maynard stumbled forward several paces before righting himself, balanced on one foot, a bottle held at arm's length to either side. He grinned, admiring his agility and the God of Fortune's good grace. A little root was hardly going to ruin his run of good luck. He had survived The Wisperal, the prattlers, and King Axil's army. He might have lost both brothers, but in a pile of steaming rubble that once had been The Cauldron, he had found two bottles to take their place. He suddenly realized one of them was empty. He tossed it into the dense undergrowth of the Dark Woods.

With continued luck, he would be in Stonybrook by late evening, tucked into his own bed, warm and snoring soundly.

I'll drink to that! Just a sip, though. This bottle has to last, you know. Yes, yes, just a sip. And how about a rest? A short one, mind you. Yes, of course... just long enough for that quick sip! There... That's a likely spot!

The trunk of an enormous tree lining the pathway ahead began to flare at shoulder height. A few of its roots—each as thick as an ogre's leg—rose into the air until their knobby knees drove them back toward the earth. Covered in blue moss, the mounded soil between them gave the spot he spied the appearance of a velvet chair with twisted wooden armrests.

He sauntered up beside it. Two hands would be needed to maneuver himself into the mossy throne, so he set his remaining bottle down. It took some navigation, but eventually, he nestled himself in between the tree's roots, his back and rear end softly supported by spongy moss.

Very comfortable indeed!

But had he placed the bottle too far away?

Dammit!

He sat up and strained to reach it, his fingertips barely able to brush its top. He inched his butt forward until his fingers tapped the bottle. They tickled its top, tipping it toward him. His hand caught the bottle's neck, and he dragged it to his chest.

He pulled its leather knot and let loose a heavy sigh.

Most comfortable! Perhaps we can afford to stay a little while, after all, eh? A short nap might do the body good!

He brought the bottle to his lips and allowed a trickle of its contents to pass through them.

What are you doing? Stuff the knot back into place, and be on your way!

But his thoughts did not spur him to action. Instead, he let the bottle's base come to rest on his belly as he studied the lush plants across the way.

Something about them needled him...

They were quite attractive, really, if one could be bothered with that sort of thing.

Which he could not be.

Even so... Bright pink with teardrop petals... Blue veins and purple dots... I'm supposed to know this. Spotted something-or-other, right? Wait a tick! It's...

A rustling in the undergrowth behind him jogged his memory.

Spotted spunge!

He held his breath.

The rustling continued.

Shite! Spotted spunge is the favorite food of—

The rustling stopped, and with it, the beating of his heart.

He strained to listen, and the rustling resumed.

Closer then, it came from somewhere right behind the tree he sat against, joined by muffled snorting, much like that of a wild pig rooting for mushrooms. But he dared not stand or try to turn around for fear of making noise himself. What would there be to see, anyway, save the trunk of a tree so wide it would take the arms of six men to wrap around it?

No! Be silent! Stay still!

He twitched as the snorting suddenly turned to squealing, and something burst from the forest to his right. *It is a wild pig!* The animal scurried across the woodland path and into the spotted spunge as fast as its stubby legs could carry it. Maynard watched its back wriggle through the pink groundcover, then blend into the forest.

Little more than an overactive snout on four legs! Gods above, how it scared me!

A mixture of laughter and nervous energy sputtered from Penniluk's lips.

Just one more drink to steady our nerves, and let's be on our way!

He stopped just shy of kissing the bottle.

Was that more rustling? Yes! Only different, and sustained. Louder than the sound of scattering leaves… more like forest undergrowth being brushed aside… the snapping of twigs underfoot. Whatever this is, it isn't waddling or shuffling; it's striding through the woods. And it's quicker than the pig, and heavier! Cra-aack! *The sound of tree limbs breaking! And bigger! Should I run? No! Don't be absurd! By the time you stand and step into the open, it will be here! Why present yourself that way? Stay hidden! It's no doubt chasing the pig. Sit still and let it pass!*

Slowly, his bottle found its way back to his stomach.

It came crashing through the woods and leaped into the middle of the pathway in a single bound. It stood upright on muscular hind legs resembling those of a horse. Covered in long, black, shaggy hair, it was much taller and bigger than a man. It had a huge head resembling that of a wolf, with three rows of short tusks on its snout. The ears of a donkey, the horns of a bull.

He had never seen such a beast, but he knew just what its name was.

Bortok! Why is it not moving?

As if to answer, the bortok dropped to all fours and put its nose to the ground. It turned its head one way, then the other, then shook its entire frame violently, as though repelling water from its fur coat. It sat back on its haunches and raised its snout into the air.

Don't turn around, beast! Please, please, gods above, do anything, but do not turn around!

Penniluk watched in horror as the bortok's head began to swivel his way.

Noggods!

One of its large eyes came into view.

Does it see me? Do not move! Do not breathe!

The bortok rose on its haunches and spun around until its snout was pointing straight at Penniluk.

It appeared to stare at him a moment before looking back at the spotted spunge into which the pig had disappeared.

Yes, yes! Go after the pig!

Instead, the beast started toward him, walking on two legs, its long, hairy arms hanging loosely at its sides. One step. Then another. Until— *this isn't happening, is it?* —the monster stood before him, almost within reach.

I should do something! Anything!

But no plan came to mind, as he could not think past the bortok's presence.

The animal had taken a clear interest in him, but seemed content, for the moment, to stare. It cocked its head to one side, as though contemplating something.

Maynard watched the coarse hair on its chest slowly rise and fall.

When it suddenly threw its arms forward, splaying its hands with claws extended, Penniluk flinched. The bortok snorted once and smiled, exposing four long rows of pointed teeth. A thin stream of drool dribbled from its mouth to the moss between Penniluk's boots. The beast's claws retracted, and its hairy arms returned to hang loosely at its side.

Don't look into its eyes! Don't acknowledge it! If only you could reach your knife!

The very thought made his hands shake. The bottle slipped from his grasp, toppled off his stomach, and rolled down the mossy slope. It bumped into one of the bortok's hairy feet before coming to a stop.

Maynard Penniluk swallowed. Hard.

And fairly soon thereafter, having barely chewed at all, the bortok did the same.

THE END

A Humble Request

If you enjoyed this book, please consider leaving a review on Amazon and Goodreads!

To stay abreast of future works, subscribe to my newsletter at rawalkerwriting.com.

I promise not to pester you, and will never share your email!

And may all seven gods smile down on you!

ABOUT THE AUTHOR

Robert A. Walker grew up in Northwestern Massachusetts. After graduating college, he packed his scant belongings in a car with rusted-out floorboards and headed west. He's lived in California ever since, and now resides along the Pacific Ocean with his wife and dogs, where he writes fantasy novels with hints of grim dark and romance.

His debut novel, *Six Moons, Seven Gods*, won wide acclaim, including The Chrysalis BREW Project's Readers' Choice Award for June, 2024; Chick Lit Cafe's Book Excellence Award for Best Medieval Fantasy, November, 2023; and a Literary Titan Gold Book Award in December, 2023. When not fabricating stories, he can be found roaming local tennis courts or working on a never-ending list of DIY house projects. Information regarding Robert's current writing projects can be found at rawalkerwriting.com.

ACKNOWLEDGEMENTS

Many thanks to editor Maxine Meyer, who continues to help me hone my craft.